THE GOD-SEEKER

NOVELS BY

SINCLAIR LEWIS

1914 Our Mr. Wrenn

1915 The Trail of the Hawk

1917 The Job

1917 The Innocents

1919 Free Air

1920 Main Street

1922 Babbitt

1925 Arrowsmith

1926 Mantrap

1927 Elmer Gantry

1928 The Man Who Knew Coolidge

1929 Dodsworth

1933 Ann Vickers

1934 Work of Art

1935 It Can't Happen Here

1938 The Prodigal Parents

1940 Bethel Merriday

1943 Gideon Planish

1945 Cass Timberlane

1947 Kingsblood Royal

1949 The God-Seeker

THE
GOD-SEEKER

A NOVEL

Sinclair Lewis

RANDOM HOUSE
NEW YORK

FIRST PRINTING

813-L676go

123734

TO the pastor of the indestructible chapel on Hesnu Street, with the hope that he will recover from his long-confining illness.

Foreword

ALTHOUGH the Gadds, the Lanarks, Rip Tattam and the people of Bois des Morts and the Berkshire Hills in this novel are all fictitious, Charles Finney and most of the Minnesota characters are historical. Some of them, particularly the Pond brothers, Edward Duffield Neill and Joseph Renshaw Brown, were truly great men who have been forgotten by a generation which is playfully diverting itself with the newest importations in Marxian guilt and neo-orthodox-Freudian-Calvinist sense of sin. Joe Brown would have laughed. I am in debt to the writings of Charles A. Eastman, James W. Lynd, Samuel Pond and others on the Sioux Indians, and to the staff of the Minnesota Historical Society, especially to Richard Sackett, for guiding me through the riches of that institution, which was cannily founded in 1849 to record state history before there was any state or much of any history.

S.L.

THE GOD-SEEKER

1

NIGHT in the dark New England hills, night and the winter stillness. Bringing the fugitive home to the meager farm and safety from the driving terror.

Deep under the hay, wrapped in a crazy-quilt, Aaron cheerfully repeated Hay-sleigh, Hay-sleigh, in tune to the horses' hoofs on the frozen road, while the runners cut through the thin snow and grated on sand. He was seven years old then, the son of Uriel Gadd, a righteous man and cold, farmer and Calvinist deacon in the northern Berkshire hills. He peered reverently at his father's shoulders, level and rigid against the star-map, and at the blot that was Uriel's old sealskin cap, worn shiny.

The sleigh jolted off the road and stopped beside a lone barn, quite dark. There were no words. A foot crunched in the snow by the barn, and an undistinguishable figure clambered into the sleigh, burrowed down beside Aaron. The horses turned quickly, almost upsetting the rig, and were yanked back on the road, whip-touched into trotting quickly.

The bundled figure down beside Aaron settled into comfort in the warm-smelling hay, then was still. Aaron fancied that the escaped slave was sleeping, then he was himself asleep; centuries had gone by, and they were drawing into the home barnyard. There were no dogs to bark. Uriel did not hold with dogs—great godless creatures that devoured enough food to keep a hired man. (Not that he held with hired men, either.)

The sperm-oil lamp in the farmhouse window showed a yard clean enough, not too clean, with a gaunt hay-wagon dusted with snow, and the dirt-and-manure banking of the house. It was a story-and-a-half white cottage, and the small windows of the attic story, just under the eaves, were diamond-shaped. They were tight-shut all winter.

The anonymous figure beside Aaron sat up and Uriel, lightly dropping down to the ground, came to give the stranger a hand, to support him into the house, as though the man might be lame or cramped with close hiding.

Inside the warmth and safety of the house, the runaway, as he drew a shawl from about his head, appeared as a small Negro, gray, rather old. He stared about the kitchen, which was also the living-room, and very modern, having not merely an iron stove instead of a fireplace, but even an indoor pump. Wide-boarded floor, pine table and chairs, they were all worn with constant and severe scouring, and the small square of rag carpet was bleached gray. There was one example of art and luxury on the wall: a carved salt-box from the Bennington Fair.

The Negro looked at Uriel and smiled as though he were begging for reassurance that now, in the land of freedom, he had become a human being. He smiled pleadingly, but the gaunt deacon stared back without feeling, and snapped, "Et anything?"

"No, sah, nothing today."

"Set down."

Uriel pushed the man toward a chair at the table. Aaron's mother, a being of calico and decency and dreariness, her crepe skin old at thirty-five, a dumpy soft woman with no expression at all except patience, automatically appeared from The Folks' Bedroom, and set out on the table before the Negro cold corned beef, cold beans and a glass of buttermilk. She faded back into the bedroom.

The man ate desperately, while Aaron and his father yawningly peeled off their dogskin coats, their fur caps, their boots. No one said anything at all. When the man had finished, Uriel impatiently jerked his thumb toward the door to the attic stairs, and led him up to a cot there, under the eaves, near to Aaron's own room, which was merely a space cut off from the attic by a calico curtain.

The fugitive must have gone instantly to sleep, with the one

4

candle still lighted. By that light, Aaron stripped to his underclothes and socks, in which he slept all winter. He was drowsy in bed before he said his prayers, but they were fervent: not only *Now I Lay Me Down* but *The Lord's Prayer,* for he was a devout Sunday-school scholar, though also a champion at stoning woodchucks.

He was knocked over by sleep. The fugitive snored lightly, mice flickered about the attic floor with a tread of infinite swiftness and delicacy, and over the roof the elm trees rubbed branch against branch like wintry fiddle-strings. For the white boy, there was a dream paradise of colored glass, and for the slave, a dreaming hope that for the first time since ever he was born, he might truly live.

That was in mid-November, in the year 1830, in Northern Massachusetts.

Though the route of escape was not yet known as the Underground Railroad, an increasing trickle of runaway slaves was dribbling from the South through to Canada, and, next to a banker and a venerable retired blacksmith, Uriel Gadd was the most trusted agent of holy treason in that entire Massachusetts county.

And Aaron Gadd was the son of Uriel.

Aaron was dazed and aching when he was called down to breakfast next morning, sharp at the usual hour of six. His father had already finished his part of the chores, and sat at the table with the enormous Bible open before him, waiting fiercely till the family should be sitting in proper rigidity. He read then from the Second Book of Samuel, as though he were the High Sheriff challenging pestilent rebels:

"Thou knowest thy father and his men, that they be mighty men, and they be chafed in their minds, as a bear robbed of her whelps in the field, and thy father is a man of war and will not lodge with the people."

Uriel smacked his lips. Aaron reflected that his father did indeed sound like a man of war, a bear in the fields, as he prayed:

"Lord God of Hosts, give righteousness un-to this household and

5

give to these, my children, obedience un-to thy will and my commands, lest in anger thou smite them for their sins and willfulness. Give, O Heavenly Father, power un-to thy servant's ordering of his household forever. Amen."

Aaron was uncomfortable and a little afraid. This, he thought, is how God might pray to his God.

Breakfast at the Gadds' was something to be hustled through, so that Uriel and Elijah might get to the fences and Aaron trot off to school. It became no longer majestic with awe, but a huddle of busy Yankees.

At the head of the table, Uriel Gadd, deacon of the Clunford Congregational Church, already venerable at thirty-seven, his face like a deep-carven gravestone in the old burying-ground, a face plainshaven except for small sidewhiskers. At the other end, Aaron's mother, with the helpless face of one who longed to be loved and did not know how.

Along the sides of the table were the three children: Aaron, Elijah and Rebecca. Elijah was, for farm purposes, a grown man—all of fifteen, eight years older than Aaron. He would be as tall as his father. He was a thin, dark boy, always scowling, not with temper but with a desire to understand people and to achieve this righteousness that his father was always flourishing and always obscuring.

The face of Rebecca was a rosy orb of goodness and acceptance. She would be married and make good butter and know sorrow and pass on, always gentle and a little boisterous. She was older than Aaron by three and a half years. Except for the volumes of Cooper and Scott which Uriel neither forbade nor approved, she was Aaron's only refuge in a rocky world devoid of dogs and neighborhood boys.

Aaron, with his rough, sunny hair, his spirited brown eyes, his uncommonly high forehead, would not be so tall as Uriel or Elijah, but he would be solider of shoulder and more powerful of hand. He had the face of a boy who would be excited about life; about women, or the perpetual quest of God, or New Bedford rum.

6

And all these varied and contentious human beings were gobbling the pancakes and their own maple syrup with zeal. But the escaped slave of last evening was not among them.

The bubbles and dough of the buckwheat cakes were almost finished before Elijah dared to ask his father, "Papa, why don't you have our guest upstairs eat with us? You never do, when you bring them in."

Uriel was harsh. "Why should I? I took him up some bread and meat: He'll go on tonight."

"He wasn't at family prayers, and I guess that's important."

"Why?"

"To save his soul!"

"What makes you think darkies have souls?"

Such a query, in a world where everybody so ardently and fretfully did have a soul and was perpetually worried about its being insured, Elijah could answer only with a scowl of wonder. Uriel went on, in a manner of ministerial urbanity:

"Many pastors and thinkers believe that darkies are like hosses and beef-critters: act real cute and knowing, all right, but not got one speck of a soul to be saved or," with some satisfaction, "to be reprobated and to writhe in eternal fiery torment. Maybe they're lucky!"

"Then if they ain't got souls, why do we help carry 'em to freedom?"

"To save our own souls!"

Uriel's stare at his rebellious and interfering son was bleak as a winter planet. He seemed to Aaron like the God of Wrath as he blared, "Salvation is the only important thing in this world! And I see my own sons and my daughter wallowing in sin and ignorance, too muddleheaded to realize they are already scorched by the flames of hell, which is the reward of them that resist the tender invitation of the Lord Jesus, and now git out and curry them hosses!"

Creeping down the stairs, edging into the room, was their guest. He was cinder-gray, stooped from years of cotton-picking. But sleep had restored his belief that God had—perhaps unreasonably—

7

created Negroes as well as New England Yankees, and that life, just in itself, was worth guarding.

Uriel said to him, quite affably, "The Goshen minister will carry you further, this evening, my poor fellow."

The Negro was grave. "Mister, I am not a poor fellow. I am a Prince. I am the son of the King of Kings!"

Uriel stared at him frigidly, Elijah excitedly, and Aaron with a revelation that there might be human beings beyond the Hoosac Mountains.

But the womenfolks looked frightened.

Uriel said, "Exactly. . . . Lije, take this fellow out and see if he can make himself useful. He goes on tonight, blessed be the Lord! Well! What you women settin' around for?"

3

2

AARON was ten, and the season was summer.

His father ordered, "Git your face washed and put on your Sunday suit. We're going to drive acrost the Vermont line to Goshen. Your grandfather, my dad, is dying. Probably going to burn in hell, and we ought to see him. He's gone whoring after Episcopalianism. Bein' a Revolutionary War veteran won't save him in the implacable eyes of a just God. Git dressed!"

No, Uriel told Elijah and the womenfolks, they were not to go. Aary wa'n't particular bright, but he knew how to keep his mouth shut, and Uriel didn't want a lot of yammering while him and the Clunford pastor were wrestling for old Hezrai's soul.

In the carryall, with the bay horses, Uriel drove into their village of Clunford, three miles away—Clunford with its one tall correct Congregational meeting-house, its inferior yellow box of a Methodist chapel, a dozen small houses and a store with heavy wooden pillars; a hamlet mostly white and green, severe as its Calvinist faith, yet humble and enduring and greatly loved, against its sharp hill of elms and beech, with meadows and little rivers all about; a place of shadiness and contemplation and hate and history.

They picked up Uriel's pastor, the Reverend Lucius Fairlow (Williams College and Andover Theological Seminary), a mild-spoken young-old man with mild chestnut hair and mild chestnut mustache and a conservative theology which stuck mildly to the pleasant certainties of God's anger and eternal hellfire. He climbed into the second seat of the carryall, and benignly addressed Uriel, his deacon:

"So your father is poorly, Brother."

"Mighty poorly, Reverend, and in awful danger of condemnation if we don't wrestle with his soul and get him conscious of his black load of sin. Maybe it's all in vain; maybe he's not one of the elect, more 'n likely. If he's whooping and hollering in the exuberance of wickedness and can't confess his evil ways, then he's reprobate for sure. Ain't that the way God and the Bible look at it?"

"Well, perhaps somewhat, at least according to the doctrines of Calvin as improved by Jonathan Edwards," said Mr. Fairlow, struck by the sweet reasonableness of his deacon but never quite sure how you *did* reconcile predestination and the value of repentance.

They now enjoyed fretting about Hezrai's defiant love for hard cider; they peeped at the question of whether his aging and pious housekeeper, the Widow Treadhill, could be trusted with his eighty-five-year-old virtue; but chiefly they doubted Hezrai's zeal in contributing to God's glory. Their road, eastward from Clunford then north across the border into Vermont, followed in part what was some day to be called the Mohawk Trail, over the Hoosac Mountains. It traced a long ridge, and Aaron looked down into wellshaft valleys which for generations had preserved men and ways from outside interference. Beyond them, the dark hills moved away prodigious, and heights of two thousand feet had the look of a savage ten thousand.

Down the Vermont slope the carryall swayed into the hamlet of Goshen, half a dozen farmhouses about the granite quarry which old Hezrai Gadd had once managed. His abode was a weather-rusted, yellow, shingled salt-box cottage of three rooms: kitchen, Hezrai's sanctum, and Mrs. Treadhill's coop upstairs.

However Hezrai may have shocked his correct son, Uriel, by breathing untamed winds of doctrine, he was querulously suspicious of any untamed winds in the house, and the windows were all nailed shut. The whole house smelled of apples, rotting wood and old blankets uselessly preserved. Aaron's puzzled head began to ache, and he wanted to run away from theology, from forgiveness, from age, from death.

Mrs. Treadhill, stringy but pleasant, met the visitants in the kitchen, and whined, "He's failing fast. Would you like I should give you some cider and doughnuts before you go in and set with him?"

They would, for this was sacred custom, also economical. But as they tried to look bland while chewing rather over-fried doughnuts, they were disturbed by an incessant cackling from the next room, the cackle of a merry and evil old man who remembered the days (they did not seem long ago) when, small though he was, he could swing a quarryman's sledge and make a woman moan with love; an aged, curious, lively elder who considered these pious boys, like Uriel, as nincompoops.

The old devil went off into a chain of bell-like giggles, and Uriel said uncomfortably, " 'Pears like maybe the old gentleman is expecting us. We must seek to comfort him, heh, Reverend?"

They teetered into the insane disorder of the bedroom. Hezrai sat up in his four-poster bed to greet them, brave in a red-broidered nightshirt, his hair and beard lovingly slicked down. He peered at Uriel, he cackled again, and he said solicitously, "How be you, Ury? What you doin' these days? Still courtin' that French-Canuck girl you used to dance with?"

To Aaron's horror at seeing his God pushed off his throne, Uriel squealed like a green young man as he answered irritably, "You know doggone well I'm not, Dad! You know I'm married and got an eighteen-year-old boy."

"Have, have ye? You still got that sly prissy look you used to have after you'd been stealing mushmelons." He pointed at Aaron a fantastically withered forefinger. "This one of your spawn?"

"This is Aaron, my youngest—ten now."

"Don't look it. Too handsome and too blame cheerful to be any of your stale leavin's. And who—" He indicated the benevolent Mr. Fairlow. "—who the hell may this pickle-face be?"

"Now, Dad, you know blame well this is Reverend Fairlow, my pastor."

"Is, is he? Board of Deacons ever looked into his morals? He looks to me like a widow-tickler. Bet he steals his sermons out of Cotton Mather. Never trust these Miss Nancy's with silky mustaches."

The poor Reverend pleaded, "Now, Daddy Gadd——"

"Not *your* daddy, thank God—or don't think so!"

Mr. Fairlow tried again: "Well, Captain, we've come in all tenderness and loving faith in God to ask you to pray with us before it be too late."

"Nope. Done my own prayin' since I was two year old. Calc'late to go right on. God and me been good friends eighty-five years now, old friends, and we don't like you slick young squirts rampagin' in and interruptin' two old gentlemen when they're talking theology. God is still mighty puzzled about the combination of determinism and the efficacy of his grace, but we're tryin' out a scheme that we want to talk over with Brahma and Zoroaster, and we don't want you apprentices disturbin' us."

As the physical sufferer may be anesthetized by the intensity of his pain, thus the Reverend Mr. Fairlow was too shocked to feel any more shock, and he could only moan, "Oh, Brother, Brother, Brother, this is Satan speaking through your lips!"

Hezrai twanged at Aaron, "Set up on the bed and let me look at ye. . . . But *you* boys go home. Don't need ye and your ministering gospel. I've left the Congregational fold, and this morning I done a job of thinkin' and I wrassled hell and threw it and was minded to quit the Episcopalopians too. I sent for the Universalist preacher up here and kind of informally joined his church—in fact, took over his finances and told him how to raise the mortgage on that cowbrindle shanty he calls a church.

"He was like you boys—wanted to give me a letter of recommendation to the Almighty, because while the Universalists know there ain't any fiery hell, they still get suspicious about that smell of smoke. But I told him that if my old friend God wanted me—which ain't any too certain—God could recognize me after eighty-five years without any secretary or hired man, like you boys, remindin' him who I be.

"But," as he turned to Aaron, "you look less sanc-ti-mon-i-ous-ly-fied, Bub. You'll be a soldier, like I was. Fit under Colonel Ethan Allen and Colonel Warner—fit *and* drunk! Ticonderoga. French wine! That was a nice English gentleman surrendered the fort to us. Always did like the English. They treated the Colonel and me real nice in prison. You know, after the war, Vermont come mighty nigh joinin' Canada, 'stead of the States.

"Boy—Aaron, d' you say it was?—they's two kinds of fun in politics: revolution against tyrants, and then revolution against the revolutionists when *they* turn tyrants. You learn that, and you won't be a broomstick, like your pop. And go west, boy. Don't stay in these stuffy hills."

This in the stuffy room, the room for a decade airless, so that Aaron was dazed with the old, stale air and the shocking heresies and the old man's glee. He thought desperately. His father was God, but here was the father of God, too ancient with old wisdoms to prefer wisdom to folly, too old to care any more for godliness or glory or morality or sorrow or anything save the memory of the joy he once had known in creation. And now the father of God was dying. . . . Must not Earth die with him?

A week later, Uriel returned to Goshen to arrange for Hezrai's funeral and for shrewdly paying off Mrs. Treadhill, without prejudice. That night, Uriel ran another fugitive slave through, and cursed him for climbing into the wagon too slowly; and though he had actually seen the thing, Aaron could not picture him irresolute before Hezrai.

13

3

DEACON THOMAS POPPLEWOOD was of the same church as Uriel, and his modest farm was only half a mile down the road. Yet the ways of his household were as different from Uriel's as Sicily from Iceland.

His was a house for small boys to visit, a house where they were fed and listened to, a house where cookies and bread-and-jam and raspberry shrub and bowls of hazelnuts marched in voluntarily, where there was a museum of entrancing novelties: a conch shell with memories of wrecks and tempests in it, a Hindu temple made of pearl shells, a peacock fan, and a lifelike bearskin in which you were positively urged to roll yourself.

The collection of birds' eggs was surpassing; there was a necklace of sharks' teeth, and an illustrated Bible with the Hebrew saints escaping through the Red Sea, very jolly. The house was small, but outside it had ingenious fretwork under the roof, and in the smooth yard was a whitewashed pear tree, with a bench around its trunk and, in the branches, a jaunty wren-house.

There actually were fewer boys in that neighborhood than Deacon Popplewood and his wife liked to see, and Aaron was a guest solicited and honored. All of a summer afternoon, when his father was of opinion that a great lout of ten ought to be working, Aaron sat on the Popplewoods' wide low porch, shaded by ivy and wild-grape vines, in a special small red rocking-chair reputed to have come from Europe, while in that restful green dimness, the enormous and white-bearded face of the Deacon and the expansive round white powdery face of his wife were flatteringly fixed on him, and their ears were attentive to his philosophy.

From Uriel, Aaron had learned the awe of God, and he had learned from Mr. Fairlow's two-hour sermons on "The Jealousy of

14

an Angry Jehovah Who Hath Weighed Sinners in the Balance and Found Them Wanting"—sermons which crawled for two itching hours, while Uriel glared at him and his bones became hot wires and his muscles were in a vise—that God was a torturer who punished small boys for sins they might commit later. God was furious also if boys read *Aesop's Fables* or shouted on the gray interminable Sabbath afternoons.

But from the Popplewoods he had a notion that God might be as decent and friendly as the North Adams stage-driver, and that the church was not merely a fortress against the yelping hosts of hell, but also a pleasant and even mannerly collection of people.

On the shaded porch, when Mr. Fairlow or the Clunford schoolmaster, a wild Irishman suspected of Romishness, dropped in to talk theology and the evils of high tariff, the Popplewoods did not shoo visiting children away. They believed that good sense from a child was not necessarily contemptible beside foolishness from a grown-up. On July afternoons, after a mere snack of seven or eight hours of weeding and pulling mustard at home since breakfast, Aaron nestled on a wonderful old velvet footstool, depicting a knight in armor composed in slightly prickly beads, with his head against Mrs. Popplewood's soft, fat, kind old arm, and listened to the thunders and minaciousness of New England eschatology.

In Massachusetts in the 1830's, the farmers, the squires, the parsons, the wandering cobblers, the East India merchants, the Jewish peddlers, if they did not reel with theology as dizzily as their grandsires had during the Great Awakening ninety years before, under the tender and brooding tyranny of Jonathan Edwards, yet they were still bespelled by all the sacred and slightly paranoid words.

Flattered at being permitted to remain in the temple, drowsy but feeling high-class and intellectual, Aaron listened to the juicy words rolling out: Perseverance of the Saints, conditional predestination, psilanthropy, premillennialism, Adiaphora, Pelagianism, inheavenation, monophysitism, synod.

To the small Aaron it was soporific but beautiful: In-fra-lap-sar-ian-ism!

One of the Popplewood treasures was an illustrated story of foreign missions, and no conceivable harpooning of right whales nor even shooting the Red Coats at New Orleans was more inspiring to Aaron than the views of missionaries in long black coats instructing grateful Africans under giant palm trees, or canoeing with naked wild Huron Indians among phenomenal rapids, bears and war-clubs.

Deacon Popplewood said that it was his heaviest grief that he had not had the book-learning to become a minister. Preachers, he explained, particularly missionaries, were greater than generals or presidents.

"To me, Aary, the deepest happiness a man could have would be to interpret the will of God to all the poor ignorant folks. That's better than coffers of gold—big coffers!"

Aaron was a man of twelve or thirteen before he could understand the ecstasy with which Deacon Popplewood meditated upon the Divine Persons. He rambled on, stroking his beard, half looking at the boy:

"I guess about my sweetest memories are the precious seasons when I've talked with my fellow redeemed about heavenly matters and the glorious prospects of the faithful, and when we've knelt down and been able to pour out our souls in prayer. Greatest bliss this side of heaven. God has always blessed me with a few joyful friends that I could open my heart with. Then there are hours when I am only sensible of the deep and awful depravity in my heart, and I'm grateful for the wise ministers I have sat under. I was too ignorant to dream of the sacred desk, but you, Aaron, you are amazingly sensible. There may open before you a holy inheritance."

Thus called, and perhaps not above enjoying the thought of himself in a fine black coat preaching to worshippers like Deacon Popplewood, Aaron went breathless to his father.

"Papa, I think maybe I had ought to become a minister."

"Oh, ye do, do ye? And what makes you think that?"

"Mr. Popplewood says . . ."

"Says—says—says! Popplewood is always saying something! If he'd do less saying and more working, be better all round! Ministers have got to be men selected of God for their sobriety, learning and strictness of conduct, men gifted for the edification of the saints and the rebuke to blasphemers and fornicators. Think you're like that, heh? You that can't even be trusted to fill the wood-box and feed the pigs! You're a damn sight too slack—always looking for fun.

"Life ain't fun. When you think that most of us are doomed by divine grace to roast in hell, to say nothing of mortgages and hail and bad crops and extravagant womenfolks, 'tain't any laughing matter! Maybe you'll get to be a storekeeper or a lawyer, seeing you're too shiftless for farming. But a holy minister? Never! Put all such hogwash behind ye!"

God had spoken.

When he was thirteen and fourteen, the Aaron who, as a little boy, had been isolated and friendless, had plenty of companions during the four annual months of schooling, when he learned Geography and the Three R's under the rum-powered Irish schoolmaster, who threw things.

He learned from his schoolmates about generation. These back-hill boys were not inferior to the city round-rimmers in their knowledge of sodomy, rape and excrement, and this harsh enlightenment may have been healthier for Aaron than twittering stories about the bees and the flowers. As he grew broader and less shy, he became the best player of three-ole-cat and king's base and the best wrestler in school, and the violence with which he could punch a nose did not seem to him at all contrary to his code as a stanch young Sunday-school teacher.

It was only his father whose ways and hatreds remained divinely mysterious, whom he could never impress, not by his affectionate smile, not by his solid fist, not by his pleasure in the sacred hymns, not even by his skill in spelling "gauge" or "incomprehensibility" right out in school. It may have been part of the somewhat puzzling scheme of Providence that Uriel's irony should have kept Aaron from becoming too glib and popular in the days from 1840 to 1870, when the country was going to worship men with stars in their heads and solid boots on their feet, men with a sense of elevated piety and of slick politics and land-options, in their violent and ever-westering lives.

4

AARON was fifteen, his sallow and worried brother Elijah was twenty-three, and it was a wet fall in 1838.

Their mother had died two years before, as reconciled to dying as she had been to living. Just at the last she had called in Aaron and, with her plain and puzzled face screwed up like a miserable baby's, she had sobbed, "Darling, darling boy, I don't know what's to become of you, but try to love your papa. Oh, I think he always *meant* to be good to you—to all of us."

She drew her breath and was dead.

Rebecca took her place as Little Mother, and tried to make Aaron refined. She made him wash before meals, and she demanded, "Now don't say 'farm critters.' 'Tain't elegant, Aary. Say 'farm creatures.'"

With Elijah and Rebecca he reveled in skating, sliding, swimming, and sometimes Uriel was tolerant enough to permit an hysterically festive evening: popcorn, dominoes and the lighter hymns, to which Rebecca played the melodeon.

It was Elijah who felt the burden of the farm, as Uriel became "crippled bad with rheumatiz," but Aaron had his share, and when he went on from district school to a couple of years in Cheshire Academy, to Greek and Latin and mathematics, he did not shirk milking and plowing. He liked it. He did not feel himself a thwarted scholar. He was blithe when he came out to milk on an April morning, with the hilltops sharp against the luminous east, with the trees delicate and distinct high up on the hills. At such a dawn, in such illumined air, he felt himself, at fifteen, the young king of the world.

But this was no April. It was a drizzly late-October morning, with the trees stripped and snow up on Mount Greylock. The farmyard was a damp cell. On the stone doorstep, quivering, begging for recognition, for food, for life, was a little red-setter bitch. Aaron smoothed the sleek wetness of its back and chirruped, while the dog recognized him as its appointed Master, and rubbed against his knee.

He had longed for pets but, by his father's prohibition, had never in his life had one. The barn-cat, a mustard-colored vixen, had a raw temper like Uriel's, and no liking for boys. Uriel was probably the only farmer in Berkshire County who forbade dogs. He may have felt it a singular act of virtue.

Aaron knew that he was sinning a great sin, but he let the dog follow him to the barn, and compounded his treason by giving it milk in a tin measuring cup.

He christened the dog "Diana," because the name sounded alien and graceful. That early morning, Uriel was still furious in bed, racked with his rheumatism, and did not suspect treachery. Drunk with wickedness and the joy of having his own confidential dog, utterly in the clutches of an evil spirit, defiant of every decency that is the foundation of domestic felicity, Aaron took a whole slice of very expensive bacon and a practically untouched slice of bread out to Diana.

She followed him as he rode to the Cheshire Academy, frisking beside the mare and looking up at him to exult, "We'll have lots of fun together, eh? Next summer we'll hunt woodchucks!"

In the Academy, Aaron was tramping through Cicero, Plane Geometry and Christian Evidences, with no extraordinary talent. He was happy in them today. At three, Diana was waiting for him, and they trotted confidently home together. Leaving her on the step, in the unwilling rain, he sneaked into the house with the low scheme of pilfering more food for her. Rebecca was out at a neighbor's, but Uriel was there, by the stove, in pain and a temper.

"What are you dodging and sneaking around the buttery for?" snapped Uriel.

Even in his folly Aaron had known that he could not long deceive the eye of God. "There's a kind of a—a kind of dog out there. It looks hungry."

"Chase it away! Food costs money. Got no food to waste on stray mongrels."

"Honestly, she isn't a mongrel, Papa. She's a lovely dog."

"You heard me!"

Elijah came slouching in from the fields then, with "What's all the row?"

Uriel said, very quietly, "This young fool wants to feed some dirty cur."

Elijah protested, "I saw it. Looks like a nice pup."

Encouraged by his brother's faith, Aaron begged, "Oh, she is! She'll kill rats! And hunt rabbits!"

"You know plenty well and good I don't allow any dogs, for good and sufficient reasons, and we don't need one, and I want you should go right out and drive her away. Get rid of her for good—take a club, hear me?"

Aaron was screaming, "I won't! I won't!"

Silent, hobbling in pain, old Uriel—hideously old at forty-five—crawled to the deerhorn rack and took down his shotgun. He looked at Aaron, then at Elijah, menacingly. He opened the outer door and, at sight of one of her own Holy Family, the little dog barked delightedly and frisked and patted with her paws.

Uriel slowly lowered the gun and blew off the dog's head, leaving a red mess where its neck had been. From the coppery fleece on the wet doorstep, blood dribbled stupidly.

Elijah stepped to his father, tore the gun from him, and shrieked, "I ought to kill you! But I'm going to leave your house this day. I'll go west, where they kill tyrants like you! Aary, I want you should come with me. This is no house for a decent man!"

21

Aaron was staring at the indecent thing that had been speed and joy. Always, all his life, whenever he saw any one mistreated, he would remember that torn body and his father's look of divine justice and divine mercilessness and divine vanity.

Elijah was going on to his still-unresponding father, like a stump orator:

"We drove out the British tyrants—and you set up a meaner tyranny! You bring black slaves into this house, to help free them, and you hate them all the while, and you keep us as slaves. I'm going. You come, Aary! We'll find the New Jerusalem!"

He stamped away and they could hear him, in his hutch of a bedroom, throwing his possessions into a carpetbag.

Aaron might have gone with him, but he saw his father's face, stubborn yet deadly hurt. Uriel picked his gun up from the floor, laid it carefully on the scoured kitchen table, and turned slowly toward Aaron. His expression was that of a blind man afraid. The boy hated him and pitied him in equal measure, and felt that to desert him would be to kill him—friendless, crippled, alone with his temper.

Aaron's training in Calvinism took power over him. Just because it would be more pleasant and easy to go with Lije, to run off and hunt buffalo and paddle canoes and kill Indians, out where the sunset had always beckoned him, just because, with Elijah gone and his father ill, the farmwork would be more grievous and he would have to leave school and never become a minister or a judge or a doctor, therefore it was his righteous duty to stay. He was the immemorial rebel who hated the king and loved the crown.

He was a boy not without logic, yet it did not come to him that it was conceivably illogical, at the moment when he hated his father for killing Diana, to want to go out and kill Indians. Through history, death has been the pat solution of all indignations, and he is but a witless reformer who cannot jeer "What we need around here is a few first-class funerals." More than a hundred years after the

22

death of Diana, and a thousand miles away, Aaron's great-grandson, the Reverend Lloyd Garrison Gadd, would stand horrified on a spring evening and see another dog killed, the dog of an obstinate Negro named Kingsblood, in mimic murder of its owner. All love is one and all hatred is one, and the echoes of the righteous shotgun of Uriel Gadd will never cease rolling, and new generations, hearing them, will think that killing is a magnificent new solution and their own idea.

Lije came out, swinging a vile and faded carpetbag, carrying an age-green overcoat and a rifle. He had become a more cool and competent and integrated person than Aaron had seen. He was no longer a sullen hillbilly but, at twenty-three, an assured man. He spoke steadily:

"Aaron, you better come along. Life had ought to be something more than drudging for a killer."

Uriel's face was neither wrathful nor hurt now, but blank, and he made no move.

Aaron mumbled, "I can't leave him to die, and there's Rebecca and the farm and everything."

Superior but friendly enough, Elijah stated, "You got to choose for yourself, boy. Give Beccy my dear love. . . . Dad, I left all the money I have, except two dollars, on the chest-of-drawers. Seventy-nine dollars it is."

Uriel was toneless: "Better take it along."

"No," was all that Elijah said, and he was tramping off into the hopeless autumn rain, walking fast, his carpetbag at his side.

As Aaron submissively turned back to Uriel and to God, he realized that his father's face was almost grateful, almost tender.

"Time to start feeding the cattle," said Uriel.

With his brother gone from the farm work, Aaron had to give up the Academy, the Latin and Greek. At night he tried to read a

Greek Testament borrowed from Mr. Fairlow, but he was too tired.

The boy liked best the tinkering, the carpentry; the creation of a solid corncrib, the nice fitting of a new fence round the pigpen. He had a wild poetic urge to be a carpenter, but he supposed himself stuck on the farm for life, and his only magic would be the neighborhood girls, pitching horseshoes and the happy gospel of Deacon Popplewood.

Then Titus Dunt, a bustling farmer-tinker, fell in love with Rebecca and wanted to take over the Gadd farm, which would permit Aaron to go off and become a craftsman. But so daring an adventure seemed to him suspicious. It might be the doing of Satan, in whom Aaron anxiously believed with all of his being except, perhaps, his mind.

He fretted over deserting Uriel and he felt guilty that they had not, for two years now, run through a single fugitive slave.

He inquired of Deacon Popplewood, "Can a man even call himself a Christian when he has left everything undone, when he is full of sloth and just wants to sneak off to the city and carpenter?"

"Why, Aary, I think it's all right for a Christian to do anything he wants to, providin' it ain't dancin' or whorin' or having truck with the Unitarians or the Catholics," said the Deacon.

"Oh, I'm safe from any corruption like *that!*" protested Aaron.

He apprenticed himself to a carpenter-builder in the perilous city of Adams, which had almost two thousand Christians and several hundred French-Canadians; he held his breath and plunged.

5

WOMEN were not allowed in the drinking-dens of Adams, that respectable Massachusetts village with its Quaker Meeting House on the hill, yet Nadine Brun was in the back room of the Pequot Tavern. And Nadine was undeniably a woman, a cotton-mill hand by day but by evening a plump, wriggling, rolling, rejoicing, inviting, shoulder-shaking, cooing, laughing, black-eyed, black-haired, black-tempered young woman, who loved all that was bright and shoddy and loud, and loved all males.

The room was low, unadorned save by smoke stains on the wall, and its fireplace was small and of iron, but it rated high among the haunts of vice in Adams. Nadine felt joyful; she had a new dress of French muslin, with the fashionable stiffened skirts—her wages at the mill had never provided that dress—and though her three companions, called Gene and Preston and Aaron, were all poor young men, innocent of social standing, there were no livelier nor handsomer beaux in Adams.

Gene Dexter was the clerk in the Petty Drug Store; he was the suavest and most airily dressed youth in town, and believed by the village gallants to know more about secret dangers than any doctor. Preston Crouse, though as a factory hand he was declassed, was the most renowned comedian in town, and wore funny hats. But the natural leader of this coterie was the un-suave, un-comic young carpenter named Aaron Gadd and nicknamed "Neighbor."

Not tall nor short, with a brush of chestnut hair, and brown eyes that were serene and markedly friendly, his forehead noble and clear as a scholar's—or an actor's—only a fair dancer but a competent drinker, Aaron showed a solidity and an impatient ability to handle people which, felt the astute Nadine, would put him ahead of the light-minded Gene and Preston.

He was on his way to becoming a Master Carpenter. He already had a precise skill with saw and chisel and tape-measure, and from the other craftsmen he had learned a good deal about masonry, plastering, painting. Though his shoulders were not bulky, he had the strength to lift the enormous barn timbers or to smooth them with the adz. From tramping to jobs for forty miles about Adams, he had tireless legs. But it was as a powerful thinker and student that he was renowned.

He was rumored to study the portfolios of Bostonian and English drawings from which the rustic carpenters learned to build their graceful New England cottages, but it was also believed by Gene and Preston that he had gone beyond this architecture into more stupefying branches. He had been heard to quote Poe and Whittier, and he was credited with having read every book that had ever been written in Ancient Greek. At least, he had showed Gene a book which, he said, was called *Xenophon*. It certainly was printed in a funny language of which Gene could not read one letter.

Now that was impressive, but it was also dismaying, for reading Greek led to studying the Bible, and studying the Bible led to becoming a preacher, and becoming a preacher interfered with singing *Lord Lovel* and *Pretty Polly* and drinking switchel-flips and arrack cobblers, and having fun with girls like Nadine.

Yet so far Aaron seemed to them safe from piety. He did go back home to Clunford, on the Sabbath, and attend the Congregational Church with his father and brother-in-law, and sometimes when he was a little drunk he babbled about "endangering the precious gift of God's grace," but on the whole he was a trusted companion.

He had once said innocently to his grinning boss, "I like to think of everybody in the world as my neighbor," and that had fixed his nickname.

They were around the table at the Pequot Tavern, drinking

shambros or hard cider with beer chasers, and working hard at having a good time. Gene became sarcastic about the morality of rich people in Adams, and Preston had a whole line of funny jokes about preachers, and generally they were being witty and getting very bored.

This was in May, late May in 1848, when Aaron was twenty-five years old.

Gene turned as usual to berating Nadine Brun. Aaron did not complain, though he was considered her lover, for Nadine would have wondered what was the matter with her this evening if no one had shown enough interest to say, "You honeyfogling swindler, what do you mean by making love with every man in town?"

Gene grated, "So Nadine can't come with us to the barn dance tomorrow night! Course not! Her ole foreman—ole Titweller, the ole sneaking skinflint!—that's the night his wife goes to the Ladies' Missionary Sewing Circle, and the ole boy can sneak out and rub his ole nose against Nadine's."

"You shut your face!" said Nadine with elegance.

"Nadine loves us wild young dastards but she also goes it strong for the old man's shinplasters," crowed Preston, who could throw off poems like that one right after another.

"You can shut up, too!" achieved Nadine.

Aaron growled, "Both of you let her alone. I can take care of my girl. She does what I tell her."

But Nadine kicked out even at him. "I do what I please, you psalm-singing chisel-pusher! Mr. Titweller and me are just friends, but he's a lot sizzlinger than any of you sheep—" To Aaron, "—especially you!"

"Why, Nadine!"

"Yes, you, you Bible-pounding hypocrite!"

"Now that isn't nice of you! I'm not religious—not cranky religious!"

"You are too! If I didn't tease you and make you take a drink, you'd wallow in religion!"

27

This was so menacing to his position as a good fellow, a ball-player, a wrestler, that Aaron defended himself: "You suppose I want to be with some creeping Moses like Reverend Chippler when I could be with you and Pres and Gene?"

"Yes, I do! You're a sneak, and I'm never going to let you kiss me again!"

She was too brash. She did not understand that in the stolid steadfastness with which Aaron regarded her there was less thought of kissing her than of slapping her.

It was at this point in their daring talk, typical of the revolutionary young generation in 1848, that the bartender came in to tack up a poster:

OUTDOOR CAMP MEETING
THE OLDTIME GOSPEL
Fair Grounds, Adams
THREE DAYS
Start Friday evening, June 9, 1848
ending with
MAMMOTH REVIVAL
3 P.M. Sabbath Day, June 11
addressed by
Rev. Balthazar Harge, Missionary to Sioux Indians
Mark Shadrock, medical missionary & former slave
Dr. Li, native Chinese missionary of the A.B.C.F.M.
Revds. Chippler of Adams, Strong of N. Adams and
THE REV. DR. CHARLES GRANDISON FINNEY, D.D.
World-Renowned Evangelist, Teacher, Theologian
COME TO THE GREATEST OUTPOURING OF THE
SPIRIT IN THIS SIN-BLINDED REGION IN 20 YEARS

All of them except Nadine, whom they considered a besotted

Romanist, were connoisseurs of evangelism, but in the decadent and overcivilized era of the 1840's, outdoor camp meetings belonged not so much to New England as to the Far Wild West, way out in Ohio and Michigan, where Indians rode on buffaloes and preachers carried pistols.

"Big show!" admired Gene.

"Aah! Where's the tigers? Where's the fire-eating lady?" demanded Preston, who was always in danger of becoming cynical.

"You better go and get saved!" Nadine jeered at Aaron. "You halfway are, anyway!"

Aaron protested, "No, I got great respect for ministers, but I'm a Byronist."

"A *whut?*"

"I'm a free thinker. I believe in not sticking in one stuffy little church, but wandering across land and sea, rescuing Greeks like Lord Byron did."

Even the faithful Preston Crouse could not stomach this. "Who told *you* about that peewee? I bet you don't know one word of his pieces."

"I do too!" Aaron was correctly indignant. "I know *all* of him, by heart—that is, all the part I know. Listen. This is from *Childe Harold's Pilgrimage.*" He looked yearningly at Nadine. "I feel like it's really me that's talking.

> "It is not love, it is not hate,
>   Nor low Ambition's honors lost,
> That bids me loathe my present state,
>   And fly from all I prized the most:
>
> "It is that weariness which springs
>   From all I meet, or hear, or see:
> To me no pleasure Beauty brings;
>   Thine eyes have scarce a charm for me.

"Through many a clime 'tis mine to go,
    With many a retrospection curst;
And all my solace is to know,
    Whate'er betides, I've known the worst."

Lost in the enchantment of his own youthful voice, Aaron had not noted how resentfully Nadine was staring at him, and he was shocked from his dream when she snapped, "How dare you say my eyes ain't got any charm for you? Heh?"

"Why, Nadine, that's just . . ."

"And you know the worst! What worst? Heh?"

"Why, it's just a poem. Fellow wrote it."

"Well, I don't like it and I don't like *him*."

Gene rebuked her, "He was a lord!" But with a superb determination to have her democratic rights as a woman, an American, a skilled weaver and a mistress, Nadine squealed at Aaron:

"And I don't like you and I don't like your friends! A nice way to talk! You so weary-all-you-meet, are you? Lemme tell you, and he's a fine gentlemen even if he is an old fool of fifty, Mr. Titweller don't get tired of my eyes!"

Then Aaron really was weary. Then felt he that it really was his through many a clime to go, as far away as possible. This lovely creature would never understand him. In distinguished despair he lighted a cheroot, and for Aaron Gadd that was no trivial gesture. Both his father and Deacon Popplewood, though they argued that there was nothing unchristian in an infrequent drink of honest New England rum, contended that smoke issuing from the mouth was a little too much like the flames of Tophet for sound Congregational practice. *And* a useless expense. In taking up the smoking of cheroots (small and extremely nasty), Aaron had felt that he was progressing, but he was never sure whether it was in stylishness or in vice.

He stared with worldly coldness at the obdurate Nadine, while Gene and Preston sought to persuade her that their friend was loyal to her and a person of superior parts. "He didn' mean you!" urged Preston, and Gene, "No, it's just a poem he read—out of a reader—like *Bozzaris! You* know!"

Nadine did not know, and Nadine ferociously did not care, and they all had a great number of drinks and became affectionate and loathing and indignant and musical. . . . And Aaron wound up in Nadine's room, at midnight.

When he came out into the watchfulness of the village elms before dawn, he did not feel masterful but unclean—unclean—empty of all grace. He tried to light a cheroot disdainfully. It was vile in his mouth, and he threw it down. He shuddered from Nadine's vulgar ladyisms and sluttish coyness and the reek of her hair.

He groaned, "Lord Byron would 've been disgusted. Anyway, St. Paul would. And this Dr. Finney that'll be at the camp meeting. I always swore if I got to be a rebel against God, I wouldn't be a cheap one, with cheap, easy sins!" He considered himself singularly unattractive in the stringent Yankee chill before dawn. And he was forlorn in the conviction that he now was lost forever to God's mercy.

He was young. With only three hours of sleep, he was able to work all of the coming day, but all the day he agonized, "Suppose a beam fell on me while I'm in this state of sin? Suppose I slipped off the roof and cracked my neck? And I don't know if I'm elect. O dear Lord, snatch me from this pit of fire and blackness and take me to thy sure abiding-place!"

He was able to restore his self-respect by the craftsman's pride; he was a good carpenter, his beams were straight and solid, his work lasted. But that night he was in agony, muttering, "I deserve damnation! Maybe it's too late now to be rescued from the just penalty of my sins. I merit it. Dear God, our father, thou didst warn me in season. I deserve only thy condemnation."

He told himself that he was only a cheerful young workman who had been doing what they all did. He told himself that he had

31

been misled by Nadine, and he worked up quite a plausible prejudice against all French-Canadians, in especial the darkly glowing women of that tribe. But it was of no use. That particular sort of coward and evader he was not, and he lay abed facing all his sins, all his slacknesses, and the merited punishment by a just and angry God.

6

IN JUNE, when the camp meeting opened at the fair grounds, the citizens of Adams and surrounding farmlands discussed the eloquence of the exhorters with as much admiration and technical criticism as the generation of a hundred years later would devote to comic programs on the radio. The evangelists were powerful, they said, and souls were falling everywhere, stricken with conviction of sin.

Aaron had soon enough recovered from his own attack of conviction to stay away from the first meeting, on a Friday, and at the Pequot Tavern he said skeptically to Gene Dexter, "These conversions are just hysterical—getting all worked up over a lot of natural faults and slips." But so ardent were the reports all round the streets on Friday night that when Aaron rode over to Clunford and the farm on Saturday morning, he fretted all the way. He felt left out of something important.

Deacon Uriel Gadd was a man of integrity, granite-rough and lichen-coated. The punishment in his rheumatism, clearly sent of God, and the defection of his son Elijah, had weakened him only in making him somewhat less contemptuous of his sentimental son Aaron. All other persons he divided into fools, scoundrels and the blessedly elect, with only himself indisputably in the last class.

Aaron said to him uneasily, "I hear there's been great goings-on at the Adams camp meeting."

"Huh."

"Lots saved."

"Huh."

"Honestly. I saw Reverend Chippler on the street in Adams this morning. He said that yesterday at the meeting there were a whole

33

lot that were stirred to acknowledge their sins and they cried out with terror of damnation and—and everything."

"Huh."

"Don't you think they got grace?"

"No."

"How's that?"

"Got grace or y' ain't got it, from all eternity, not because some preacher copycats the everlasting truths that was known from before Adam. Man's fulfilled of grace or he ain't, and no playactin' and kickin' up your heels and confessin' about it."

"Don't you think you might like to come over tomorrow, Papa; the Lord's Day, final meeting? Hear the world-renowned Dr. Finney?"

"This fellow Finney—probably an abolitionist; wants to get us into civil war, 'stead of getting rid of slavery slow and cautious, like I been helping do all these years. Flannel-mouth! The missionaries at the meeting—some sense to *them*—take the glad tidings to them black heathen that are perishing in the darkness. But what's the use of a loud-mouthed evangelical like your Reverend Chippler, the Arminian hound, with his drums and cymbals and loud lamentation and general circus whoop-tee-do? The Lord ain't deef! Son, I want you to good and plenty meditate and realize that it's only in the secret recesses of the soul that the battle is waged, and not in no hell-hollerin' hullabaloo!"

Disturbed, Aaron rode on to Deacon Popplewood, who was gentle but firm:

"Aary, sometimes it's the Devil himself that works up all this spiritual tumult and ostentation, like amongst them Shakers over to Lebanon, with their dances and professions and monkeyshines. Camp meetings may be all right for them poor ignorant savages out in Wisconsin, but not in the great Commonwealth of Massachusetts. No!"

He determined to stay away from his little coterie of hell that

Saturday evening, and it was with considerable irritation that he found himself with them at the Pequot at seven o'clock, an hour after supper, and discovered that all three of them were so pleasant this evening that he could not take out his inspired irritation on them. He had to transfer it to the local mill-owners and lawyers: "the damn aristocrats" he called them. "Bunch of slavers, that's what they are. Lot of 'em make out like they're abolitionists and help the darkies escape North, but you know why? They try to keep 'em here for cheap labor and pull down the wages of the rest of us. And none of you white slaves get in a feeze about it!"

Preston begged, "Why, Neighbor, you're in a terrible stew to-night! What 'a' we done? Honest, we agree with everything you say, even if we don't believe a word of it."

All three were beaming at him so appealingly. He groaned, "Oh, I didn't mean to be mean, but I'm flummoxed. Listen, you heathen. I've been running away from the pleas of the Lord. He wants me to go to that camp meeting, and I been balking. And now we're going, the whole kit and boilin' of us!"

They were not embarrassed by his piety. The more earnest young men in New England of that day, when they were choosing professions, were more likely to instance the approval of the Almighty than to urge that they could "make big money." Gene soothed him, "Sure, we'll have a look at your holiness outfit, if you say so."

"And don't get funny about it. All three of you need a bath in the cleansing spirit. You're all dirty infidels—like me. O dear God, like me, too!"

Nadine screamed, "I am not! I'm a good Catholic and I've never failed on my Easter Duty and I won't have you Protestant skunks wetting *my* religion!"

"All right, all right," Gene chirruped. "We know, Nady. You bathe in holy water."

Hours then of blasphemy and fury and debate, all in the theological terms that seem shocking to the literate citizens today, who

35

believe in God but just don't care to mention him or any of the other lowly friends they knew before they went to Yale.

Aaron ordered, "Everybody go home to bed now, and we'll meet at the post office at two tomorrow afternoon and go out to the meeting."

"It'll be awful funny, all them preachers wrasslin' with God. Maybe we'll rough up the meeting a little and start some fun," glowed Gene.

"You will not. You're drunk. Go home," said Aaron.

He did not worry. He had been able to talk himself and drink himself out of his earlier fear that a just God and an angry God might suddenly become just and angry.

THAT Sunday morning, he went to church in Adams.

The Reverend Mr. Chippler, who had organized the revival which would wind up this afternoon, was a leaping little man, fuller of friendliness, optimism, go, zip, imagination, ingenuity, cheeriness and oratory than the nobler and slower animals. In joy over his camp meeting, he was jammed with exuberant wrath at sinners, this bountiful June morning. His text was from Job: "For the arrows of the Almighty are within me, the poison whereof drinketh up my spirit: the terrors of God do set themselves in array against me."

He barked, "It is of me that the Bible speaketh, warning of the sorrow to come—of me and you and you and *you!*" He seemed to glare straight at the alarmed Aaron, in a pew halfway back. But what pierced Aaron, so that he took up the sermon and preached silently to himself, was the pastor's denunciation, "Sin is cheap. It's like living in a dirty cabin with a pigpen in the front yard when you might dwell in the marble halls of the Lord and stroll amongst gardens of the finest flowers."

Aaron was smitten by this thought of Cheapness. He wanted to build houses that would stand for three hundred years, to have a gang that worked like a steam engine, a worthy wife and clean children who liked going to Sunday school, the ability to read Greek, and a large gold watch chain with a bear's claw on it. These fruits of the spirit, and not the cheapness of barroom jocosity, he wanted to display before Uriel, who was God.

To achieve all this splendor, Gene and Preston and Nadine would be of no help to him.

He scolded himself then: "So you just want to *use* them! And is that all you want to be: a fat householder—an old he-sow, sucking skimmed milk? Don't you want to dance and fight and pick up cripples along the road and drink the north wind like Byron?

"Yes, I do, but I won't get that out of sitting around the same table in the same tavern with the same crew, boasting what highbinders we are!"

Everything seemed confused and contradictory, and he longed for one clear command from a divine martinet.

As the four young people—Gene and Preston gaily, Nadine speculatively, Aaron sullenly—tramped out the Old Fair Grounds Road, amid dust and the dry smell of dust and lavish fields of buttercups and devil's-paintbrush, the camp-meeting audience was moving thick. Farm wagons with the children on boards across the box and surprising numbers of female relatives in lace-trimmed Sunday bonnets. Insane small boys stopping to do unsabbatical somersaults. A crippled old woman pushing her crippled husband in a wheel chair. Upright citizens trying to strike a balance between a look of salvation and a look of bank-credit. Mothers in Zion with leather-bound Bibles rubbed from black to brown. Young men flaunting London Style vests but agitated lest secret practices be mentioned at the meeting. Pretty girls with smooth-muscled beaux.

To get out of the dust, our friends took a side path, and on it they met, coming across fields, a cricket of a little man, shining with holiness, carrying a dozen hymn-books. He stopped to play his curiously innocent smile on them and to pipe sweetly, like a cheery little bird, "Such a lovely Sabbath afternoon, folks, and are you all saved?"

Till of recent years, when they had become mature men devoted to sitting and drinking, Gene and Preston had been noted for a device in which one knelt behind a wayfarer while the other operator suddenly pushed the victim backward. Aaron saw them preparing this celebrated prank now, and stopped them with "Quit it, you!"

So they had to take out their proud young cruelty in wit. Preston, the clown, said pompously to the little man, "Peradventure may I presumable to impetulate your making that intrapaloosa again?"

The little man's sparkle faded, but he squeaked bravely, "Why, boys! I just wanted to know—evangelistic meeting—are you saved?"

Preston yelped, "Why, sir, do you mean to insult my manhood and the virtue of my Great-Aunt Betsy's sister, Hepzi-bah-bah? How dare you!"

And he slapped the little man, lightly, not painfully, most humiliatingly, and with that he went pop out of Aaron's friendship. Aaron gripped his arm, and grumbled to the little man, "Excuse these boobies. They're drunken fools."

The victim begged, "Please don't stop them! I've always wanted to be bruised and striped for the love of our dear Lord, and till now nobody ever wanted to. I'll gladly turn the other cheek!"

Gene roared, "Oh, you make me sick, you pukefish!" and he finished it up to Aaron, "And you, too! Just stay with your sobbing friend!"

Preston and Nadine and he stalked away. Aaron almost ran to join them, almost ran from the saint, embarrassed by his otherworldliness. From the camp meeting, just beyond the trees, was coming the first hymn: "Alas, and did my Savior bleed, and did my Sov'-reign die?" Its unearthly sweetness made shaky all that was masculine, rough and belligerent in Aaron, and he was as faint as he had been among the tuberoses at his mother's funeral.

When he had caught up with the apostates, Gene explained, not at all affectionately, "What's the matter with you? We wa'n't going to hurt your little Miss Nancy. God all fishhooks!"

"I know. Excuse me, Geney. Got the blues. But I do think we ought to grow up now and quit these baby tricks."

They looked at him with virile contemptuousness.

The great hymn from the growing multitude beyond the trees was rising and imploring now, "The debt of love I owe. Here, Lord, I give myself to thee. 'Tis all that I can do!"

The Fair Grounds lay below a hill of uptilted moor-grass scattered with barberry and scrub cedar and edged with birches along an old stone wall heaped by stony New England farmers. But the flatland had become something out of the Far West. Hundreds of backless benches half circled about a wooden platform and beyond them were the tents and wagons in which slept the worshippers who had come to spend the entire three days. Here, farmwives in aprons had cooked their beans at outdoor fires, and unsabbatarian dogs were still sniffing for scraps.

A hooded Conestoga wagon stood with oxen tethered near it. Aaron fancied that it belonged to a caravan ready to start off tomorrow, bound away for the wide Missouri. Some family was forsaking the bright familiar glens and maple groves for the dark wilderness, but they longed to know again, this one last time, the savor of rejoicing with their old neighbors in the glad assurances of the oldtime gospel.

In this Yankee audience there was not so hot a rejoicing, such bitter mourning, as there would have been in the naked West, yet already, before the speaking, a few young women were crying aloud, shaking with guilt and loneliness. Their sobs mixed with the yip of dogs, the yelps of the children playing over and under the benches. But the village dignitaries, treasurers of the local temples, white-sidewhiskered, cool, devout and pontifical in white chokers, looked suspiciously at women who whooped with grief in public, and each trustee whispered to his stout pure wife, "That wench there must of been up to some funny doin's, carryin' on like that!"

These elders, Aaron did not notice. With the benches, the Conestoga wagon and a stray Stockbridge Indian in overalls, he was in the West, he was with his brother Elijah, and they were crossing the red sands to the very couch of the setting sun.

On a bench at the back of the half-circle Aaron and his troop lounged, and while the incorruptible Nadine went on thinking of nothing but the bonnets and young men, Gene and Preston became almost as uneasy as Aaron. At first they scoffed, with the light mocking wit of all Parisians, all Romans, but they grew strained. Suppose

—they had heard of such surprising mischances—suppose they were suddenly caught by the power of the Holy Ghost and their pride overthrown, and they became weak with piety and could never enjoy light girls or dark rum any longer?

"Let's get out of this!" quaked the sorry Preston, but he was too awe-bound to rise. But he tried to look amused.

The exhorters were all on the platform now, except for the great Dr. Charles Grandison Finney, of whom it was whispered that he was on his way from another meeting. Among the preachers Aaron noted a Negro and a Chinese.

Negroes? Yes, they were all right—the ones his father had smuggled through. But Chinese? Could they ever learn to speak English? Probably not, living in porcelain temples and drinking tea and wearing queues, as this fellow on the platform was doing, along with a blue silk blouse and skirt. And that was too bad, for Aaron wanted to like all races. He fretted about this through the second hymn.

Mr. Chippler of Adams opened the services rather drearily, as though he was trying to remember what he had said in his church this morning. Aaron felt fortified against any discomforting attacks of salvation, and he smiled back at Nadine's smiles, while Preston giggled ostentatiously.

Then, on the far side of the arena, Aaron saw his father, grim, the Reverend Mr. Fairlow of Clunford, blank, Deacon Popplewood, happy at any Christian meeting, and his sister, Rebecca, looking as though she wanted to weep and making Aaron think of his mother and her unending futility. He was embarrassed, and he was relieved that they were paying no attention to him.

Mr. Chippler introduced a local Methodist lay preacher, a cobbler who was given, during the twelve hours a day when he sat hunched with only his hands and elbows moving, to furious joy in a Heaven where a professing cobbler would be enthroned above frivolous bankers and where fine ladies who were nasty about the stitching of kid slippers would grovel before the leathery saints.

From the platform the cobbler screamed that the Day of Retribution was nigh onto coming. A power of folks who thought big of themselves on this side of Jordan would learn that the Lord was lying in wait for the purse-proud and silver-tongued, to show 'em that nothin' don't count over yonder but an umble heart and keepin' the Lord's commandments.

So bitter was the speaker that the Aaron who had recently been denouncing the same purse-prouds began to think rather well of the fine manners and benevolence of all old gentlemen in carriages. But then the cobbler got down to the practical business of sinning. He flung at them his contempt for taverns and trollops, and Aaron stopped sneering at the sneers.

He thought of himself lusting for Nadine, noisy with hard cider, sick-drunk and weaving, and he whimpered, "Nice public spectacle you must of made of yourself!"

Yet he noted (in those days one did constantly note one's moral pathology) that his disgust was only of the mind. He sighed, "I ought to be busted right down into contrition, but my heart is still hard as a stone—frozen—like a lump in my breast. Maybe I'm too far gone in evil for the Mediator to be able to help me any longer!"

Cold and lonely he felt, in the wintry street outside the warmth and love of the tabernacle.

The cobbler, with the power of really meaning it, was hammering:

"Silly faces of loose women grinning! You despising yourself, and everybody despising you!

"Foolish women at home, too lazy to lift up their babes to the eternal light!

"You all thinking you're so cute and you can fool the old Devil, and him laughing inside himself, ready any time now to snatch you right off to a real, literal, torturing, searing hell of hellfire!

"So, you generation of vipers, you think you're too smart for both God *and* Satan! You fools, you fools, what a come-uppance you got coming!"

Aaron saw that Gene and Preston were much less dapper and

mocking; that when the cobbler shouted "God will thrust forth into the light that sin you hid so well!" their mouths slid open and they dared not look around. He saw that, across the meeting, Uriel looked disapproving, Deacon Popplewood was rejoicing, Rebecca was slowly weeping. As for himself, Aaron felt that he was choking and stinging and scarified with burning sulphur, that the vengeance might burst on him now, and he would never see his people again.

At the clamorous end of the cobbler's address, the gentle little man whom Aaron had saved from assault climbed up on the platform. He led the meeting in *Rock of Ages*, to the new tune. His voice lifted so clearly, the audience followed it so gladly, that when they all yearned together, "Let me hide myself in thee," Aaron felt his frozen heart warming.

He had always been such a friendly and tail-wagging pup, fond of everybody, known as "Neighbor." He could not resist utterly the singer's invitation nor the passion of the bruised and anguished cobbler for a just world.

Mark Shadrock, the Negro, and Dr. Li, Chinese Christian minister, followed, but in them there was only serenity.

Mr. Shadrock was grave, magnificently confident, a man of thirty or so who had been bought out of slavery and educated by the Quakers. He was now attending the new Albany Medical College and going back to his own race as a medical missionary, like Dr. Li. And that celestial, it was revealed to a chagrined Aaron, actually could speak English, although, as this was the first time that Aaron had ever heard a scholar from Oxford and Edinburgh, he did not understand Li easily.

In a sensitized hour, his impressions of the two men were important. He sighed, "That's a wonderful gentleman, that Chink. If I could only talk like him! Maybe it is true that heathen people can become just as good as *us!*"

In any Yankee, such humility and imagination are to be prodigiously honored and considerably doubted.

Dr. Li explained that it was a little harder to carry Christianity to the Asiatics when he had to admit to them that the white Americans did not seem to believe in it.

Couldn't they, Li demanded, see those pleading faces uplifted—faces of sweating Chinese coolies pleading with them to help, but first to dedicate their own lives to Christ—upturned, dumb, pleading faces, begging the white people to take the bread of life, so freely offered, then pass it on to the hungry people of the darkness—faces pleading, begging, in dumb anguish?

Aaron writhed.

He had suffered under the gentle complaints of Li and Shadrock, but he suffered more under the harsh indictment of Mr. Harge, missionary to the Sioux, and he thought of the implacable Uriel Gadd, looking down like the God of Wrath upon the coaxing, cowering red setter, and the abominable blast of his shotgun.

8

W E SHALL now hear," Mr. Chippler had said, "from one of the most stalwart missionaries of our time, the Reverend Balthazar Harge, founder and still superintendent of the famous Bois des Morts Mission among the Sioux Indians, in a Western frontier land called Minnesota. Brother Harge gave up a large law-practice in Pennsylvania, when he heard the call of the Lord, and gladly went way out there to face the savage barbarians, the ferociously cold winters, the hunger and loneliness. When he returns to his station, as he will shortly do, you will remember having looked upon one of the great message-bearers of our age, hero and soldier of the Cross—Mr. Harge!"

The missionary was a square, stubby, tallish man with powerful arms and shoulders and, under a hard mouth and weathered cheeks cut with ravines, a wide chin beard, not a common clerical adornment in that decade. But he was clerical in his long frock coat, and as he got up he handed to the little singer (who took it and meekly cherished it) the high black silk hat he had been holding on his knees. For all his broadcloth and starched white shirt, Mr. Harge seemed like a farmer to a farmer like Aaron, who noticed that under his somewhat billowy black sateen trousers, the missionary wore stout boots.

His station, said Mr. Harge, was on a river sometimes called the St. Peter's, sometimes the Minnesota, a Sioux word meaning chalky water. It was in a wilderness too formidable ever to be settled, and his labors were surrounded by the Sioux or Dakota savage Indians, hell-flamed, gorge-raising, murderous, adulterous, Sabbath-breaking sons of Belial, who nevertheless kept begging like scared children in the dark for someone to bring them the healing gospel of Christ

Jesus and give them a chance to climb to civilization and to see on their dark and rugged prairies the light of the kindled cross.

(Prairie! To Aaron the word meant incandescent noons and great starry nights and the freedom of limitless space, and Indians riding after the thunderous herds of buffalo.)

Mr. Harge had come east, he explained, not only to stand lonely at the grave of his old mother, and to have a few more pages printed in the Dakota language for the Indians, but also that he might take back with him two or three young people who were God-minded enough to see the glory of gaining for themselves not palaces nor jewels here below, but greater palaces and jeweled crowns above. Today, of course, he was here primarily to help Brother Chippler bring mourning souls to the great surrender, but if on top of that some of them should decide to devote themselves to the Indians, oh, this would be a day of triumph indeed!

"Come out and help us! On that far river in the lonely land, we shall be waiting so desperately for you, and your faces shall be as the faces of friends and angels!

"Yet I know how many of the supposed Christians here, as in my own beloved but tragically cold-hearted Pennsylvania, are only willing to grab what they can out of life, and never learn the peace and pride and joy of sacrifice! But do you think the Lord God of Hosts is so easily deceived? Ye of little faith and little love, do you know that the terrible sentence may right this minute be thundered from the throne, and that awful hand stretch out to seize you? Fools!"

But the missionary's wrath dissolved in pity, as he begged, "Oh, you can't hurt God, but you can hurt and destroy yourselves, and in all love I beg you to flee to him for safety!"

In Aaron there was crystallizing a plan of brotherly communion all around the world, and a voice was urging him, "Will you come and help?" when from a million miles away he heard the tiny jeering of Nadine Brun: "That missionary looks like a rampaging goat. I'll bet he's a terror with the women!"

46

Aaron could only snarl, "Shut up, you infidel!"

She told him what he was, then. There were so many good points to her remarks that he almost lost the momentum of regeneration which Mr. Harge had started rolling.

A few anxious suppliants had come up to the bench before the platform and knelt facing the speakers, moaning, "Praise God" and "Give me grace" and "Oh, my sins are black—oh, help me bear them." The meeting began to sway in rhythm to the cry "O Lord, dear Lord!" as Mr. Harge finished his address, as he pleaded with them to accept the gift of mercy. More and more worshippers straggled to the bench, and each one Mr. Harge welcomed with "God bless you!"

Aaron could feel his whole body moving in his desire to rise, to go forward, to share in that neighborly exaltation of lifted sins and lightened sorrows; he could feel his shoulders sway forward, his legs flex; but all the while he was afraid of Preston's snicker, of Gene's disgusted "My God!" and he sat sweating, all one guilty mass.

Dr. Li was talking again, beseechingly, lullingly. Aaron saw teafields and upcurved roofs and high hushed mountains, saw the mystic orb of grace, all nations redeemed in one rejoicing band, washed clean of pride and envy....

He found that Gene was peering at him, and he froze again.

Dr. Li broke off, to stare westward—Mark Shadrock and Mr. Harge sprang up to stare—Mr. Chippler trotted to the side of the platform, holding out his hands—and a handsome carriage drove smartly in from the North Adams road. Out of it, hatless, wearing an urbane gray suit with an almost theatrical stock, sprang a man who leapt up on the platform and shouldered across it, powerfully shaking hands all the way, and Mr. Chippler cried, "My friends, Charles Grandison Finney!"

He was tall as a pine tree, straight as a pine tree, clean-shafted and sure as a Norway pine; he overshadowed the smaller figures on the platform as if they were shrubs and Mr. Harge as if he were a stump. He was the prince come to take command of his army, he was the actor triumphing as Hamlet, yet Aaron felt that he was not without humility and could work among humble men with his hands and shoulders, and not with his sunrise smile alone, or the voice which was a cello played by a happy angel.

For an hour he played that cello, with an occasional and astounding drum.

They had all known people—said Mr. Finney—who were ashamed of being weak and ugly, but some people were ashamed of being beautiful and strong. They wanted to become toads and hide in the dust, so that no one would notice them. They felt safer so.

He himself had done that.

"When I was a young man, I understood the reality of atonement, and I saw that all I needed was to get my own consent to give up my sins and accept Christ. I said, 'I'll accept him today or die in the attempt.' I went into the woods and knelt down, but I could not pray. My heart was too heavy. I felt too weak even to continue on my knees.

"Then I thought I heard somebody coming, and I was ashamed to be seen kneeling there. But the most overwhelming sense of my wickedness in being ashamed of communion with God swept over me, and I grew angry, and shouted, 'I will not leave here till I have utterly made my peace with the Lord Jesus Christ and felt his blood fall healing on my lips! I will not leave if all the men on earth and all the devils out of hell surround me and threaten my very life!'

"Oh, I was still afraid, but now I was afraid of fear—ashamed, but only of my shame. Then I heard a kind voice, as if someone stood right beside me, and it said, 'Worry no longer, my son, but lay all thy worries upon my breast. It is even I!'

"I fell forward upon my face then, as though I had been smitten by a glory that was too vast for me to bear, but as I lay there I had no more shame, no more fear, but only glory—glory—glory—and joy such as I had never known—excelling joy in the presence of the living and all-merciful God, who is here now, right now, calling you to glory—*come!*"

Mr. Finney's long forefinger seemed to reach down through the multitude and hook out Aaron's soul.

Early in Finney's discourse, Aaron had worried about his sins, without being quite clear as to what they were, and had wanted to get rid of them. Then he was not sure that he could. He felt that he was corroded clear into the chambers of his heart. He determined that he would not fret about his sins, but throw them away, and he saw what they were: unclean and irreverent talk, inattention to the church, failure to revere his father, the slimy touch of Nadine, liquor and cards and the perilous dancing, pride in his carpentry and his strength.

It seemed to him then that his sins were gone, mysteriously, completely. His mother was standing beside him, looking at him beseechingly. From a great height he saw that his sins lay scattered on the ground, foul and stinking and broken; that Gene and Nadine and Preston were far down below him, staring up with terror; that he was dying of agony and at the same time dying of an uncontainable and inexpressible joy; that he had to flee—that he had died—that he had come to life and was again in the flesh, kneeling at the mourners' bench, with the solid hand of Missionary Harge on his shoulder holding him safe.

As Harge moved on to other candidates, Aaron saw that kneeling beside him was a stranger, a young man who might be a teacher, an apprentice lawyer. He stared at Aaron, and said clearly, though he seemed to be speaking only to himself, "We have experienced it! It's true—wonder of reconciliation with God, the mystical union of the soul with Christ. I wanted to believe, but I couldn't. But now I know, for I have walked with God!

"I was always so proud of my mean *reason!* I would never yield myself to faith till now, when Mr. Harge begged for our help, when Mr. Finney made me conquer fear! Then, you know, it was as if someone had picked me up, held me way up above the earth, and I was spun in a whirlwind, in spirals of terror and exultation driving each other, rising and glittering spirals, and then I seemed to rest in a great cloud that was yet an invisible person, and I smelled an odor of fresh violets and of a fresh summer wind, and heard something like a silvery spray of bells and a voice like cooling water was saying, 'Come—rest—be quiet—struggle no more against the abiding love!'

"You know, I suddenly understood all the problems in the world: democracy, authority, poverty, illness, everything. They were made by man's own sin-created blindness. They just *seem* like problems. They will all be solved by man's union with the power that makes mountains and, in his good time, overthrows them.

"My eyes are open now. I can see that the material world is only a drifting thought in the mind of God, and yet it is shining and glad— every rock and weed is transformed by a new beauty now, and I am thus transformed, and you are, my friend, and we can never again know sin nor sorrow. You see all that. Don't you?"

Aaron could only mutter obligingly. Out of his sweeping experience he now retained only a memory of cleansing, a distaste for barroom lechery and shiftlessness, a belief that all men could work together under the captaincy of God. A shaky exaltation remained in him, but he felt that he was still only Aaron Gadd and always would be Aaron Gadd, the son of Uriel the son of Hezrai.

9

BUT the whole world had a new light on grass and leaves and hills, with a sound that might be the wind and might be great harps singing.

He was snatched back to the common earth when he heard Mr. Finney, after busily looking at his watch, gloat to Mr. Chippler, "Got to hustle on now, Brother. Due in Springfield by midnight. Fine outpouring today. I calculated nineteen souls saved. Last evening, in Bennington, I figured twenty-one. Well, God bless you and the work. Be seeing you!"

A brisk sound of hoofs, and the angelic visitor was gone. And gone the young stranger who had knelt at the mourners' bench.

Aaron would have moved away—the heavenly light on hill and rock was colder now and dustier—but the Reverend Mr. Chippler gripped his arm, and cried, "My boy, this is the great moment of your life! Ever been converted before?"

"No, sir—not really."

"Now is the time when you have grown up and become a man. I've seen you in my congregation, but are you a church member?"

"Yes, sir—Congo—in Clunford."

"But now that you're with us, in dear old Adams, you must get a letter to our meeting, and take some earnest part in our Sunday-school work, and come and counsel with me often, and make your calling and election sure!"

"Yes..."

Chippler had bounded away, but Aaron's own people were standing there, curiously in awe, and his father, looking wistful for the first time that Aaron had ever seen, was hesitating, "It's good, my boy. It's all right. I never was converted, myself. I'm one of the once-born. But I was pleased to see the flood of blessings poured upon you. Very fine."

Aaron was reduced to boyhood. "Oh, do you feel so, Papa? I'm glad! Say, when Mr. Harge was talking, I almost wished I was a missionary."

"Well, that's a noble work—I guess—for those as get a call for it." And Aaron's zeal was instantly dimmed.

The others were silent; Rebecca kissed him, Deacon Popplewood and Mr. Fairlow shook his hand, restoring some of the confidence and maturity which Uriel had pilfered from him. They moved off together.

If he could conceivably become a missionary, it would give him a chance to defy God, who was his father, and to obey God, who was God. . . . And missionaries stood a lot higher than carpenters in Massachusetts society; almost as high as a judge—anyway, a local judge. . . . He hotly told himself that such ambitiousness was vile and corrupt. But the son of Uriel would have to think of stability and power. Was he, Aaron considered seriously, mad? Would a sane man have to start being converted all over again, so soon after conversion?

He saw Nadine, Gene, Preston, standing beyond the benches, looking his way, whispering together, seemingly frightened. That pleased his vanity of righteousnes. But he rebuked himself for feeling superior to these tried friends, and he started toward them, with warm but badly defined notions about getting them into the fold also. He was stopped by Mr. Harge, now stately again in tall silk hat.

Though he was square while Uriel was lean and rangy, Mr. Harge seemed to Aaron very like his father.

"Sit down, sit down on this bench," he said. "I noticed you at the mercy seat. Fine strong young fellow, thinks I. I was wishing we had someone like you at Bois des Morts. It's a combined Presbyterian-Congregational mission of the A.B.C.F.M., under the Plan of Union."

He assumed that any young man of the slightest decency would understand that the cabalistic initials meant "The American Board of Commissioners for Foreign Missions," and that he need not explain that the Presbyterians had split into the New School, which was for union with the Congregationalists in missionary work, and the Old School, which considered Congregationalists disgusting about the finer points of Eternal Damnation.

"The Bois is out on the Minnesota River, two hundred miles west of the Mississippi River and Fort Snelling. It's beyond the reach of the whisky-sellers and their so-called civilization. Your heart would be wrung if you could see how critical for all future time is our work among the Sioux—or the Dakotas, as they presume to call themselves. They are clotted with evil. They don't feel any obligation whatever to worship God according to the plain instructions in his holy word.

"They're all dirty, superstitious, and awful gamblers; all liars, adulterers, thieves, murderers, and you can't get any of them to observe the Lord's Day, no matter how you warn them of their awful danger in breaking it. And I doubt if there's a single chaste woman in the whole seven fires of the Sioux nation, except the few that have accepted Christ as their savior.

"What a chance for a missionary to reap a harvest of souls and of glory in the world-to-come! There will undoubtedly be a treaty taking over all of the Suland west of the Mississippi, but now no whites are allowed there except such traders and missionaries as are licensed by the Indian agent. Once the treaty is made, it will be too late for you to see that land just as it came from the shaping hand of God. It will be swept by grog-sellers, by railroad-gangs cursing and boozing and fighting, by the godless Roman Catholic Irish and German Lutheran farmers. But now we still have our chance to administer a power directly derived from God.

"He has never in history put out such a strong call for missionaries

53

as he is doing now, and we need strong and virtuous young men as helpers, need 'em bad! ... What's your schooling, Sonny?"

"Oh, couple years Latin and Greek and so on at Cheshire."

"What's your job?"

"I'm a carpenter. Done a little brickwork and plastering, too."

"And farming?"

"Born, brought up on one."

"Oh, my boy, my boy, never was the hand of God clearer in history! You're what we need most urgently! We're ordained ministers at the Mission, and some of us are as familiar with Greek and Hebrew and the tongues as with our own boyhood palaver, and yet —with the aid of our farmer, Jake—we have to build our own cabins, plow our garden, cobble our shoes and ... Married?"

"No, sir."

"Boy, it's ... What's your name?"

"Aaron Gadd. Some call me 'Neighbor.' "

"Neighbor! Aaron, my dear boy, it's destiny, my being here to summon you to the fields whitening for the harvest, on the very day and hour when the plan of salvation was revealed to your heart! It's a miracle! Neighbor, you are going to be a missionary!"

"Well ..."

"And those grand prairies, millions of acres, right up to the bastions of the Rocky Mountains; buffalo and bear and beaver; riding wild horses—not stick here, wedged into a village! And the ecstasy of leading grateful souls right up to the heavenly sheepfold! Maybe if you don't come with me, maybe if you turn a deaf ear to the Lord's tender pleading, hundreds of Indian souls will be lost and writhe in hell, all through your indifference!"

Aaron shuddered. "That would be bad. I wish I were a minister and had the training ..."

"You come with us, Aaron and you'll get it, free! Mr. Speezer, my collaborator, and I will instruct you in theology, Greek—everything!

54

Also both of us speak and preach in Sioux—to some extent. You shall study under the best conditions, free from temptations. What we need is a pure young man who's a blame good farmer and builder, and in return we'll give you of our learning.

"Don't you see it? Don't you see how maybe God has personally chosen you for this sanctified calling? Come try it. If you really are happy in your work there, you can be ordained by the Presbytery right in Minnesota—the Congregationalists permit it. That's what we're doing this year with Gideon Pond, who was a carpenter too, come from Connecticut. I feel in my bones that God calls you to the holy eminence of the pulpit! Why, Jesus was only a poor backwoods carpenter, too. Maybe that's why he picked you out.

"I was a lawyer once, like Brother Finney. Oh, I was a vain and pompous sinner, clean outside the circle of God's mercy. I didn't do so bad, at that. I was a county attorney, down in Pennsylvania, when I was in my twenties. That's why so many of the brethren call me *Squire*.

"In fact, I might of got to be a judge. But God smote me and showed me politics wasn't nothing but a pushing cattle-pen and an empty holler. He led me like a lamb into divinity school, and out to the perils of the wilderness. Not but what it's mighty interesting, these peculiar Indian doings, like the sun dance. Don't it tempt you?"

"Yes, it does, Squire."

Mr. Harge seemed pleased to hear his title. He urged:

"I want you should come and see me, soon, at Eliot House, where I'll be staying a few weeks. That's a home and school for missionaries' children, over near Hawley, near here. That's how come I could attend this camp meeting. My daughter Bessie is there. What a sanctified little miss she is! Had a strong conviction of sin at five, and used to go off and pray in a closet—always kept the door a wee mite open though, for air. She'll be a great missionary, some day, where her father has been an old bungler. She learned all that my dear wife, Mercie, and I could teach her, so she's been continuing her studies at Eliot. They tell me already—she's eleven—she has a fine sense of hermeneutics and the Greek particles, and now I am taking her home to lighten our declining years. . . . Mercie isn't well; couldn't come with me.

"Also at Eliot House you'll meet the daughter of our only white neighbor at the Bois, Caesar Lanark, the fur-trader. Selene, her name is—Selene Lanark."

He called it "See-lean." He thought about this young female, and shook his head.

"Selene is bright enough, but she's like her father, who is a scoffer and a man of wrath. Oh, yes, he may look so gentlemanly and cultured and all that, but he sits right down with the unredeemed Indians and drinks red-eye with 'em! Selene has never been under conviction, though she must be nineteen or twenty now! Maybe you can rouse her to a sense of her dreadful peril before the judgment of God —strong, earnest young fellow like you!

"You try it. May help you accept your calling as a missionary, and come to us. . . . By the way, we can't pay you any of these fancy Eastern wages. I hear where carpenters getting as much as a dollar-fifty a day! I don't know that we, that is, the Lord, can pay you anything except board and keep, along with the chance to learn Sioux and Greek and the divine mysteries, and chance to teach the young Indians, and preach if you feel moved that way. To do the noblest work allotted to man! How about it?"

"Why, Squire, as a missionary I wouldn't expect to get much."

"Not in hard cash. But what a joyful experience can be yours— bride of the lamb—oh, strike while the iron is hot! When can you fix it to come over and see me at Eliot House? Too bad you can't make it next Sunday, but of course there is no sin more destructive than needless travel on the Sabbath. How about next Wednesday? Couple miles west of Hawley."

"I'll be there!" said Aaron.

To be picked out as a missionary within half an hour after his conversion! To go west! To bring order and civilization to the aborigines, under the word of God! And perhaps Squire Harge was wrong—a noble man, but old-fashioned—in thinking the Indians degraded. Perhaps Aaron would be the first to understand them, love them, unite them with the whites in a titanic new race of men.

He saw Dr. Li and Mark Shadrock talking with women worshippers beside the platform. Li was a symbol delicately carved in old ivory; Shadrock was quick-spoken and a little amused, an easy and superior man out of the great world. Months afterward, Aaron wondered if he had actually ever seen human beings called Mark Shadrock and Dr. Li. Perhaps they had been angels in a vision, brown angel and saffron angel, benevolent and gentle but of a nobler blood.

His soul had been a lonely little dog, like Diana, trotting in the darkness, lost, but it had found a master who promised shelter within the warm walls. Whether he would like those walls he had not yet considered, nor whether the master's God, the God of the Mission, would tolerate him, even on the doorstep in the rain.

10

He SCAMPERED over to Nadine and Gene and Preston, the friends who had been waiting for him so faithfully, and found that they were not in the least faithful or friendly.

"So you had to go and do it, hand yourself over to a lot of sneaking hypocrites!" snarled Preston, and Nadine, looking at Aaron as though she had seen him somewhere before, reflected, "Maybe the priest won't give me hell for going to these Protestant doings, and won't he be right! Lot of old women in pantaloons crying about their poor little souls!"

Gene finished it: "We just waited to tell you we hope to God we never see you again, you rat!"

Thus forcefully got rid of, Aaron could only be human enough to wonder how he could get rid of *them,* and free his shining new righteousness from such boozing, fornicating, loose-talking pests.

Nadine leaned with relish against Gene, and murmured, "Oh, honeyfoot, I got to have a drink, to get the taste of him out of my mouth!"

They walked off, leaving Aaron uncontaminated and considerably surprised.

"I'll never see that Nadine again, no matter how much I'd like . . . No! That's over!"

He was still saying the same thing at midnight, as he stood by the window of his little straw-matting room at the Widow Plummer's. But he was so distraught that he lighted a cheroot. Suddenly he threw the cheroot out of the window, and a whole paper of them after it.

"There's one sin I can tramp on for keeps!" he thought, with wild and innocent viciousness.

He was embarrassed and considerably pleased at church, the next

Sunday morning, when Mr. Chippler announced that during their harvest of holiness, one of their fine young members, Brother Aaron Gadd, had been led to pledge himself to God's great work of missions, and would immediately be leaving for the land of the Sioux. Till that minute, Aaron had not been at all sure about this point, but it seemed now to have official sanction.

He was accustomed to the obsequiousness of customers who wanted a door rehung, quick, but the quality of reverence with which the congregation shook hands with him after meeting elevated him to a noble imbecility. That sober splendor continued when (since he was going home this did not count as breaking the Sabbath) he tramped to Clunford, and stopped at Deacon Popplewood's.

The Deacon bubbled, "Oh, yes, Aary, now that your feet are set upon the way, you must go on and become a missionary, and when the Last Day comes, I know it will be counted for my poor credit in heaven that perhaps I have influenced you."

"Oh, *yes!*" cried Mrs. Popplewood. "Will you have a caraway-seed cooky, Aary, like you used to when you was real young?"

But, at home, Uriel was flint.

"What's this nonsense about you taking up the sacred work of missions? You're too sloppy. Never used to could get you to even keep the wood-box filled. And you laugh too much. No laughing matter, saving the miserable souls of a lot of murdering savages. You suppose Jonathan Edwards ever laughed?"

As he walked back, Aaron vowed, "I'll show him!"

With a notion of defying somebody—he was not quite sure whom—he went to vespers at the Episcopal church in Adams, late that afternoon, but the twilight round the gaunt church, the tenderness of the trees, the gentleness of the service turned his irritation into resolution. On Monday morning he abruptly told his astounded boss that he was going to take off the whole of next Wednesday—a debauchery unheard of in those good old days, when an honest man worked eleven or twelve hours a day, six days a week, at whatever wages God was pleased to give him, and no crazy European ideas about wasting his own time and his employer's hard-won substance by taking "vacations." If you had time off to see your family on Saturday, it was because you had worked extra hours all week.

"I never heard . . ." said the boss.

"I'm going!" said Aaron.

He must have been a good carpenter, to take off a whole day without being driven out of this decent community.

As it was only sixteen miles over to Eliot House, Aaron did not have to get up early for his walk—not before five A.M.

The exhilaration of his free day, the shine of mid-June on the rocky hillsides, sage-green and woolly with lichens, so touched his cheeks that he came up to Eliot House like a young lover. He was too happy to note that the establishment looked like a county poor-farm, with a shaky wooden barracks set among suspicious trees. A feeling of charity and soap and tracts was all over it.

At the cracked door on the long, naked porch, he knocked and knocked till it was opened by a round-faced, skeptical-looking girl who openly jeered at anything so uncommon here as a stalwart young man.

"I'd like—oh—Reverend Harge—I'd like to see him." Aaron's tongue was crippled.

"You would? I declare!"

"Yes, I would!" He had noticed that most young women were zealous about doing whatever he wanted (speaking in a pure way), but his masculine conceit did not penetrate this female cynic. He guessed that she had been sent home from the field by missionary parents, and might be acquainted with African fever-ports, Burmese jungles, or the palaces of St. Petersburg and the polylingual but unredeemed young noblemen there, to whom earnest souls were carrying the gospel of Massachusetts.

She looked him over without prejudice, and sniffed, "I'll send down the matron."

That lady was middle-sized, overaged, corded and very resentful.

60

"Judge Harge is engaged in literary labors. I don't know as he would wish to be disturbed."

"He told me to come."

"What was the name, please?"

"Aaron Gadd."

"Aaron?"

"That's it."

"God?"

"No, Gadd!"

"And what was the first name, Mr. Gatts?"

The door was shut in his face. This portentous visit, he felt, was to decide whether he would be one of the giant missionaries of history, with bearers holding a jeweled parasol over his head while thousands of dusky faces were reverently bowed to earth before him, or be a Berkshire carpenter, busy with a saw. If Squire Harge was as sniffy as the matron, he would tramp away. . . . Could he win back Gene, Preston . . . Nadine?

Squire Harge absent-mindedly opened the door, head down, looking over his spectacles at nothing at all, and audibly muttering: "*Unk* prefix with *pi* suffix as in *unkoiepi, unkoranpi*—heh?"

Aaron was not so defiant as he had intended. Not so easily could he give up the buffaloes, the Indians, the great winds challenging the prairies. He said diffidently, "Squire—Aaron Gadd—Neighbor!"

The man lighted. "Oh, my dear boy, I was expecting you! I ain't sure but what the old, the gettin'-old folks don't wait for the young critters more anxiously than t'other way round. I was so mixed up in this pesky Sioux grammar—kind of stuff a wild hyena of an Indian *would* invent! Come in, come in, my boy! . . . Oh, here's my little Bessie coming!"

Hop-skipping down the dingy corridor was a picture-book fairy child of ten or twelve, goldilocks, strawberries and cream. Her father shouted, "Bessiekins, here is Aaron I told you about. My, doesn't he look like a big, stout fellow to take you sliding! I'm hoping he'll be coming to us just after you and I get back. Isn't that nice?"

Bessie confidingly took Aaron's wide hand, looked up at him sunnily, and with the utmost gravity she said, "Are you saved, Aaron? Because if you aren't, you'll go right down to the agonized groans of the damned, even if you are a good slider on earth. Have you known conviction and wailing?"

"Wwwwwwww . . ."

"Dear Aaron, we'll have lots of time to find out at the Bois. In winter there isn't much to do there except to have a true examination of our souls. You know, Aaron, being a church member don't save you from the wrath to come, if you betray reprobation by having naughty thoughts, dear."

"There, there, there, chickabiddy!" Mr. Harge chuckled. "You know, the dear babe is so engrossed in her future mission career, to carry on my labors, that she can't help practicing. She gets the old gardener here quite mad. . . . Run along now, Papa's bunny, and Aaron will have dinner with us at twelve. See if you can't get that uppity matron to give us something besides hash or chipped beef. Honest, she ought to, us with a guest!"

"Goodygoodygoody!" yelled the happy prodigy. "Maybe I can get the old hexe to give us some punkin pie. I'll see you soon, dear Aaron!"

"And tell Selene that Aaron is here," Mr. Harge shouted after her.

"Selene?" inquired Aaron.

"I told you about her—daughter of our only white neighbor at the Bois, Caesar Lanark, the trader. Princess Selene, *he* calls her! Handsome girl, but vain and worldly. Even at the age of twenty, she's got no sense of her tragic sins. Oh, I don't mean she's *got* any sins, not especially, but still, who of us ain't, in the sight of God?

"Mr. Lanark will be a very rich man some day—he calculates to trade in Minnesota land, when we get to be a territory—and Selene will know every luxury. Crying shame to think that she'll probably devote herself to hideous voluptuousnesses, theater-shows and imported china and beefsteak every meal, instead of helping out some poor mission. I got her took in here at Eliot House as a favor to Mr. Lanark. He helps us get in our mail and supplies and gives us grub wholesale, though he's a raving infidel. The thought weighs heavy on me. Maybe we shouldn't have a pagan like Selene here."

The heathenish given name of this young woman was pronounced as Say-lay-nay by herself and her father; Aaron later compromised on Say-lane; most people, including the Bois missionaries, called her See-lean. That it was an appellation of the swift moon goddess (something that Aaron never knew and Selene may not have known) was not too unsuitable. She lunatically intruded on Aaron's missionary ardors before he ever saw her.

For when Mr. Harge had led the way to the enlarged cupboard which had been lent to him as a study—a cubicle with a pine table, two wicker rockers, and a steel engraving of the Reverend Dr. John Witherspoon—Selene kept slipping into their talk.

Said Mr. Harge, "What makes it so bad is that she isn't really under the rules here, like my poor Bessie is. Why, they make Bess stop singing hymns at nine o'clock! Selene is just living here to be properly chaperoned. She's studying French and piano at an academy in Shelburne Falls. Goes over by coach, all by herself, free and hoity-toity as you please! But I must say she's a pleasant young woman. She's nice-looking, in her funny way . . ."

"Nice-looking? She's a thundering beauty!" quivered Aaron. For a girl who could be no one but the Princess Selene stood posed in the doorway.

She was on the tall side, slender, rather tanned: olive-brown of skin with a wonderful smoothness to it. Her nose was uncommonly straight and decisive; her mouth wide and emotional. Her eyes had the tint of black glass, but they were not opaque; they were vigorously aware of everything.

Selene Lanark was all vigor, speed, tautness. Her dark energy would have made the briskest housewife seem slack and uncontrolled. She wore what was, to the farm-bred Aaron, a fabulous dress of brown delaine with a demure fichu of lace, and the wide skirt of the day, stiffened and arching like a bell. Where Rebecca pasted her hair down and Nadine scrambled it up, Selene's black hair was erected in a snailshell crown; where Nadine's idea of holiday elegance was a flutter of muslin, with badly sewed seams and things pinned on things and falling off, Selene's costume was severe.

She seemed to Aaron older than her twenty years. She was the imperious princess who had never heard of anything so nasty and uncomfortable as revolutionaries, and who was kind to the peasantry with a flavor of disgust in it. Then, as he saw the secret interest in her eyes, he understood. She was a child superbly playing at being grown-up, and she wanted her applause.

11

SQUIRE HARGE rumbled, "I have a couple of things to attend to, and I think I'll leave you two young people together a second. Oh, I got an ulterior motive—my, yes! See-lean, you remember what I told you about this boy—Aaron Gadd?—Neighbor? Well, I hope you'll try and persuade him to join us at the Mission. He ain't a minister, but he's a fine, steady worker, a carpenter, and a moral influence on all his group of thoughtful young Christians. He'll bring noble thoughts to the Indians. You tell him what a beautiful country Minnesota is—also highly recommended for all diseases of the throat and chest. . . . Selene will be finishing up her mastery of music and joining us out there by next spring, I hope, Aaron."

He tiptoed off like a ponderous pussycat.

Aaron said to the girl, resentfully, "I'm not that good. Noble! Are you?"

Selene's superiority dissolved at once, and as she perched in a wicker rocker, brown hands clasping a knee, she whooped, "Oh, Aaron, my good young missionary! Do you suppose Daddy Harge is trying to make a match between us? Isn't that too wonderfully absurd!"

Aaron could not see anything absurd about it, and he hated her fluting pomposity. He had a flat-footed Yankee suspicion of princesses, anyway. He considered that this haughty young woman was too rich to be able to pass through the—what was it?—camel's eye? needle's eye?—of friendship. He sat offensively forward in his rocker and, catching suspicion from him, she became prim again, though her eyes were inquisitive, her lips parted.

She was so young!

He tried to be more obliging. He said tolerantly, "Squire Harge allows you're quite a princess, out there on the prairie."

"Oh, that's just silly! Princess—pooh! Just because some people call my papa's trading-post 'Lanark Castle.' Of course Mon Père is an important fur-trader—all these mink and beaver and otter that the ladies wear in London. He has hundreds of Indians trapping for him. He gives them orders and he sits and reads and reads and looks out of the castle window at all his lands and rivers, and he protects the scary people at the Mission from the marauding Indians —oh, *kind* of a king—*you* know—not really!"

Aaron remembered the engraving of Warwick Castle he had seen at Deacon Popplewood's, with a man-at-arms looking over the battlement at an obsequious village of thatch and stone. He was more humble than ever he had been to his father, as he inquired, "Do you feel the Mission, Bois des Morts, does a lot to civilize the wild Indians?"

She put her head on one side, in the best manner of the best Parisian salons. "The missionaries certainly do a lot in making the wild Indians pretty dull! It's years since I've been back home, but I remember how my father laughed at Sioux scalp-hunters trying to sing Sunday-school songs. The missionaries are such awful naggers, especially the Presbyterians."

"What's your church?"

"Why, I'm a Catholic—well, no, more sort of a ritualistic Episcopalian, you might say. Uh—incense."

She was, he saw again, still a child, and however pretentious and snobbish and inclined to lying, a gay and charming child, if you gave her the chance. With her, it was absurd to keep up ponderosities about civilization, and when he burst out, "I'll bet you're a slick skater!" she was his friend forever.

"When I was a little girl out there, I used to put on a red cap and red mittens and skate way up the Isanti River. Daddy was horribly afraid. He said the Sioux would kidnap me and make me a chieftainess."

"Now!"

"Honest he did! *Something* like that, anyway!"

"Look, See-lean . . ."

"Say-lay-nay!"

"All right: Say-lane! That's the best I can do. . . . If I should go out to the Bois, would you . . . We'd skate together."

"I may go. Next spring. Then I hope I can get Daddy to take me to Europe."

"Oh . . . *Europe!*"

"He has so many important relatives in Scotland, barons and all, and then we'll go to France—I have some French blood as well as Scot—of course my ancestors were with Charley-over-the-Water—and then study music in Italy, so beautiful with their mustaches . . ."

"Stop gabbling and tell me if you think it would be sense for me to become a missionary."

She looked as though she would laugh or be sympathetic, whichever he preferred, and he said urgently, "I'm awfully earnest about this, Selene—a world in darkness and suffering because I don't heed the call to carry them the free word of God!"

She decided to be sympathetic. "Oh, yes, it is our duty to help these poor ignorant Indians. *Noblesse oblige!*"

"I do so know what that means! But it isn't that. I've got more shavings on my coat than stars for *noblesse!* But . . . I'm glad you think it might be worth while."

"Though you *ought* to be a lawyer or—or *something*. In politics, or with one of these great merchants. Not a missionary or a carpenter! Honestly, I think you might look slick as grease, if you got some Boston clothes!"

Aaron was still choking at this tremendous compliment, new and, to him, by no means contemptible, when Mr. Harge returned and croaked, "Well, well, hurry now. Dinner is ready."

He escorted them to the Eliot House dining-room, which was a slightly widened corridor, white-plastered, with surly iron pillars. Bessie had not been successful in her solicitation, and the dinner

67

was hash, with no pumpkin pie. The actual eating took less time than Mr. Harge's rather expostulatory grace-before-meat. Yet it lasted long enough for the Squire to make a plea which, coming so humbly from so aggressive a man, moved Aaron with guilt and longing, with a desire for Selene's distant country.

Harge was lamenting, "Aaron, I'm not so young, and neither is Brother Speezer, at our shop, and you might look forward to being the gallant captain of our ship of salvation. The Lord says Come. I am just a faltering voice, trying in my humble way to pass on to you the petition of the Master!"

Aaron had thought that his father and Squire Harge were of the same metal, but Uriel had never in his life begged for anything. He warmly reflected that here might be a new father, with livelier affection.

He was fascinated by the way in which Bessie was sticking out her tongue at the daughter of a respectable missionary in Peru. But such conduct on the part of the holy child did not long shock him. He had a feeling of all these children and their parents as belonging to one family all over the world, praying for one another, loving one another, extremely curious about one another, and of that family he longed to be a part.

When dinner was finished, Selene rose smoothly and, with all her boy-and-girl gaiety gone in a ghastly maturity, she said, "Very nice to have seen you, Mister Gadd. Good-bye." He sprang up explosively and seized her hand, but she looked at him with the most silken indifference, and their handshake was nothing more than fingers crossed on chilly fingers, a network as lifeless as dry twigs, and she was gone, not looking back.

But Bessie kissed him with a healthy smack, and crowed, "Brother Aaron, you'll be coming out to us and to God's work, won't you!" And Squire Harge, accompanying him to the small square entryway, with its hard varnished wainscoating, its slippery varnished black floor, and the solemn black-and-gray portrait of the Reverend Hezekiah Ripley, D.D., said hesitatingly, "We hope you like us, Son, because we sure have cottoned to you! We need you, we'll be looking for you, and I'll write you. God's peace be with you, Neighbor!"

12

FROM Ripley, Ohio, that Presbyterian shrine, Squire Harge wrote, "Turn not thy hand from the plow. He that turneth his back, once his face is set unto righteousness, the same shall be eternally damned. If you get no salary, still will fully share whatever humble comforts wife & I have, and Bro Speezer will hand on to you his store of theology, logic, Ancient & Modern History, ethics, homiletics, Gk, Latin, Hebrew, French, German, Dakota language and etc., and agriculture of maize or Ind. corn. Bessie says tell dear Aaron we are waiting and longing for him."

At just this time, Mr. Chippler came along to complain, "Brother Gadd, we don't see as much of you in church as we'd expected. Oh, he that falls by the way and backslides shall know tenfold more torment than he that never heard the Word spoken!"

Aaron was worried then about his state of grace, and he attended the "concert"—the prayer-meeting. There were two women who sobbed all through it, and Aaron was as uncomfortable as a small boy who has blundered into his mother's bedroom while she is dressing. He wondered whether he had got himself into a greater duty of being good than he could bear. But he noticed that all the women looked at him reverently, and after service a pretty girl whom he scarcely knew caught up his hand, as they stood on the church steps, and panted, "We're all so proud of you that you're going to be our very own agent in the mission field. And you so young!"

He thought that he might have kissed her, with just a little constructive effort, and he found it extremely pleasant to be a hero and a saint and young. But on his way home he came out of it, and scolded, "I've been thinking more about Selene than about experimental religion. I'm not good enough nor pure enough to go. I simply got to scourge the flesh, so my soul will be free from this awful burden of carnal desires. Dear Lord, help me to drive out the devils of sloth and vain imagining!"

So began his season of mortification and of hunger and visions. The heavenly hosts must have smiled down tenderly, in memory of their own youth, as they saw this sturdy young carpenter kneeling half the night, trying to turn himself into a frail beadsman.

Whenever he thought of Selene's lips, of her breast, he writhed with the effort to convert it into a prayer for the elevation of her soul. He went at his business of mortification as busily and methodically as though he were building a wall on the edge of a dangerous cliff.

It was no task at all to give up smoking, drinking, his unemphatic little blasphemies. They had never meant so much to him as his joy in strong arms and quick-running legs. The trouble was to give up precisely that pride in arms and legs and youth and health and friendliness, which seemed to him to be menacing his soul. He had been a contented eight-hour sleeper, but now he tortured himself awake till one in the morning, and yet was up before six, as a man should be.

His prayers were artless: "Oh, dear Lord, honestly I am not just seeking after my own salvation only. I want to know whether it is thy will that I help the Indians—yes, and the white folks who don't understand that all of us, Indians and Chinese and black folks— like Mark—should be brothers with the same rights. Oh, *tell* me what you want, God!"

He read the Bible for hours—that is, his eyesight passed faithfully from word to word, even if his brain didn't. He carried a pocket Testament to work and read it at noon hour, perched on a bundle of shingles, while the older men nodded fervently and the young ones snickered and he tried to make himself ignore them both. His most precious indulgence was permitting himself (though he was not quite certain that he might not get into trouble with heaven for it) to skip the begats and the cubits, and revel in the tales of Job and Ruth and Abraham.

He went about muttering, "A new race and a new life in a new land." No one in this Calvinistic world was alarmed by his muttering—they were relieved that he kept off sandals and a beard. To slay his desires, he tried cold swimming in the deep abandoned quarry north of Adams. At first it was a bath of fire, but he soon enjoyed it; he floundered and splashed and sang aloud, in a rather bubbly voice, and to his mortification it did not contribute at all. He tried sleeping on the floor, and while it was true that most of the impurity of his thoughts about women left him, he was in a temper about the ache of his shoulders.

He tried putting a pebble in his shoe, but that made it hard to walk (which had been the intention in this mystical device), and while he wanted to drive out the soft enticement of evil thoughts, he certainly was not going to interfere with getting to his job. He would put in a pebble again next Sunday, when he was not working (only, perhaps, a smaller and less sharp one). But he forgot it, and in all this there seemed to be no spiritual progress whatever.

He had heard Deacon Popplewood tell of the visions of eternity that came to him when he sat still in his rocker and let the brutal noises of money and political fame fade out. Aaron invited such contemplation. In the still village midnight, he composed himself in a chair in his room—but a severely straight chair, no treacherous rocker, for he was sleepy after the day's work. With some erratic notion about robes of purity, he had draped a white bed sheet over his nightshirt. He had discarded his cloth slippers, and he planted squarely on the floor his square, bare young feet. He folded his hands on his chest, and tried to drive from his face the grin that came when he thought of Rob Gorion, his working partner, slipping on a wet plank and making a windmill of his arms while he protested to heaven.

Quiet, controlled, suspended, Aaron waited for the visions. And they did creep slowly across the lighted ground-glass field of his mind, but they were singularly unspiritual.

He saw the new auger that his boss had bought, and wished he had one.

He saw Nadine's way of drinking cider, with small tentative screams, and felt warm and happy about seeing her, and had to chase her out of his vision.

He saw the Adams banker driving his red-wheeled buggy and Deacon Popplewood plowing with his slicked oxen, and he wanted the buggy and the oxen and the fields to plow and the Deacon's cheerful patience . . . and the banker's money.

He saw Harge's humorless, heavy face set on its base of chin-whiskers.

He saw the ripe dish of pork and beans he had had for supper, and wondered if he was really hungry now.

He saw Selene's supercilious, worldly leer, and the play-acting child behind this objectionable female, and Selene's well-set ears and her narrow, wedge-shaped hands, and her manner of sitting, balanced and sure, and he was conscious of a liking for her quite different from the heat he had known for Nadine, and the nearest that his anxious soul came to soaring was its flight to Selene's presence—to Selene, Selene. . . .

He sprang up and said, like a hurt small boy, "I don't seem to get one single celestial vision! I am the greatest of sinners, Lord; I am unworthy!"

He persuaded himself that the sensible thing would be to see Selene—oh, not as a lovely girl, but as the one unprejudiced person who could tell him whether he would do well to go to Bois des Morts. He argued that this would be sufficiently holy work for the Lord's Day, and on a Sunday he suddenly started and tramped over to Eliot House. But when he crossed that poor, patchy lawn, he came on a setting of abashing elegance.

Selene, in ruffled yellow muslin with a tiny, flowery bonnet

73

perched high on hair that was now a riptide of ringlets, was sitting in a hammock, daintily gesturing with a lace parasol, talking to a burnished young gentleman with blue frock coat, side-whiskers, a cane with a tassel, and no face. And the stringy matron herself was leaping to serve them with tea and buns.

"Hel-lo!" said Selene gaily. "Mr. Frothingberry, this is Mr.—uh—Gadd. A missionary."

"Howdo," said Mr. F, superciliously.

"Howr," said Aaron.

"So you are a missionary!" purred Mr. F, and winked at Selene.

"No, not exactly. More sort of in training, you might say," lumbered Aaron. To talk to this youthful aristocrat was like heading into level-flying sleet.

Mr. F said easily, "Oh, splendid! I'm sure you will be of great inspiration to the Cuffies or the spicks or the poor-lo's or whatever unfortunate race you decide to minister un-*to*."

"Are you interested in perfectionism, Mister?" demanded Aaron, the by-now almost-reverend Aaron.

Mr. F giggled. "Oh, dear me, no! I'm afraid I'm a sad dog, more given to iced hock than to holy water. My avocation is the theater."

Selene was looking at Aaron apologetically—but not very apologetically; she looked now at Mr. F admiringly—but not too admiringly; and she said bouncingly—but with only reasonable bounce: "Oh, I saw Mr. Forrest in *The Gladiator,* in Greenfield, not over two months ago. Just wonderful!"

Mr. F was amused. "My dear, entrancing, naïve child, Forrest is a very poor, bombastic actor! I fear we Americans can never acquire the English ease. Macready is the man! There's culture! I saw him in *Hamlet.* The way in which he waved a handkerchief to indicate his simulated madness was simply too subtle. But," to Aaron, "I assume that you don't care for the naughty theater."

Aaron said nothing in particular, meaning nothing at all. He was pondering, as carefully as though he were drawing a building plan, "If I hit him in the nose, it will be unchristian and make

74

Selene awful mad, but if I don't hit him, it will make *me* awful mad. I dunno."

"Though really," flowed on Mr. F, "I'm not sure that I prefer the theater to such delicious tidbits of poesy as Mr. Longfellow's *Belfry of Bruges,* or that too entrancing excursus on the lands beyond the sea in his *Outre Mer.* Ah, Europe—'in the hollow lotus land, to live and lie reclined.'"

"You always talk like this?" Aaron snorted.

"Aaron!" wailed Selene, while Mr. F protested, "Now really!"

"What's your stand on abolition? Huh?"

"My charming friend, I take no stand whatever on such disagreeable topics. I'm what is quaintly known as a 'gentleman,' and in my hours of ease, I trust I'm a poet."

"You trust wrong. I'll bet good poets work at it. When I get to be a missionary, I'll call you a 'vain infidel,' but just now it'll be enough to call you a blithering damn fool. Bye, Selene!"

He tramped away, heedless, and down the road. He had not known till this moment that he had been expecting (after a handy miracle or two) to marry Selene; also he had not known that this was clearly impossible. She would marry Mr. What's-his-name, or some other rich flunky. She would never stray out to Bois des Morts at all, and if he went there, he must go without romantic hope.

Then, angrily; he *would* go, and for his own sake, his own soul, his own God, not for Selene or Uriel or Squire Harge or Dr. Finney. He trudged steadily at four and a half miles an hour toward the Sioux who were going to be his only friends.

He heard a pattering beyond the stone wall which he was following, but ignored it in his fury. A swift figure vaulted the wall, then sat on it, crosslegged, holding out a hand—Selene!

"Oh!" he remarked.

He was near to embracing her, but he had just come from being-made-a-fool-of, a thing he did not relish. She looked at him affectionately.

"Aaron, I had to say good-bye to you. I'm glad you slapped Mr. Frothingberry. He's scandalous rich, but he's a pudding-head."

He sat on the moss at her feet, his contented head brushing her dangling legs, and he implored, "Not going to marry him, are you?"

"I didn't know, till now. No, I won't! Aaron, you go to Bois des Morts. I think maybe you'll become a dandy minister, and *some* ministers are almost as much fun as lawyers and—I just thought of it—you can curse people you don't like and scare 'em into fits and still get credit for talking holy! You wait for me at the Bois, and I'll be coming along in a year or so. Perhaps by then I'll have some sense. Father has promised me a few months in New York, next fall, staying with an aunt. I'll learn lots—I'll have to—the rustic maid from Yellow Medicine River!"

"Oh. Then you'll become such a fine lady you won't talk to me at all. You'll see receptions and routs and the theater and ... Do you realize that actors are the agents of hell?"

"Who told you so?"

"Well..."

"You ever see a play?"

"N-no."

"Or an actor?"

"Certainly not!"

She was nodding her head to herself, a triumphant young lady, and she condescended, "I've just been reading *Hamlet,* on *his* recommendation, and it's a very fine moral lesson. A lady named Ophelia commits suicide because of her sins. It doesn't say there in the book what they were, but I think it was opposing her rightful lord, the King."

"Don't sound like sin to me! I'd oppose any king that came around here!"

"Oh, that was long and long ago."

"But now you'll be seeing a heap of plays, and *not* moral ones, but where frivolity—where the fair jeweled hand of woman, holding the sparkling wine cup, beckons you downward into the fiery pit!" He laughed, suddenly and enormously. "I guess that's all I *have* got to say about play-acting, and I heard it somewheres else, and I don't know one doggone thing about it, and I guess I'll have to let you go to New York. But you'll become so wonderful that I'll look like even more of a clodhopper to you than I do now! You won't hardly talk to me then!"

"Oh, no, no, no, Aaron! Squire Harge told me how you'll be studying Hebrew and Greek and everything, and you'll be terribly wise and think I'm just the silliest little squid! I'm scared of your learning already, before you even got it!"

"If you only were. Scared!"

"Aaron darling, you will work hard? I'll be thinking of you studying in that little Mission. Won't you!"

"Oh, yes, I will, Selene! I'll be thinking of *you*. And I'll do what I humbly can to help those sin-encompassed, ignorant, dirty savages, those poor Sioux."

"Not Sioux, Aaron. You should say Dakota."

"Oh—you must have seen some of them out there, as a little girl."

She sounded curiously dry. "Yes. Yes, I've seen them. And they're not all of them dirty and ignorant. There's some Dakota warriors like knights—in *Ivanhoe*." She turned passionate then. "I won't go on denying the Dakota! They're so brave and kind, and they've been betrayed by the white men! It *is* true—maybe—I guess—that my father is related to the kings of Scotland, but—— Aaron! I'm a half-breed."

It meant nothing to him, at first, and his grunt was merely friendly.

"I'm half Indian. My mother is a full-blooded Dakota, and I'm not sure she was ever married to my father, except by Indian rites, and a lot he'd care about *them,* if he ever wanted to get married

77

Christian to somebody else! The elegant Say-lay-nay, the fine lady, with her fair jeweled hand holding the sparkling beaker! A miserable brulée—a squaw that ought to be toting wood! That's me!"

"Dear, dearest Selene, I love you for being an Indian! I love the Indians for being part of you! They shall be my own people!"

He stood beside her, as she sat on the wall, and kissed her as tenderly as though she were his sister. They were a singularly innocent and trusting pair of country lovers, by the gray stone wall and the aromatic pasture thick with juniper. As passionless but eager as he, she rubbed her eyes against the slightly worn blue of the Sunday Best coat he had put on for her.

"Red Bud, my mother, is *kind* of a princess—just a teeny princess. She's a M'dewakanton of the Island People band. She's a sister of Cloudman, a wonderful chief. She must have been lovely once. She ran away from my father, Mr. Lanark, because he was so haughty to her, and she went west, toward the Missouri, and married Iron Thunder, a Sisseton. The Sisseton—well, you know how they are—a lot better than the Teton and Yankton, anyway. But still, my gracious! That Red Bud—what a vagabond! I haven't any idea where she is now. And so now you know what the Princess Selene really is!"

"Now I know, and I love it! She's human, where I thought she was just another label!"

On the wall they sat hand in hand. Her hand was dark and fragile and smooth, that of an ancient Hebrew heroine out of the Bible, of Ruth amid this barren New England corn.

He insisted, "You're proud of being part Indian, aren't you?"

"I'm clean flummuxed about it. Sometimes I love the whites—they're clever—and hate the Indians. Sometimes I love the Dakota, because they don't just grub for houses and carriages, and I wish I were more like that—clean of things. And sometimes I hate them both!"

"I wish I could do something to reconcile them. When you come

78

out to the Bois, maybe I'll know something about the Dakota, and we'll be able to sort of study them together."

"I don't know hardly anything about the Dakota part of me. Isn't that funny? My father's had me here in the East most all my life. When I was out there, I never even went to see my noble Injun relatives, except with the lordly Père Caesar along to keep me pure. I never learned ten words of the Dakota language."

"Some day I'll teach you."

"Maybe you will. Oh, you and I could do such things at Bois des Morts—ride over the prairie and chase buffalo and maybe even find a grizzly. Would you be scared of a grizzly?"

"Yes."

"You're darling! There's one lovely young Indian out there, re- lated to me, Black Wolf. He speaks English. So handsome . . . ."

"Um."

"Oh, he's all married; don't worry. Maybe Father will let the Wolf guide us. I'd *like* to know the Dakota. Wouldn't it be funny if a sour Yankee like you, all codfish and maple syrup, were the one to teach me about my own people! Oh, Aaron, they are so unhappy, so plundered! The whites are such covetous swine, especially my own father, who may be a great merchant baron but who's certainly a great scoundrel and a great tyrant. I think I hate all the Big Knives, the whites. Except maybe you."

"Why, you can't hate Mr. Harge! And Bessie!"

"Oh, yes. I could. I hate to be *forgiven* for being an Indian! I warn you: the Squire is a hard driver; if you go to the Bois, he'll have you working eighteen hours a day. Can you stand it?"

"If you'll come."

"I will . . . maybe. Good-bye, good neighbor!"

She was gone, popping back over the stone wall, with a flicker of yellow muslin skirt and prim white underskirt and the latest in lace stockings and a smile intimate but uncontractual.

79

13

WITH all this he might never have gone west if he had not met Gene and Nadine on the street.

"Oh, God, there's that missionary!" remarked Nadine.

Gene addressed him with great reasonableness, "Hya, Neighbor! Come have a drink."

"No, thanks."

"Still afraid to go around with real men? Still wearing your knees out praying?"

"I am."

"Better get one of the holy sisters to brush you off."

"Gene, this looks like a fight. I know I can lick you, but I want you to see that the Lord can lick you, and your sins—you poor little half-pint chuff! I forgive you and bless you!"

At such sanctimoniousness, Gene looked sick, Aaron felt sick, but the eternal woman was enchanted, as what woman in all ages has not been by the warrior-priest? Nadine said to Gene sharply, "Don't be a fool! Of course he can lick you!" and to Aaron, fawningly, "Dearie, why don't you come around and tell me about religion? Honest, I'd love to hear it."

Gene, who was as awed secretly by religion as he was derisive of it publicly, complained, "Aw, gee, you couldn't do that, Neighbor!"

It is not easy to put off the robes of priesthood, once you have known their authority, and though he was distressed by his own smugness, Aaron said gravely, "I would carry the Word to even the poorest of God's creatures. I am a missionary!"

Nadine languished at this, a mass of soft corruption, and as he contrasted her with Selene's hard clarity, he could not endure her. He walked rapidly away, groaning, "I guess I'm chosen, and all

I really *want* to do is to be a rich builder and marry Selene. I'm in for it. God help me and help those I preach to!"

Now that he was going, he found joy and adventure and humility. "I won't be a sniveling Pharisee, as I was with Gene. I'm going to be a plain soldier in the army of the Lord. I just hope I'll become a friend of her folks."

He would win the nervous hand of Selene out there, and he could see the two of them as veteran missionaries, bent and humble and rejoicing, revered by everyone in a city which they had seen grow from prairie trail to boulevards and towers and friendly bells.

"That city shall be holy and our love shall be holy!" he vowed.

He had four hundred dollars saved; he was prepared to use it for his fare, his salaryless stay at Bois des Morts and his frontier outfit, on which he had extremely vague information. He sent to Springfield for a Greek Testament and a map of the Middlewest and a pair of new boots. He had an Adams tailor make him a suit of black wool, decorous but not quite ministerial. In the *Missionary Herald* he had seen pictures of missionaries with sun helmets and extra-long black coats, and it tickled him to think of himself in such dignity, but he kept to a black jacket and a thick black bow tie and a black wide-awake hat.

He was shaky with excitement. In all his life he had never been farther from home than Albany.

He thought constantly of going over to Eliot House for another farewell to Selene, but she would distrust him if she saw him again before he had achieved all his promises; had journeyed clear out to the Mississippi, which was approximately the same as journeying to China, and had become fluent in sermonizing in the Dakota language. No, he must see her next in his glory as a practicing missionary.

Deacon Popplewood urged, when Aaron came to say good-bye,

"Let us kneel and offer prayer together!" Aaron was embarrassed yet happy as the Deacon petitioned, "O Spirit Omnipotent, when I come to the final judgment, let it be remembered for me that despite all my sins, which are abominable in thy sight, I have sought ever to set the feet of this young man in the paths of righteousness, till now we behold him as a mighty bowman, heroic to front the monsters of iniquity for thy sake."

Aaron felt crawly and his neck itched, but as the Deacon went on, long minute after minute, Aaron was lifted by the Hebrew poetry, noble, moving and meaningless; and when he had to pray in response, he heard his own voice, unguided, making what seemed to be the same tremendous music, and he was gratified.

But his father, Uriel, said only, "Hope you'll do all right. Mebbe you will. Mebbe so."

"Dad! I always wanted to ask you: why did you quit running in fugitive slaves?"

"Never did quit, once I got over the rheumatism. Ran in one last week. More 'n you done!"

"Oh! You did? Why didn't you tell me?"

"You never asked. You were too busy with them Adams girls and your self-glorification as a missionary! Well, time to start for the stage. Bye, son. Bye!"

14

IN THE year 1848, when Aaron Gadd set out for Minnesota, he did not know that this frontier, for all its battles between Chippewa and Sioux, was a valley of peace compared with the culture that he was leaving: the hostilities of abolition, socialism, transcendentalism, women's rights, spiritualism, mesmerism, phrenology, vegetarianism, and the Millerites who believed that the world ought to have ended in 1843 and would make up for it right away. These yeasty heresies had utterly shocked or loftily inspired everybody in the United States, except perhaps the people thereof.

In 1848, the holy crusade of the Mexican War was just ending and the California gold rush, more practically holy, was just beginning. The Mormons were comfortably settling in Salt Lake City, and Thoreau had left Walden Pond. The Free Soil Party was organized; the first labor party nominated Gerrit Smith for President; and the Whigs nominated Zachary Taylor, who won. Lucretia Mott spoke at the first Women's Rights Convention, and William Tweed fathered a volunteer fire company which would father Tammany Hall.

It was by chance that Aaron had not gone to Mexico or California or Utah or the women's convention or the labor caucus but had been enticed into a more pious venture by Squire Harge's petition and by Selene Lanark's coaly eyes.

In 1848, all over Europe the events were preparing immigrants to follow Aaron to the prairie. Under Kossuth, Hungary revolted against Austrian rule, and was defeated by a Russian Army of Unliberation. Metternich and the Austrian Emperor had to flee from Vienna in an insurrection. In France, the country rose against

Louis Philippe and proclaimed a revolution which was echoed by the students and workers in the severed states of Germany, who went so far as to demand trial by jury.

In the union of Sweden and Norway there was more liberalism, but not enough to hold the plowmen on ten-acre farms, once they had heard of America, where a county could be had for the asking. In England, the Chartists were parading enormously, making a point against starvation as an imperial practice, and in Ireland there was a wild year of revolution, with habeas corpus suspended and the leaders transported or hanged, while from 1840 to 1850 lasted the Great Irish Famine, during which, to celebrate the reign of the young Queen Victoria, a million people died of hunger and another million chose the milder ordeal of emigrating to the United States, though Uncle Dickens had just proven that all persons who went there died early of ague, tobacco-poisoning or duels with bowie knives.

And during the year 1848 there were sixty-four revolts of Russian serfs; and Karl Marx's *Communist Manifesto* was published; and Darwin was preparing *On the Origin of Species;* and one Abraham Lincoln was an inept and lonely Member of Congress.

In a scarce-mapped wilderness bordering on Wisconsin and Iowa, in a solitude called Minnesota, there were fewer than a thousand white men: traders, lumbermen, missionaries, soldiers, trappers, with half a dozen farmers along the St. Croix River; and all of it save a sliver was held by the Dakota and Ojibway—Indians corruptly and popularly, or unpopularly, known as the Sioux and Chippewa. Not till six months after Aaron's arrival would the district be recognized by the Congress as a Territory, and Aaron believed that he had come at the beginning of the beginning. He was luckily ignorant that French traders and missionaries had threaded the whole land two hundred years before.

This decade of revolutions in Europe and of unease on the Atlantic seaboard was a reasonable one in which to bring forth a new state dedicated to the proposition that storekeepers and farmers and carpenters and doctors may be as wholesome a population as bishops and judges and financiers and patroons.

It is true that within another generation and a half, the carpenters and farmers and the more guileless storekeepers and doctors would hand the control of their eighty thousand square miles of land (so recently lifted from the Indians) over to energetic Maine lumbermen, New Hampshire millers, Canadian railroad-land jugglers, New Jersey bonanza-farmers, and to top-hatted investors who were too portly or too anemic to follow the marshy trails westward, but who had found that dollars fly over marsh and river and forest faster than any moccasined foot, since they are unimpeded by stone bruises or by the heartache of the homeless.

But Aaron Gadd, in 1848, could not know that the first battle for a free frontier had been lost before there was any clearly marked frontier, nor that he should seek for his newer testament not in the great room of the prairie but in tight compartments of old iron safes in Boston and New York and Philadelphia and Cleveland and Montreal and London and Amsterdam and Hell.

15

WHEN Squire Harge had gone out to found the American Board Mission at Bois des Morts, in 1835, it had taken him five weeks from Philadelphia to Fort Snelling. But in August and September, 1848, Aaron rattled out from Adams to the Lower Landing, St. Paul, in a mere seventeen days.

He was awed by the giant five- and six-story buildings in New York, Pittsburgh, Cincinnati, St. Louis. He talked to people, from a Lieutenant-Governor to a red-plush-vested seegar-salesman (who was the Lieutenant-Governor's cousin). He traveled by ferry, river steamer, canal boat, railroad, with twenty-four hours in a stagecoach from Cumberland to Wheeling, across the mountains in rain and fog.

As he contrived his way westward, he was embarrassed by the increase of spitting, sherry cobblers and politicians, but delighted by people who told him that he was a fine young fellow and ought to settle in their town, which, just now, had only a hundred and fifty citizens but was destined to have an opera house and a university within three years. They needed him, they said; and as no one back in Massachusetts had ever indicated that they needed anybody at all, his neighborly spirit grew large with enthusiasm.

No railroad had yet been extended to the Mississippi, and it was by way of the Ohio River that Aaron came to the Father of Waters. He was overwhelmed by it. The Mississippi was a prairie in passionate motion; it was a mad bull of a river, tearing with furious horns at the trees on its banks. From the mouth of the Ohio up to St. Louis, the Mississippi was sallow with mud from the Missouri, but northward it became fresh-colored and cheerful. The steamer's bow butted snags and sawyers, and they scraped over shoals with the chandeliers in the salon rocking and the chairs leaping and gamblers not even looking up.

The passengers wolfed salthorse and pork and beans and three kinds of hot-bread at a narrow but immensely long table. Silence, except for chewing and spitting, was invariable during the eating, but afterward everybody talked, all at once: about the money they were going to make out of Indian land, gold mines, stagecoach companies, buying gingseng; or about the Roman splendors of their favorite politicians.

In St. Louis, Aaron had his smell of the real West, in the warehouse of the ducal family of Chouteau, with precious furs piled in dark alleys smelling of musk, with voyageurs in dark-blue capotes parading in and out, bright-eyed from conflict with the Mandan and Crow and Yankton Sioux on the Missouri. He saw his first Western Indians: Sac and Fox and Winnebago, their deerskin feet squshy on the plank sidewalks, their arms folded under enveloping blankets, their faces so indifferent that Aaron thought hopelessly, "How can one ever get into their dark minds and give them the message of the Lord's mercy? And how can they be so fearless without it?" He was like a savage looking at a violin and wondering how the player ever got it to make such powerful sounds.

From St. Louis he steamed on a second boat to Galena, for the last stage of his journey before Minnesota. That mining settlement lay between the bluffs and the narrow Fever River as if at the bottom of a well. Pigs of lead were piled on the landing and pigs of pig reveled in the canyon streets; every other house was a saloon or a gambling-house, and red-faced men, showy in frenetic plaids, swaggered out of them and stopped to whisper of the threat of cholera. It was a breathless and alarming place, and Aaron was delighted by it.

At the wharf was his final steamboat to St. Paul: the *Dr. Franklin* of the Galena, Dubuque and Minnesota Packet Company (M. W.

Lodwick, master; Russell Blakeley, first officer and clerk). This challenger of the furious river Aaron was some day to love as a man might love a fast horse or a great battle. With her lofty twin stacks, of artfully scalloped tops, her ornamented wheelhouse, her upper decks edged with wooden lacework, her huge side-wheels and their handsomely painted semicircular housing, she was not unlike one of the fantastic mansions that Minnesota lumbermen would be building in the 1870's and 1880's.

Looking down at Aaron from the top deck as he crossed the landing was Captain Blakeley, beardedly benevolent but firm as Uriel Gadd. When Aaron found, afterward, that Blakeley had been born in his own North Adams, in the Hoosacs, he felt that all this shaggy new land was really his, that it belonged to his own lodge and that he might take command of it whenever he wanted to.

His bunk on the *Dr. Franklin* was in the omnivorous men's cabin —not for a poor missionary a stateroom like a little house with the deck for balcony and the racing brown river for garden. He pushed under his bunk, a flinty shelf that was one of a line of thirty, his small tin-covered trunk containing his Bible, a shotgun, no great store of shirts and a completely idiotic fringed buckskin jacket which he had youthfully been lured into buying in New York.

It came to him that as he was now less than a fortnight from his Mission, he would do well to begin learning a little of the Message which he was to give the Indians. Panting in the stuffy cabin, which smelled of too many unwashed adventurers, he hauled out his trunk again, opened its double lock and took out his Bible.

Before they left Galena he sat on the hurricane deck, his back against the wheelhouse, and tried to read *Second Kings*. But the sound of uninhibited miners playing poker in a room above a riverside saloon distracted him. The old Jacobean words, the distant and sandalwood-scented Orient air, seemed only museum arts in this fresh, raw, violent, neighborly world at the end of civilization.

Farther down the deck he saw, sitting on a blanket-roll, another

Bible reader, making an impression of large earnestness by muttering the verses aloud, but constantly taking sly glances over the top of his book. Now this fellow-student was of Aaron's own age, pathetically neat in a patched linsey-woolsey jacket, without tie or collar, and he was unwholesome, like a stalk of overgrown celery. After fretting a little about the young man's general airlessness, Aaron felt that they must exchange improving discourse, as he had at Deacon Popplewood's.

The *Dr. Franklin*—which Aaron was later to learn to call the *Old Doctor,* when the *Dr. Franklin No.* 2 made its presumptuous appearance on the St. Paul run—gave a blast which rolled up through the gulley-streets of Galena. It began to back and fill, turning on the Fever River, mightily bothered by the narrow draw of the new bridge. Released, it slid through a small land of hills and marshes, and went butting into the full current of the incontinent Mississippi.

Last lap to St. Paul!

By now the bibliolatrous youth on the blanket-roll was staring at him hungrily, and Aaron felt it his fraternal duty to go over and (they said it in churches) fellowship with him.

"Hello," said Aaron.

"Ah—Brother."

All Aaron could think of was "Ah."

"My name is Reverend Cudway—Reverend Noah Cudway."

"Well! . . . Aaron Gadd."

"I saw that you were trying to read the Word of God."

"Yes—trying."

"I didn't think you was what you might call real attentive."

"No?"

"Are you saved?"

"I hope so." Aaron sounded like a boss carpenter.

"Do you trust utterly in the sanctifying grace?"

"Yes, I——Sure. I think so. So you're a preacher."

89

"I am. Though all unworthy, I have been privileged to follow the strait and arduous path of the Master and what state you come from?"

"Mass."

"The East! A hotbed and cesspool of pride and vice and volupting! Thank God, I come from Indiana, which is bad enough, reeking with every vile corruption, but a whale of a lot of sanctifieder than New England! I thought you were a Yankee—I thought so—them expensive pantaloons. Thank the unmerited mercy of God, I'm Scotch-Irish, all the way through."

"And a yard wide?" Aaron was astonished but considerably pleased to find himself a suave, cool, reasonable man of the world, an intensively cultivated Easterner, linked to the best families. Extraordinarily like Mr. Frothingberry.

"Yes—yes—yard wide? I'm a missionary.'"

"Oh."

"Going out to carry the Word to the wild and terrible Menominees —a word that means 'rice-eaters.' In Wisconsin. I get off at Prairie du Chien."

Aaron faithfully did not say "Good!" In his elegant new manner, sounding intolerably baronial, he condescended, "And what is the denomination?"

"I am an ordained minister of the Covenant Baptist Brotherhood."

"I don't know that one."

"You *will* know 'that one,' as you put it. We Covenant Baptists are destined to be the one only Protestant Church in America, the only out-and-outer and cover-to-cover Christians, obeying the injunctions of God down to the least, littlest ioty—yessir *and* foot-washing! What's your church?"

"Congregational."

"Oh, woe to the Congregationalists for that you are all weak, wabbly, halfway-covenanting Laodiceans! Letting in a batch of

unredeemed brethren with unsacramental baptism—the very mugginses of hell!"

"Now you look here now, Cudway! We Congregationalists are
just as tough about hell as the old-line Baptists!"

"Old-line Baptists! Woe un-*to* them—hypocrites, all uncleanness
and lying! Methodists! Woe un-*to* them, puking out their vile
blasphemy that righteousness shall be attained by works and not by
faith alone! Presbyterians, that think faith without works is the
caper! Episcopalians—a gang of fancy fellows that're going to hell
right along with the Catholics and the Jews, unless they all fall
right down on their knees with a mighty wail and beg God that by
his surprising mercy he let them hearken un-*to* the Covenant
Baptists! In God's own time, we shall bind all true believers of
every denomination (providin' they aren't drinkin' and whorin'
men) in-*to* one millennial choir, one dread army of Gideon, that
will arise and wipe out all atheists and Turks and bibbers in one
mighty holo—uh—holocaust, bless his merciful name!" Sharply:
"Why don't you say Amen?"

"Amen!" bleated Aaron.

"This church-union you hear about—that's us! All they got to do
is join us. *Amen!*"

"A——Now you look here!"

"But I don't know as a strict constructionist like you could ever
ketch the idea of holiness, anyway."

Aaron became powerful: "See here now! I'm a missionary myself
—practically."

"You don't look it!"

"I was given a special invitation by Reverend Balthazar Harge
and Charles Grandison Finney!"

"Him? Finney? Just an Athenian, spending all his time in vanity
and fine clothes! Always telling some new thing, instead of the
unchangeable hard pan of the gospel. I'm plain folks, and I don't

91

hold with these false evangelists that ain't nothing but private chaplains to the court of Mammon. No, *sir!* Folks as works with their hands, folks as works with their brains, folks as works with their sanctified hearts, that's our line of goods, not fancy lawyers like Finney, that take up the gospel like it was another bastardy case they was hired for. *No,* sir! Poor stinking Indians I'm a friend with, poor niggers, poor farmhands, but not no fancy preachers with a white choker!"

Never could Aaron feel so much like giving up all his quest for God as now, at this caricature of himself and his raceless utopia. It was a notable moral event; it was all education in one hour. He would never be so smug, hereafter, about his own virtue.

Brother Cudway demanded, "Where's your blanket and the rest of your duffel?"

"Under my berth, in the men's cabin."

"You mean to say you go and waste money on a berth? A fine missionary you'll be! I just got deck passage; sleep out here, unafraid in the face of the night air. You're a voluptooary, that's what you are, reveling in Babylonian sloth! You ain't going to mission nobody! You need a good missioning yourself, my friend!"

Noah Cudway turned triumphantly back to his Bible, another good work done with professional finish, and Aaron stood scratching his chin. A young man not without merriment and balance, he yet saw nothing funny in having his cornhusk mattress called an object of Babylonian sensuality. Maybe it was—maybe Brother Cudway was right—maybe he was not a good-enough Christian to get the proper zest out of mortifying his indolent flesh.

That night, in the communal stuffiness which pressed on his nose like folds of dry dish-towels, he lay in his berth deciding, from moment to moment, to get right up and sleep on deck, in the rain.

He awoke to feel himself saying, "No, if my darling Selene were with me, I wouldn't ask her to sleep on deck, but myself . . . Yes. There's some big thought I must get hold of—must get—so sleepy!"

16

THE *Dr. Franklin* stopped in at Dubuque, with its good clean line of brick buildings under the bluffs. Noah Cudway followed Aaron through the town, and punctuated their walk by gleefully pointing out how inevitably each of the local citizens must land in hell.

As they steamed on to Prairie du Chien, Noah quivered with a crusade. He was certain that they could not get in by Saturday evening, that they would be steaming on Sunday, and he planned to summon a mass meeting of the passengers and explain how much viler was Sabbath-breaking than incest or murder.

The others, fur-traders and army officers and farmers, stared at the two young men, including Aaron in their irritation, as Noah shouted along the deck, "Single-handed I will make the great wicked company that runs these steamers buckle to the will of the Lord and keep his day! I'll show 'em! I'll bring 'em to their sinful knees!"

Had he, Aaron writhed, boasted thus to Gene and Preston?

Noah tried to interview Captain Lodwick, who was a godly man and thought well of church-going but who liked to run his own steamboat, and who said, "We won't discuss it." Having the pleasure of thus tasting martyrdom without discomfort, Noah was encouraged to address an unwilling crowd in the saloon. He screamed that if the *Doctor* broke the laws of creation by failing to tie up on the Sabbath, the Eastern newspapers should hear of it, righteous nations like Germany would stop sending out emigrants, and probably the *Doctor's* boilers would bust and destroy everybody aboard except the indubitably virtuous, of whom there seemed to be only about one.

Then, with shocking abruptness, the *Dr. Franklin* arrived in Prairie du Chien on Saturday evening, with the intention of staying till Monday, and Noah's revolution was spoiled. He went ashore, stating publicly and loudly that he did not intend even to say good-bye to Captain Lodwick or Captain Blakeley. At Aaron he shrieked, "You never give me no help whatsoever. Cursed shall he be in Canaan that saith Lord, Lord, but taketh not the Lord's work upon him, and when you land in hell, you'll remember this day. Adoo!"

The outpost of Prairie du Chien, with the palisades of Fort Crawford and its great log blockhouse, the trading-posts of log and stone, and Hercules Dousman's elegant Villa Louise, was a village of islands and waterways and bridges over which passed coureurs de bois and Winnebago Indians in buckskin leggings. In its tiny rough pine way, it was a medieval Venice trading to far-off forests and unknown heathen towns along dangerous ways. Aaron half-determined to dash ashore, offer himself as a trader's clerk, and be sent off to self-reliance among unknown tribes.

The rancid taste of Noah Cudway had for a time made him bilious toward any notion of becoming a missionary. He was a reasonable youth, and he tried to reason himself back into mystic passion, a feat never yet accomplished in the annals of religious ecstasy. He insisted to himself that it was not fair to judge gospelers by so perverse an example as Cudway. What about Adoniram Judson, or Marcus Whitman, who had been murdered in Oregon just last year? But the flavor of these heroes did not drive out Noah's. Aaron fretted that the holier the language used by a fool or a scoundrel, the more moldy and sick-smelling the result.

His meditations upon Noah drove Aaron to demand of himself what, away from the camp meeting and Squire Harge, he veritably believed. What was his vision of God? Had he truly been seeking him, had he found him?

(A quiet young man on a river boat, looking out at a canoe by the levee at Prairie du Chien.)

Jesus Christ he saw as God completely transformed into a man, rather like his brother Elijah, as quick to defend the distressed but quicker to understand a boy's bewilderments, and more serene, more often smiling.

His childhood picture of God, as lean and arbitrary like Uriel yet bearded like Deacon Popplewood, was gone, and he thought of God now as an overwhelming light with streamers that reached out to pierce a man's soul; and as for the Holy Spirit, it was a smaller light, darting from the central glow on incomprehensible missions.

He saw that what he had called his "conversion" had been little more than a lonely desire to be a very good young man. He had had none of the sense of God as a tangible presence which the man beside him at the mourners' bench had received. His own impression of an unearthly glory had passed away within an hour, and had never returned. God was fire, and as unapproachable as fire must be. He sighed:

"But if I understand that I haven't yet completely surrendered to God, isn't that a sign that I shall?"

He was somewhat comforted.

He tried to be clear about just what must happen when God did triumph over his stubborn will. He was content to be a carpenter— that was the trade of the Lord Jesus! He would make his living by honest tools, and be a volunteer preacher on the side. He wanted any cabin that he might build to be so solid that, beholding it, every Indian would be inspired to give up his flimsy tipi and his rickety gods. That Yankee log cabin, that Yankee Calvinism, should be the first structure in a new City of God that would be ready to welcome all the distressed Europeans who might come fleeing to Minnesota.

It was as well for his exaltation that he did not know that log cabins were not Yankee in origin, but Swedish; that his Calvinism had originated not in Jonathan Edwards' New England study but in the gray propriety of Switzerland; and that his zealous belief in human perfectibility was not sound Calvinism at all, but belonged rather to the heretical Methodists.

In all of his meditations appeared Selene, as one to whom he had to justify himself, and with her often came Mark Shadrock and Dr. Li. From Mark and from all the Negroes escaped from the hot checkered fields of the South, whom he had seen as a boy, he had a feeling that the "colored peoples" were valorous and wise and patient.

"These people I love," he thought, "and my faith mustn't be insurance, but something that binds me to them."

As the *Dr. Franklin* chugged on up the Mississippi, Aaron turned to the passengers, hoping that they might forgive him for having endured Noah.

At toy wharves with hillocks of cordwood, under the river bluffs, the boat landed repeatedly to take on wood for its boilers, often paying in barrels of pork. The more powerful of the male passengers got exercise by trotting up the gangplank with sticks of poplar, and of these Aaron was valiantly one. Among his colleagues was a captain of dragoons on his way to Fort Snelling: Captain Amos Pipman, a swarthy, burly desperado of a man with a martial mustache which would have adorned Ajax. No one could have had a taller or cockier uniform cap or more buttons shining on his dark-blue tunic, over light-blue breeches with a gallant yellow stripe, and no one, not even the mate, was noisier and busier at the wood-landings.

True, Captain Pipman did not so demean West Point as to touch a stick himself, but he hustled a couple of army troopers magnificently. Aaron had heard that he was a tough customer, a veteran of the Second Seminole War in Florida, a Mexican War hero wounded in the charge at Molino del Rey. He was sure that no one aboard would so despise his piety as Pipman, the eternal man-at-arms, reckless, cruel, mercenary, materialist, loud-jeering, and presumably long-gambling and deep-drinking. He was imaginatively sure that among the roisterers in the saloon, Pipman must have snorted, "Have you talked to that pair of perfectionists, Cudway and Gadd—Good-God-Gadd? They're going to convert the Indians. Let's get those peewees in here and question 'em. I think there's something the matter with 'em. Then we can throw 'em overboard!"

Aaron had listened to this quite fictitious insult with such indignation that he grasped a stick of cordwood lethally when, on a wharf, Captain Pipman shouted, "Like to talk to you!"

"Well?"

"Hear you're a cub minister."

"Well!"

"I'm in the army. Fine body of men. Darn brave. But not religious. Poor fellows, I guess most of them are going down in sorrow even unto Hell. Drink and whore and blaspheme and play cards and get into fisticuffs—dreadful! Except for a few like Colonel Loomis and Captain Ogden, soldiers are in a shocking state of morals.

"I do my best with them. 'Gentlemen,' I tell them, 'Jesus is our commander and his book is our manual of arms.' But they answer ribald. I've had to show some active disapproval. I've given that up, though, since the last one went to the hospital. I try to pray for them at mess, but I've known even colonels to throw buns! I belong to the Baptist communion. Could we slip away somewhere on the boat and pray a little together, this evening? Brother, you can't know how thirsty I get for the sparkling waters of the eternal word, out on the winter trails, or in the great loneliness of battle!"

The shame of unctuousness which Noah Cudway had poured all over Aaron was gone.

Captain Pipman and he prayed together briefly, in the darkness at the stern, their stammering pleas lost in the pleasant gurgling of

97

the sidewheels. They talked then, and Aaron told his new friend how confusedly he was seeking for a clear chart of God's will.

"Me, I just *accept* him," said the simple captain, "like I accept the fact that America is the greatest country in the world, and we'll have to lick the English again pretty soon, and then there'll be universal peace and I can take to keeping bees and read my Bible clean through every year."

But the quiet keeping of bees would not have satisfied an Aaron who was seeking to find out what he was seeking.

"I'm to do some exploring for the Government, in Minnesota up toward the Canadian border," said Captain Pipman, "and I hope, along the way, to speak the good word of the saints to the Indians. But how I envy a real missionary like you!"

That was better!

To a Berkshire-dweller like Aaron, it was not strange but homelike and comforting that the bluffs along the Upper Mississippi should be lofty rock faces, with demure grassy valleys between peaks, with the sumac and scrub oak radiant now on the dry, bright, exhilarating fall days. There was promise of the great autumn coloring to come.

He made none of the comparisons to temples, domes, castles, which were customary, perhaps obligatory, among all tourists who were spirited enough to make any comparisons at all. What astonished him was that the cliffs were not proper hills at all. They did not go down on the other side as a decent hill would. Their summits were part of the almost level prairie down through which the Mississippi basin had been cut. That was his own prairie, calling him westward.

There was a new fear on the river steamers, this fall of 1848, along with such excitement about farms and future titles that everyone was a little parched and feverish. River steamers did blow up and catch fire and sink with their bottoms torn out by snags. Sioux and Winnebago did fire on steamers and ambush wood-landings. Suave gentlemen did prove to be gamblers or forgers or villains who, to break up the journey's tedium, might seduce your wife. But this particular fall, there were cases of the epidemic Asiatic cholera found virulent on steamers every few days.

Captain Pipman prayed about it, but neither he nor the other passengers seemed timorous, and Aaron was impressed and proud, more eager than ever to be accounted part of them. Pioneers become as used to fear as they do to cold and weariness and turnips and coffee made of cornbread crusts, and all of this prosaic company on the *Dr. Franklin,* including Aaron Gadd, were in the spirit of the Vikings, without the runes, the armor, or Longfellow.

And Aaron was really too busy for fear. He was trying to crystallize his social faith as he had (he believed) his theology. If he could unite the warring Dakota and Ojibway in one cheerful tribe— though in these two hundred years not even the golden Sieur Du Luht had found that possible—then he could go on and unite those more viciously belligerent tribes, the numberless sects claiming to represent Christ.

Never since the Puritans came to Boston and highmindedly turned a wilderness into a prison, thought Aaron, had there been such a chance in history as this opening of the North Middlewest. A great new life in a great new land! Bring in the Greek books and the Lord's Prayer and the habit of bathing, but leave behind the horsehair sofas, social dinners, slavery, stock companies, genealogies, and all titles, such as Colonel, Honorable, perhaps even Reverend.

All this he would do!

Aaron did not phrase his rebellion quite so definitely as this. He actually knew very little about the Puritan theocracy which had chained his own ancestors, but he remembered Deacon Popplewood saying, "Our forebears ought to of loved the Baptists, but they drove 'em out. If you ever get to be a minister, Aary, you love wrong Christians just as much as you love right Christians. The shadow of the same cross falls on both of them."

They were approaching St. Paul. At Remnica, under the barn bluff, they saw the log chalet of the Swiss Mission; then the Methodist Mission at Red Rock, and Little Crow's village at Kaposia, with Dr. Williamson's American Board school.

Aaron was aggrieved that there were so many rival outposts, but Captain Russell Blakeley assured him, "Once you get a few miles west of the Mississip, you can be just as lonely and heroic as you want; lonely as a Jew trying to do business with Philadelphia Quakers. I got out of North Adams, Mass, at the age of two, and traveled west (with some assistance from my family) to Genesee County, in York State, and I've been traveling west ever since. That's what we do out here, Mr. Gadd: travel west. They say Joseph Renshaw Brown—Joe Brown; the Horace Greeley *and* the Samuel F. B. Morse of Minnesota—is figuring on a kind of steam horse that would pull carriages right across the plains. I'd like to drive one of those things and go on westward till I hit the crest of the Rockies in the sunset and look down on the Pacific Ocean and the girls on the Sandwich Island beaches and hear the Chinese temple bells, and *then* go on! That's pioneering!"

17

I N FRONT of the Chapel of St. Paul, founded by the brave Catholic padres and so artfully constructed of logs that it resembled a charming Gothic chapel reproduced in oak and from which softly rang the Angelus, strolling or taking the air in jingling carriages, passed and repassed the gay throngs: gold-laced soldiers swinging great sabres, bright-eyed ladies with silk parasols chattering coquettishly in a dozen melodious tongues, statuesque Sioux chiefs with jewel-adorned eagle-feather war-bonnets and fathomless eyes, watching the cheerful bustle of their white acquaintances, the flower of Minnay-Sotor or the Land of the Sky-blue Water.

An Indian princess, with a tiara of antique carven Inca silver round her raven locks, flirted with trappers and half-Indian buffalo-hunters in buckskin, singing in chorus their French ballads redolent of romantic days in le pays des chateaux. Prosperous Eastern financiers in broadcloth talked to gamblers with gold nuggets sewed to their waistcoats and English adventurers whose bearing suggested many a family of the highest titles.

Amid this colorful scene, so wistfully seeking to be inconspicuous that every bold masculine eye was drawn to her, was a little maid in a demure gray cloak that revealed the exquisite proportions of her womanly form—Agnes, the toast of the trappers, the brightest ray of the Etoile du Nord (Star of the North).

Thus invitingly had Aaron seen the Lower Landing in St. Paul, Minnesota, described in a tale by Mr. Whistleton, the celebrated author of Historical Romances so justly popular in 1848.

The *S.B. Dr. Franklin,* with its whistle unhappily blatting, came in a cold rain up to the muddy landing at St. Paul. The only buildings at hand were Louis Robert's old log store and a moldy warehouse. A swampy trail led up the bluff to a little log Catholic chapel, like a rough stable. A couple of log stores were up there, and a few frame houses, but most of St. Paul was composed of disheveled cabins roofed with bark or with damp, discolored hay. It was not a village at all. Evidently some giant had tossed a handful of timbers over a rising series of hillocks, and they had stuck wherever there was a level resting-place. Farms stretched up from the Mississippi in strips, and the white population of St. Paul, farmers and all, was less than two hundred.

. A few citizens, all male, had ambled down to meet the boat. Most of them were clerks or farmers in greasy caps and canvas jackets and moccasins, talking in Canadian French. There were one soldier and one Indian—the first Sioux that Aaron had ever seen nearby. The soldier was a private, with his tall cap askew and his tunic unbuttoned. The Indian wore cloth leggings and a breechclout and moccasins and an aged military jacket, but not one feather, not so much as a sparrow. Both of them were very friendly and both of them were very drunk. As Aaron passed them, the Sioux remarked, with the universal whine of the beggar, "Gimme two bits, Mister. Hungry!"

Aaron did not take a jingling carriage, because there was no jingling carriage to take; just Henry Jackson's strictly private wagon, drawn by oxen.

But he was here, and he was young, and the land was young.

The St. Paul House, the only hotel in the settlement, was astonishingly large and very old for the time and period: two years old and two full stories high. It was built of tamarack logs elegantly hewed square, and its barroom was the most fashionable drinking-place in town. Jake Bass, the proprietor, was a Vermonter, a Braintree man, and a friend of missionaries. He had married a daughter of Elder Alfred Brunson, the first Methodist superintendent in Minnesota, and Mrs. Bass loved all ministers.

"Oh, yes, Son, you go to Jake Bass's. Tell 'em you belong to the cloth. They'll offer you prayer and a drink, and carve a chicken for you," Captain Blakeley had said.

When Aaron had struggled up the hill to the St. Paul House, with his small tin trunk on his right shoulder, his carpetbag in his left hand, and mud seeping up the leg of his clerical new black trousers, Mrs. Bass, at the pine desk in the dining-room-office, wailed, "Oh, now, Reverend, that's a shame. Every room is taken—six people sleeping in Room One. But I can give you a nice clean mattress on the floor of the dining-room here for tonight—just a few other people sleeping here."

He accepted, and disconsolately walked through the village. The streets were mud trails which disappeared among the scrub oak and hazel brush after so short a stroll that the community seemed to be only a series of clearings which the derisive forest was reclaiming. There were a souple of log stores for trade with the Indians, and Aaron tried to feel encouraged by Dr. Dewey's drug store, by the log schoolhouse in which Miss Harriet Bishop taught the young half-breeds, by William Nobles's energetic blacksmith-shop and wagon-building works (the works being one man, one wagon, at a time), and particularly by that symbol of urbanity and art, a tailor-shop, as kept by Mr. Parsons K. Johnson.

But beside the Catholic chapel stood the priest whom he later knew as Father Ravoux, a cadaverous-faced and needle-eyed cleric in cassock and biretta, and he stared at Aaron as though he were an intruder among the French Catholics. (Which he was.)

He told himself that this was all very hearty and fresh-smelling and vigorous, a village filled with valiant yet highly educated frontiersmen, and that he was going to have ever and ever so many friends. But that was all; there was nothing beyond but the dripping woods and the restless river; and never had Aaron been half so lonely as when he straggled back in the bleak wet twilight to the joys of the St. Paul House and its barroom lighted by sperm candles set in saucers.

The first man he saw there, a trader in a pilot-cloth jacket, welcomed him, "Have a drink, Friend?"

He longed to toss down the burning applejack, the fantastic switchel-punch, to shake hands, to tell stories about the ghost of Stockbridge, to sing, and be universally accepted as a new friend of importance. But he had to say, "No, thank you," at which the stranger looked contemptuous.

He sat at a pine table, alone, unloved, unwanted. He was no longer a good companion, but a missionary.

Why?

He was joined at his table by a Phenomenon: a man who was a Yankee but smooth and plump; who was drinking bourbon but pleased to have a companion for whom he did not have to buy drinks; who asked the three obligatory questions: Stranger here? and What state y' from? and How y' like our town? but who had no further catechism.

"Lively town, lots of fun," he explained. "But it's gettin' too civilized. The old settlers claim you ought to seen it in the good old days, at Pig's Eye Parrant's, back in the thirties, when everybody drank straight rotgut and they wa'n't none of these fancy drinks like ching-ching, and the Injuns would get obfuscated and bite each other's noses off and tumble in the fire and singe! Nobody drinks the real old oh-be-joyful any more. Whole damn country going Oberlinite!"

But for Aaron even this year of 1848, which was mildewed with age and culture and sinking into the death of civilization, became sprightly enough when the somewhat soggy company was stirred by a cheery young man in the splendor of a black tall hat, a black tailcoat cut in at the waist, a cerise vest and a fabulous black cravat sweeping clear down across his white shirt. His lapels rolled as heavily as a shawl and he carried a thin cane with a tassel.

"That's Billy Phillips, our first lawyer," said Aaron's companion. "Now we got a lawyer, we got civilization, which I understand to mean that a man has a chance to get rich without working. Now I always worked, myself. I got a farm over here in the St. Croix Valley—my name's Hiram Gunstead, from Maine—but I got better ideas. Once the Suland, west of the Mississip, is opened to the white farmers, I cal'late to quit plowing and make a fine living by selling land to newcomers."

Counselor Phillips had thrown open his coat, the better displaying a watch charm which was a golden dog with ruby eyes, and he was shouting, "Gentlemen and friends, shall I now entertain this court by reciting *Marco Bozzaris,* or by melodiously rendering *Flow Gently, Sweet Afton?*"

They bellowed for *Afton.*

Billy Phillips had a true tenor, and he sang imploringly, like one remembering other days: "How lofty, sweet Afton, thy neighboring hills."

In this raw barroom, Aaron thought with anguish of the burly hills of Berkshire County, kind with beech and elm and maple, of unexpected, nestling valleys, of white houses with the tolerance of age, and of Selene at the center of it all. He had wilfully given up all this for a flat and ragged and unseasoned land.

Why?

Every face in the tavern was turned away from Phillips, and every eye was abstracted, as they too thought of old green lands. The homesickness of the frontiersman is more poignant, recalling more loves and dancing feet and friendly handclasps and new mounds in the graveyard, than that of any greensick girl sent off to school.

Aaron wondered of what Farmer Hiram Gunstead, across from him, was sadly thinking: salt marshes and lobster pots, or the prickly Blue Mountains? Without any clear intention, Aaron said suddenly, "But this'll be a better land—no rocks—and it'll be ours, not the bankers'!"

"That's it!" Gunstead said gratefully.

Looming into the room like a Roman statue walking came a man at whom all the habitués yelled, "Hey, Joe!" or "Have a drink, Major?" He was a nobler Dan'l Webster, taller, less plump, with commanding eyes, a great blunt nose, a tight mouth and a wave of dark hair down about his ears. He carried an abashed linen hat, but his dark, baggy suit suggested a conservative judge; and a black bow tie crouched under his huge gaping collar. He was Leadership incarnate.

Gunstead exulted, "That's Joe Brown himself—Joseph R. Brown. He's bound to be governor, when we get statehood, and then, more 'n likely, president of the nation. He makes things zip. I hope he gives us a speech. Quiet fellow, mostly, but when he gets going— watch the elephants!"

Aaron noted, with a stare, that Major Brown seemed to be drinking nothing but lemonade. Perhaps he was one of those (highly economical) souls who are born intoxicated, so that they have had six drinks before they take a drink. He was talking to a shy-looking, rustic Frenchman whom Gunstead named as Vetal Guerin, who had settled on a farm in the future St. Paul back in the hoary era of nine whole years ago, which made him a contemporary of the last glacier. But everybody was listening to Major Brown, Aaron with them:

"Vetal, *mon vieux!* Ah, you didn't know I speak French? Like a Spanish cow, Vetal. I'm just back from a quick journey to Big Stone Lake. There will be a kingdom there, some day—terraced gardens above that luxuriant expanse of water. And I have some very neat trading interests.

"Vetal, all the way I have been thinking that we did a statesmanlike bit of shenanigans at the Stillwater Convention. And we're going to pick out Harry Sibley for our delegate to the Congress. Mark me well, Sibley will show the stiffest collar, the stiffest classic metaphors and the neatest foot in the best-blacked boot in Washington. He will demonstrate to those conniving coons the sort of men Minnesota turns out, and he will, inspired by the hortatory epistles with which I shall bedevil him on every mail—that is, once a month!—make them put through a bill, and Minnesota will be a territory within three years, a state within fifteen—a legitimate brother to Majestic Virginia, to Lordly Maryland (the happy font of my being) and to Nimshibustious New York."

By now, Major Brown had given up pretending that he was talking only to Vetal Guerin. His gestures, half oratorical and half humorous, took in the world. His glance had spotted Aaron and the other newcomers, and he welcomed them with the hot claret of his confidence while he sipped the cold lemonade of his glass:

"Gentlemen, we stand here on holy ground—though it needs a slight brushing-up. Head of navigation on the imperial Mississippi, two jots and a hop-skip from Fond du Lac, at the nobler end of noble Lake Superior, with the boundless bosom of the winsome West somewhat immodestly displayed as it rolls on past the envious Rocky Mountains to where nightly (in good weather) the sun gives his nuptial kiss to the languorous Pacific—yes, and north to a land which, however hard on the ears and toes in January, produces the furs that adorn the voluptuous shoulders of duchesses—all of 'em—every single doggone duchess has got to show a pelt handled by the J. R. Brown Lac Travers Outfit or the people rise in their frenzied might and yank her right smack off her throne onto her—indignity. Yessir!

"And right in the center of all this munificent wealth stands St. Paul, which the good Father Galtier prophetically named after the greatest of the disciples. The ineluctable power of Destiny had chosen it to be the most mammoth, gorgeous and powerful metropolis on this globe—say what they like, up in the jealously hissing hamlet of St. Anthony, or in that city, named after the stinkweed, huddled in its squalor on the southernmost tip of Lake Michigan! And you St. Paul boys got to admit that's handsome of me, considering that I am the founder of the vivacious rival villages of Stillwater and Oliver's Grove! Look, all of you—look up!"

They did, in alarm.

Joe Brown was pointing his great arm straight upward, and he

107

said solemnly, "Do you see that parallelopipedon along about one hundred foot straight up there, that singularly bright and salubrious bunch of air? Note it—mark it—long remember it! For there, you mark my word, within one brief century, will be the audience chamber of His Excellency, the President of these United States. There he will receive the obsequious ambassadors of the degenerate human herds of the Old Country. The proud descendants of Saladin, of Capet, of Marlborough, of Rurik, will come here to pay obeisance to America, to the Great Valley—to St. Paul!

"And I'm damned, gentlemen, if I don't think I mean very nearly a quarter of this! Oh, it's a good country—Minnesota. You can plow your own honest earth, cut your own trees, swim in your own lakes, as joyful as a king in fairyland!

"Except for those tan rascals, Vetal's brulé cousins up round Grand Portage, I reckon I'm about the first arrival among the pioneers now, and I ain't but forty-three, that's how new we are here. I come to Fort Snelling as a drummer-boy (*and* skilled fifer) in 1819. I've been an army sergeant, a trader, a whisky-seller, a lumberman, a farmer, a printer, a town-developer, a road-builder, a friend of the Dakotas and their many sorrows, a friend of the missionaries and a foe of their bigotries, a foe of the politicians and a friend of their ideals, when any. I've wandered this fair future state from the glorious hills that dip down to historic Wee-non-ah to the winter-howling plains that embower Joe Rolette's morass of Pembina. I've seen it all and loved it all.

"Gentlemen, we are raw and rough and rude and somewhat ridic'lous, like a muscular young man. Shake hands with that youth. The hair on his chest is the prairie grass and his legs are the white pines and his voice is now the April zephyr and now the devastating blast of the blizzard. He's going to be a lusty man, a mighty champion, yes, and kind-hearted as God's own sunshine. Let's drink to that wonderful boy, son of all of us, father of all of us, purpose of all of us—drink!"

He drank his robust toast, in lemonade, and Aaron Gadd drank with him, in water.

Years afterward, when he read *Martin Chuzzlewit,* Aaron realized from his memory of Joe Brown that half of the oratorical rambunctiousness which that British tradesman of genius, Mr. Dickens, had heard and indignantly noted down had been mocking exaggeration intended to mislead the innocent Victorian tourist.

No more, at least on that first evening, did Aaron long for the tight valleys of Massachusetts. This was his own West, to create or to destroy, in freedom.

He was stumblingly saying his prayers that night before it came to him confusingly that all his freedom now was supposed to lie in joyful obedience to the supreme will of God.

18

SOME of the mattresses were filled with hay and some with fresh corn husks, and there were nineteen of them, on which slept twenty-three persons of all ages and sexes, and Aaron was one of them. There was a good deal of mutter and whimper and stirring in the room all night, and the air was acid and filled with tired ghosts, and in the corners were the personal luxuries of the immigrants: trunks, bundles of clothes tied in bedspreads, music boxes, axes, framed wedding certificates.

Aaron's pillow consisted of his boots rolled in his black trousers. (This ridiculous garment seems always to have ridiculous names: trousers, pantaloons, pants, breeches, bags, slacks, buckser, byxor, housut, Beinkleider.)

He was accustomed to a solitary room and some edge of the mountain breeze in it, and tonight the breath-stuffed air seemed to fill his head like handfuls of old fluff from under bureaus. He wanted to argue with Major Brown about the freshness of the bold new land, wanted to be back with Selene in a cedar-flavored lane.

Everyone was aroused at a quarter to seven; the mattresses were piled in a corner; and in this same room Aaron had breakfast of coffee and fried pork. For supper he had had fried pork, johnny cake, turnips and coffee.

Today the murk of rain had dissolved in blue and gold. In a coach that was an open wagon drawn by horses that seemed incessantly scared of Indians and wolves, Aaron took the grand tour through St. Anthony Falls. They crossed the river on a ferry, and beheld the chief historical monument of the region: the ur-ancient Government Saw Mill, a pine-slab structure going clear back to 1820 and now a ruin, even if not a very picturesque ruin. They swished through prairie grass and came to lakes like round shields, called Harriet and Calhoun. Aaron, the builder, tried to persuade himself that some day there might be villages on their shores. It was, he insisted, a sightly land: great river, fresh lakes, fertile prairie with elevations for drainage. All this region might, with sweat and prayer, be broken into comfortable farms.

The driver said that Lake Calhoun had long ago been taken over by the whites. Fourteen whole years back, the Pond brothers, missionaries, had built a cabin here. As Aaron stared at Calhoun, in the autumn tenderness of light, he noticed a Sioux woman hoeing. On her back, upright in a swinging cradle decorated with porcupine quills, was a baby, contemplative and wise, looking out through a mosquito netting over its toy howdah.

"Cute lil pickaninny—papoose, I mean," thought Aaron, with the inanity suitable to tourists.

The baby eyed him back, and registered him as a decent-enough young man possibly worth an infant's philosophical study. That was in the fall of 1848. In 1949, that Indian baby is still alive, a retired grocer and a Civil War veteran, slightly over a hundred years old, still dwelling within sight of Lake Calhoun, in a twelve-story Minneapolis apartment house.

Before he could settle at the Mission, in Sioux territory, Aaron had to have permission from the Indian agent, at Fort Snelling.

He tramped to the Fort, through the oak and tamarack, and crossed in a boat ferry, rowed by a wild-looking French half-breed, to the west bank of the Mississippi, to a region which had belonged to France, to Spain, to the Territory of Missouri, to the Territory of Iowa. Of course, all the while, it had really belonged to the Indians. That was why the fort was there—in case the Indians got a notion that they might have a right to their own land, and treacherously try to drive out the whites who had taken it over on the constitutional grounds of being white.

III

The fort had never fired a gun. The stripped Indians had looked at it and seen that they must be wrong.

Its two stone towers and massy stone walls looked down on the junction of the Mississippi with the Minnesota River, which would be Aaron's future highway westward. He was excited, for this was the most medieval, looming, warlike and undeviatingly peaceful castle he had ever seen, and he was betrayed into unmissionary thoughts of Selene living in a gray tower and of himself leading his brave men over enemy corpses. He was so awed that he gave up any thought of calling on his steamer acquaintance, Captain Amos Pipman, and went direct to the agent's headquarters.

The log council-house, the agent's story-and-a-half stone dwelling and the armorer's hut, where blacksmithing was done for the Indians, lay a quarter of a mile west of the Fort, on the prairie.

The agent was called Major Murphy. Indian agents were called Major automatically, as the owners of newspapers and racehorses have always been called Colonel and all congressmen against whom it has never been quite proven are called Honorable.

There had once been an agent at Fort Snelling, Major Lawrence Taliaferro, who had protected the Sioux and Chippewa and learned their languages, which was annoying to his affable superiors in Washington. He was got rid of, and since 1840 the Minnesota district had had the same pleasant custom as other parts of the Indian country. The agency was given to some deserving politician who, as he knew nothing at all about Indians and spoke no language except traces of back-street American, would not be prejudiced in Indian affairs and interfere with the highly informed traders.

While Aaron was humbly waiting on a wooden bench outside the Major's office, a gentleman in clerical garb rushed up to him, bubbling, "Mr. Gadd? I'm Ezekiel Gear, chaplain at the Fort—Father Gear they call me, though the Dear Lord knows why, because I'm not at all fatherly. Dr. Williamson, the moderator of the Dakota Presbytery, sent me word on Elder Harge's behalf to keep an eye out for you. Splendid people, the Presbyterian missionaries. They are the sugarless oatmeal in the sound Christian diet. They consider me, as an Episcopalian, the strawberry tart. As a matter of fact, you will see him and his brethren at once. They have been holding a meeting of the Presbytery at Kapoja—or Kaposia, as you doubtless call it—and they're to stop in here to make their usual faithful attempt to evangelize the agent.

"Riggs and Williamson are worthy leaders and Mr. Hopkins, who's stationed at Traverse des Sioux, is a fine athletic young fellow, splendid swimmer, not much older than you but a veteran of five years' service in Minnesota missions. But the Ulysses and Achilles of these warriors are the Pond brothers—Red Eagle and Brown Bear, the Sioux call them.

"While we are awaiting these argonauts, would it, uh, offend you if I suggested that we adjourn to my modest quarters and if I offered you a very mild glass of wine? . . . Ah, quite so!

"Now Mr. Gadd, far be it from me ever to proselytize. The astonishing endurance of the P.E. church has come from its civilized *laissez-faire* philosophy. But if you should become weary of the logs and clods at Bois des Morts, you come back to me, and I'll give you a letter to my bishop, who will explain the *authorized* apostolic priesthood. Pompous though 'Father' may be, I like it better than 'Hey, Reverend' or 'Hi, Doc.' *You* know!"

Father Gear had scarcely finished his mild laughter when Aaron's colleagues trooped in, welcoming him.

Thomas Smith Williamson, M.D., was a broad, rocky man, rather like Squire Harge but sharper of eye. Stephen Return Riggs, the translator into Sioux, was gentler, more insinuating, but it was Robert Hopkins, high-stepping and eager, who seemed to Aaron most of his own kind. Largest among them all bulked the Pond brothers, Samuel William and Gideon Hollister Pond, the Connecticut farmer-scholars. They were men near forty, men like Great

Danes, just as courageous and formidable and honest, and just as unsympathetic to the smaller and more playful animals.

After fourteen years of not-too-meek service in lay-preaching, farming and carpentering at various missions, exploring, teaching, and tracking down new Sioux words like a detective, Gideon Pond had just yesterday, on September 14th, been ordained as a Presbyterian minister (he had been reared as a harmless Congregationalist), and he was going back to his mission at Oak Grove with the sanctity now of being a Reverend. He was exalted about it, and a little sardonic, and he took in Aaron with an astonishingly powerful slap on the shoulder, and told him to go and do likewise.

They were all brave and eager, these missionaries, and worn with toil and cold and bad food. There was nothing of the holy, hushed mystic about any of them, except for moments in Gideon Pond. They had the explorer's patient boldness and outdoor self-dependence. There was nothing for which to pity them.

The pity went to their wives, who had all the privations of the frontier farm-women with the distressing added obligations of having to look piously cheerful when the Indians had just shot the new calf, or taught the children a new curse.

Of having to look clean and well dressed during a season of dust-storms when no missionary box from home had arrived for a year.

Of having to look edified when husband preached for the tenth time his sermon fervently presenting an entirely erroneous view of the sacraments.

Margaret Poage Williamson, Sarah Poage Pond, Cordelia Eggleston Pond, Mary Longley Riggs, in heartbreakingly neat blue or brown delaine dresses and modest homemade bonnets—they all looked as though they had been pretty girls, then eager schoolteachers, and thereafter constantly hopeful that some time they would not have to work seventeen hours a day, but only fifteen.

One of the missionary wives was different. She was Agnes Carson Hopkins, and she was still only twenty-three, two years younger than Aaron, though for five years now she had been toiling to keep a mission station attractive, never quite out of hearing of the Indians drinking rotgut whisky brought in by white traders. She was still soft and gentle and gay. Aaron had an unclerical thought that if he invited her to go to a dance (in entire purity, however), she would be distressingly shocked, and then go.

He had a lively sense now, one that he had longed for at Eliot House, of belonging to the whole family of missionaries. They called him "Brother" and "Aaron" and "Neighbor"; they patted his arm, and urged, "Lad, you come break bread with us whenever you can. We won't have much to offer you, but we can always put another potato in the pot and spread out another buffalo robe on the floor, and show our dear love for you as one of the communion of saints!"

Outside the agency, the missionaries' children were highly vocal.

Aaron had not yet seen his Mission Family in hunger and threatened death, but only just after that most joyous time when they had gathered at a conference. For this they ride, by horseback or mule or behind creeping oxen, through days of bog or mountain pass, and as they come wearily in, they are greeted by the spiritual kinsmen whom, with cholera, flood, savage rifles, they had not hoped to see again. They pray together, they sing together, and as they exchange ideas about the shrewd business of being a missionary, they begin to hope that perhaps they will, by God's grace, really be able to save a few souls, and that *next* year, the Board will send them the money for the wash-tubs, the slates, the bell, the altar.

Their children meet old playmates again, and boys who are pretty dreary in algebra speak familiarly, in a dozen dialects, of Rangoon and Fort Laramie and Mount Tupungato, of mahnomen and curry and pahklava. Later they will marry the girls they first met at the conferences, and with them go on in turn to Honshu or the Mackenzie or the Brahmaputra and, among other dust-storms and famines forty years later, still will ride to the annual conference.

Aaron had found his Family. And he was convinced that they would take in Selene and that she would take them in; blissfully convinced of it, even though he did not believe it.

19

WHEN Major Murphy, the agent, came out to greet the missionaries, he made a speech to Aaron, for the Major was a politician, and politicians do make speeches, even in bed. He was proud to license Aaron to go into Indian territory; in fact, he congratulated the Sioux on their luck in having this new brother, who would elevate their morals and improve their domestic architecture, while upholding the arms of the older missionaries, weary from so many years of self-sacrifice.

Aaron was impressed, until he saw the Reverend Mr. Samuel William Pond wink derisively at the Reverend Mr. Gideon Hollister Pond.

Dr. Williamson said to his colleague, "Brother Riggs, there's about twenty lodges of Wahpekute Sioux camped out behind the agency. Been loafing and begging round here all summer—scared of the Chippeways. Let's show our young friend Aaron what the savages are sure-enough like."

Aaron strolled with them to a huddle of lodges supposed to be made of bark. (It was only in the cold months that the Sioux used their buffalo-skin tipis.) They were as patched a litter of huts as was ever seen on a dump heap after a war: shanties of moldy bark, of broken boards stolen from the Fort, smeared bits of cloth and worthless muskrat skins pierced with shot. The ground was scattered with gnawed bones, broken bottles, excrement. Out of the huts buzzed half-clad children like agitated wasps, sticking out scabby hands to the three white men, shrieking, "A penny—two bits—a penny!" and dancing shamelessly, grinning witlessly, rubbing reddened eyes, while among them barked and growled a whole flea-camp of dogs.

Through this delirium could be heard adult Indians drunk in a shanty, singing, yelling, banging tin cups. A few men leered out, naked but for breechclouts, leggings, moccasins. One of them had been painted in stripes of vermilion and black, which had run from rain and sweat, like a fantastic skin disease. He galloped over, whining, "Gimme pork—gimme bread—starving!" An Indian woman crouched in front of a lodge; her blue cotton dress was decent enough (decided Cadet Gadd) but dirty, and her hair had never been combed.

"There's your Sioux!" snorted Dr. Williamson. "I don't like the Wahpekutes as well as the M'dewakantonwan, but all the Sioux campfires are just about as bad."

Aaron was sick; he was as low in resolution now as he had been high when he had been adopted into the family of the cross. Had he come from clean, severe Adams to live with these dirty beggars?

Did Selene have contaminated blood like this in her heaven-blue veins?

"Few Indians as degraded as these," sighed Williamson, "but before you risk the road into Suland, I want you to see what they can be, to make sure, for Brother Harge's sake and your own, that you will stick through the weary Day of Small Things even unto the final day of glory. Have you got that kind of courage? Huh?"

Aaron tried to look extremely courageous . . . . It was too late to turn back.

Williamson lectured, "Satan has, literally and scientifically, and I speak as a physician, made these people his own. Especially the men. Sometimes they cut to pieces the clothing of the Indian children who attend our schools, and slash the nice modest new dresses that their womenfolks make for themselves at our sewing classes.

"Possibly we ought to let *all* the Indians, except a handful, perish, like the sinners of Sodom and Gomorrah. Lewd, corrupt of heart and unrepentant, these Sioux, except for a few who have listened to the

Gospel, are ineradicably damned, without a single virtue, without a single hope!"

"But aren't they extremely brave?" faltered Aaron.

Mr. Riggs sighed, "I'm not even sure of that. They don't stand up to battle, like white men. They're all sneaks, hiding in ambush and potting the enemy like dogs, and then running away. There are Sioux Christians, like Simon Anawangmane and John Otherday, who are just as good as white men, in their *place*—but keep them in their place!"

In the comparative privacy of his mattress, back at the St. Paul House, Aaron tried to salvage some of his crusade.

"I'm learning! I am by God—by Godfrey! I'm getting a finger on the worst spring of evil. The way Reverend Riggs talked, and Williamson—that's how my father talks about the French-Canucks, and how the Canucks talk about the Irish construction gangs, and how the Irish talk about the Nova Scotia bluenoses, and how the bluenoses talk about all of us Yanks that aren't rich. I smell murder somewhere. I'm going to find it!"

At a table in the barroom, in his tall, thin, clear script, he wrote a communal letter to his father, his sister and her husband, and Deacon Popplewood:

"I hope you will all excuse me for seeming to be so slothful in writing to you, have not forgotten you for a minute but oft in the stilly night and of course daytimes I think of you going yr accustomed ways in dear old Clunford which seems ever more fair & green, as well as the hills, the farther I get into this flat (though high bluffs along rivers &c) country, so now at last I take my pen in hand in St. Paul at the St. Paul House which is the best only hotel in St. Paul, though crowded &c, but the props Mr & Mrs Bass very kind, he was born in Vermont but she comes from Ouisconsin, her father was a missionary.

119

"Well you will all be wanting to know what this country is like. From what I hear they grow only Indian corn, turnips, potatoes, beans & a little wheat, it does not seem to be much good for rye, barley, or veg. Also settlers make money picking cranberries and ginseng root, which is shipped to China, for medicine.

"There are many lakes, rivers, &c. Coming up the Missipi whole valley is just a deep cut in prairie. Lake Pepin a beautiful body of water, it is not really a lake but an ~~enlarg~~ widening of the Missipi, soon this will be a territory but in answering as hope you soon will my address will be

Mr. A. Gadd,
Care of Rev Balthazar Harge,
Bois des Morts ABCFM Mission,
Upper Minnesota River,
Ioway Territory.

"This country is claimed to have much less ague than Mich, Ohio, Illinoy, &c. very healthy for pulmonary diseases. Have met Major Joe Brown, one of the early settlers, they say he will be a millionaire some day.

"The Minnesota River used to be called the St. Peter's River and many oldtimers still call it that, perhaps change of name shows how R.C. influence is dwindling.

"Now I am sure you are asking about the wild indians, yes, I have seen some of them, a little discouraging, dirty &c but after all that's why we are here and the Lord has his own purposes and he that is last shall be first and the corner of the temple, I hope it will be like that with inds. When I feel faint of heart at prospect of failure I denounce myself, O thou faint of heart, do you not trust in the Lord God and do the errand to which he has set yr hand.

"Oh, we are all sinful in his sight, slothful, stiff-necked, & blind & deaf to his clear purposes. O pray for me, my dear friends, that I will be uplifted from my cold sullenness and enabled to do the work of the Lord, however hard."

To Miss Selene Lanark, at Eliot House:
"Beloved Miss Lanark, or I would call you Selene if I dared.

"Well, you will be surprised to hear from me from so far away. I think of you daily and pray the Lord to grant you sweet peace and serenity and if you go to the perilous city of New York, maybe you are already there, to guide your feet faithfully along all its dark ways and manifold temptations.

"I haven't seen much yet of your own people, I mean your own in *part,* the Scioux or Dakotas, but my most earnest wish is that God will find something for me to do for them.

"Oh, Selene, I certainly do long and wish to see you. Do write your stupid friend Neighbor, who needs badly to hear from you and often, Selene, and God keep you, and I so long and hope you are happy."

By direction from Mr. Harge, he was to go to the Santee Outfit at Grey Cloud Island, where the monolithic trader, Pascal Jones, would arrange for transportation up the Minnesota to Traverse des Sioux, on the way to Bois des Morts.

The only vehicle that Jacob Bass could find for him that next day, Saturday, was a canoe which a couple of powerful young Sioux women were going to paddle down the Mississippi to Grey Cloud. "You can trust yourself to 'em; either one of them heifers could lick you and me together," said Jake, to soothe any male pride that might be troublesome in Aaron.

The two young ladies did not look formidable, nor did the fragile birch canoe, bobbing beside the lower landing, with its swooping bow and stern and its scarlet drawings of little men, look safe. He stared out at the whitecaps on the cruelly broad river . . . Well, he could swim.

The girls wore blue shortgowns—clean—and no ornaments save hair-ribbons. They were comfortable girls, round-faced, brown-faced girls, nice girls, good girls, not unlike Rebecca, but when he climbed in before them and by his arm-whirling, foot-shifting awkwardness betrayed that he had never been in a canoe before, they screamed with boisterous zest, and one of them sprang to hold the canoe, the other to steady him and pat him down into place like a rumpled pillow. They swung his trunk and carpetbag into the canoe like veteran furniture-movers and slid into their places, and all the while they sized him up, every inch, and hooted and discussed him in Sioux, intimately and, he thought, not unflatteringly.

As they shivered out into the downriver current, it seemed inevitable that they should be swamped. The fresh waters hurried and gurgled beside him, a millimeter below the gunwale. But he was tired now of surprises and doubts and humiliations, and he grew stubborn. Let it sink! Probably these blasted seegar-colored heroines would save him like a doll—confound them and confound all canoes and confound the whole confounded Mississippi River, from Cass Lake, or whatever it was, clean confounded down to New Orleans!

He grew easier as he saw how gaily the bow canoewoman, with her strong, muscle-sliding back before his eyes, kept looking around to continue her merry inspection of him (poor heathen white boy!) and to announce her findings, right over his shoulder, to her giggling mate in the stern.

He said silently, "You girls wait till I learn some Sioux, and I'll preach to you on my new theory, that Satan must be a woman."

They passed Pig's Eye, they passed Dr. Williamson's school at Kaposia, where the South St. Paul stockyards would some day show their splendor. They approached a line of softly wooded bluffs, and the forward canoewoman pointed her paddle, and announced, "Glay Clow Islan."

He was disappointed. He had rather hoped that they would upset, so that he could show these Westerners that he was a mighty Yankee swimmer, trained in the deepest and coldest quarries in the Hoosac Mountains.

When they landed at Pascal Jones's log pier and the girls happily looked for him to fall overboard, he got out with painful precision, walked up to the bow paddler, seized her shoulders and kissed her firmly. And now the delighted shrieks of the two girls were altogether for him.

Pascal Jones, in his log warehouse, was by look a severe Yankee schoolteacher, with a slim spike of gray chin-whisker. He had an immense reputation for sobriety and for running whisky.

Yes, he has heard from his friend, Brother Harge, and he will send Reverend Gadd as far as the Traverse on a bateau that will be starting up the Minnesota at once, with three fine voyageurs and a winter's supply of goods for his fort on the Blue Earth River. At the Traverse, Reverend Gadd can get ponies—oh, yes, everything modern and convenient now, not like back in 1830, when you *walked* to Bois des Morts.

Mr. Jones turned on Aaron like the sharp but grammar-loathing New Hampshire schoolmaster that he had been at sixteen.

"Tell me, Reverend: You're a Christian—sure-enough saved and sanctified?"

"I hope so . . . But it isn't 'Reverend,' yet."

"Oh! Well, Brother, you got to do a whale of a lot more than *hope*, want to git to Heaven. Got to lead an industrious Christian life. Going to try the missionary line, eh?"

"Seems so."

"Licensed to preach yet, Brother?"

"Not yet."

"Then look you here, Son! Ever thought about the fur business and what'll come later—land and lumber? I could use a nice-talkin', polite, eddicated young man of sober habits that could whale the tar out of the uppity coureurs and sneakin' unlicensed traders, if the Lord or I called on him. Like to make money?"

"Not just now, Brother. No."

"You ain't doin' so bad, Boy. I've knowed you ten minutes now, and you ain't told but one lie—though that's a thumper. Well, come to me when you get sick of Brother Harge and Brother Speezer tryin' to explain vicarious atonement to a lot of concupiscent Sioux!"

He slept in the warehouse loft, with the three lively voyageurs from Big Thunder's gang of half-breed kinsmen, who were to give him a lift.

He had wondered what would be his sacred duty if Pascal Jones planned to have them start on Sunday. Doubtless Squire Harge, like Noah Cudway, would have called down fire if Aaron had traveled on the Lord's Day. But Pascal was much too pious, and insisted on Sabbath rest and worship, which in his own case meant lying in a hammock, drinking rye and reading *Sam Slick*.

At sunrise on Monday, they started in the bateau, a great barge filled with boxes and barrels and propelled by sail, by oars and, later in the more shallow reaches of the Minnesota, by poles. They passed Fort Snelling, and Aaron was melancholy at leaving this old, old home, where he had so many familiar and tested friends—Captain Pipman and Father Gear and Major Murphy. He ought to swim ashore and stay there. But they turned into the Minnesota River, turned toward the Mission and his destiny.

The Minnesota, itself not wide, flowed through the wide valley of the ancient River Warren, which had drained off the vast northern lake left by the last glacier. Along it had camped nameless Indians, so civilized as to do their murders with flint knives three thousand years before the Great Pyramid was built. And here Aaron discovered the prairie, which is a separate experience.

He had seen only patches, but now he was immersed in it wherever the Minnesota crept from groves of cottonwood and aspen out into the gigantic grasslands. Sometimes, at sunset, while the voyageurs were getting supper, he skipped to the top of a bluff and all his senses were absorbed in that rolling vastness.

It was not, he thought, as everybody had said, like the ocean. The surface of the prairie, though it was darkened with storms or painful with snow or checkered with swift cloud shadows, was forever there, unchanging, as self-contained as a rock mountain, while the ocean (such a small but disconcerting slice of it as he had seen on the Sound steamer to New York) broke up in senseless waves or, when it was calm, became only a pale annex to the mirrored sky. The prairie was absolute, like fear or hunger or the North Star.

Nor did he find that it "stretched away from him, endless." Rather, from every point of the enormous circle of horizon, seemingly from every acre on the entire earth, it swept *toward* him, and he was the center of the whirling universe.

But not a powerful, controlling center, he admitted in new evangelical humility; merely a speck of dust in the center of that gigantic clock-face. But, since he was clearly the center of the flat earth, he must be just under the center of the sky. And there dwelt God. Yes, but every other wanderer on the prairie must also find himself exactly beneath the throne of God.

"I could make a sermon out of that!" he exulted, and then the incorruptible soul of Aaron Gadd said coldly to him, "Yes. You could. Certainly. And get praised for it. Even by Samuel Pond. But it would all be words, it would all be bad poetry. No, my son."

He wailed, in protest against his soul, "Can't I have faith in myself? Can't I seek God and report thereof as confidently as the Ponds or Squire Harge?"

"I doubt it," said his soul.

He had always had elm rows and houses and hillside rocks near at hand, for assurance and guidance; and it reduced him to a small lost animal to be absorbed in a waste where the nearest landmark was a tree five miles away, and everything in between was a radiant nothingness. Yet the autumn prairie was warm-colored and diverting; and in early morning the meadow larks went mad with summer's last happiness.

Out of the long buffalo grass, with the sharp scarlet of sumac edging the swales where wolves could hide, sprang exuberances of goldenrod and fireweed and purple asters. At the edge of long marshes were open slews, brilliant with green scum, and here the red-winged blackbirds tilted and sang, and at twilight the ducks circled down.

There were jackrabbits furiously humping themselves across the plain, and gophers, and coveys of prairie chickens with whirring sudden flight, and passenger pigeons in clouds, and once or twice, a distant small herd of buffalo. And rattlesnakes and eight-foot bullsnakes—plowed under now.

It was adventure to help pole the bateau through this welter of new land, walking back, pushing on the pole, then running forward.

The voyageurs were dressed like any other workmen, in denim and corduroy and worn wool, but all of them clung to the bright Pembina sash. They accepted Aaron as one of them. They told preposterous stories after supper, and laughed at his doubt when they asserted that, back in St. Paul, the waitresses kept crawling into their beds all night long. After two days, they announced that they did not believe he was a preacher at all, but an honest carpenter with a lively future in the expanding state-to-be.

When it did not rain, there was the soft gold of the prairie autumn, bathing him, washing out all the careful meannesses of the tight-folded hills; soft gold, radiant gold in waves, and the high cumulus clouds overhead. It was at night, after the voyageurs had told their gallant and pathetic lies and gone to their virgin blankets, that fear came sliding in.

It started with the mosquitoes, which were more testy and demanding citizens of the prairie than even the blackbirds or the wolves. By day, too, the mosquitoes were furious in the shade of the cottonwoods that marked the course of the small creeks, so that you ran from their armadas, but at night they seemed to fill the air solid, all screaming their tiny, slashing war cries. Campfires had to be kept smoky with handfuls of buffalo grass, and netting was staked out over the blankets.

Aaron told himself that the prairie sunsets were the torches of the heavenly host, lighting him on to the Mission, but they were snuffed out swiftly, and over the drab immensity of the land came the prairie fear, the fear of solitude with no walls to shut it out. The stars were too large, too near, all night long, and the breeze was full of voices. It was a relief when he could identify them, as wolves or crickets or the ridiculous night-chanting bullfrogs, and be fairly certain that they were not, after all, the spirits of Indians and padres and trappers dead in the wilderness these two hundred years.

But daily he leaped up at the huge sunrise, and they went on—westward.

20

THEY came to Indian villages along the river, and Aaron discovered a world of Sioux unrelated to the drunken beggars he had seen at Fort Snelling.

Elm bark for lodges was not easily come by on the prairie, and even in summer many of them lived in tipis of clean, taut buffalo hide, translucent when they were new. The men were grave and erect, and they looked at such intruders as Aaron not with lewd petitioning, but indifferently or with hostility.

Their moccasins were ornamented with beads and quills; their leggings, white and green and red, were worn taut; their hair was in braids, decked with ribbons or, among the young dandies, with small mirrors and bead brooches; and the blankets which they wore over all were as dignified as togas or as jaunty as evening capes. The women were modest, and their quiet eyes resented the leering voyageurs. Even the dogs seemed one or two per cent. less raucous and flea-gouged than at Snelling.

Aaron's imagination went to work, and he admitted, though only to himself, that these tall and softly stepping men did not seem inferior to God's own chosen people—the Yankees.

He asked the voyageurs, "How come these Indians up the river are so different from the vagabonds at the Fort?"

Georges, the most English-speaking of the three French half-breeds, shook his head, looked doubtful, decided that Aaron could be trusted and poured out, "The more the Dakota have to do with the white, the worse. The whites give him whisky to get his furs and bimeby he don't want to trap so many furs but he want plenty more whisky. The white traders take his girl, and all he get in swap is a disease. They take his land, and all he get is a leetle annuity so he don't do any work and starve slow. The Indian gets white man's gun and he is drunk and kill his own brother and they call him sinful. That's what he get from the white man—fine kettle, fine gun, fine blanket, the big pox, the small pox and religion."

The tyro missionary was horrified. He thought, as a disciple of Squire Harge and Dr. Williamson:

"Suppose this *is* true? Suppose, through the whites, a thousand Indians get diseased or killed, but one single Indian, hearing the true word of God, is saved, and his soul preserved for the heavenly choir? Isn't that worth while?"

He guessed how Harge would answer it, but for himself, he did not believe that he had the fortitude, and he was more doubtful when they came to Traverse des Sioux. For there, hanging about the two or three traders' posts and Robert Hopkins's American Board Mission, were another set of drunken, dependent Indian beggars.

But, having decided that the fur-traders were all traffickers in vice, when that veteran trader, Narcisse Jupon, welcomed him and told him he was a brave young fellow and an apprentice saint, Aaron loved him and was grateful for his favors.

Aaron's three companions shook hands and insisted, "You come back with us! You no missionary! In twenty year, you learn to be pretty good voyageur, and we find a nice M'dewakanton girl for you."

Selene was half-M'dewakanton.

Narcisse Jupon reigned blandly in a shaggy log cabin, with his three-quarters-Sioux grandchildren hunting rats in the muddy yard. He had been trading with the Indians ever since 1816, when Fort Snelling had not yet been built and you were more likely to see a British flag here than an American. Some day, when Aaron would be hearing fine speeches about how the Yankees had founded Minnesota and practically laid out the lakes, he would remember M. Jupon, who had been born behind a white pine log in Quebec.

Narcisse was to furnish Aaron with two ponies, one to ride and

one to carry Aaron's trunk and the mail and more precious pack-
ages. The rest of the Mission's winter supplies, brought by Pascal's
voyageurs, would be fetched by ox-team.

He stayed overnight with the missionaries, Robert and Agnes
Hopkins, in their trim two-room cabin. They had just come in with
Brother Riggs; and how, they wanted to know, had Aaron done,
traveling with the heathen?

"I had a fine time with the voyageurs," said Aaron.

"How could you? They're probably Catholics!" said Mr. Hopkins.

"I'm used to French-Canadians."

"Really? I was brought up in Ohio and Indiana. I suppose a fellow could get used to them, but they sure talk queer! Tell me. Did
you use your Heaven-vouchsafed opportunity on the trip to convert them to Protestantism?"

"I guess I never thought of it."

"You *did*-ent?" mourned Hopkins.

But Agnes just laughed.

"Maybe I was too busy thinking about the Indians. Brother Hopkins, do you suppose the whites, with their whisky, are responsible
for the degeneration of the Indians? Does the religion we bring
them make up for the evil we bring?"

Hopkins, the hearty and athletic and extremely pleasant, laughed
contentedly. "My gracious sakes alive! So many of you young
tenderfoot missionaries go and bother your heads about that question!" (Mr. Hopkins was a venerable thirty-two.) "Oh, there *are*
ungodly white folks out here that sell licker, but the Injuns don't
have to *take* it and swim in it, do they? No, no! They won't listen
to the missionaries, and see that they only have to start plowing
and put on pantaloons and accept the Gospel."

Mr. Hopkins lowered his voice, as if his hyperorthodox teachers
at South Hanover College, Indiana, might be sneaking around the
cabin to listen for heresy.

"Same time—and mind you, the older missionaries would claim
this is blasphemy—*I* believe that if an Indian has never had any

chance whatever to hear the True Word and yet has always been God-hungry and unselfish, maybe he might be elect and go to Heaven! Does that strike you as dangerous doctrine, Brother Gadd —Aaron?"

Aaron didn't—well—he didn't *think* so . . .

Neither of them knew how ardently that point had been discussed by ecumenical councils since *circ.* 400 A.D.

Aaron was again convinced—perhaps a quarter-convinced—that the white invaders had been only a blessing to the Indians. Why, of course! They were *white,* weren't they?

All in good time and weather and all alone, guided by glimpses of the Minnesota River, he rode over the houseless prairie on the three-day journey from Traverse des Sioux to the Mission. The ponies' hoofs made a clean, long swish in the high buffalo grass, or a cautious sucking sound in the bogs. Two nights he slept out, under an immensity of stars that swung low to inspect him, and it was a comfort to have the two ponies staked there, as a protection against unknown monsters.

Along the trail were scattered the pulverizing bones of the buffalo slain long ago by the Indians; and once, among them, he fancied that he saw a heap of human bones.

As he rode he made up a story of meeting a raid of Chippewa; squat, ugly scoundrels, not like his own true Sioux. They stole (in his story) his trunk and bag and all his possessions: his new good black suit, his new Greek Testament and his Bible from his mother and the Testament from Deacon Popplewood, his fine new toothbrush, the pair of razors that had been his father's farewell, his leather-bound Byron, a calotype of a girl which he had purchased in New York because it resembled Selene and the handkerchief he had stolen from Selene by the stone wall at parting.

Aaron rode coldly away from the Chippewa, unruffled, a white man with the courage of the master race. He never did figure out why they left him one of the ponies.

The story served wonderfully to keep him cheerful on the slow journey, and to give him an excuse to talk aloud to the ponies, which were surprised at first but began to gather around to listen to him.

And then, in the middle of an afternoon, from a bluff looking down on the junction of the Minnesota River with the shallow brown Isanti, he saw the end of his trail: the Mission where he was to live for years and years . . . where he might die.

There were a few small structures: a frame chapel with a tiny steeple; two frame houses, one notably the larger; a house of white-washed logs; a corncrib and two log buildings which might have been stables, workshops or warehouses: altogether, seven primitive shelters, huddled beside the union of the waters, stray commas on the unwritten page of the wilderness.

There were twenty or thirty acres of recently cultivated farmland, with wheat stubble and corn stalks, in the flat valley by the mouth of the Isanti where the Minnesota widened out in what must be Lake Bois des Morts, edged with reeds and willow-groves.

The river bluffs at his feet were gouged with deep ravines, seeded with hazel brush and ash trees and scrub oaks, and atop the opposite bluffs, across the lake from the Mission, were the bark lodges of a Wahpeton Sioux village.

That was all: blocks scattered on the nursery floor, nothing human visible beyond, in a land surely too rough ever to be settled. There was no glimpse of any Lanark Castle. Perhaps it did not exist, perhaps Selene Lanark did not exist, perhaps he was enchanted in a fairy story and had, himself, no existence otherwise.

He smacked his pony, yanked the rope of the other one, and trotted down the bluffs to the Mission of Bois des Morts.

21

HE HAD guessed that the larger white frame house was the dwelling of Squire Harge. It was on the simplest plan; two-storied, rather long. Only the front doorway suggested the East or differentiated it from a large-sized piano box. It was of boards set vertically, probably a sheathing over logs.

As Aaron rode up, shouting, "Hello, hello!" Mr. Harge popped out of the front door, demoted from squiredom in overalls and a straw hat, his black chin-beard aggressive, his two stout hands out, crying, "Neighbor—Son—you've come!"

After him tumbled his daughter Bessie, yelling, "Brother Aaron! Goodygoodygoody! Darling brother! Could you make a model of the temple at Jerusalem out of pasteboard? Did you keep the Sabbath all the journey, the *whole* journey, did you?" And she galloped to him and held up her flushed face to be kissed.

Half a dozen Indian girls in black cotton dresses followed her out. Bessie sharply clapped her hands, gave a signal with an authoritative forefinger, and they broke out in a welcoming Sioux hymn to the tune of Aaron's old favorite *One Sweetly Solemn Thought*.

He vaulted off the pony, shook Harge's hand, kissed Bessie again and waved his hand lavishly to the Sioux children, who giggled. He had come home.

He saw that Harge's house was not white-painted but white-washed, streaked and seedy. He happily planned to paint it.

The Mission grounds were not untidy with rubbish, like Jupon's post at the Traverse, but they were grassless clay, like a school-lot back home. There was just one hollyhock bed, which must have been tended by a homesick woman. This was a place of industry and strict duty, a place in which to get through life carefully, without offending God.

Harge was bellowing, "Come in, come in, my boy, and meet the folks!"

He led Aaron down a narrow, matting-floored hall into the living-room. It was white-plastered, eighteen feet long, twelve wide; the floor was of unpainted wide pine boards, grimly clean; it had bookshelves and a huge sheet-iron stove, a long homemade pine table, three or four stools and a few chairs made out of barrels, and just two pictures: Moses on Sinai, and the rustic Pennsylvania courthouse in which a young Mr. Harge had once been a promising lawyer-politician.

You remembered the room as glaring white, and completely empty.

The Indian girls had settled on the floor in the living-room, cross-legged in a semicircle about a pleasant young woman who was seated in a kitchen chair.

"Our teacher, Miss Huldah Purdick," said Harge.

Huldah Purdick had warm brown hair, not too neat, a face round and fresh and often dimpling, earnest eyes that could be gay with people whom she trusted. She was three years older than Aaron, but she did not look it. She was in some peril of becoming too plump and heavy-breasted, but she fought it with vigor and cheerfulness.

She never was anything more than what you first saw, but she would never be anything less. She was born in Woodbury, Connecticut, and her father, the stage-driver, was related to the clergy. She was passionately and mystically religious, as mystical by nature as St. Theresa, but she also considerably liked men and cooking and the idea of a Home.

That was all there was to Huldah Purdick—plain to read and impossible to forget. She had visions of Christ and the angels, but she had never had a psychosis, a longing for political leadership, an interesting tendency to dipsomania or to Lesbianism or a false tooth in her life, so that a hundred years later, she would have been considered very dull. She was as earthy as Anne Hutchinson or Joan of Arc. Aaron did not particularly notice her when he met her, and for weeks thereafter, he noticed nothing else so acutely.

She taught English and Bible and rather elementary arithmetic and geography to the Indian girls and boys and to the children of the missionaries; she wrote business letters for Squire Harge; she helped her sister Anna, who was married to Jacob Wherryman, farmer at the Mission. Anna and Jake, with Huldah, taught spinning, weaving, dressmaking, cooking to the Indian girls, farming and washing the face to the boys . . . except that mostly the adult Indians did not wish their children to learn these arts from the emissaries of what they astonishingly considered an alien, false and hostile God.

Huldah said, "Welcome, Brother Gadd; I hope you'll like it here," and all he had for answer was, "Oh, yes, I'm sure I will."

Squire Harge grunted, "This is my sitting-room and this next is our kitchen-dining-room, and here's the rest of my young uns."

The adjoining room was neat enough, but bare as a trapper's log cabin, with a small cook stove set on a huge flat rock, a homemade sink, a pail of water and a tin dipper and a tin dishpan for plumbing. Aaron met Bessie's brothers: Jefferson Harge, a year older than Bessie and equally evangelical, and Fred, two years younger and the despair of all because, at the advanced age of nine, he was still unconverted, and stubborn about it. (Jefferson was to become a missionary, a shining pillar among the exiled Sioux in South Dakota and Nebraska; but the abominable Fred was to be a livery-stable keeper and expert small-town gambler.)

"I'm the real cook here, not Bessie," sighed the Squire, "though Huldah is real kind about lending a hand. My dear wife, Mercie, always used to take care of us real good, but she's upstairs now, awful sick. Bad chest. She come down with it just after I left for the East, this summer. She'd been ailing before that and thought she better not go with me. I'll holler up and see if she's ready to meet you."

"Oh, no, no, don't . . ."

135

"She'll be real pleased to lay eyes on a stranger. Mercie is a sancti-fied soul, but she ain't never lost her liking for pretty tricks and vain worldly possessions. 'God, not gauds,' I often tell her. Ha, ha! But don't make no impression, seems like . . . Poor girl. She is so sick!"

While the Squire was shouting up the rudimentary stairs off the kitchen, "Dearie, our young man, Aaron, is here," young Bessie seized Aaron's sleeve, tugged him to a varnished pine cupboard in the corner of the kitchen and drew aside the red calico curtain.

She whispered, "These are Mummy's lovely things. Oh, dear Aaron, help me pray for her!"

The three inadequate upper shelves of the cupboard were filled with English porcelain, all gilt and posies, a Wedgwood platter of gray with figures of Greek dancers, a cheap but graceful pressed-glass vase and a dozen thin old spoons.

"They all belonged to Mummy's Dad, the General, back in Maine. She used to use them for dinner when folks came in. I don't guess she'll see them any more now," whimpered Bessie.

Squire Harge was back, rumbling, "Mercie—Mrs. Harge—she allows she'll be real glad to meet a handsome young fella, but she says she better make it a little later. She feels . . . I guess maybe . . ."

The sound of death was in his voice.

"That'll be splendid," quaked Aaron.

"We hope it's just a fever, but it could be consumption. And she's only thirty-three. Kind of frail, and just as fond of titivating and feathers and fripperies as she ever was as a girl. 'Why,' I said to her just now, 'I never did see such vanity! Wanting to dress up to im-press a young man, and him a stanch young Christian!' I told her, but she said anyway she's going to wash her face. Pshaw, course she'll be all right!

"Now, Aaron, we'll go see the others. There's the Speezers—Reverend Herbert Henry Speezer, M.A." (Aaron thought he em-phasized the M.A. with some irony.) "Dartmouth graduate he is, and Lane Seminary. Congregationalist, but just as rigorous in the faith as a real Presbyterian. And his good wife, Luna.

"And then Jake and Anna Wherryman. He runs our farm and does our carpentry and brick-laying and blacksmithing. 'Jake,' I say to him, 'maybe you ain't learned in Hebrew and exegesis, like us, but in the art of fertilizers and midwifery to the cow animals,' I tell him, and it certainly does tickle that humble fellow's heart, 'in those things you're a true minister of the Lord.' And by golly I ought to know! I was brought up on a farm!"

He looked gratified when Aaron dutifully said, "No! Honestly?"

"Yessiree, and except for the little red schoolhouse and reading law books, had no education except the treasures of God's word. And believe me, that's all you need, and the Speezers can *keep* their Plato and—and what not!"

Jake and Anna Wherryman rolled in then, he in overalls and she in gingham apron. Jake was short and fat, with curiously diminished Yankee nutcracker features cramped together in the middle of his orb of red face. His eyes were humorous and calculating, and the hand which wrung Aaron's was like a rock. It was natural that these two should greet each other, at once, "Howdy, Aaron—welcome, fellow-chips!" and "Glad see you, Jake."

Anna, sister of Huldah Purdick, was a rolypoly and a butterball, with pink-and-white plump cheeks. Said she, "Welcome, Mr. Gadd! Did the Squire tell you you're to room and board with us? (Free! Charged to the Mission!) We're awful glad, Aaron!"

Then there stalked in, very pleasant, altogether high-class, somewhat as though they were slumming but didn't mind, the Reverend Herbert Henry Speezer (M.A.) and Luna Davenport Speezer. He was bald and whiskerless, dry, sparkling, scholarly, lightly humorous; she thin, energetic, hawklike and (considering a missionary's salary) elegant, with black jet earrings.

Mr. Speezer held Aaron's hand and breathed, "Mr. Gadd, you cannot possibly know how fortunate we deem ourselves in having a new companion who may constitute a new audience for our little jokes and eschatological theories! We shall do everything we can to make you happy and ... *Where's the supplies, Squire?"*

Suddenly, just at a mutter of the word "supplies," the kitchen was filled, with Huldah Purdick, Bessie Harge and brothers, the Speezers' twins, and Anna Wherryman's four bouncers, including Martha, aged one, carried by Putnam, aged ten.

Traveling with Bessie, the Squire had not been able to carry much booty back on his return journey. The winter food and heavy clothes, brought by Pascal Jones's bateau, were to come from Traverse des Sioux later, by tote-team, but Aaron had brought with him, in panniers on the pack pony, a surprising treasure. They all hurried out to that stoical woolly little animal, lifted off Aaron's trunk and began to unpack the panniers, with moans of such delight that Squire Harge in his evening prayer would have to mention their grievous greed.

For the women there were gloves, handkerchiefs, combs, precious toothbrushes. Luna Speezer had an exquisite bonnet of French plaited straw adorned with beadwork, as handsome an object and as unsuited to a Minnesota winter as the subtlest brains of Paris could conceive. For Mercie Harge there was a pink knitted bedjacket and, as they looked at it, even the newly come Aaron felt wistfully that this was the last mantle she would ever wear.

Squire Harge's wardrobe had already been richly adorned in the East, but Mr. Speezer and Mr. Jake Wherryman were gloating over new satinet pantaloons and flannel chest-protectors, along with a new set of wood-files, a mold for bullets, and handsome linen dickeys for Sunday. But most distinguished of all were the books: for Harge, *Thaddeus of Warsaw, The Conquest of Mexico, Lalla Rookh,* and the Reverend Dr. John Harris's *The Great Commission, or the Christian Church Charged to Convey the Gospel to the World;* for Speezer, Locke's *Human Understanding,* and Epictetus in Greek; and for Jake, *Family Letters on Chemistry,* by Baron von Liebig, and *The Workman's Popular Com-*

pendium and Handbook of Handmills, Steam Mills, Horse Tread-mills, with Tables & Appendix.

And for Harge, the new set of false teeth ordered in Philadelphia, and for all the children, wooden dolls and very small toy wagons.

The Squire in his culpable glee took out a plug of tobacco, bit off a luxurious chew and spat. Aaron looked with amazement at this unchristian practice, which he himself had given up in the dawn of his enlightenment. The Squire ducked his head, looked rueful and contritely confessed, "Oh, Neighbor, you have come upon me in my most sin-soaked habit. I've prayed about chewing real hard, but I've never been able to give it up more 'n a day at a time. But with the Lord's help, I reckon I'm going to get shut of the horrible vice this winter! Help me with your prayers, Brethren. Phut!"

22

DOWNSTAIRS in the Wherryman log cabin were two rooms: a bedroom for the four children, and an apartment which was parlor, sitting-room, kitchen, dining-room, workshop and Jake and Anna's bedroom, with a billowy bed resting on a single post and on pegs driven between the logs of the two walls in a corner. The chief luxury was the possession of not only a mud-and-stick fireplace but a sheetiron stove for cooking and heating. But this was not an enervating luxury, for all the rest of the house was kept warm—that is, kept from going much below zero—by ducts from this one room.

The low second story, reached by a staircase that even in New England would have been considered steep, had Huldah's room at one end and Aaron's new all-contained home at the other, each with the splendor of a window (with real glass) two-foot square.

Though he was used to cold and barren lodging at home, when he was first shown to his bedroom-study-library-prayerchamber at Jake's, Aaron was annoyed. The room was unceiled, showing the inside of the basswood shakes which covered the roof; the floor was of unnailed boards, which were likely to fly up and hit you, and on the log walls were beetle-trails and the gray wreck of a wasp's nest. The only furniture was a straw mattress on a base of hay on the floor, a puncheon stool, a packing-box for wardrobe and table and, for light, a cotton wick lying in grease in a hollowed turnip.

"Well," Aaron thought mildly, "I'll be away from here and outdoors a good deal."

"That's right. When it drops to forty below, you'll go outdoors to get warm," commented an inner voice clearly coached by Satan.

Between Huldah's room and his, there was only the windowless attic for storage. Their rooms were remarkably close together.

With his newest family, Jake, Anna, Huldah, the pup, the kitty, the tame crow named Josephus and the four children, Aaron was in a transplanted chunk of New England.

Huldah said little, but with quick-coming dimples and admiring eyes, while her hands fluttered with knitting, she encouraged the others, and was excited by even their least studied remarks on crab-apples or straw-stacks. But Anna chattered like a farmwife with Sunday-afternoon company.

"Oh, yes, we get *some* results at the Mission, both in farming and saving the dratted Indians' souls," Anna gossiped. "Mostly it's the Sioux womenfolks that accept the Master, but we have taken in one man—Isaac Weeps-by-Night. He's a real, redeemed, praying Christian, and he ain't any nasty beggar, either. He's a fine deer-hunter and a wonderful warrior—he's scalped ever so many of these wretched Chippeways. He's got two wives, but we're hoping to kind of ease him into monogamy, and officially our church don't recognize but just one of them.

"Of course he does get awful drunk and shoot out our windows once in a while, but my, Isaac is always so repentant afterwards, and begging for the soothing grace of God's mercy, that you just got to forgive him, after you discipline him a little. When he ain't hitting it up, he's an elder in our church here. If he just wouldn't snicker so when poor Squire Harge tries to preach in what he thinks is Sioux language—poor dear man, for years now the Indians have never understood one word the Squire has preached!

"Oh, yes, we don't always have it easy here, the rats and bedbugs, for instance, even though we are guided to carry out God's mysteri-ous plans. It's hard being hundreds of miles from any doctor. The children get restless and fretful and feverish, and then they die, poor things, and there's nothing you can do but just stand and look down at them and . . . Jake and me have lost two. I pray that in their baby way they repented of natural sin and were admitted to the meadows of Heaven and not punished forever, poor scared babies that they were, so sick they couldn't laugh any more, even when Jake tried so hard to make funny shadows on the wall with his hands. And moaning so steady, on and on. . . .

"I guess maybe I've had less trouble with Martha—that's the baby—than with any of the others. She's so lively; a real terror to goodness. But she stopped wanting to nurse real early. That time, I got awful weak from nursing one of Isaac Weeps-by-Night's young uns. When Martha was just a few days old, I suffered quite a good deal from full breasts, so I hired Florantha (that's Isaac's first wife, a Wahpeton, kind of a fancy name but she picked it out herself when she was baptized)—I hired her to come here at night and let her baby draw my breasts, and after I begun that, I just never seemed to find a stopping place. Sucking that way, it nigh killed me."

Huldah flushed, but she listened placidly enough to this frankness, and the embarrassed Aaron fretted, "I suppose a missionary has got to learn about All These Things. But my gracious!"

Jake relieved him by sputtering, "Aaron ain't interested in baby business—yet. Beats the Old Ned what midwives all women is, even the sanctified ones!"

Bessie Harge danced in then with a message from the Squire: Aaron and he were to have supper at the Speezers', right away now; getting late.

Aaron hastily changed to his good black suit and, under a sad prairie sunset, in the growing autumn chill when everything about him seemed alien and unfriendly, he trudged over to the Squire's. He tried to make the Mission his own; in ninety seconds he had built a dairybarn and a tall church with patterned windows, and Selene had come to relieve his loneliness.

At the Manse, the Squire, with tender clumsiness, under the bossing of Bessie, was preparing a tray to take up to Mercie. He had put one purple aster into an old ink bottle. In a corner of the kitchen, Jefferson, aged twelve, kept arguing that the Persians needed the Gospel more than the Sioux, and besides, in Persia you could hunt elephants, hippopotamuses and pashas.

"Here, you take this tray up to Mercie and surprise her," Harge said to Aaron. "I'll follow you up."

"Maybe she'd rather not be surprised."

"Oh, she's expecting to be. These women!"

In an old-fashioned spool-bed, Mercie Harge sat up smiling at the shy, tray-bearing Aaron. Flushed with illness, Mercie's was a flower-like face, very soft and even, with flutters of acorn-colored hair about it. Selene Lanark was haughtily and irregularly beautiful; Huldah Purdick was comforting; Nadine Brun was theatrically bold; but Mercie Harge was the soul of delicacy and femininity and innocent perversity, pansy-faced with traces of kitten and of sharp flint. In blue-ribbon-drawn muslin cap and her new pink bed-jacket, she did not seem more than twenty-five. But she was thirty-three and tired with living.

On the old trunk that had to serve as her bedside table there were horrible squads of gummy patent-medicine bottles with flourishing optimistic names.

Her voice was everything clear and gentle that a girl's should be, with a diminished Yankee quack in it to make it funny and endearing.

"Aaron, I do apologize for not coming down to welcome you. I just don't feel very well, these few days. The Squire says you are called 'Neighbor,' and we were real neighbors: I come from Maine. I shall never see it again."

The Squire bumbled, "Nonsense, nonsense, dearie! You'll be downstairs again any day now, and I'll get emergency leave from the Board and take you right back to Maine—your ole coves and harbors and that stink of seaweed! And till then, you can ride horseback with this young skeezics here. Personally, I never could get along on horses, the clumsy things, even though when I was on circuit, as a lawyer, I had to ride. I never could get a horse to listen to reason. They're as bad as these Indian codgers: rather pay attention to the voices of their personal devils!"

Harge chuckled on, trying to be gay, while Mercie shook her

143

head at Aaron as though they were both sorry for Harge, as though they had known each other for years and years and only Aaron understood that she would never again go riding.

They shook hands quietly.

"I'm glad you came, Aaron. You bring the salt New England air in with you," said Mercie.

Before they went to the Speezers', the Squire proudly showed the rest of the Manse.

"You may wonder at our hogging such a big sitting-room, but truth is, it belongs to everybody. Anna teaches spinning here, and we hold prayer concerts when the church is too cold, and sometimes the benighted Indians sleep here on the floor—benighted in both senses—land sakes, that's a pretty good joke! So I got a little room of my own, my study you might call it, for literary labors and prayer and meditation, when the spirit moves. In here."

The study was an unplastered catch-all with a desk-table, a shelf of unworn books of theology and envelopes of garden seeds. Half of the room was filled with a workbench at which the Squire happily lost himself in cabinet-making. Hot with love for his own creation, he showed Aaron an oak reading-stand, ornamented with tiny Gothic arches, which he was making for their church. Around it lay seed corn, fancy and impractical devices, with springs and bells, to keep the blackbirds from their crops, a St. Augustine in Latin and a lone snowshoe.

"I come in here when the financial cares of the Mission drive me mad, when I am discouraged by the stubborn devotion of the Dakotas to the wiles of Satan, when some woman communicant says her husband has threatened to cut her nose off. I tell Mercie—and for once the dear girl doesn't laugh at me—I tell her that I can pray better with a plane or a chisel than with my stupid tongue."

The Squire sighed, plagued by memories.

Then he brightened: "Let me show you! We got a guest-room

here! Only one, I sh'd say, between Fort Snelling and the Pacific Ocean! Here!"

He opened the door on a twelve-foot room with a genuine detached army cot, a chair, a mirror, a packing-box cupboard and a pot painted with bluebirds. The only flaw in its exemplary neatness was that Fred Harge, aged nine, was asleep on the cot, together with a mongrel pup obviously half-Indian.

The Squire protested with the utmost helplessness: "Now how many times have I told you brats you can't sleep in here? It's kept for guests!"

Fred and the pup each opened one eye to look at him, and went back to sleep.

"I'll tell Bessie on you, that's what I'll do!" grumbled the Squire, as he softly shut the door on them.

"Yessir, planned to have you sleep in there, this first night, Neighbor, but Jake 'lowed you'd better get settled, so you can start digging 'taters tomorrow morning bright and early, say about six. But ain't but mighty few rooms, even at the White House, where there's been more distinguished guests entertained: Henry Hastings Sibley and Joseph Nicollet and Joe Brown and George William Featherstonhaugh and John Charles Fremont and Martin McLeod and Norman Kittson and Dr. Williamson—yes, and Little Crow, thinking about his intrigues, no doubt. Son, back in the Old Bay State, you saw where history was made. Here, you see us making it."

"Oh, yes!" said Aaron, with zeal.

The Speezers' house was smaller than the Squire's Manse, but more worldly. It was sided with narrow, dovetailed boards set horizontally, and it was really painted. Mr. Speezer must have blown in his own money, and wildly, to have had white paint.

And they had a sitting-room in which no cooking was done! It was lavish with a Brussels carpet, a rug of lambskin dyed red, a red plush couch, rocking chairs and real brass andirons. The point of interest (the twelve-by-twelve room was a little crowded) was a

145

center table that was also a desk and a bookcase climbing in diminishing tiers.

"Squire Harge made that for me with his own hands," purred Mr. Speezer. "He's an artist, as well as a great Christian leader."

"Ur—uh—nothing at all!" fluttered the Squire.

"This room is also my study," said Mr. Speezer. "I hope that some day some wandering scholar will be pleased to learn and remember that here I finished my work on Dakota syntax."

"Brother Herbert, we shall be remembered, if at all, only for having shown some lost heathen soul the true road to redemption," growled Squire Harge.

"Oh, doubtless, doubtless, Squire," said Mr. Speezer soothingly, as one who should say, "Speak for yourself, my unalphabet friend!"

They supped in the kitchen, and magnificently, on boiled turnips, boiled potatoes, cornbread and maple syrup. Most of the time they teased their young friend for his innocence in thinking that he was now a Minnesota pioneer. They explained that, actually, he had come at an era of decadent luxury.

Harge told of his explorations back in 1835, when he was seeking a site for his Mission and traveled by birch canoe, with mile-long portages through mud-oozing swamps or over gashing rocks. His first house and chapel had been a cave over there in the hillside, with a blanket for door and with mosquitoes for his congregation.

Aaron noted that in the kitchen-dining-room was the cobbler's bench at which Mr. Speezer repaired the boots, children's shoes, moccasins and harness of the Mission. His own superiority in representing youth and experiment and modern science he forgot in admiration for the veterans' endurance.

But as they talked around the fire in the sitting-room, he was embarrassed by the nakedness of their piety. Even his boyhood of listening to neighborhood theology had not trained him to feel easy before such brisk unclothing of the Mysteries. And Huldah Purdick came in and played nurse to the ghostly medications.

Said Mr. Speezer, "Brother Gadd, I hear you were converted and found the joy of yielding yourself to obedience at a revival where Brother Harge spoke."

"Yes—I did."

Huldah thrilled, "Oh, Aaron, can life ever hold such ecstasy: to feel yourself pierced by the holy spirit, to be all on fire, to rise clear up to the clouds and to float down in ineffable peace and abide in the temple of the indwelling Trinity! . . . You experienced all that, didn't you?"

"Yes—oh, yes—I think I did."

Luna Speezer said blandly, "Maybe Brother Gadd feels things too deeply to want to chatter about them."

"That's so," said Huldah vaguely, not looking at Sister Speezer, while Aaron decided that there was something not altogether holy here.

Harge roared, "Great revival, but Brother Finney didn't lambaste sin enough, and bring souls to the mourners' bench screaming for mercy!"

Speezer said comfortably, scratching one knee which was cocked up over the other, "You're always so right, Squire! Man in his natural state is lost—oh, immeasurably!"

Aaron wondered a little why they seemed to regard this as news.

Squire Harge fretted, "On my trip east I thought most of our churches were full of criminal coldness and inactivity and a lot of the pastors shooting off their mouths about abolition. Aah! I don't believe in keeping slaves, but the pulpit is where you tear off the garments of iniquity and pride, and show the black, clotted evil beneath the shining raiment.

"Neighbor, Son, each year you'll study more on the tremendous work of God's redemption; the wonders of justifying faith. Oh, truly, his footsteps are upon the sea. Don't it give you a heartache when you see young folks dancing and full of light laughter? If they knew how Hell lurks behind them, they would scream with

147

terror, the sweat would pour down their brows into their eyes and sting their breasts! Oh, we must save them—we must! Us that have been miraculously chosen.

> "Why was I made to hear thy voice
> And enter while there's room,
> While thousands make a wretched choice
> And rather stand than come?"

Huldah wailed, "Oh, yes, yes, yes! And yet, even knowing we're elect, how hard it is to follow the path! I am a wretched rebel against the government of God!"

Then Luna Speezer made Aaron gasp by hurling herself into it with a fieriness which he had not expected in that cautious lady:

"Huldah, you'll keep on to sanctification, but me, I'm always on a zigzag course, thrown to left and right. The dear Lord Jesus broke the power of iniquity in me and bruised the head of the serpent, and yet it is continually striving for dominion over me and I go my way after my heart's lust! I indulge myself with a superfluity of naughtiness! My heart is filth and pollution, contaminated with loathsome softness and decay! I love the glittering serpent of sin, and toy with him as with a shameful earthly lover! I vaunt myself, I display my weak delight in music and complain that out here there are no musicians, no libraries, no art works. I boast of my many talents, and all, all is ashes and vanity—woe is me!"

23

WHILE Luna's hysterical voice still circled the room, her husband cut in, coldly, very reasonably:

"Our young friend, Gadd, must realize that we aren't often raised to such a delightful peak of frank confession as tonight. Mostly we are pretty matter-of-fact folks, but maybe the presence of his fresh, virgin page has helped us to express our longings. Uh—I hope he has been cleansed and refreshed by the experience!"

Aaron hesitated, "When I hear all of you, I feel kind of guilty— so practical. Squire, do you think it might be a good idea for me, tomorrow, to start my work by devoting the whole day to prayer and fasting?"

Harge stared at him, long, then guffawed, "Brother Speezer and I and the women can take care of all the praying that's necessary around here! You start right off tomorrow morning digging potatoes and turning the grindstone for Jake. Tools awful dull. You give your attention to *them!* If you feel called on to pray—and I guess that's a fine idea—you can do it in the evening!"

Aaron thought that the titter had come from Luna Speezer.

He flushed. He stumbled, "I just meant—I meant, because the Mission is so religious and I've never done much meditation and so on, and I thought maybe if I could start in a—in a holy spirit . . ."

Huldah cried, "I think that's beautiful of Brother Aaron! I don't believe you appreciate that, Squire!"

Luna hastily got into it with "You're such a superb manager, Squire, you can't understand the whisperings in the soul of a boy poet like our dear Neighbor!"

Aaron was distinctly sick.

Harge stuttered, "Oh, nobody appreciates prayer more 'n I do. But the boy can rise early for it; get up at four-thirty instead of five-thirty. . . . You can pray *any* time, Aaron, but if them potatoes don't get dug now, they'll spoil, and fasting may be a good idea for these profligate Romanists, but I find you can pray a lot stronger on a good boiled potato!" He burst out with the laughter he had been confining. "No, no, Boy, don't you worry about plenty prayer gettin' done here without *you* takin' charge!"

Aaron felt that he had begun not as an acolyte but as a booby. He was grateful to Huldah for praising him and only a little alarmed at Luna's gurgling fount of perfume but in this sick-sweet odor of sanctity, he wanted to be outdoors, with Selene—with Nadine—with his own natural and sinful self.

Harge was explaining, "You know, Neighbor, we're counting on you—and mighty grateful, you understand—for quite a lot of things.

"Husk the corn and shell it and finish the fall plowing and get up some fence posts and flail out the wheat and boss the Indian women while they dig the rest of the turnips and potatoes and move that big stone under my kitchen stove and put a new floor in my sitting-room and there's some repairs on the cart and we need a new privy and a couple of ox-yokes and I have a clock that won't run and you might butcher some pigs and a calf and salt down the meat and maybe help Anna dip some candles and make soap and fix our little grist-mill so's it'll go by bands instead of ropes and put a movable partition in the church so's we can have two rooms for school classes.

"Course Jake and you will do these together and Brother Herbert and I will give you a hand whenever we can take the time from teaching and studying and instructing candidates for admission to the communion. There is one job that might take a little effort: build out another lean-to on my house so Bessie can have a room of her own. She's a pure-minded girl, but still and all, it ain't quite decent for a girl her age to sleep in the same room upstairs there with two boys, even if they are her own brothers.

"I wish it was possible to get some tin and have you cover our church spire so it would be bright and shiny—maybe attract some of these sneering Sioux and Catholics with all their folderol. What you think? Maybe we could get some tin out from the States next year."

"Rust," was all that Aaron had to say.

While Squire Harge took up the rusting of tin in all its aspects, Aaron brooded: *Next year!* Would he still be here next year, butchering calves?

"And some day," said Harge happily, "we'll start a brickyard. That'll give Jake and you something to do. Then after that, you can begin to learn Sioux properly, and start your theological studies."

Luna Speezer purled with especial sweetness, "So you think our young friend will be able to begin conning his books in not more than five or six years? Or perhaps seven?"

Aaron was certain that there was malice in her, but whether it was against himself or against the Squire, he could not tell.

Harge was defending himself:

"Well, I haven't given as much time to the books as I'd like. My father—he was an M.D., of course—he wanted me to go to college but I wanted to get into the law and I guess what I learned as a lawyer about the devious and wicked heart of man stood me in as good stead as anything else could for sniffing out evil spirits and standing up and fighting them. Yessir, I went to Brush College and I learned my psychology from sizing up folks, not books! Welllllllll—— Time to be headin' for home, I guess."

Luna said brightly to Aaron, "You must sign our guest-book. There's some lovely names in it. A bishop!"

He was not too youthfully hard for pity when he saw the guest-book: a faded ledger which Luna had tried to decorate with little crayon pictures of the prairie flowers.

Outside, Harge snickered to Aaron, "Sorry I had to put Brother Speezer in his place about his colleges and his languages and all that hocus-pocus. There's no more earnest Christian alive than he is, for all his highfalutin ways, and no truer witness to salvation, but when he gets uppity about his supposed learning, I just take it on myself to remind him that God and his angels know almost as much as college professors!"

Jake Wherryman said, "God all fishhooks, Aaron, it's near nine o'clock! What you and the reverend clergy been up to? Kissin' games? Which was smarter at 'em? Luny or Huldy?"

"You keep still, Jake," Huldah said with aristocratic disdain. "Aaron was so sweet, sitting there listening to those old mugginses lecturing. They're saints, but they're so long-winded."

Aaron inquired, "There's one thing I have to do. Say, where is Castle Lanark? How far from here?"

"Castle *what?*" wondered Jake.

"Caesar Lanark. The trader."

They chuckled, and Jake explained, "Castle? Oh, my land o' Goshen! It's a bunch of shacks in the next ravine west'ard."

"I met Selene, and she said . . ."

"Sleen's a sly minx. Ain't seen her since she was a girl, but . . . Sly!" was Anna's opinion.

"Oh, no, she was a smart, bright young un," said Huldah.

"Her father, Mister Caesar Lanark," said Jake, "is a four-horse-power bastard."

In Anna's face was dread. "Mr. Lanark makes fun of our Mission and he tells the Indians what to do. They got such twisted minds they think *we* got the wrong religion! If they ever get real mad at us . . . Sometimes when their hunting don't go so good or they have an epidemic, they think it's because we pray to our gods against them, and they come and shoot our cows. Shining Wind, their *wakan* man here, hates us, and if the village all got drunk some time and Mr. Lanark said they could, they might skip over and massacre all of us."

"Still, I guess I have to see him, if he's Selene's father," fretted Aaron.

Jake argued, "Maybe you can get around him, newcomer like

152

you. He laughs at the rest of us. A cold-hearted man, awful mean; a Scotty; looks down on us Yanks. He'd like to see us all weltering in our blood."

Anna contradicted herself: "Now you be still! The very idea! Weltering! He's a real nice, polite man." But she did not sound convinced. "Land sake, I never expected to like a breed like Selene better for the Injun half of her than for the white half, but that man . . . Oh, let's go sleepy-by."

Was it possible, Aaron was worrying, that Selene did not understand the unfortunate ways of her own father? She had seen but little of him since she had grown up.

Before they went to bed there was an embarrassment about taking turns in going out to the privy. Huldah was graceful and casual about it, but Jake had to snort humorously.

Aaron climbed up the alpine stairs after Huldah, who said a somewhat lingering good night in the musky storeroom which separated their chambers. "You can see we've taken you right into the family. Everybody loved you. Good night and sleep tight, Friend Aaron, and the angels hover round your head. See you tomorrow!"

On his trunk, which would serve him as writing-table, there was a block of sulphur matches, which were torn off singly and which lighted with a diabolic stink and a purple sputter. He kindled the wick floating in the hollowed-out turnip, but the glow was so watery that it merely filled the darkness with coiling likenesses of Harge preaching, Huldah smiling and a Caesar Lanark who was a squat, black-bearded Macbeth with a copper crown, waving Indians on to the slaughter.

He stood by the turnip lamp, cold with melancholy. Why was he here?

Huldah, Jake, Anna were his friends, with the frost of New England hills preserving them. But the others considered him a theological child, a tenderfoot and a good deal of a fool. Back home,

153

his boss thought him a good carpenter, and even his father snarled at him as one worth chastising and rearing.

He undressed, wrapped a blanket about his shoulders and, since for years he had always said his prayers with his arms resting on his cot, he knelt by his pallet, his elbows on his thighs, his hands tense on that low bed which was just a mattress.

"I came here," he thought, "to do a little something toward making the world into Christ's kingdom, where all men should work together. And then Harge talks like he expects me to be a slave—and a comic one. All right! I *am* a tenderfoot! I haven't got anything so important to do that I mind carrying out his orders and sounding my penny whistle for God's glory and not for mine. Christ Jesus help me to rejoice in being a clodhopper and a fool for thy sake! Amen."

No longer lonely and futile, comfortably conscious that his friend Huldah would be sleeping a dozen feet away, he slipped between the sheetless blankets, dozed in journey-weariness, and was instantly yanked awake again by the jamboree of sounds from the Indian village across Lake Bois des Morts.

A persistent thud of drums, the screaming boast of young braves, the wail of the women's mourning-song—a shrieking chorus in mounting and falling waves—and behind it the drum and the rattle and the flutes.

The howling of the *wakan* man fretting the sick with his gourd rattle, and his lamentations to Onktehi and Wakinyan, the evil-dealing gods. In a lull, only the red-cedar flute in serenade of a soft-limbed Indian girl. Then the tune for the bullet-and-mitten game, the death-song of the women, the bellowing of vainglorious young warriors, the flute, the rattle, the drum and, sudden, a million ragged dogs in cacophonic chorus.

Selene was half-Sioux. Perhaps some cousin of hers was mangling that drum, that sonorous parchment head on a powder-keg.

154

His Dakota friends had no churches, no libraries, no cities, no cannon; only love and fury and trade guns; but perhaps God loved them as much as he did Herbert Henry Speezer, B.D., M.A.

Aaron was asleep, looking young and bright headed and defenseless.

24

Breakfast at the Wherrymans' consisted of acorn-coffee and fried pork with flour gravy. So did the other meals.

Jake explained that they were supposed to have family prayers before breakfast, but they all got so doggone hungry out here in the wilds . . . Usually, the service was conducted by Huldah, for Jake was, he said, no great hand at praying.

Would Aaron take a shot at it this morning?

So Aaron made his first public appearance, and had stage-fright before an audience consisting of Huldah and six Wherrymans, of whom only Martha, aged one, was hostile. She eyed Aaron malevolently all through his reading from *Ezekiel,* occasionally remarking "Baa!"

When he came to pray, he was sure that he could never become a minister. It occurred to him that most clerics asserted that in praying they were veritably talking to God, an even shakier ordeal than talking to President Polk. True, they sounded as though they were addressing the assembled deacons rather than Omnipotence robed in thunder; but suppose God *was* listening?

He prayed, "Lord God, let us be the kind of Christians that you would be if you were a Christian. Amen!"

He had screwed up his eyelids so tight that they hurt, but a sense of power came to him, in a dusty darkness with streaks of saffron. Yes! He *would* be a minister!

When he opened his eyes, Squire Harge was in the room, peering at him, not approvingly, and blurting:

"Well, boys, want you to get busy, get busy. Set those lazy squaws to digging the potatoes, and then start preparing the boards for Bessie's room. Her and Jefferson are studying mighty hard; real diligent about the work of the Lord—that's the idea: diligence! Already they hear the mighty summons of mission work, only they want to go to Africa—claim the climate here is too con-cerned cold. I tell 'em, 'I wish I'd picked a warmer location myself, but you'll go just exactly where the Lord calls you, and no if, and, or but about it!' "

Jake sighed, "Boards, heh?"

Aaron petitioned, "Would it be all right if I went to Lanark Castle —Mr. Lanark's fort, I mean—some evening? You remember you introduced me to Selene, Squire."

"The *Princess* Selene!" said Harge. It was a sneer.

"Would you like to go over there with me, Squire?"

"I would not! I see just as little of that man Lanark as the Lord will let me. He's helped bring in our supplies, and couple times he's translated hymns into Sioux, but Caesar Lanark ain't what you'd call a Christian, not even a Unitarian. I suspect him of laughing at our poor efforts. I can't forbid you to go there, Neighbor, I suppose." (He spoke as though he supposed he certainly could.) "But I'd be just as glad if you didn't never do more than just pass the time of day with him.... See you later, boys!"

Jake said, "Ain't that delightful! Some more sawing! I'm thirty-nine and I ain't been sawing boards but thirty-six years now. And these, y' understand, Aaron, ain't been through a mill. We saw 'em right out of logs. The Squire is a saint; prayingest fellow I ever knew; but when he *ain't* praying, he's always figuring out some finicking new addition to that house of his, or wanting that dad-blasted slab of rock under his cook stove moved again. I've moved it three times already, and wa'n't any use putting it there in the first place.

"Now he'll have us hammering there, and his woman so sick. He'd never think of that. Real nice girl she is, too, Mercie; real friendly.

"Some ways, the Squire is more pigheaded than Lanark, who's a

157

nice-spoken galoot, anyway. The Injuns think Lanark is a king, because they claim he keeps 'em from starving by giving 'em credit.
Fact is, he helps 'em starve, by fixing his own prices, buy or sell, and
they never see what he puts down in his books—couldn't read it if
they did—only educated Injuns here are Isaac and a fellow named
Black Wolf, and Lanark has him bribed, I guess.

"Well, it's all a Gehenna of a situation, if you ask me, so let's go out
and see what the squaws are doing with the potatoes. Potatoes!
There's one fruit I like nigh about as much as I do sawing boards!"

A dozen Indian women had come over from their village, in two
dugouts, to dig potatoes for the Mission. They were busy in the field,
cheerful and mocking, in shortgowns well smeared with earth. They
looked at Jake and Aaron and said something peppery-sounding and
giggled.

Jake protested, "Now that last slam they took at me, I don't know
what it was, but it's a lie!"

"How do you pay them?" Aaron wanted to know.

"In *potatoes!* My God, them women like them things!"

Jake showed the church, a bare little chapel with backless wooden
benches, but, on the wall, a head of Jesus pale against goldleaf, which
Aaron associated with Luna Speezer. Jake led him to the log stable,
windowless, hay-smelling, with its half-dozen cows tramping straw
into the muddy earth floor.

"I done the milking and let you sleep late this morning, Aaron—
till six. But guess after this, you better be up in time and take over
all the milking."

Aaron was willing, though not too inhumanly willing.

With the long, two-handed saw they started cutting boards out of
a tamarack log. The task was sore to the muscles and, in the strain of
keeping the boards even, shocking to the nerves. And it did go on
so! Beside it, building a house seemed to Aaron like playful wood-
carving. He felt that however substantial his faith, there was no

future in sawing out boards. It was as unadventurous as working in Adams, though the straw-thatched log stable and the bark-roofed workshop, between which they were sawing, and the pathless river-bluffs behind them did remind him that this was the fabulous West.

He demanded of Jake, "How did you ever get this done before I came?"

"Brother Speezer helped me some. He kept saying 'Oh dear!' And the Squire did. When he got a splinter in his hand, the Squire would yell, 'Oh, *habeas corpus mandamus*' and then wink at me! Oh, the old gent is pretty human, once you get past his idea he's going to get the biggest jeweled crown in Heaven for saving Injun souls.

"I'm a good Connecticut Christian. When I got converted—in Waterbury it was, on a Thursday—I hollered about my sin-ridden condition so loud it like to scared the preacher out of a year's growth. I give up coffee-drinking for eleven months and four days! But after thirteen years out here at the Boy de More, I begin to wonder if all this missioning is worth while. I dunno. God how I hate boards! 'Druther draw manure!"

They were interrupted by a dugout-load of Indian husbands who were clearly no friends of economic emancipation. They demanded that their several wives return at once, bringing the potatoes which they would have earned if they had gone on digging. Mr. Speezer was summoned, as the only staff member who knew the Dakota language well enough to deal with such complexities. He looked drier than ever, yet he so placated the husbands that they went off, leaving their women to labor but scrupulously taking every potato that, by Jake's count, they had earned to date.

The Aaron who had been doubting Speezer and admiring all Indians as Cooper heroes turned right around in his ethnology. And the saw went achingly on.

The Squire stopped them next.

"Mrs. Harge—Mercie—would like to see you, Neighbor. She feels a wonderful lot better this morning. I want you to tell me frankly how she seems to you. Not having a doctor here. The Speezers do annoy me, talking about her maybe having consumption. General debility, that's what it is. And I've been giving her a real good tonic: ivy leaves and hyssop boiled in skimmed milk."

But among the country people at home, Aaron had heard of this as a tonic for the thirty-year consumption.

The Squire left him with Mercie uneasily, as though he was afraid of what they two might say about him.

She was gay in a Persian shawl with passionate roses on white silk; her hair was parted and demure; her eyes were interested. Only, as Aaron sat on a stool by her bed, he saw that the flush on her cheeks was too intense, that silver was too thickly woven with her chestnut hair, that the shawl was threadbare and on the white ground was one drop of blood.

"You're really going to be a missionary, Brother Aaron?" she piped, and in her voice there was a good deal of the exuberant child. To Aaron she was every age; she was all women of every age.

"I don't know yet, Mrs. Harge."

"My good gracious! *Mercie!* Plain fellow Yankees like us!"

"Mercie."

"Oh, *be* a missionary! I do believe on the Lord Jesus. He's been a great solace to me, these days. He smiles more than any of them ever tell you. It's a glory to be a missionary and bring light to my poor Indians in their darkness. I love light, every ray of it, from the first dawn. I lie here (poor Harge has to sleep on a trundle bed now!) and reach for that first ray. It's better than cold water.

"But don't get proud of your gospeling. The missionaries all claim they give God the credit, but they don't sound so."

Aaron tried to be professional: "Pride isn't my trouble so much as coldness of heart."

She laughed, like aspen leaves. "You won't be cold! Wait and see. ... Have you got interested in Huldah Purdick yet?"

"Why, I think she's a nice young lady."

"You keep her like that, will you! You're fresh and good. Don't get a family too quick and get shopworn. And it wouldn't be fair to her."

"Never even thought of such a thing!"

"Of course you have! Huldah's a devoted girl; just the kind that will wear her life out fussing. Send her back to the States and have her marry a nice Episcopal rector that's a widower with two pretty children and glass fingerbowls. Don't spend your life in a muddy slew, lost, tramping in circles, and don't let Huldah, either. You stay here, but send her back."

She burst out, and now she was not smiling:

"Missionary work is hard on the men, but it kills the women. There's a kind of small-town girl—they're very pure and enthusiastic; they love to sing in the choir and do needlework and wash the neighbors' children. And they write verses about loving God, and when missionaries flock east, looking for new batches of wives after they've worn out the old ones . . ."

Aaron was gasping.

"You know it's true! Well, these brown moths flutter a bit and then get caught. They think it's God calling them. They get taken on, some as wives, some just as helpless helpers. They go out to the frontier or to the jungle, and write lovely little articles for the church magazines and the home weekly about the savage scenery and the quaint customs and the continual goodness of God. There's two kinds of them: the hysterical and the consumptive—that's me—and I don't know which is the more quivery. The consumptives are excited about the love of men or the love of God, and then they turn cold, so suddenly. Harge goes on being optimistic. I just go on coughing blood."

"Oh, no!"

"Yes. Good thing all missionaries' wives aren't like me. Some are

the sensible kind, like Anna Wherryman—lots of 'em. There needs
to be lots, because missionaries use up wives awful fast. Harge's first
one only lasted a year.

"Yes. They die. But it's kind of hard on them before they go—before they fold their hands and smile contented and say, 'I hear thy
call, Jesus; I come with joy.'

"All the cooking. Oh, the food has to be dainty, even when it's the
same old turnips. Mending. The Reverend has to be neat; seems
God gets irritated otherwise. Bearing children, and bringing them
up—and they're a Reverend's little pledges, so they have to have
their noses wiped. . . . Children! Time for you to grow up, Aaron. I
want to talk as if you were my brother. I haven't anybody else here,
and now, I never will have."

"Huldah?"

"No. She'd think I was raving. She'd say, 'There, there, dearie,'
and pat me. How I hate to be touched, except by a man I love!

"Oh, I do love children. Bessie is the cutest trick alive, the sancti-
monious little swindler! But a reasonable supply, Aaron—please!
Missionaries like Harge are so powerful about not tippling or soiling
the Lord's Day, but how they do love to make love, and the more uplifted they feel, the more affectionate they get. And there you are
with another precious coming, and no doctor, and you're no longer a
girl—even if you aren't but twenty-odd by the calendar. You're just a
combination of scrub-woman and stock farm, and you're supposed
to yell Hallelujah about it. Three of mine died. Partly, I was too
weak to nurse them, and one, she was such a pretty thing—diarrhea.
Sickening!"

Aaron was neither embarrassed nor horrified. No one had ever
been so close to him, and her bitterness, her distress, were his anger
and his wretchedness.

"Aaron dear, if you marry Huldah . . ."

"I've known her less than twenty-four hours!"

162

"Doesn't take long. Matrimony moves fast on the frontier. Only fun there is!"

"Never even thought of such a thing."

"*She* has! Handsome young man, nice smile, and Harge and Herby and Jake all occupied—for the moment. And when you do marry her, be kind. Don't feel you must be restrained, under the judgment of the Lord, in everything except the tired body of your own wife. Please!"

"Oh, I will." Just what he was promising, he did not know.

"It's so hard to decide what to do with the children, on the frontier. You want them to love your pet savages, and yet you don't want 'em to learn too many heathen war-cries. It scares you. *Scared!* That's the word. A woman is scared here all the time—lie in the darkness and listen to the scalp-dance song or to the everlasting drums—bung, bung, bung, bung—all night long.

"Not quite so bad right here, with other missionaries around, but Harge and I spent two years at another Western station, with no white helpers, and often the children and I were alone in the house, with the Indians looking in the window and laughing. They'd come right in, begging, putting their fingers into the pot and yanking out the one piece of pork that was all there was for me and the babies.

"Oh, they never hurt us. They were much more likely to ride the babies on their knees than they were to brain them—ride a cockhorse to Banbury Cross. But I was just as scared, and Aaron, all I'm thinking about now is, I haven't had anybody to do a good complaining to for three or four years, till you came along."

"Go ahead, Sister Mercie."

"I intend to, Brother Aaron. Silly nickname, 'Neighbor.' Like you were a county politician. I've been devoting myself to thought on that for hours now. And—but—sometimes the Indians got drunk, and one night when I was alone, they came into the yard and shot our only cow, and Harge way over at Mendota, busy with the Lord, that didn't need him, but . . .

"Don't you and Huldah have any children while you're missionaries at a lonely post.

"Oh, my Balthazar ... What a name! Like a Jewish king with a red-gold beard! He does love me, tenderly. He's so puzzled that I don't worry more when the poor Dakota can't get a conviction of sin for the crime of hunting on the Sabbath. And he can't understand why I'd rather he'd just pat my hand and not get passionate.

"Poor Aaron! To have all my griefs poured out on you! But I have to talk to somebody, as I used to talk to my father, this one last time before I die."

"Now you're not going to ..."

"Don't talk like Huldah! Of course I am. . . . You know what Harge and Herb Speezer are? They're town pumps. They think you can get the bright waters of salvation only from them, when all over there's little creeks with birds lighting on wet stones. I like creeks better. . . . 'Cricks' I still want to call them.

"New England. *New England,* Aaron! At home, we had a real Maine house, all white and square, with a pyramid roof: as plain and solid as a block of Maine granite. But there was a lovely clutter inside: rag rugs and gilded pine cones and china dogs; and outside, there was a regular jungle of lilac and snowball and spiraea. And a Concord-grape arbor, like a tunnel, and you could look right down through it and see the salt inlet and the lighthouse and the waves mocking at winter.

"My father, General Frost—he's still alive but I don't suppose I'll ever see him—he got his rank in the War of 1812, where he did valiant work buying cordage and drinking brandy punches—he thought all children should have ponies and Punch and Judy shows. And I had a serious kitten that slept in an old green-plush cap right under the kitchen stove.

"I know this is childish. But ever since I was married, I've been so highly grown-up. I've done my best to groan and holler over my sins, to please Harge, even when I couldn't figure out what they were, but

164

when I see you with that nice, fresh New England face, not all yellow with Ohio River ague, it takes me back to Maine.

"You know: on that inlet you could see an old careened schooner. And the waves were always changing. The prairie is so pitiless and so everlasting. There isn't a thing on the prairie to hold your eye, except the big clouds sailing over; there isn't a whitecap or a dory or a dune with the sand blowing. Nothing.

"You hear so much from the pioneers about how excited they are over their new homes, and that's right; yes, they ought to talk that way; it's a big, free land, with a chance. But you don't hear so much of how the women and the older children get homesick for Back Home and the sea and geraniums in old earthy pots on a back porch with vines on it and a swing.

"You've let me go home, Aaron. I'm grateful!"

He thought of taking her back to the grape arbor and the inlet, but Squire Harge was not one to accept interference from advisory young men. He kissed her cheek and went back to his evangelical labor of sawing out tamarack boards. What confused him most was that it seemed to him that it was Selene whom he had just left.

When he saw Huldah next, Mercie's warning made him look at Huldah with interest.

To AARON, sawing boards, appeared Leon Simonet, and he said that he was the voyageur for Mr. Caesar Lanark.

He displayed more of the traditional costume of French voyageurs than had the half-breeds with whom Aaron had journeyed in the bateau: a long blue blanket coat, red-striped and hooded, a crimson sash and a pouch for pipe, flint and steel. He did not so much mispronounce his English as give it a flavor, like sage.

"Mr. Lanark weesh me to tal you he is the father of Mees Say-lane, and he present his compliment and he would be very 'appy if you would come to supper tonight at seex o'clock."

Aaron was enchanted, and said so, though Jake was leering. "But how did Mr. Lanark know I'm here, and that I met Miss Selene?"

"He 'as 'ees ways. He makes it 'ees business to know everything that 'appen west of Snelling. I come later for show you the way."

Harge consented to all this, but sulkily. Aaron reflected that this was the first time since he had left the house of Uriel that he had asked permission to go out in the evening.

For this social occasion he put on the Good Suit, the new black one, with an unclerical blue-silk stock.

He followed Simonet on a thin trail westward along the Minnesota bank into a ravine and up to a plateau of bayberry and ash trees. His venture seemed a mockery when they emerged before a wall of upright logs, rough and mossy, more a stable than a castle. But he had a sense of Indian-fighting and the Wild West, gold and romance and mountain passes, as they came to a heavy log gate in the palisades. Through it he saw four log buildings and a littered yard.

Simonet showed him the store, piled with Indian-trade goods.

Like all tourists, Aaron had supposed that the Sioux swapped their furs and wild rice for nothing besides guns and tomahawks, and he was astonished by the possessions which were bartered for by the artless and possessionless Indians:

Blankets, white and blue and scarlet. Guns and soap and wheat-flour and Carolina rice. Opodeldoc liniment and hawk-bells and blue-edged porcelain platters.

Medals with the face of General Washington. Tomahawks and scalping knives—only, if he had been back in Clunford, he would have supposed them to be small hatchets and kitchen knives. Nails and sassafras and augers. Mosquito bars, awls, bullet-molds, iron pots, brass pots, ear bobs and gartering by the yard. Chests of tea, strings of wampum, military caps, vials of peppermint, pitch for repairing canoes and stylish strings of beads—beads of gypsum and glass and brass and elm.

He was aware then of a great Indian kingdom and imperial trafficking. "It's like my white-man's impudence to think of the Indians as doing nothing but sleep, fight, hunt, dance," he sighed.

They saw the warehouse, with its fabulous bins of buffalo, deer, brown bear, fisher, wolf, lynx, coon, otter, mink, muskrat, and the stable, with a real riding-horse for the Lord of the Manor. Aaron was prepared for grandeur now, and it was with considerable respect-fulness that he came into the main house, into what was as much throne-room as living-room, into the baronial presence of Caesar Lanark, Esquire, the grandson of Sir Priam Fortesbarrow, who kept a carriage, and of Angus Lanark, who kept pigs.

It was a big room with a big stone fireplace. Along two sides was a bench on which Indians were loafing, looking up at Aaron with squinting condescension. In the center, facing the fire, in a teak-wood armchair, was Lanark, tall and slender, with a Marcus Aurelius brow and, though America in this decade was almost beardless, an immense beard of brown silkiness. It was probable that he was not over fifty, but more probable that he was hundreds of years old: amiable, learned, sharp-eyed, disposing of petitioners with a glance.

He was somewhat romantically clad in low black shoes—as rare as ivory sandals on the booted frontier—in shepherd's plaid trousers, a gold-embroidered green silk waistcoat, but with them a braid-bound jacket, a round-looking jacket with the air of a Boston brokerage house.

Two sperm candles, in brandy bottles, stood on small tables on either side of his throne.

As Aaron came in there was a murmur of Dakota all through the room. Apparently Lanark was speaking it with the Indians, who wore blankets over colored skirts, or buffalo hides over naked chests. A couple of them were fashionably painted, in streaks of red and green and black, with different patterns on each cheek, and a couple, but only a couple, wore eagle feathers. (Which may not have meant that they had killed anybody at all, but merely have touched an enemy's new-slain corpse.)

Lanark nodded, and observed, "I have heard from Say-lay-nay. She is staying with my sister, in New York. Permit me to welcome you to Westward Ho."

"Ho!" said one of the Indians, but it seemed to have no connection.

Ignoring Aaron then, not introducing him, Lanark went on talking with his court of Indians, who were passing a small pipe from hand to hand. Aaron wanted to know them, and he suspected that they had more humor and shrewdness than any Harge.

He sized up the farther end of the room. It seemed to have been planned for Selene as her private apartment, with a square piano, a marble-topped table, a whale-oil lamp. But the case of books must be her father's, with Macaulay, Carlyle, Fielding, Charles Chauncy.

A youngish Indian came rapidly into the room; a slim man, active

168

and fierce, with a silver band round his black hair. Lanark addressed him in English:

"Black Wolf, this is Aaron Gadd, a new missionary come out to join Elder Harge."

Black Wolf stared with his hand on his mouth, the Sioux gesture of surprise, while Lanark went on to Aaron:

"The Wolf learned English at the Mission and then he went along to Oberlin College for a couple of years. He is the most eloquent orator among the Isanti River Wahpetons, though they're all given to spellbinding, curse them! It's probably his trace of M'dewakanton blood."

Aaron rose from the little reed rocker in which he had been a wallflower, and Black Wolf gravely shook his hand, saying clearly, "Our friend Lanark is mistaken. I am forgetting all the English I ever learned. I have reverted to the low redskins. Plenty reverted! I like hunting and a free foot better than Brus-*sel* carpets and boiled cabbage!"

Aaron said urgently, "I want to get acquainted with the Indians, if it's possible. I'm not a missionary. I'm a carpenter."

"You shall do it," promised Black Wolf, and turned away. He had made no visible sign, but the other Indians followed him from the room.

Caesar Lanark said, "You have impressed the Wolf. My congratulations. He is wise and brave and foolish and unhappy."

Aaron was making a dutiful "I'm glad" when through the inner door of the big room came a Catholic priest, and Lanark muttered, "Father Bonifay—Mr. Gadd."

Aaron had never spoken to any Catholic priest except to grunt, "Mornin', Fath" on the streets of Adams. Bonifay was stranger to him and less natural than Black Wolf of Oberlin College, and more disturbing. Now that he was saved, and was adjutant to an enterprise for spreading pure Christianity and smiting the heresies of Rome, ought he not to do something about this agent of the Vatican?

Father Bonifay was round-faced, casual, spectacled. He might have been a schoolteacher, a merchant, a postmaster. There was, Aaron fretted, nothing ascetic nor interestingly vicious in his look. He wore a clerical collar, a rabat and black vest, with a small gold crucifix, but also a fringed buckskin jacket and high boots that were creased and tired-looking, as though his feet were tired.

Aaron said with agitation to Lanark—the father of Selene!—"I didn't know you folks were Catholics."

"I'm not, my friend. I am a Positivist, under the patronage of St. Auguste Comte."

At this, Father Bonifay smiled, rather smugly.

Aaron thought, "I have a good chance of being humbugged by these wise old scoundrels. I don't think there is such a sect as the Positivists, but there might be. Neighbor, be careful. Don't let these pagans show you the elephant!"

Mrs. Vilac, the cook-housekeeper, who bobbed to Father Bonifay every time she came near him, had been setting a folding table in the parlor half of the throne-room. Now she yelled, "Everyt'ing servi!"

The table was of fine cabinet work, and it was spread with thin china, crested silver. For dinner they had roast wild goose, wild rice and dried figs with hazelnuts, and it may be interpolated that it was the last really good meal Aaron would have in six months.

Father Bonifay said, with only the faintest whisper of accent, "I hope your work here will be interesting, Mr. Gadd."

"Father, I hope I won't be saucy if I say what wonderful English you speak. You are French?"

"Born in Auvergne."

"Did you learn it in New England?"

"No, in London, and then in Australia, among the gold-seekers, and then in Iowa, with his Lordship, Bishop Loras."

"Oh ... Which way you headed, Father? Going back East?"

"I hope to have a look at the Indians along the Missouri River and beyond: the Teton and the Mandan and the Gros Ventre. They have not had much propaganda."

"Much ... ?"

"Missionizing you might call it, or evangelization."

"I didn't know the Catholics were around here. Reverend Harge never said a thing about it."

"We Catholics have been working among Wisconsin and Minnesota Indians ever since Father Allouez, in 1665, a hundred years before any Protestant layman or catechumen, even Peter Pond or Jonathan Carver, set foot here. By the perfidy of British and American politicians, we were long kept from taking instruction and the blessed sacraments to our suffering children, but now you will hear the mission bells again.

"Your Mr. Speezer—our Church would be glad to have such men to teach the Indians to plow; and Mr. Harge—oh, yes, an earnest man; he was a law-clerk, I believe; very well-meaning, but of the most stiff-necked pride and afraid of the adventure and discomfort of thinking."

"I think Mr. Harge is a great spiritual force!" stated Aaron, more stubbornly than angrily, while the other voice within him said, "Do you?"

"I'm sure of it, Monsieur," Bonifay agreed suavely.

Aaron realized that Caesar Lanark was silently laughing at both of them.

——Mister Harge! Law-clerk! I suppose to this priest, the Squire is no more of a minister than I am. Anyway, I'm not going to let them make Selene a Romanist. Hm! Maybe the Sioux feel about my religion the way I do about Father Bonifay's. I can see why a Sioux

171

lover would slash his girl's new clothes if *his* Selene hankered after *my* religion!

——I'd better quit thinking like this, or I'll never be a missionary. And I better listen to this idolatrous Papist. I might learn something. That wouldn't hurt me!

He said politely to Father Bonifay, "Don't you find it hard to get converts?"

"Why, no! Instead of confusing the poor fellows with a lot of man-made Protestant theology—Forensic Justification and Sabbatarianism and such fantastic make-believe—we just tell them about Christ's love for them and the healing of the sacraments, and they gladly offer themeslves for baptism.

"Two hundred years ago, a lone Jesuit with a portable altar on his back would steer his canoe down an unknown lake to a new tribe; in a month he would learn their language, and in two he would baptize the whole blessed lot of them! . . . Do you know anything about Catholicism?"

"I can't say I do."

"When I come back from the Missouri—if I ever do come back!—I must explain our faith to you. You seem to be free of the Presbyterian pomposity of Mr. Harge."

Lanark jeered, "I thought you European priests were proud of being tolerant. Would you proselytize this defenseless young man?"

Bonifay said cheerfully, with a sound that had the body but not the soul of a laugh, "I haven't your joy in cruelty and dramatic attitudes, Caesar. Does it surprise you that a humble priest should want to keep an amiable young man from going to the Protestant heaven which may, perhaps, be identified with the Catholic hell?"

Aaron was bothered. Perhaps this round, placid soldier of the cross, with a hooker of whisky before him, was a magician who could entice him out of the stockade where he had been safely singing with Deacon Popplewood and Mr. Finney and Squire Harge and Huldah, and pen him in a heaven where he wouldn't know one soul except Nadine, who would give him away to the angels.

Lanark was chuckling, "Father, I'm glad to hear that your monolithic church has become 'humble.' When did you tear down the Vatican?"

Father Bonifay was grave. "No missionary priest has a Vatican in his soul, but only the terrible sins and longing of unredeemed men in savage places. . . . Mr. Gadd, why have you been afraid of our church?

"Excuse me, Father, but the Roman Catholics seem so foreign, in America."

"Did you ever think how foreign your hymns must seem to the only true Americans—the Indians?"

"Ye-es . . . "

"What astonishes me is the way you Protestants fail to use the rich quality of Faith that already exists among the Dakota, as shown in their *hambeday* trances, their seeking after the presence of God.

"When Louis the Eighteenth was King of France, after the Napoleonic wars, I was old enough to understand what you might call the post-war milk-sickness in my land; the boresome intellectuality of the revolutionists who weren't brave enough for barricades but who sold their birthright in the Church for a mess of very nasty modernist pottage: homosexualism, artistic insanity, socialism.

"But I thought that worse than any of these wet souls were the highly moral amateur clerics who rewrote the angelic code and dressed up God in Calvinistic small clothes, with a ruler instead of a heavenly scepter. They were such clever debaters, while we Catholics were simple souls. Yes, yes, every man his own Pope, they said—but that showed, you see, that they believed in *having* a Pope! Sooner or later, every one of these reformers who had a sense of humor and had read a little history came back to us . . . *You all do!*"

Lanark was teasing, "Father, when you two clerical gentlemen

173

have agreed on a scheme of theology, perhaps you will reflect how well the Indians got along for several thousand years without either of you."

Aaron was eager: "Do you thing it might have been better for all the savage races if the whites had never come at all?"

Father Bonifay rose, his smile cordial. "No, my son, for whatever pitiful human frailties we may have had, we brought to what you call the 'savages' the inestimable gift of the Holy Cross! Good night, gentlemen. I must be up at three."

26

SAID Lanark, "Bonifay looks so well-fed and cozy, but he's a courageous man. He'll get up early for the purpose of going out and risking death among the Western tribes. He is also a man of education. Unlike Fathers Galtier and Ravoux, in St. Paul, he has read books—though not as many as he would like you to think. And he is more dangerously single-minded than even the fanatical Mr. Harge. I'm never sure that Bonifay won't convert *me*, some day."

Aaron was alarmed as he thought of Lanark leading Selene into a Roman fortress which the son of Uriel, son of Hezrai, could never blow down with his Calvinist trumpet.

Lanark talked now. He could be silent; often, surrounded by his court of Indians, he silently encouraged them to tell dirty stories, to boast, to betray themselves. He could also be loquacious as only a lonely man who has been reading many books can be when he snares a listener.

He courteously made it evident that Selene belonged to a caste unreachably above a young missionary who sawed out boards:

"I'm glad you called on my daughter and brought her a breath of reality. The trouble with that young woman is that she's almost too talented—music, French, everything. I'm afraid she will not become less complicated when I take her for a year or two on the Grand Tour of Europe, as I shall. I want to get her away from a man who has been too attentive to her in Massachusetts—old family, rich, Harvard, that sort of thing, but not clever enough for her."

"Mm," said Aaron.

"Aside from giving her a wider scope, I shall enjoy seeing Europe again myself. And what I crave is not the great cathedrals or the

Dukeries but a certain plain little chophouse in Edinburgh called the Whistle & Wet, where they knew my grandfather, Sir Priam, and remember me as a boy. Oh, yes, I never forget them, on my trips to Britain and the Continent."

Providence, which had singularly let Aaron down in his contest with Rome, went back to work and presented him with the speculation: I wonder if this fellow has ever been in Europe at all?

"My only worry about having Say-lay-nay meet the lairds and that sort of grandee is that one of them may snatch her away and marry her, and she never will return to our tatterdemalion frontier at all."

——This man wants to use her for his own glory—get acquainted with these pesky counts and what-nots through her . . . Well, Neighbor, what do *you* want to use her for?

"But let's not waste any more time on my wayward girl, Gadd. So you're at the Mission. A good Presbyterian?"

"Congregationalist."

"Same thing. One has indigestion and the other has spiritual corns. My grandfather's brother was a Scotch dominie: hard on sin and harder on his family."

"Tell me, Mr. Lanark: what did Mr. Bonifay—Father Bonifay—mean when he said the Indians have a lot of faith already?"

"He was referring to their rite of *hambeday*—or it can be transliterated *hanmdepi*—which means variously dreaming, fasting, consciousness of divine power or God-seeking. As a sign of maturity, the young male Sioux takes the *inipi,* the steam bath, in a lodge of cedar boughs, very fragrant and healthful, too. Then, sometimes for two days and two nights, he stands on the highest point of land nearby, naked and silent and alone, fasting and ignoring rain or hail or the chill of night.

"His only variation is to hum a sacred song or—this may seem comic to you, but perhaps your rite of the Lord's Supper seems odd to the Indians!—he may smoke the sacred pipe, with tobacco mixed with red willow bark; just a few puffs and hold the pipe up to show God that it is a humble offering.

"He is awaiting a message from his God, Wakantanka, who is like your Hebrew Yah-weh except that he's less literary, less intrusive and less vindictive.

"If he gets no message, sometimes he comes down and tortures himself, dragging a buffalo-head from skewers stuck through his flesh. But I don't know that this self-torture is more abnormal than the early Christian mystics. Of late, it has become a pretty bloody show, but that seems to be the influence of the whites and their interference with the original purity of the Dakota religion. Just as the primitive medicine man took no pay for his herbs and incantation, but has become a charlatan now, under the malign example of mercenary business men like myself and creed-mongering mullahs like you—Catholic *and* Protestant."

"Us?"

"Oh, yes. You substitute an unventilated chapel for the open woods which were the Dakotas' tabernacle and a dreary staff of paid text-parrots for the Indian grandparents whose delight it was, in the old days, to instruct children in the duties of tribal morality and in the delightful myths about their demigods.

"Oh, yes. We white people have taught the simple Dakota that it pays to lie and steal, and by providing them with firearms, we have transformed their mildly lethal contests with the Ojibway into some very neat exhibitions of murder."

Aaron worried, "My voyageurs *said* we gave them the pox."

"My dear boy! Just a beginning! We have given the Indians consumption, influenza, measles, syphilis, and the hymns of Charles Wesley. With the guns they get from me, they are exterminating the buffalo, which formerly provided food, shelter, clothing. They will soon have to turn to farming, and I shall buy their wheat and sell them plows and bushel-baskets—at *my* prices.

"Oh, personally, I have never been too dishonest with them.

Very few of the older traders have—Sibley or Joe Brown or Norman Kittson or Hazen Mooers or McLeod or Philander Prescott. But we've pioneered the way for a lot of scoundrels who want to butcher the Indians at once, instead of gently pasturing them and milking them over the years. And this shyster competition has forced us veterans, the Medicis and Rothschilds of the frontier, to extend credit to such a dismaying point that we shall have to recoup by making the Government pay us out of the money that will be awarded to the Indians for their land in future treaties, so that they'll lose all the land and get nothing for it but our receipted bills.

"Then will come the time when you Christian missionaries will be useful. When the Indians have lost everything—land, food, faith, self-respect—then they will believe Elder Harge's admonition that it was the fault of their heathen gods. Instead of any very determined insurrection, they will be half convinced and half scared into becoming Christians, and for their future history from then on, *vide* the history of the domestic fowl."

Aaron protested, "You can't believe all that about *yourself!*"

"You mean, about Selene's father? You err in supposing that I take any discredit for what you would call Ruthlessness but what I call Realism. It is not I but the March of Civilization that is ruthless. The Ojibway stole the Mille Lacs region from the Dakota. We Canadians and you Down Easterners take it—or steal it—from the Ojibway. The Germans and Swedes and Irish will take it from us. The Poles and Italians and Slovenes will take it from them, and after that I think happily of the Chinese and the Hindus, and a final triumphant return of the rattlesnakes and gophers who were the real aborigines. Progress is power. I don't believe in sniveling pity. I am a Swimmer, not a Thresher, not a man who waves his arms and sputters and pretends he can fight the current, instead of sliding smoothly with it, head proudly up above the foam, seeing where he's going.

"Such bold swimmers get called 'predatory.' Well, the world admires the predatory lion, not the rabbit. Don't be a Thresher, Gadd! Don't you think that Elder Harge is a slightly ridiculous spectacle: a hefty man with sea-captain whiskers bleating to the scornful Dakota warriors, 'Come be Jesus's little lambs'!"

"I suppose you think all abolitionists are Threshers!"

"Naturally."

"And Women's-Righters!"

"Aren't they?"

"Well, I think Mr. Harge's effort to do *something* is better than being a—a . . . "

"A cynic? From the Greek word for 'dog'? Precisely what your friend Father Bonifay calls me. He points out that at least Elder Harge is *seeking* the true path—meaning the R.C.'s private toll road—while infidels like myself confuse the admirable seekers by heaving bricks out of the thicket."

"And maybe he's right!"

"Could be."

"Do you think Father Bonifay is wiser than Mr. Harge or Mr. Speezer?"

"Oh, no; just more strategic in stealing your converts after your spade work is done. But with both factions: the amount of time and passion that theologians have spent on defining fairy-story words would, if sensibly applied, have eliminated all war and bad cooking. Don't you think so?"

But Aaron had no opinions now except that Caesar Lanark was a cruel man with a wonderful memory for the many playful books he had read in the Minnesota winters. And that to show indignation would be just the youthful sort of clownishness that would delight Lanark.

He was in a dream of thinking, and it did not seem unnatural that a Sioux, certainly drunk, perhaps insane, should be steadily walking into the room now, pointing a shotgun at Lanark.

179

The trader rose easily from his throne, smiling and pouring out amiable and soothing Sioux as he walked toward the Indian. His hand was on the gun barrel, and as he yanked it away, with the other hand he slammed the warrior down on the long bench. But he kept on laughing. He poured a drink, bore it to the Indian—and handed back the gun.

The Sioux walked out, obviously proclaiming that Lanark was his friend.

That was more than Aaron could do.

He made motions of going. Lanark said dulcetly, "So soon? By the way, you haven't told me your particular hobby in religiosity. Humility, like Harge?"

"I'm crazy enough to believe in a world without race divisions."

"But so do I! The only difference between us is that you think all races are equally good, and I think they're all equally bad and slovenly and in need of being controlled by their superiors—by which, no doubt, I mean myself."

"Oh."

"B' the way, do you ride horseback?"

"About like most farm boys."

"When Selene comes, next spring or summer, you might like to ride with her."

Aaron felt a jump of the heart, but he tried to be mannerly. "Maybe this young Indian that speaks English—Black Wolf, is it? —would be a better escort."

"He would. But there's a hitch. The Wolf is a patriot, a hater of the invading whites, and he particularly hates me, though he has worked for me in the store and I have given him a bountiful measure of my philosophy of Inevitable Power. I imagine he intends to kill me some day. He is so ungrateful."

Aaron wanted to think, "I'd like to kill you myself," but he dared not think it, because he felt that Lanark sardonically expected him to.

He got himself away awkwardly. When his host said cordially, "Good night. Hope I shall see you again. Find your way in the darkness?" he answered indignantly, "Of course I can."

Feeling coltish and impotent.

Outside the log fort he stood still, above a ravine filled with sinister, moving branches. Had it been youth in him or cowardice or the hobble of his own deep sins that had kept him from denouncing Lanark with evangelical thunder? But the pious fret was less irritating to him than the revelation that, because of her father's malign character, because of the high place she would occupy among the fripperies of Europe, Selene was not for him, ever.

He turned to a warm thought of Huldah, the tender, the dependable, the pure of doctrine.

27

IS feet had been sufficiently trained by night tramping in the Berkshires to feel a path through the soles of his boots and to let his feet and not his fallible eyes guide him. But at home, though a bear had been killed on Deacon Popplewood's hill within the past ten years, there were no wolves, no rattlesnakes. Aaron would not have admitted it, but he was healthily scared.

It was not that, by the stanch tradition of night panic, every stump (and there were an unreasonable number of stumps) was either a bear or an armed Indian. It was that the ravine and the trail along the Minnesota were prickly with small noises so vicious and undecipherable that he would have been glad to recognize them as coming from respectable Sioux and grizzlies. He walked spellbound through a world of whispers, mutters, conspiracies, evil.

When he saw a light and decided that he was near Squire Harge's house, he suddenly so loved that firm abode that he was sure he would stay on at the Mission till he was a very old man, the honored veteran of God. . . . Only now it could not be with Selene growing old beside him . . . What about Huldah?

He came into a tidy ash grove which he remembered as bordering the Mission. He stopped bolt, as he heard a groan, and stood apprehensive. Then he made out Squire Harge's rough voice; he realized that the Squire was alone, praying aloud in a woodland cell:

"Lord God of Hosts, thou didst command that we carry thy word, but you know that we are weak. Oh, try me no longer! Give me the souls of these heathen as the seal of my ministry. Deny not this, my one petition, and make Mercie well and able to help me as she used to when . . ."

Aaron tried to move on softly. A sharp voice: "Who's that? Huh?"

"It's just me, sir. Aaron."

Harshly: "Oh. Come here. This way."

Squire Harge was kneeling by a stump. He turned and sat on the forest floor, his back to the stump, and Aaron realized that for his vigil the Squire had piously put on his tall silk hat.

"Neighbor—Son—you have come upon me in one of my hours of despair. Maybe it's just as well for you to know what you're facing. Preaching here is like sowing in a desert of rocks, though he who clothed and quickened the dry bones can raise up even out of rocks and fallen trees children to Abraham, if it is his will—only sometimes don't seem like it is.

"It's sixteen years since I was converted and freed from the worldliness of law courts. It's thirteen that I have worked here at the Bois, with seasons at other stations in between. And—and this is dreadful to me—I have no sure evidence that I have been instrumental in the actual conversion of a single lost soul. Of the Sioux women who come to our meetings and Isaac Weeps-by-Night, I'm not dead sure that any of them have accepted Jesus fully.

"Thirty-seven people have been admitted to the communion here. Some remain, some have drifted away, and some have been gathered by the Lord to bloom in his shining garden. But not one of these has ever intimated that it was I that finally brought them to the truth. That may be because of a kind of blunt, cranky way of talking that I reckon is natural to me. I've prayed about it, passionately, but I can't seem to eradicate it. I always mean to sound pleasant and full of brotherly love, but the grouchy words jump out by themselves, before I can think.

"I do love the Lord God with my whole soul, and I want to make a savory sacrifice to him, but Satan comes and makes me botch it and there's a stench of sulphur round my offering.

"Lately, I've had serious doubts about whether it's my duty to

183

continue in missionary work at all. Maybe my bad temper and my inability to learn Sioux real good have kept precious souls from the healing grace. Oh, if I was convinced of that, I would get right out—do something—go back to the bar, though I've forgot so much.

"Son, if I did help some in your conversion, by bearing testimony —and I did, didn't I?—then we're sort of bound together in Christ Jesus. So tell me honestly if I seem to you a stumbling block and not a means of grace. Speak up, Boy! Let's have it! I don't want to go on hurting these frightened seekers after God!"

Aaron cried, "Honest, Squire, you must be an inspiration to the Indians as you are to me. You've done everything you could. If so few of 'em come around, probably it's some mysterious plan of God that we don't understand."

"Maybe."

"I was telling Mr. Lanark how noble you are."

"Did, eh? Bet a penny he didn't agree."

"Would you want him to? I wonder—he talks so much about power and ruthlessness—I wonder if that doesn't show he's weak and uncertain inside?"

"Well, now, that's mighty deep of you, my boy."

Thereafter, though at suitable times Harge was to regard him as insubordinate, heretical, saucy, idle, he considered Aaron a profound and possibly dangerous thinker. It is fortunate that Aaron did not too enthusiastically share this illusion.

At his doorstep the Squire mourned, "I can't go on lying to myself. I think Mercie is dying. I'll be so alone! When she goes to see the King in his beauty, in the kingdom that's so near and so far, it will be hard on my kids. Honestly, the Board pays me so little that I don't know how I'm going to manage Jeff's education. It seems to me that Satan undoes everything I get started. We touch the hearts of the Sioux, and then our booze drives them crazy. Boy, you never really answered my question: Ought I to quit?"

"If you do, sir, we'll all have to quit. You're our skipper!"

In the darkness before the house, with the mean light of a dip candle shining out, Aaron saw the elder snap back his head as he bit off a chew of tobacco. He spat mightily, then blurted, with a cackle of mirth, "You don't mean one word of it! You're too smart. You know I'm a slew-footed boor. But bless you for lying, and as long as you can stand me, I'll get along. God bless you! Good night!"

Aaron reflected, "When I know them enough, I think I'll laugh at the Squire, and love him; and I'll admire Mr. Lanark, and hate him."

That was all he saw clearly after the evening when, for the first time, he had talked to a very competent priest and to a fairly competent atheist.

In his room, he was too sleepy for more than a patter of prayer.

There was a dazzle behind his closed eyes, and faces in it. They were not the faces of Harge or Lanark, of Selene or Huldah, but of his brother Elijah, swinging a scythe on a Berkshire upland, and shouting, "Religion is not peace in a valley but fighting on the windy hilltops."

He was angry when he awoke at three to hear himself protesting, "And even *that* is just words! I've got to learn all the words, out here: the Squire's and Lanark's and Black Wolf's words, and learn to taste them without getting drunk on them ... Dear Selene!"

28

IT MIGHT, except that there was no crucifix nor proper altar, have been an early California mission, with its benches, its hewn rafters—this church at Bois des Morts where Aaron attended morning and afternoon services on Sunday. The staff and their children were the congregation, with a few motionless Indian women masked in shawls or blankets, and one man, Isaac Weeps-by-Night.

Aaron had expected in him a humble brother, but Isaac was taller than most of the tall Sioux, wide, fierce-nosed, erect. When he sang the hymns, which he did mightily, he stood poised, a warrior.

In the morning, Harge preached for an hour and a half, in Sioux, but Aaron managed to keep awake most of the time.

They had the Lord's Supper, with the polished silver cup of water on a clean linen cloth, and tiny squares of wheat bread, which Aaron had proudly sliced in Anna's kitchen. The Indians came up to kneel in front of the plain pine table which was pulpit and altar, and Aaron knelt with them, wishing that he had some way of reaching the sardonic Isaac, the mute veiled women.

The lavish late September, the bright river bluffs seen through the uncolored windows and beyond them the ceaseless prairie, with this humble room, these shabby people meeting in loving commemoration of Jesus—Aaron had a feeling of tenderness and consecration. The smell of the earth, he thought, was in the room, and the simplicity of a yearning for holiness.

In the afternoon, Mr. Speezer preached, more briefly but more airily; twenty minutes in Sioux and five in English; and Isaac prayed; but now Aaron had no satisfaction of earth and sun and devotion. Brother Speezer was too handy.

In the midst of it, Aaron looked back and saw Black Wolf, the refugee from Oberlin, on a bench. The Wolf minutely turned his head to stare back, but he showed no recognition, no liking, no hate, nothing but irony, and Aaron was afraid, and bothered that he could not determine what he was afraid of.

For themselves, the staff had a fervent Experience Meeting at Harge's that evening. The Squire grunted, "Brother Aaron will now have his first chance among us to testify to his sins and his merciful deliverance. Go right ahead, Lad."

It was not the visible audience, of fourteen adults and children, which flustered Aaron; it was the thought that just above the plaster ceiling, in her bed, Mercie Harge must be listening, flower-sweet yet ironic as the metallic Black Wolf. He had to get into a defiance even of her, before, leaning heavily on the table, he could blurt:

"I guess I'm not much used to talking in public yet, and I guess all I can say is that I guess I never felt right about my life back home, and drinking (some) and using bad language and girls and so on and so forth, and I believe it was God's hand that led me out here, and I certainly hope I can bear testimony to the Indians of God's goodness."

He sat down with a bump, and Mr. Speezer rippled, "Somewhat brief, but very sincerely and well put, Aaron. Oh, yes, very good."

But Aaron did not feel comfortable.

It must have been on the day after this very successful Sabbath that, for reasons apparent only to his own tortuous and rebellious mind, Black Wolf produced a small keg of whisky which he had brought in and hidden weeks before. In sequel, there was bellowing from the Indian village, and Isaac Weeps-by-Night backslid with unusual speed. He swam across the lake, he heaved a rock through a church window, he stood on the church steps and blasphemed against the Sioux syntax of all the missionaries, and he demanded a round of pork of Anna Wherryman, who chased him out of her kitchen with a flatiron.

For these several crimes, the church session tried Isaac *in absentia* and demoted him from elder, but though he had been prouder of his eldership than of his four eagle feathers, he remained drunk and unrepentant for a week. The following Sunday, Satan directed a few buffalo near the village, and Isaac crowned his misdeeds by hunting, riding and whooping on the Lord's Day.

This time, when the session met, they dismissed Isaac, permanently, from the communion of the church. In a couple of days, the whisky was all gone—and the buffalo meat was finished—and Isaac was taken with powerful remorse. He came over every day and sat on the church steps, looking dejected and imploring, but the members of the Mission paid no attention to him except for saying, as they stalked by, that Isaac certainly looked like eternity in hell.

Though he was the only male convert they had to exhibit, it was a month before Isaac was readmitted to the fold and four months —not till he came in injured from the winter hunt—before he was reinstated as elder, and almost a month more before he got drunk and demoted from a state of grace all over again.

Said Squire Harge, "Aaron, ever since our talk in the darkness, I have been thinking that my fault is not only in my impoliteness but in my lack of energy and excess of pride. I have felt too proud to go to the Indians—let them come to me, I said. Now I am going to seek them out and beg them, in the alarming condition of wickedness in which they stand convicted, to come to our services, to let me help them, and now, before they're off for their winter deer-hunt. But I, uh, sort of hate to go alone. You come with me . . . And shall I wear my tall silk hat?"

Aaron persuaded him to go in humility and a low-crowned

wideawake. Harge agreed, though he sighed, "Ever since I've been a boy, I've associated eloquent ministers with silk hats. I got this one in Philadelphia on my last trip, and the man at the store said it was the latest thing for clergymen. All right."

They crossed the river in the Mission dugout—and Harge was a far better paddler than Aaron—and landed at the Indian village. Near it were wabbly scaffolds on which the blanket-wrapped bodies of the dead were exposed, and, close by, a granite boulder with many worn coats of vermilion paint.

The Squire croaked, "That rock is an idol—Tunkan. Disgusting! And the abomination of those corpses! Sometimes they come and ask us and we make coffins for them, and then the deceased can have holy burial—in the earth, as God commands. But most of them are too proud and nasty to ask us—even the ones that beg for potatoes. Shows what stubborn infidels they are!"

Outside the village the braves were practicing their ball game, a forerunner of lacrosse. Thirty men on each side, naked but for moccasins and breechclouts but painted green and black and yellow, they were running like elk, screaming, trying to knock the ball from the cupped net of the carrier's hickory racket.

Very solid in his wide black hat, his black broadcloth frock coat, his large black boots, his well-rounded black chin beard from end to end of his lower jaw, rather like a black-granite Presbyterian church on a restricted residential avenue, the Squire watched the game.

Aaron expected a blast of disapproval of this worldly dissipation, but he realized that the Squire was beginning to mutter, all unconsciously, "Good run! A nice one! Get him! Trip him up! Kill him! Oh, a beauty!"

The Squire came to, peeped at Aaron and said primly, "If these heathen would devote that energy to fighting the wiles of Satan instead of running aimlessly with little sticks, we might build a Christian community here, like Scranton."

He marched into the nearest bark-covered hut. Along three sides of it was a blanket-scattered bench which was bed, couch, table; and in the center was an Indian woman, stirring a pot over a fire. She half bobbed to the Squire, and looked over his shoulder apprehensively, as if she expected a disapproving husband.

Mr. Harge was the least patient of men, but by his longing for spiritual conquest he had today made himself the most patient. He argued with the housewife in Sioux, and from his gestures Aaron guessed that he was telling a parable. He stumbled on his words, he wiped his hot head, but he rolled on, a Missouri River of earnestness, while the half-dozen dogs lay quiet, somehow amused.

Indian men began to sift into the lodge, entirely silent, sitting on the circumferent benches, listening but expressionless. It was Aaron's hope that Black Wolf would be among them, for on that whisky-toting Galahad he depended for learning the language, for youth's eagerness with youth. But the Wolf did not come.

Turning from man to man, Harge seemed to be coaxing them to do something, and they answered with simpers and shaking heads that half promised, half refused. He shook hands all around the lodge, beaming, and charged out.

"Trying to get 'em to attend our Sunday services once or twice. Maybe some'll come. If not, I've swore it won't be for want of trying and humility—and humility ain't my natural mood!"

In humility and irate cheerfulness, the Squire went to a dozen lodges before he gave up. "The blockheads!" said he.

To Aaron's gratification and the Squire's ecstasy, some half a dozen new braves did appear at the next Sunday services, and four of them a week later, sitting upright on the backbreaking benches, just glancing at one another when Harge and Speezer got tangled up in Dakota pronouns.

The fall flight of ducks came then. Since the summer supply of corn and wild turnip and *psinchincha* was low, the Indians were counting on that flight for food till they should go off on their late-fall hunt. But this year the ducks seemed to avoid Lake Bois des Morts and the nearby slews, and Isaac Weeps-by-Night reported to Harge that Medicine Spider, mother of Black Wolf and the most influential woman in the village, was explaining that this bad luck was due to the evil spirits of the missionaries, and to the anger of her favorite god, Unkteri, against the Indian men for attending the heretical Christian church.

This prejudice led to a race riot against the despised white minority. The young men (Isaac whispered to Harge) had a meeting of the soldiers' lodge and talked about killing all the Mission staff. The exhilarating motion was lost by a small vote. But they did swarm over to the Mission, hammer at the windows, scare all the women into a white shaking, and kill three venerable hens. They were not so hysterical, however, as to believe that the slain fowl were filled with the malicious magnetism of the missionaries; they sensibly roasted and ate them, with potatoes lifted from the Mission garden.

For the twentieth time they cut into bits the dresses made by Anna Wherryman for the women who had been going to church. On the Sabbath after this riot, there was only one Indian woman at services, and no male at all, not even Isaac, who kept leaving messages for Mr. Harge to the effect that, though he did not care to have his ears cut off, he was secretly praying—out in the woods.

Through it all, Harge groaned and was impatiently patient, as he had been these many years, and so were Huldah and the Speezers and the somewhat unevangelical Jake and Anna. Only Mercie wept and was angry. She begged, "Dear Aaron, get out—leave us—we're all doomed and mad!"

Watching his betters read their *Missionary Herald,* Aaron was moved by their enduring patience; years, decades, generations, waiting and laboring in America, in Africa, in China, in India, while all the isles the silver seas distress still hear the heathen vaunt their wickedness, sea-flashing isles that greenest beauties bless yet black with sin.

He suggested to Harge, "I think I might get hold of Black Wolf for a Social Function, say something like supper at Jake's, and we could ask him how can we touch the hearts of the heathen."

The elder doubted: "But it was his mother started all this ruckus."

"Maybe that shows she's a woman of deep religious feeling. All we got to do is to switch her from Wakantanka onto the true God."

"That's so, that's so, Son. You do that now. You're beginning to show signs of the true mission faith."

After such involved plans for securing the person of Black Wolf as having him kidnapped by Isaac and spuriously rescued, an imaginary scene of great drama and delight, to be played out on a dark evening with unseasonable lightning, the genius of simplicity was given to Aaron and he merely sent a note over by an Indian girl who still stubbornly came to learn spelling:

"Dear Black Wolf: I would like to get acquainted. Please to come over to supper at six next Thursday night. Yr friend, A. Gadd."

Black Wolf came.

The trusty Anna had a magnificent repast: not only potatoes and turnip but a small piece of pork and the sensuousness of squash. In honor of the house, Black Wolf had put on an aged scarlet British uniform-coat. Aaron preferred not to speculate about how he had got it.

They were a friendly company: the Wolf, Aaron, Huldah, Anna, Jake, and they cheerfully discussed spiritualism, the Atomic Power of the day. It was the emotional Huldah who was the scoffer, while both Black Wolf and Jake had actually met ghosts—the latter the spook of General Israel Putnam, very profane.

They stopped their happy wrangling as they saw the outer door of the dining-room-parlor-kitchen edging open. This was a land where an opening door might mean danger. Then, evangelical but lugubrious, all in black, Squire Harge, Mr. Speezer and Luna purposefully plunged into the room.

Black Wolf leaped up and backed to the wall, his hand on the knife in his girdle, and Aaron, feeling that he had betrayed his guest, shot up to stand beside him.

But at Harge's "Welcome, Blackie, and the peace of God be with you," and Luna's insinuating, "That's a beautiful coat you've got, Mr. Wolf," the Indian unsmilingly sat down again.

They relaxed around the table, a social gathering seated on stools, boxes, an antiquated trunk and a sawbuck.

Aaron had usually been modest and somewhat wordless among his superiors in piety, but he felt uncomfortably that this gathering was his responsibility, and that it was rather slippery. He said gravely, "Black Wolf has been explaining to us the Sioux belief in the souls of trees and rocks and animals. It's a mighty poetic dodge."

In a manner which he felt to be jocose and neighborly, Harge demanded of Black Wolf, "Now why do you go fooling around with kid ideas like that, Blackie? Ain't you got any better use for your expensive college education?"

Black Wolf must have heard comic anecdotes when he had been at Oberlin. He looked at the Squire with deliberate insolence, and answered, "No spika da English."

Luna crooned, "Why, I've heard you speak it like a meadow lark!"

Harge snapped, "Blackie, how'd you like to be a teacher for us? Mighty hard to get the spondulics out of the Board, but guess I could fix it to pay you handsome, maybe twenty-five a month, just to go round and tell the Wahpetons true stories out of the Bible, like Jonah and the whale, instead of these silly Sioux lies, like the one about Heyoka and the rabbit. But you'd have to ask your ma to not go on caterwauling about her superstitions being better than the sacred canons of faith. Twenty-five a month! I guess *that* would set your wife up in beads and looking-glasses!"

Black Wolf was deliberate about rising, shaking hands with Aaron and, with his moccasins surprisingly loud on the puncheon floor, moving toward the entrance, from which he addressed Harge:

"Judge, it's unfortunate there's no code of law in this barbaric Indian country and no penalty for attempted bribery, except the Springfield carbine. Good night, my friends."

29

FINISHING Bessie's lean-to room, repairing the shakes that covered Jake's roof, doing the last fall plowing with oxen that were only untrained cattle, hauling wood for fence posts and for winter heating, building a pigpen, all of it alongside Jake.

Squire Harge helped them, strong, clumsy, faithful; Mr. Speezer helped them, crafty but careless. The Squire was silent and probably prayed. Mr. Speezer talked in a light, brisk, modulated voice, full of friendliness and malice. He prattled to Aaron, "I envy you and the Squire for your strength. That may be your advantage from not having gone to college."

As he discoursed, was it not natural that he should put down his hammer? For he was giving his higher thought to the theory that since God scattered mankind and gave them different languages at the Tower of Babel, if they could all learn one language (he could not decide whether it was to be English or Hebrew), that would be a sign that God had forgiven their contumacy. So, he explained, it was proven both that the Second Coming could not be far off, and that the study of languages in college was a very fine thing.

But he did work, he did bruise his thin hands on boards, he did cobble all the boots and brew herb tea for the sick children.

Sometimes the staff seemed to Aaron not so much to be building a mission station as to be rebuilding their Eastern homes. They were all mutely longing for nests. Yet they would be transferred and have to build all over again; they would never see the blooming of the maple trees they planted, nor their grandchildren playing under them. They were professional and talked like professionals, like old soldiers, old actors.

Even the sensible Anna, changing Martha's diapers or smacking her for her soul's sake, would muse, "Do you suppose cherubs wear

195

didies? Or haven't they any bottoms? . . . Oh, dear, I do get so tired working! Sometimes I say to Jake, the old chouser, 'I could go and rest on the Lord's bosom right this minute, and let you fry your own pork.' Well, it's all the work of the Lord. Anyway, it's *work!*"

The Squire stopped Aaron, plodding with a sawbuck on his back, and inquired, "Neighbor, do you feel you're getting along on your pilgrimage? Are there times when you seem to be marching through darkness and you find it hard to pray as much as your duty requires?"

Aaron was rather irritable: "Maybe I could pray more fervently if I could start in on my theological studies. I like plowing all right, but if I ever am to get ordained . . ."

"Yes, yes, yes, just as soon as we get this place a little settled! Next spring, maybe."

An early task, done in the evenings on his own time, had been to make his own room habitable. He had nailed down the loose floor boards and built a broad log bed, covered cheerily with his mother's star quilt. His Sunday Best black suit and his Second Best blue suit hung under a calico curtain which Huldah had stitched for him, and he had nailed up a shelf on which were his dozen books of poetry and theology.

He had also built a handsome plank bed for Huldah, whose room was of the same size as his own but magnificently decorated with daguerreotypes from home, woodcuts of Connecticut pastors, pressed flowers, dried cattails, a scarf said to have come from Mount Lebanon and a rag rug woven by Anna. There was in it a scent of cedar boughs and of Huldah.

Once a fortnight the Mission staff had its own "concert," for prayer and the most-beloved hymns, held not in the church but in the Squire's living-room.

Outsiders were not forbidden, but they were not encouraged. This was their own hour for the faithful, for the encouragement of the weak in trust, for remembering young faces in chapels back home, long ago. Though Luna Speezer might have been snippy to Anna just that afternoon, though Jake might have been grumbling to Mr. Speezer that he couldn't build no bookcases till he'd made a door for the privy, at the concert they were one sacred body, full of mutual love.

The candlelight was gentle on their plain faces, on the old steel engraving of Moses receiving the tables of the law, on the Rogers group of a barefoot boy with a springing pup. Aaron stood beside Huldah at the melodeon, and their voices seemed to journey together as the staff sang, low and sweet:

> Jesus, the name that charms our fears,
> That bids our sorrows cease;
> 'Tis music in the sinner's ears,
> 'Tis life and health and peace.

But one night at the concert they gasped when the door opened on Caesar Lanark, his beard the color of wild honey, his frock coat hanging with exactness, his silk hat higher and friskier of brim than the Squire's.

"It's Satan come for us!" muttered Huldah, and Aaron protectively laid his arm across her shoulder. Her muscles seemed to rise and snuggle against his inner arm. He hastily took it away, not because he had been repulsed but because he distinctly hadn't.

Lanark sat down sedately, holding his hat, looking civil and amused, and as the hymns went on, he sang. He had a mildly operatic voice while the uncomfortable disciples stumbled like amateurs. They were the more embarrassed when he shook hands all round, afterwards, and told them that they were, to a lonely man out of civilization, a treat and a blessing.

To Aaron he said, "Come for supper again, next Friday?"

As interpolation, Aaron did go, and he heard much the same

197

lecture on the beauties of power. Lanark's only news was, "I'm not sure that Selene will come out here at all next spring. I have given her perfect freedom, and like all these Modern Girls, she abuses it. She thinks she can go anywhere, do anything, spend any money that she pleases. This new Transcendental Education is ruining all our girls—opinionated, undisciplined, think they know everything, won't listen to the voice of experience or to anything their fathers say.

"I tell you, when I was a young man, in 1820 or thereabouts, women learned something useful—cooking and nursing and old-fashioned songs, and tried to make a real home. They didn't get all mixed up with women's rights and Grahamism, and want to become amanuenses and clerks in stores and all these new-fangled professions that are so unsuitable to a womanly woman. Rights and privileges, that's their demand now, not duty. I tell you, by 1860 or so there won't be a woman in the country who's willing to cook a man's meals. I put my foot down, but Selene just doesn't notice it. . . . She's her father's daughter, the little vixen! . . . I suppose I'll have to go to New York to see her!"

When he had walked home with Huldah after the Lanark-infested concert, though they were two feet apart it seemed to Aaron that she was leaning against his arm, and when they came home, he was nervous. He liked her; she was to him a sister Rebecca plus temptation, a Nadine without poison.

Whenever Huldah said good night, she had a way of touching the back of his hand with two fingers that drew his soul out. Because she was so pure and good, because she seemed so defenseless in her thin-walled room two strides from his, he had been careful of propriety with a fussiness that Miss Nadine Brun would have gaped at. He tried not to go up the alpine stairs just after Huldah, and when they were in their adjacent rooms, even when he was moved to agitated prayer, he tried to be as quiet as a moth.

Tonight the Wherrymans put a dishtowel over the tame crow and went to bed early, leaving Huldah and Aaron in the living-room. Though the one-poster bed was actually in the same room, Jake and Anna managed it with Congregational modesty by drawing a calico curtain around the bed.

Huldah murmured, "Brother Aaron, tonight when Mr. Lanark came in, I knew—I'd guessed it before—that you are very brave and generous."

"How's that?"

"When we first saw him and thought he was some unknown gambler or something, you wanted to shield me."

"Oh, well—I just—you know."

"Oh, now, Mr. Aaron Gadd, I *do* know, you know!"

He was not one of your men who detect archness and run to safety.

"Aaron, I've always wanted to talk to you about . . . I'm a good Hopkinsianistic Calvinist, but same time I'm a little different in my religious feeling from any of these saintly people here. No matter how hard I work, I take some time each day for Contemplation, absolutely quiet, not trying to force good thoughts but just letting the divine spirit flow into me. I guess I'm what they call a mystic. And the Lord gives me wondrous visions. It's the real practice of the presence of God. I think you have something of the poet in you, too. *You* could be a mystic, if I instructed you. Come to my room, and let's try."

He was alarmed as he followed her up the stairs.

30

IN HER room, she looked at him a moment with her finger crossing her lips, then whispered:

"If the visions are to come, you must forget your body; make it comfortable and let it melt away. Sit—see, like this: on the floor, with your ankles crossed and your wrists crossed, in memory of the cross of Christ. Oh, I won't let the Papists take my cross away from me! Try it."

He sat after that manner, and felt namelessly apprehensive.

"Your body will seem to float off through the window, leaving your spirit here, and by and by a presence that you *know* is the Savior will come into the room, all kindness and forgiveness. Sometimes I have heard a rustle of his garments and a tiny sweet fragrance—he is with me, and then the visions come.

"Once—and I was wide-awake—I saw the heavens. There was a great square stone, oh, miles long, all of flaming colors, with a luster on it as if it were mirroring the glory of God's countenance, and then I saw a heavenly host standing on the stone, of various ranks and heights, and suddenly they were not angels at all, but buildings of flashing marble with many stories, and then I knew that I had seen the City of God.

"And sometimes—have you ever felt it?—the Holy Spirit strikes you right on the head, like a very soft hammer, and the quiver goes clear down your spine into your toes. Oh, there are ecstasies greater than charity or human love or even fear! I want you to know them!

"Before we're ready for the visions, I always read something from the Bible. I'll read now, and just let yourself sail with the divine current. Try it!"

She looked at him with such gentleness, and her face, which was neither pretty nor ugly, was transformed to beauty.

She was two or three years older than he, but so trusting, so willing to strip her soul bare before him, that she was a child in faith as she was motherly in understanding. Without resistance, with no audible snarl from his inner malice, he sought to slip into an overarching nothingness.

She was reading from the Sixty-third Psalm, in a voice low and shaky:

"My flesh longeth for thee in a dry and thirsty land . . . My mouth shall praise thee with joyful lips, when I remember thee upon my bed and meditate on thee in the night watches . . . in the shadow of thy wings will I rejoice."

Her kind voice faded, and they crouched side by side in the silence of the fall night on the prairie. Even the Indian village was quiet now. A wolf howled, far off, and was still.

He thought that he felt around him a presence, an undistinguishable sound, not voice nor footfall nor murmur of robes, a vibration so delicate that his ears could not identify it. He believed that something incomprehensible, outside him yet not quite outside, was drawing him into its warmth and, without quite picturing her, he thought of Selene.

He did not know when he uncrossed his hands and slid his arm along Huldah's shoulder. There was nothing consciously predatory about it. He felt that they two together, not moving, were yet soaring through mounting crystal streams of air. He was recalled to his body with a thud; he seemed to drop down a thousand miles into it, as Huldah's hand touched his. Her exhaled breath had an echo of a sob in it. He stared at her uncomprehendingly; they stared at each other as they both stood up, in no perceptible agreement.

She seemed to be waiting for a word from him but he was still in a trance, far from her.

"Didn't you feel some strange presence?" she whispered.

"I think so."

She stared again; she shook her head; she spoke as if with effort:

"It's late and . . . You try to get the presence by yourself some time. Good night, dear friend. Oh, you must go *now!*"

He clasped her hand and heard her sob. He fled.

In unmissionary luxury, he had built for himself not only the beautiful pine-log bed but a rough table beside it to hold a candle-lantern made out of a pierced gourd.

It was viciously chilly tonight. He was drained by his seeking after visions, and his prayer, when he knelt by the bed, was hasty. But as he lay snug, with the candle still lighted, his thoughts were long.

Yes, he *had* known the scent and movement of some alien being beside them in Huldah's room. He was stoutly certain of that, and then he was not certain at all. His inner voice came, not mocking and malign but with the sound of the extremely sensible carpenter from Berkshire County.

——Sure! You were trying to feel something divine. You'd make yourself feel it. Look here, Neighbor: if you go getting visions along with that good, decent girl, first thing you know you'll be fooling yourself into believing you're in love with her. And she hasn't got any other young people here, and she might get fooled same way. Mustn't let anything like that happen. No! You're pledged to Selene!

——Oh, the hell I am! That's silly! Selene is a rich young woman with a snotty father. She's half gypsy and half snob, and she probably doesn't even remember that I exist. The other night, when I was thinking how the same moon was over both of us and she must be looking at it, too—she was in some elegant parlor, dancing the polka. Or whatever it is.

——It would be much more sensible to marry a girl who shares my longing to spread the gospel; love each other because we both love God and . . . Let's see what the Book says.

He turned to a passage in *The Epistle of Jude* which he had never read before:

202

Raging waves of the sea,
Foaming out their shame;
Wandering stars, to whom is reserved
The blackness of darkness forever.

——Why! It's a poem! Maybe greater than Byron! But it certainly don't tell me what to do. Got to try again.

He turned to *Ecclesiastes* and "I considered all the oppressions that are done under the sun, and behold the tears of such as were oppressed, and they had no comforter; and on the side of their oppressors there was power."

——There it is! All clear! Admonition to me to comfort the Sioux, that are oppressed by Lanark and that whole gang.

He meant to get out of bed and thank God that all doubts had been washed away, but he had been digging stumps that day and the candle was going out, and while he dreamed that he was on his knees, praying, he was still in bed, asleep.

Next morning, Jake snorted, "Heard you 'n' Huldy chewing the rag upstairs half the night. What you up to? Settin' up with her? Good luck!" And winked.

Mercie Harge sent for Aaron and she said sweetly, "That must have been a nice concert, last evening. I could hear the singing."

"Oh, yes. I think the spirit did really move us."

"Mm, yes. I'm sure it did. I hear Mr. Lanark was there, in his best checkerboard pantaloons."

"Yes."

"Aaron darling, don't you be a fool and try to snub Brother Lanark, the way Harge does. The missionaries depend on him to carry their mail and supplies and give us a barrel of pork now and then, but just because he doesn't keep groaning about his soul, they claim he's an infidel."

"Well, isn't he?"

"Maybe he's got a religion of his own. Harge wouldn't recognize it unless it had John Calvin as vice-president of the Trinity. And his daughter was such a lovely child. Don't let any of these doting hens cluck you into becoming a family man before you meet Selene again."

"She'd never look at me—her father certainly wouldn't."

"I know. You'll have to leave the Mission—don't go while I'm still here, though—and become a banker. You'll be a nice banker. You're so tidy!"

"Look here, Mercie. Mr. Lanark robs the Indians!"

" 'Then we, the jackals at the feast, should call the lion kind, at least.' Oh, I know that isn't fair. Harge is as independent as a cat. But Lanark is a realist, and as I slip away, I'm tired of these screams of enthusiasm about the joys of evangelism, which has cost me my home, my children. When Bessie comes up here, she wants to know how my soul is resting today. . . . Mercie! Quit whining! . . . Now skip along. I'm tired again. I'm tired so much. I don't want to be tired. I want to be dancing. And I never shall now, not even with you!"

He encountered Luna Speezer supervising the Indian women who were doing the Mission washing. Over her dress was a calico wrapper but her hair was up, her steel earrings tinkled. She always made Aaron think of Boston and ships to Europe.

She squawked, "I hear you're quite the favorite with the ladies—Mercie and Huldah and no doubt all the pretty half-breed girls."

(Did she refer to Selene? What did she know? But what, on this tight island, was there that everybody did not know?)

His bumpkin awkwardness could not have been more complete: "Aw, you're trying to make fun of me!"

"I wish *I* could be attractive; fragile like Mercie and charitable like Huldah and competent like Anna. But ah me, ah me! I have learned too much theology from my good husband. I am so unfortunate as to know that it isn't these little virtues that God wants us to seek. No matter what we do, we are utterly vile in his sight,

204

and it is solely by the virtue of the Mediator that righteousness is imputed unto us. Mankind are walking in bitterness to their doom, and good works are of no merit save as testimony. Against our wilful wickedness, God rages incessantly. Doom!

" '*Phugein apo tes mellouses orges*'—that's the Greek Testament for 'Flee from the wrath to come,' you know. But I wish I didn't study so much and have this ghastly gift for prophecy. Happy Huldah—to be so carefree and jolly!"

Mrs. Speezer's slant eyes looked satisfied, she shook her head, her earrings clinked and glistened. She turned from Aaron to her washerwomen, but as he hastened away, she frightened him by yelling, "But doom is doom—doom is doom—inevitable doom!"

31

ISAAC WEEPS-BY-NIGHT was the only member of the Isanti River band who had taken to white men's ways; that is, to Civilization. He had a two-room log house and he grew barley as well as corn. He wore trousers instead of leggings and he worked for the Mission now and then; hauled supplies from Traverse des Sioux, plowed, tanned hides.

He sang loudly in chapel—when he was in such a state of morals as to be allowed in chapel—and he was notably honest. He stole nothing except melons and pumpkins, which never have counted anywhere. Like pencils.

And it was from the Laodicean Isaac that Aaron began to learn the Dakota language. Isaac, like a newly ordained Doctor of Philosophy, after years of being nagged into learning rejoiced in being invited to stand up and look important and teach. He was astonished by his own erudition and by the fact that his class of one did not walk out.

Aaron and he did not labor over syntax. They clove to the theory that "Me want bed and cow-meat" will get a traveler all he needs in any language.

Isaac delivered new words not merely by shouting them but by whispering them, moaning them, repeating them, with gestures. One by one, beating his forehead with the heel of his right hand, Aaron learned the commoner nouns, leaving the verbs and adjectives as bright promises of future bliss: *ma-za*—iron; *mi-ni*—water; *ma-ka*—earth; *na-pa*—hand; *co-tan-ka*—pipe; *i-san*—knife.

Isaac followed up his instruction ardently. Amid the decorum of Sunday morning service in the chapel, while Mr. Speezer was explaining the baptism of infants, Aaron was alarmed to see the nearby Isaac apparently in the grasp of a fit. He realized that, with comprehensive physical illustration, Isaac was audibly advising him that *do-te* meant throat and *ci-zi* was tongue.

Aaron was diverted to have Luna Speezer, beside him, repeat to herself: "Oh, yes; *do-te, ci-zi—do-te, ci-zi* I see." After service, she bubbled at him, "You are such an earnest young man, but I must say it amuses me to see you trying to learn Sioux!"

He wanted to know the Indian village, to talk with Black Wolf, without the spiritual slumming of Squire Harge. Unlike a good many of the villagers, Black Wolf never came to the Mission to beg for potatoes, or to ask Jake or Aaron to repair a gun or fashion an axe-handle.

Aaron unscrupulously ran away from the task of making an ox-yoke and crossed to the village on the thickening ice of Lake Bois des Morts. He came on a group of young men sitting about a scarlet blanket, playing bullet-and-mitten, very much like the shell game at a fair back in New England, and chanting to it the ancient ritual tune.

Black Wolf was among them, his hair fancy today in two braids. He motioned Aaron to sit down.

Now that the Indians were too busy whooping with pleasure at winning or with fury at losing to pose for the intruder, they did not seem to Aaron either the romantic woodlanders of Fenimore Cooper or the degenerate heathen of Harge, but just young men, entirely human young men, who might have been Clunford farmers or students in the nearby Williams College. Most of them were a little darker than the devout young gentlemen of Williams, more flexible and stronger, more matter-of-fact and sure of the proper behavior, and Aaron wanted to join them, not preach to them.

Black Wolf got up, and threw at Aaron, "Come!"

They squatted by a rock that was a shelter from the autumn wind, and the Wolf said gravely, "I am glad to see you by yourself. We are an exclusive people, you know. We don't like strangers. The white men come in to trade whisky for our furs or pantaloons for our souls, and the Ojibway drop around to murder us—oh, in return for some slight murders on our part. It is refreshing to see a friend with nothing more threatening than curiosity."

"Wolf, I want to meet your mother. I want to know why she hates the missionaries. We mean only good."

"She shall tell you. (Medicine Spider, her name is.) Come."

They approached a bark lodge from which came a sound like a stampede of moaning cattle through shifting sand. Black Wolf grinned. "It's my father, Shining Wind, the conjurer and doctor, healing somebody. He's good at it."

They stopped at the door. Inside, an Indian with bare breast lay on the ground, while above him, leaping, stamping his feet, shaking a gourd rattle, bellowing, the medicine man was making a maniac show. He was painted green and orange in spirals and circles, and in his feather headdress nestled a pinioned live garter snake, writhing its separate insane dance. As Aaron watched, Shining Wind touched the patient's chest with his lips, then sprang up to spit a scarlet stream into a birchbark dish. As he raised his head he saw his son, and waved to him as casually as a white surgeon after an operation.

Black Wolf laughed as he urged on the horrified Aaron.

"The old man is giving a good show today. Scarlet spit—that means he's drawn out the demon of bilious lung fever. The patient will be cured, and our little family will get paid a couple of deer later, and some buffalo hides."

"Surely, surely, Wolf, you don't believe in that disgusting *wakan,* even if it is your father!"

"Certainly not. Neither does he, except that it's what you white philosophers call a faith cure. By the way, before my people ever saw the white men, the *wakan* man rarely did any of this comic swindling. He used healing bark and roots and the steam bath. But he learned from the white blackrobes and traders how to make a circus and get paid for it. Mockery and money we've learned.

"So let us seek wisdom in the lodge of my mother. Among us, the women own their houses, you know. Their husbands are only tolerated guests, who can be kicked out. Our women are not owned by the men—they're merely free and equal, not like Mrs. Harge."

"Now you look here, Wolf! I'm sick of your perpetually claiming that the Sioux are perfect and the whites are stinkers!"

"My friend, don't you find it an agreeable change from hearing the opposite, as you have all your life?"

"Well, maybe there is . . . Yes!"

The mansion of Medicine Spider, Mrs. Shining Wind, was of such superior luxury that it had a door at each end. On the wall bench, on blankets spread on dry hay, several warriors were smoking tobacco and dogwood, while Medicine Spider sat in the center by the fire, mending a pair of moccasins. She sprang up. She was light and quick and determined, like her kinswoman, Selene; she was much wrinkled, thoughtful but quick to anger. She wore a plain shortgown, with a man's crimson sash over her head.

When the Wolf, in Sioux, had introduced Aaron, the braves walked out, with immense superciliousness, and the Spider sat down again, muttering.

The Wolf said amiably, "You can see we are a Beacon Street family and too rich to share everything, as most Indians do, though my wife and I live in a much plainer lodge. That is my father's war bonnet there, in its case, and his beaded fire-steel bag, and the beautiful gilt mortar beside my mother is the final proof of her wealth and standing, because it is expensive and absolutely useless."

"My friend," said Aaron, in what he hoped was Wolf's own rather literary manner, "stop chattering and ask your mother why she hates the Christian religion. She looks like a good woman."

"I think in many ways she is," the Wolf answered, most seriously, and went off in a Sioux address to his mother, while Aaron, studying Medicine Spider, suddenly knew where he had seen her— seen her all his life.

Though she was not portly and large-bosomed like most of them,

Medicine Spider was the true Mother in Zion, the female pillar of the Protestant Church, such as he had known in Clunford and Adams, at church services and church suppers and church sewing-societies. She was the support and the terror of the pastor, punctual at meeting and critical of the girls in the choir and the pastor's wife's clothes, mighty in making flannels for the poor but inappreciative of their adulteries, a saver of money to meet the mortgage interest, a baker of great balloons of bread.

She was (here in Bois des Morts or at home in Berkshire County) orthodox in theology and fiercely regular in politics, rich in gossip, unimaginative as a boiled potato, tart in criticism and generous in deed, a worshipping daughter, a corrective wife, a credulous mother, and a magnificent grandmother—the Matriarch, the Salt of the Earth, the Guardian of the Temple and the Hearth, half wolf and half pigeon and altogether woman, and as infertile a field for alien doctrines as could be found between Bangor and Danbury.

This was the Medicine Spider, whom he had been considering a "heathen Sioux squaw." Anna Wherryman was her sister, and Huldah would be, unless she should be skillfully betrayed.

Through her son, Medicine Spider outlined her heresies, curtly and firmly:

The Christians are devil-worshippers. Their supposed chief god is a devil, which is proven by the fact that he rules them through the fear of hell and not by inspiring them to courage and battle. In envy, he leads them to persecute the Indians.

All white people are constantly angry, from overeating and over-heating.

All white women have a miserable time, even aside from the fact that their men are bald on top and ludicrously whiskered on the chin. Among us, women merely do the cooking and hoeing and bring firewood and erect tents, while our men take care of all the dangerous labors, such as hunting, and fighting the Ojibway and the Sauk. But among the whites, the women have to clean and mend too many possessions, and have to travel exhaustingly; not, as with us, for sensible hunting but because white men are restless and discontented.

White women actually dress up to please their husbands, instead of, as is normal, the men showing off to please the women. And white men spend all their time inventing new ways of lighting, so that women can sit up and work half the night while the men snore.

It was too bad, Medicine Spider finished at farewell, that Aaron could not marry an Indian girl. Perhaps he could. There was no fundamental reason why a white man could not be as manly as a Dakota, if he would just take off his clumsy clothes and be reborn, re-educated.

She held up her hand in blessing.

In the autumn dusk, Black Wolf walked back to the Mission with him. They stopped at the Wolf's own lodge and spoke to his wife, "Her Door," a round and cheery young woman who lost her cheer and tightened her lips when she saw one of the hated white men. Their son was playing by the central fire with a toy bow and arrow —rehearsing, Aaron sighed, for the day when he would try to kill Aaron's son.

They insisted on his eating a hunk of rabbit out of the pot, and Her Door served him with the punctiliousness of hatred.

The new ice of the lake was lonely with star-shine and icy reeds clattered on the shore. Aaron slid and staggered in boots, while Black Wolf's moccasins clung to the ice and made him sure as, in everything, he seemed to be more sure than anyone else at Bois des Morts.

He said, "Look up at what you call the Milky Way. We Dakota believe that it's the soul's pathway to the land of the dead."

"Do you believe that? Do you honestly believe the Dakota religion?"

"Do you believe the Christian religion—that God talks only in riddles, and if you don't have the answers, you are tortured forever?"

"That's not a fair picture of my faith."

"And no picture you ever had of the Dakota faith is fair. It's Shakespeare."

"It's what?"

"When I was in college, I liked Shakespeare. And by the way, though it was hard to understand his world, it was no harder for me than for my Anglo-Saxon classmates from Illinois river-bottoms and Ohio pig-farms. Well, Shakespeare's humor seemed to me more Indian than it was Yankee—full of rough jokes and beautiful dirt. I suspect some Dakota got to Stratford-on-Avon a year before Shakespeare was born.

"If you study his wild characters, you will understand the minor Dakota gods. You certainly believe in Juliet; she's more real than any lady missionary; yet you know that Shakespeare invented her. It isn't that the Indians are more superstitious than the whites—they're more poetic.

"And different Indians believe in different god-heroes, and laugh at the ones they don't believe in—like your Catholics and Protestants. There's some amusing Dakota gods; Unkteri, who rules the water, and Wakinyan, the thunder-bird—some of us pray to him for good weather, just as your preachers pray to whichever Christian god it is that will provide a sunny day for a Sunday-school picnic.

"Then we have Heyoka, the god that does everything backwards —he's like Caliban; and Iya, the god of big eating—like Sir Falstaff; and Taku-skan-skan, who's as crazy as Lear. He's the god of movement and of brains and of war, and yet his symbol—your fool missionaries call it an 'idol'—is a motionless boulder which we paint red and call our 'Little Grandfather.' He also watches out for our maidens' chastity—almost too successfully!

"There's a dozen others, along with the spirits of the animals, the birds, the trees. We're childish in that—and poetic! It may be silly, but it isn't foul, as your evil-minded Harges would have it. And do *I* believe all that? Well! Do you believe in Hamlet?

"Like all peoples in all times, we worship the divine power of

212

the sun, Hunkayapi, only we don't just loaf in the light of his glory, but make a dance. And behind all these symbols there is the one great mystery, the power that made everything, the God Almighty. One of his names is Wakantanka. He is the king; he is all good; he is as bland and quiet as the sun in summer. He doesn't waste time on sheep like you and me and Harge and Isaac Weeps-by-Night. He gives his orders to his under-chieftains, whom you call our 'gods.' Unlike you ghosts, we really do have only one god—what do you call it?—a monotheism.

"Wakantanka—sometimes I think I really do believe in *him!* I know Isaac does."

Aaron squealed, "You mean that Isaac still chases after your gods, as well as the true ones?"

"Yes, friend. Isaac is a fool, but a skillful warrior. He never used to be scared of the Ojibway, and, among us, the only real sin is cowardice. But you finally *have* scared him, with your mysteries, your hell, your confusion about keeping only one day holy instead of all of them, as we do. You've broken him down. No wonder he gets drunk in such a silly way. Harge promises him heaven but lets him see that what he's bound to get is hell. What a trick! It's like the cheating that Lanark makes with his account books. Promise a convert a future life, with lots of pork and singing, and then break the treaty."

"What about you? Do you believe in a life after death?"

"I don't suppose it's impossible."

"What do you think it will be like?"

"I don't have your idea of it—that the Archangel Gabriel will be secretary of state. I don't have *any* idea. Unlike you, we don't seem to have travelers coming back from death to report what it's like—how many harps there are and how high the sapphire walls and which of the four souls get rations."

"Four?"

"You whites have three souls apiece: the one that goes right up to heaven and the one that stays in the grave—which makes you all so scared of graveyards—and the third that haunts houses—a lot of your best clergymen have seen them at it.

"But we beat you by one. A Dakota has one soul that dies with the body and one that lives near the body after death and one that goes south—some say it's west—to the unknown afterworld. (No Indian, by the way, believes this Happy Hunting Ground yarn; that's the Caucasian contribution to the poor Indian with untutored mind.) Then we have a fourth soul, in a lock of our hair, which our friends carry over and throw into enemy country and it turns into an evil spirit and plagues hell out of the Ojibway, and a fine thing, too!"

"Do you really . . ."

"Of course I don't! Any more than you believe in a Holy Ghost that looks like a pigeon."

Very feebly for so grave a young man, Aaron complained, "I'm not quite sure what I believe yet. But you have nothing but mockery. Is that all you learned at Oberlin College? I wish I could have gone there! Weren't you happy?"

"I hated it. They treated me like a bright child ten years old who had some chance, but not much, to become a janitor. And the cities I saw on my journey to the States—Galena, St. Louis, Cincinnati—all noise and stink and thieves. And I hated your women. They acted as if they were scared of me and yet wanted me to make love to them. They shocked me. I'm a warrior, not a hairdresser. So I came back here. I love hunting and riding the prairie and the ball game and women that don't titter and men that don't live to wear white collars. I shall never go back to Babylon. Good night, my friend."

32

A T A LATE and extremely cold second supper at Jake's, he would say only, "Interestin' place, all right, that Indian camp."

That evening they gathered at the Squire's for community prayer-meeting. Before it, Aaron consulted two experts on ethnology and the good life: Mrs. Mercie Harge and Miss Bessie Harge, aged eleven-going-on-twelve. Mercie said, "I know. Listening to Harge talk against the Indians, you get contrary and want to think they're all lovely. But don't! They're so hard. I believe—and Harge and the Indians don't—in all the soft, civilized things: blue ginger jars and Mozart and fanlights and clipped hedges and low voices. And I think the story of Bethlehem and the star and the shepherds by night is better than dragging a buffalo head in the sun dance."

Bessie was less complicated: "The Indians are dandy. They're dirty pagans and of course we got to convert them, but they got so much more sense than Papa or those ole Speezers."

At the prayer-meeting, Aaron did not give testimony about his spiritual progress, as he was bidden to do, but announced an illicit crusade:

"I have an idea—I hope you'll all excuse me if I seem pretty green; probably you've thought how all races and nations ought to get together, the way it says in the Bible—anyway, I guess it does. But I been thinking what a wonderful chance we have to start it off right here, with the Indians. I learned something about them today, and maybe they're a lot more reasonable and moral than we've been supposing."

Already there was from Harge a minatory rumble, and Aaron hastened to get in before the storm:

"Maybe we haven't understood that their Wakantanka is really our God Almighty, and I was wondering . . . Why don't we have

Black Wolf here more and ask him to teach us and maybe we could learn a lot about his religious ideas while he was learning ours—quit trying to *convert* him; unite the two religions and . . ."

It was Huldah, and fondly, who interrupted him: "Oh, Aaron, what a mad thought! Mad! You'll learn that when these heathen try to pretend they have a holy religion of their own, they're just being mouthpieces of Satan!"

The sky darkened and Harge thundered:

"Young man, after the prayerful interest we have devoted to your welfare, I am shocked to find that the seed has fallen by the wayside! Here you had a chance to spend hours with this so-called Black Wolf—though I must say, with Bessie's room not plastered and the repairs on the chapel roof not even started, you might have employed your time more usefully!—and what did you do? Did you, as it was your plain and unmistakable duty, press him to acknowledge his manifold sins and accept Jesus Christ as his personal savior? Did you, heh?"

"No, I haven't yet."

"No! You prefer what you consider your own intelligence to the plain warnings of the Gospel! You don't see what, confound it all, is right there before your eyes: that the Indians are demons in league with Satan to rise up and wipe out our precious Christian institutions, led by their *wakan* men, making a desperate attempt to roll back the glorious tide of Christianity. They are charging upon the thick bosses of Jehovah's buckler, but they will be dashed in pieces like the potter's vessel!

"And they claim they can't understand when I preach in Sioux! They understand, all right! They just don't want to admit they're all going to hell.

"And how you get this socialist idea about the union of races out of the Bible is something that neither me nor any other lifelong student of Holy Writ can understand! But maybe you've cooked up a new idea and got wiser than God!"

216

Aaron could find no useful answer.

Now Squire Harge was a man pious and humble before God but he was also the old prosecuting attorney, trained to send malefactors to the gallows for the public peace and the prosecutor's career. He blasted at the indicted Aaron:

"Good God Almighty, how many times have I got to tell you that when any of these outlaw breeds—niggers or Indians or Jews or the Ytalians or the wild Irish or any of them—seem like they're bright and decent and even religious, they're just imitating us, like monkeys! Except that the merciful Lord has given them one chance that monkeys don't have—I suppose. He has sent us missionaries to them with the wonderful tidings that if they turn to Jesus like little children—and if by God's will they are elect—then they may be saved just like regular folks. What a lavishing of mercy to send us to them!"

Aaron said flatly, "I don't think we're that good."

"You . . ."

"I believe the Lord would be glad to have Black Wolf in his kingdom if he'd never *heard* of the Gospel."

The heir apparent, Bessie, bobbed up with a happy scream of, "Goody, goody! Black Wolf gave me a buckskin doll. I'll bet he's elect like anything!"

"Dry up!" said the Reverend Mr. Harge.

"Yes, Papa," said Miss Bessie, entirely unimpressed.

Aaron's heresy had been so profound that the Squire went on somewhat shakily: "In my long years of evangelism, I've seen missionaries who were ingrates, liars, idlers, weak in faith, even those that turned from the Lord's work to traffic in real estate. But I never before met one that blasphemously stood right up and asserted that the heathen can be saved without Christian intervention and the hearing of the word. Because that's God's only program for regeneration. Only possible one! And I want to tell you right here and now, young man; I'm going to tell you . . ."

With unexpected force, Mr. Speezer stepped in. "Brother, now Brother! You're beginning to fly off the handle. You do, you know, in your Christian zeal!"

Harge looked devastated. "Am I? Forgive me. 'Tain't just my annoyance at Aaron's stubbornness; it's my wrath at the way the Sioux still defy God. And the time is so short that we'll have the field to ourselves. Once these foreign cattle like the Irish Catholics and the German Lutherans and all the Scandinavians intrude here, the true theology, as handed down by the Presbyterians—and I suppose by the Congregationalists—will be adulterated, and the Indians won't know *what* to believe."

It was Mrs. Speezer who soothed him, "Oh, Squire, don't worry about the Germans and Scandinavians and all those foreign peasants. They never can possibly be anything but hewers of wood and drawers of water to us real Americans, and indeed thus they'll leave us more time for Higher Work."

"Oh, yes—more time for Religion and Culture," said Huldah happily.

Harge protested, "But if you admit a Norwegian or a Swede or a Dane, how can you keep out the Jews—those Jew atheists and moneylenders and pork-eaters—I mean, they refuse to eat pork—and all claiming the true Sabbath is still Saturday!"

Speezer said maliciously, "Of course some real Americans, followers of William Miller, have got up a sect called the Adventists, and they claim the Sabbath is still Saturday."

"Might be all right for Men of God to choose their own Sabbath, if they're redeemed Christians and white men, but for a lot of Jews and Indians to think they can go sashaying around picking out any day of the week that pleases 'em for pleasing God, that's just blasted impertinence, and you let that be a lesson to you, Aaron, about freethinking, and it's time we all went to bed now and no more argifying!"

At home, Huldah said, "Oh, Aaron, don't try to get the Squire confused! He's such a valiant soldier of the cross."

"I know," said Aaron, slightly ashamed, and not at all clear as to what he was ashamed about.

Her hand pressed his slightly as they said good night.

His room had seemed to him only too fresh, with the autumn wind nipping in about the window and between wall and roof, but tonight the air tasted stale and thick and sour, and the heavy-breathing presences of Jake and Anna, audibly sleeping downstairs, were like dough. Even the warm girl, Huldah, was like sweet dough. He wanted to be with Black Wolf in the thin and spirited air on the icy lake, in his thin and spirited skepticism.

33

IT WAS unfortunate that when he went to see Black Wolf again Aaron should come upon him dressed in imitation of a real wolf and engaged in a Feast of the Raw Fish. All the tribesmen, in costumes of fur and feathers, were prancing before a couple of large pike, painted blue but entirely raw, then tearing off pieces with their teeth and swallowing them bones and all.

The Wolf came to him, stripping off a wolf's-head mask and looking more sheepish than wolfish.

"Is it a game?" snapped Aaron, able for the first time to be superior with his friend.

"No, it's an old religious rite of intercession—this time because of rumors about the Ojibway. Didn't you think we imitated the animal noises well?"

"I thought it was disgusting."

"So did I. Like that abominable habit of the whites, eating raw oysters."

"Christians don't do it as a religious ceremony."

"How do you know? Maybe they do in China."

He didn't know. All that day, that evening, he fretted that he did not know anything. He sighed, "I have sought the Kingdom of God a little, the Squire has sought it terribly, but we haven't even a map, and after what I saw this afternoon, I know the Sioux are as barbarous as we are. Is it possible that nobody ever has known—that there never has been a completely civilized man, and won't be for another thousand years?"

It was not consoling to go to Caesar Lanark's for dinner and to discover that that pirate and scoffer at righteousness was, to eye and ear, more civilized than Harge.

No, said Lanark, it did not look to him as though Selene would come to Bois des Morts at all, unless he bullied her and threatened to cut off her income, and that he did not want to do. He could never quarrel with so estimable a daughter.

He held up to the light his huck glass. (Only it was filled with rum and water.) "Oh, yes, neither you nor I can ever understand her. We can only regard her with envy."

——That's his way of warning me off.

"Her very obstinacy in pursuing the arts should rebuke us, here on our somewhat grubby frontier. Aren't you getting sick of it at the Mission?"

"Oh, no."

"All these servile jobs? Gadd, I think you may just possibly have, still quite undeveloped, some of the qualities of a great trader-explorer, an Alec Mackenzie, with his honors and social position. Such a man may confidently meet *any* one."

——Meaning Selene.

"And wouldn't you be doing more for the world in throwing open ten million acres of prairie and forest for settlement by white farmers, for the site of future cities, than by trying, and failing, to get Black Wolf to say his catechism?"

——Wait, wait now! Lanark hasn't thrown open any ten million acres! Or one!

"I think you might like to work for me, Gadd; to learn the Dakota language thoroughly; to begin by exploring clear up to the Assiniboine River. In four or five years, you might have a minor partnership. Wouldn't you like wealth and mature responsibility, and New York and Montreal and London waiting for you when you are ready for them?"

But Lanark was too oily. Aaron fronted him with considerably greater ease and confidence than he would have shown a month before. "Mr. Lanark, you remember the story about Satan taking Our Lord up on a pinnacle and offering him the world."

"Quite. But you are singularly different from Our Lord, you know, and also, we've never heard Satan's version of that story."

——Words! Harge's words and Lanark's words and Black Wolf's words against all of us! Can't I get a philosophy that isn't built of uncemented words?

As to the prospect of being a new millionaire in a fur collar defiantly modest in London, he was not much tempted. He would rather be old Harge, ridiculous on his knees in the night woods, circled round with the glory of the Lord.

34

(*Editor's Note:* The few pages of a diary here published form all of the only journal ever kept by Aaron Gadd. At least, no other similar document has ever been found. They appear in a school-exercise book with worn light-brown Manila cover. Mr. Gadd's script is unusually clear and exact. S.L.)

1848

November
1st—Wednesday

Huldah Purdick suggests I keep day book to record & better realize spiritual struggles on the way to some degree of mastery. So shall try, though am not much of a hand @ writing. 1st snow of yr. Lake B d M ice thick. Busy all day, repair traps for Inds, oh, they scoff at our Bible teaching but ready enough to beg us help them. Finished making ox yoke, butchered pig, not a job I like when they look at you like traitor. Made coffin for Ind child.

Have offered make coffins for them. Seems Sq Harge had refused, because of their stiffneckedness. They have trouble digging graves when ground froze, no proper tools, one reason for dead left on scaffolds, some get habit so do it even in summer. Admit it does rile me as it does the Sq to have them *demand* such help. They say if we really believe Christ's teachings, why don't we divide everything we got with them, *they* divvy up all property with each other. What impudence. It takes Xian fortitude to bear it. Especially as I can't think of any answer.

Learned couple new words Dakota lang from Inds here today but no more. Oh when shall I have a chance to learn theology &c? I feel gt distress abt it and hate being so ignorant of all that for which I have come here willing to give my life to God if he so wants it.

223

Sq H keeps telling me I must not despise *the day of small things.* Out of that comes the gt temples &c. But, oh, I do want to get down to work on the theology books, I want to *know* the deep mysteries, but every time I open one somebody starts hollering, "Hey, we got to have some wood!"

Played dominoes with Huldah this evening for 1st time PS she plays a very fine game she says she does not think the game is wicked, never heard of gamblers playing dominoes, but we certainly won't go & ask the Sq what he thinks!

My room is pretty cold tonight the weather has turned snow comes in thru roof but it is more than I have a right to expect, good roof over me while Ind hunters often sleep in snow

Lord give me patience & thru thee may my sins be forgiven & I be cleansed from all unrighteousness & find increased faith on thy Son. Is this not Holy Ground, our abiding place & that of the Inds whom I love as I do my own people, they are very brave, suspect they have plenty more humor than I have.

2nd—Thursday

Butchered another pig it looked at me as I cut its throat & I felt horrible & for a moment fell into sin of thinking oh what is use of our religion if we kill & hurt, we are no better than Inds with such vileness as raw fish feast

All day long I have failed to be as prayerful as I should be, my mind on this world's concern & Selene & Mr Lanark & Huldah &c, and have indulged in a morose temper of mind. Shall I ever learn to be diligent about the Lord's business & get over this self indulgence & always leaving things 'til a "more convenient season"?

Tho so late in season spread manure on a field where snow blown away, Jake down with diarea so finished plastering Bessie's new room. Also it took hours, seems like, finding stray cow & driving it back, fell thru ice got soaked and ran like the dickens to keep feet from freezing rest of the time threshing barley in stable, seemed monotonous, am not even making start in theology

But stopped & thot how Sq H, Mercie, Mr & Mrs Speezer, Huldah

&c have endured this tedium for yrs & all for the glory of God then felt ashamed to be always lamenting & bellyaching, but had to smile when remembered how I told Mr Lanark missionaries brave to be doing mere farm work when they want to be engaged in spiritual endeavors & he said "Nonsense, they are not preachers who started farming but farmers who started preaching." Got mad & asked him, Were his folks not farmers like the rest of us, he said "They had every vice but that." He is a vainglorious & worldly man but tells interesting stories about Paris, France &c but I bet he has never been there. Played dominoes with Huldah & *won!!*

3d—Friday

Ran over to village, saw Black Wolf, learned Scioux words for hunt, fish, walk, run

Fixing plaster in church made a table for Mrs Speezer, she says she wants to drink tea afternoons, where does she think she is? Splitting shingles, splinter in finger, Mr Sp took it out neat but he laughed at me they are vainglorious & worldly people or certainly would be if were not faithful followers of the master. Huldah takes cup of broth to Mercie every couple hours, M cannot talk much now, very weak.

My increase in fervor & in knowledge of God so small as to be despicable I feel much anxiety to know what the Lord designs for me in the future

Mr Sp very good to sick Inds, crosses over to vge to doctor them & explain gospel, he has a chest of medicines & books &c. Maybe I was saucy with Speezers. Seems as if all day long I have had such a cold indifference towards God & caught myself thinking of Huldah bodily, how she would be elastic to squeeze & maybe would not object oh I fear sin has complete dominion over me.

Dominoes w Hul she won

Prayed in room against sins of spirit & flesh and being bad loser at anything!!

Nov 4th—Satday

Joining & matching boards, had to do Anna's share of milking,

225

diarea. New board in Sq's sanctorum & he wanted stove moved I did it but stove was all right right where it was.

Some Inds came over from vge on ice, ventured in my bad Soo to try to tell them of Christ's longing to have them receive the Great Gift of the Redeemed and Purified Spirit but they did not or wd not understand & listen but I did learn some words.

Oh when will I be let off this incessant manual work & be able learn enough Scioux to give them the message? And *when* do I start Greek &c!! I hint abt it to the Sq but no signs. I suppose I could make love to Huldah, longed to this eveng, clenched my hands to keep from going to her room and felt strongly my unspeakable tendency to sin & resisted tho alarmed by my overpowering corruption. Shd not play dominoes with her so much, even danger reading Bible aloud with her. My hand has a tendency to creep along her arm as if it had an evil life of its own.

So hurried to my rm & read "The Great Commission" by Rev John Harris, borrowed it from Mr Sp, he has big library at least 70 bks, tho all bound in brown & black & look gloomy. About theology &c. He says there are thousands such all based on searching thru the Bible, but they do not agree on what they find there, wh worries me.

Rev Harris claims all the heathen (wh wd include our Scioux here) condemned to eternal torture because even tho they never had a chance to hear the word of God, still there ancestors must have perpetrated the first act of idolatry, in defiance of God's will. Not sure what that means & sometimes I get impatient even with such clear expositions of the Truth as Mr Sp makes & want to throw out all these books & look at things directly like I wd size up a beam to see if it was right size for a barn and not go look in Bible & try to find out.

But Sq H says, that is how you get into the devil's snares by trying to use your own pretended reason & experience oh why can't I see the guidance of the Bible clear like Huldah? Bessie comes over & gives sermons to Jake's kids & makes them put cookies in collection

226

bag which she has made on end of long stick just like I used to see as boy at Clunford, those were happy times & Selene near though did not know it. I think of her all time & yet not like to put down her name here seems too hopeless.

5th—Lord's Day

A storm this morning, dark in church, we had service by candle-light, & Lord's Supper. No Inds present, admit that easier, I felt much moved, all the faces seemed dear friends, the Squire's face like a kind father, Mr and Mrs Sp smiling gently at me, Jake & Anna solid & honest, dear Huldah esp. All my beloved family so close to each other out here in the wilds leagues from anywhere, all comrades in a far & gloomy land, so patient thru the Day of Small Things, spreading God's Peace, enduring cold, hard beds, worry over kids, all for glorification of God alone. If Black Wolf cd only have understood us and been there, & wife.

Nov 6, Monday

Sq Harge started for Traverse des S to bring in the last of the winter supplies he says as he grows older he can stand the cold less, ha, I don't like cold any too well myself when am out rounding up cows get wet in slew not frozen over. Felt chastened as thot how the Sq gave up everything for Christ, he might have been a judge

Most of the Inds at vge gone off on fall deer hunt, some left 2 weeks back. They will be back in Jan or Feb, then fur hunting here esp muskrats & make syrup from maples but also, never heard of this in New Eng, from birch & box elder wonder where my Brother Elijah is, would Selene and him like each other?

Then in summer Inds will plant & hoe corn, pick berries, make clothing & weapons, gather wild rice & cranberries, then in early fall harvest corn, hang ears to dry. There's your "wild" Indians!! They have as much routine & settled & busy as at home in Mass and yet how much happier they wd be if under God's law. Black Wolf not gone on hunt yet, staying to help Mr Lanark while voyageur away

Made window for Bessie's room, I would like to have a daughter like B. Made coffin for Indian.

I wish Huldah wasnt older than me. Don't know what is the matter with her this eveng, she seems unhappy abt nothing in particular. Could it be because I was talking so praisingly about Mercie? See Mercie every day.

7th—Tuesday

Bessie taking care of her mother. Huldah looks in all the time, too, she had a funny joke today about how the Ind *idols* are very *idle*. When she tells one like that she has a very sweet trick of laying her hand lightly on your elbow & looking up at you.

I am entirely destitute of grace. I will try to improve my time diligently, remembering that it is short. Will keep this acct of my advance or retrogression every day and seek to cast all my cares on God.

Nov 8—Wedn

Heavy snow, some sleet.

Joining & matching boards. Shall have to make new floor in Speezer brats' bedroom, the twins, Rex & Regulus. They ask too many questions. These young gentlemen, aged 6, informed me that a man who has not gone to college is a goney.

Floors for everybody, I guess, I feel disposed to weep. I know not what to do about acquiring the languages. Too tired by evening.

A few minutes with Mercie. Why does she remind me of Selene when they look so different?

Dominoes with Huld. *Won*. This evening my mind was wickedly ruffled by the unreasonable conversation of reasonable beings. Huld & Anna kept nagging at each other about the children getting their feet soaked &c. They were both touchy and here it is only nov. Fear we may all be jangly by next spring.

Nov 9—Thur

FLOORS—FLOORS—FLOORS!!

For the rest of this fleeting month may I be constrained to grow in Knowledge & true holiness.

Either I got to marry Huldah or quit this business of holding her hand. Wd be a tough job to go thru winter storms to St. Paul or wherever you get a license, maybe Prairie du Chien, oh this is madness, do not love her that much, tho as grow more & more used to depending on her, dont know what may happen My heart is all filth & pollution. Without doubt I am one of the chief of sinners.

Jake says tallow & beeswax best to keep snow water out of boots. Wonder is there any big Eastern manufacturer of Ind moccasins? Might be good money in it.

Shd have been reading my bible all evening but Satan always finds a 1000 diversions, gossiping with Anna, Bessie

10th, Friday

Mr Sp touch of influenza I tried to teach his class of Ind girls in English, only 3 of them with others on hunt, all abt 10 years old and very cute, they laughed at me & we had a good time together though Mrs Sp always claiming they are all stubborn heathen brats, oh do you have to be a prig to be a good Christian

Mercie not so well Huld has moved over to Sq's house to take care of her. Missed Huld's good night. Wish I could think more frankly about her she is true Xian and if were married to her would be influenced to fidelity & not wandering evil thoughts yet my kind feelings towards her are so mixed with horrid sudden desires to fling myself down and cohabit with her that I am aghast. I never felt that way about Mercie or Selene, with them I am like a brother, though don't know what wd happen if saw more of them. O guide my retrogressive steps!

And all here think I am a "nice boy"!! If they only knew the deep corruption of my wretched heart!! Everything I do is defiled. If God shd spurn me from his presence I would only rejoice in his justness. I am utterly cold & polluted. My heart is literally harder than the millstone. My mind is as dark as the Egyptian darkness that could be *felt*. Can it be that Christ could die for one like me? I believe I am the most vile and contemptible man living when I think how pure & sisterly Huldah is towards me and I repay her with heated thoughts. Maybe I could even commit the unspeakable deed of slowly corrupting *her* thots. The other day when we were walking together and she was all innocense I put my arm around her waist as if carelessly and pressed her side to mine and for a moment she seemed to melt right into me, before she realized how lewd that might seem. Then she muttered "Oh, don't" and pushed me away, though she did not refuse to go on walking with me as I deserved. I neither have the courage to propose honorable marriage to her, because I don't want to get tied up all my life, or yet stay ~~strickly~~ strictly away from her. Oh, unstable as water! It is hard to write. My hands get raw, chapped, even bleeding, working without gloves as I often have to, fixing carts &c.

Swept Huld's room for her as she at the Sq's. Not very neat, I must say, but was touched by her schoolgirl drawings, houses, churches &c.

Finished up a pen for Jake's sheep. He has to have them if is to get wool & teach Ind girls to spin, weave, but everything is after those sheep—wolves, bear, Inds, and the Sq looks longingly at them & talks about the lamb chops he used to have in Philadelphia—yes & with beer too, I bet! I think Jake will have to give up keeping them. Must all our mission work be given up, little by little, & all our quest of God? That wd please C. Lanark & his master, Satan!!

Nov 11—Sat

Squire back from Traverse his whiskers all hung with icicles. Fixed the cart. Fixed the Sq's washtub. Sq tried to wash some things for Mercie, I finished it for him & he was glad. Mercie's clothes are pretty & frilly but badly worn out but I am afraid they are going to last her through.

Repaired Mercie's little daguerreotype, it is of leather with a brass clasp. The hinges were broken from so much moving and I guess from often looking at it. It is a picture of her father, very erect, long straight mustache & torpedo beard, with Mercie as a little girl, with a big sunbonnet down her back & small terrier in her arms, so active-looking and smiling and so *young*. Selene must have looked like that at same age, only thinner, darker.

12—Sabbath

Jake, Anna, still unwell, did all the milking, fed chickens, found an egg with like a cross on it, is that an omen? Gave the prayer in church but no Inds there and Harge and Sps not interested, only Huldah. I sounded so cold. O Lord why cannot I lift my voice to thee as I truly do my heart? This day I made three *Resolutions:*—

To pray & read my Bible at least 1 hour every evening and *not* feel sleepy.

To not be irritated by the Speezers' pussycat smiles and their hints that I am a mere country bumpkin, but read fast & catch up with them on education.

To inquire courteously of Mr. Lanark would it be of help to Selene in her moral conduct amid the glitters and perils of New York if she got letters from me?

Nov 13—Monday

I was so damn mad today I could have spit.

I don't know but what my whole Christian career is ruined & ended. I was talking to that stylish slut, Mrs Speezer, who had called me in just when I had a necessary task hauling firewood. She asked me to put up a shelf for her, right away. I asked her why she did not have her old man do it, he has plenty of time. She says Herbert Henry is too busy, cobbling the shoes, and translating an English tract called "Little Nelly and the Coachman's Humble Home" into Dakota. It is awful. What Black Wolf will do when he reads about Little Nell weeping into her dainty snotrag, I don't know. He'll probably cut Isaac's throat and shoot Herbert Henry in the behind with a burning arrow Luna smiled and said very polite that the trouble with me is not so much that I am uneducated as a cow but that I have no humility. I ought to get right down on my knees and thank God I have a *chance* to help out Herby.

So I guess I talked mean, and I came home and read what I have written in this diary.

It makes me sick. I would burn it up, only I want to keep it and remind myself what a sanctimoniouslyfied fool I can be. Writing about "cold & polluted" and "contemptible"!!

I never really felt shameful & crawly like that at all. I got to writing so because it's the way I hear them all talk here, except Mercie—and maybe Martha Wherryman, aged 1½. The fashion. First time I was ever fool enough to kneel down to Fashion.

I do want to serve our Lord and esp defend the Dakotas, but nowhere in my Bible did I understand that you got to talk about being so humble and shameful that you ought to go roll in the manure pile, and when I heard Harge & Speezers mumble that stuff, I should have seen that the Sps are a couple of play actors and Harge is sincere but a slave driver.

I do want Mercie & Huldah & Selene & Black Wolf & Gene & Preston & Elijah & my dad & Deacon Popplewood & Mark Shadrock to be my close friends and Bessie, and I want the Savior to be our leader and that's all the program I got & my feelings towards Huld are not shameful at all, just a healthy passion for her & probably will marry her, Selene being plumb lost, & guess this is 1st & last diary I am ever going to write. Amen.

35

Clunford, Mass.
Oct. 15, 1848

MY DEAR dear brother;

I suppose it will be a long time before you get this letter, I should have written to you long ago, and indeed, dear Aaron, I do think of you daily and of how blessed you are to carry light to the heathen, but my heart is heavy for our little Charles has been taken from us, and my husband can scarce go about his tasks.

Some say it was the cholera now creeping through the country, perhaps it is a warning to this wicked generation. It was some kind of a sudden fever that took Charley. He lingered but a day and then his spirit fled from earth. We try to tell ourselves that he is safe with the Blessed Ones, where sin and suffering cease, but our hearts are sore even while we try to realize the mercy of God and the wisdom of his chastening hand.

I am afraid we loved our dear boy too much, not regarding the injunction "keep yourself from idols." God saw fit to show us how empty is earth and all its charms compared with Himself. He has mercifully left Sabrina to us—a little gray-eyed thing running about on all fours, so noisy & affectionate. But we comprehend now that she is suspended over eternal burning only by the brittle thread of life. Should that break now, before she has accepted God, she is lost forever. Yet God's arm is not so short that it cannot save, and I know you will join us in prayer that Sabrina will be preserved till the saving grace has flowed over her.

Titus joins me in all affectionate greetings, Father says in his gruff way that he is so well he now expects he will last forever. But I think he is truly saved. His rheumatism does not keep him from working daily. I hear that girl you knew in Adams is married to a millworker.

God keep you and give power to your Message.

Your loving sister
Rebecca Gadd Dunt

In his soreness from the chafing of Luna Speezer's theology and manners, Aaron was less grieved by his nephew's death than angered by the abjectness in this first letter to come from Rebecca. But he was lured back into the religious sweetness of his youth by a letter from Deacon Popplewood which came in by the same mail, carried by a passing trader, Martin McLeod.

Clunford
Octob'r 2, 1848

Dear Neighbor Aaron:

I suppose I have to be respectful to a real missionary and maybe I should call you Mr. Gadd now but when I think of you as a toddler running down the road I feel more like saying Dear Aary.

You know about Charley's passing, Rebecca bears up wonderfully, praising the Lord. Your father is still like one of our pasture rocks.

I wish I could tell you that our church here is "walking in the fear of God & in the comfort of the holy Ghost," but many are slothful or lost in the quest of pleasure. The multitude are sporting giddily along the broad road to ruin.

I do think Reverend Fairlow is a good man, and I agree with his firm refusal to introduce wild doctrines in the pulpit, like women's rights, which he says are not warranted by Scripture, & abolition, non-resistance and so on.

Lately I have had great delight in sitting on the vine-covered little porch in the evening, not too chilly with the old knitted afghan over my knees, until the stars come out joyously to share my thoughts, meditating on a passage from the Book, "We shall be like him for we shall see him as he is."

234

That I may be transformed into his glorious image helps me to bear up under the infirmities of age.

Well, this is the first Monday in the month, when so many hearts are sending up prayers from every point of the compass—from every continent and island, and many a ship that is sailing the great waters, and today the tenderest affections of the heart are brought into lively exercise. How many prayers have met and mingled before the mercy seat.

How I would like to visit you and see the wigwams and wondrous costumes of the chiefs, and then have heavenly conversation with you about our inheritance. Perhaps some day when Dr. Harge and your other teachers of holiness have finished training you and you have been ordained as a minister, you will come back to us and fertilize these barren fields with your zeal. Come before it is too late for you to be seen by

Your old friend

Thos. Popplewood

Aaron was homesick.

Huldah studied him as he sat by Mercie's bed and found him scandalously gay. He proposed that Black Wolf start a mission with classes in archery and scalp-taking, and Mercie laughed. When he had straggled away, Huldah coursed after him and drew him by the sleeve into Harge's study. She held both his forearms, and looked at him with moist eyes.

"Dear Aaron, you're discouraged here."

"What makes you think so?"

"Mercie and you were so wild, and it was a sick wildness. I always think of you as steady, like a good horse, and when the horse starts to gallop down hill, I'm uneasy."

"Oh, I have to liven up my chores."

"Aaron! You're not going to leave us?"

"Why?"

"If you do—I think I'll go, too!"

"Oh, no!"

"You're not the only one that gets sick of chores and chores and bad food and bad beds and the Indians jeering and no thanks and no reward anywhere—except in the Life Everlasting, and maybe I could get that just as well in Connecticut. Anna and I know as well as you do that the Squire is an old grizzly and the Speezers are sly. Having you with us, it's been a voice from home. If you went, Anna and Jake and I might quit, and that would just about kill the Mission. You couldn't do that to God's work, could you?"

"Well . . ."

"And to *me?*"

He kissed her cheek, but did not greatly note it, in the stress of making himself say, "No, I guess that would be wicked. But look here now! I'm not going around any more saying I'm a worm and full of corruption! Like they all do here—even you!"

"Why, Aaron Gadd, you dear silly, that's just a way of talking—trying to show our humility, our worthlessness in comparison with the perfection of God. It's like—if we had a king in America, you'd be one of the first to bow to him when he walked by, because you have such nice manners—when you remember about them. Don't you *see?*"

He didn't, particularly, and he had an immediate dislike for that ambulatory king, but he must not hurt the faith of Huldah. He felt that it would be shrewd to take a few days of vacation from being a censored but unpaid combination of farmhand, janitor, carpenter and lay preacher.

If he could go off hunting with the Wahpetons?

He gave Huldah loud assurances of nothing, and hastened over to Black Wolf's. He found that in a couple of days the Wolf and his wife and son would be joining the band in their distant deer hunt, and that he would be willing to take Aaron along.

Aaron explained to Harge that on such an expedition he would be able to learn more of the Dakota language and become more nimble at evangelizing them. Harge was shoveling manure and earth around his house, to bank it from the winter cold. He leaned on his shovel; he sized Aaron up with the insight of years as lawyer and minister.

"You want to run away from God's work pretty early, don't you!"

With an "Oh, no!" Aaron had started the denial that was expected of him when the inner malice snarled, "Oh, let him have it!" and he said firmly, "Squire, I'm not going to do *any* of God's work among the Sioux if I don't get a chance to learn their lingo. I don't want to be brash, but I've got to choose between going on this hunt and going back home."

"Oh, my boy, of course go, if you feel that way!" sputtered the Squire, and he seemed curiously lonely and tired and hopeless. It was only by a rigid exercise of will that Aaron kept from giving up his hunt, his freedom, his self.

Luna Speezer brought him an article clipped from a magazine, and tittered, "I believe your friend Black Wolf is proud of how well he reads and writes English. Give him this piece—it's by a very talented traveler and maybe Mr. Wolf will learn something about his own people from it. I'm sure that you and he and that dreadful witch his mother will enjoy it evenings, during the hunt."

The very talented traveler, Aaron found, reported in extensive detail of the Western Indian nations, including the Dakota, that they were idolatrous, lazy, dirty, improvident, murderous, adulterous and given to gambling and begging.

Luna simpered, "I'm sure Black Wolf will have some lovely answers to this, because after all we've tried to do for him, after going to college, he has deliberately returned to the blanket. Be sure and show it to him!"

Aaron grunted.

36

To FIND himself not too rustic but too urban was for Aaron an embarrassing pleasure. Black Wolf looked at his buttoned pilot-cloth coat, fur cap and leather boots, and scoffed, "What have we got here? A professor from Cincinnati? I thought we could make a decent Indian out of you, but you've got pug-dog blood."

The Wolf himself wore three cotton shirts, buffalo-skin mittens, a coat of blanket-cloth lapped in front and fastened with a coil of steel wire, and Her Door a coat of dressed deerskin with a blanket over it. Both of them carried buffalo robes, and with these wrapped about them they looked not like romantic pictures of Indians but like oleographs of winter-bundled Russian peasants, jolly and warm and round.

They made Aaron swap his boots for moccasins and lent him a buffalo robe for emergencies. The truth was that these dispossessed Indians owned, and now carried with them, rather richer possessions than Aaron had ever owned. On a travois, cross-framed poles with ends dragging on the ground behind their one pony, they had a collapsible tipi of buffalo hide with the hair scraped off, a rifle, ammunition, blankets, cooking utensils, an axe, a heavy short hoe. But for food they had taken only a strip of bacon for their son to suck, because they would be shooting rabbits on the way to the winter camp, or perhaps a belated goose, and have a load of deer meat afterward.

The bourgeois Aaron, along with his own rifle, was carrying a skin of pemmican and a johnny cake (Anna), and when no rabbits obligingly came along on their first eight-hour tramp, he was able to offer pemmican to his condescending hosts. The Wolf looked surprised, "Oh, no. You keep it. We're used to going without eating

238

for thirty or forty hours." Aaron had to beg before they would take a share.

Then, held up by a snowstorm, they were all without food, empty as winter crows, for another twenty hours. After the storm they tramped over prairie that was not earth at all but a dirty gray cloth forty miles long. Her Door, grave, dark-eyed antelope, kin of Selene, trotted and kept up with the Wolf's loping, and their son, aged three, ran half the time and the rest, rode on Her Door's shoulder—rarely on the Wolf's, Aaron had to admit.

They came at dark to the hunting camp of the Bois des Morts band: an eruption of tipis among the iced willows on the bank of a creek. They were greeted with shouts, with the firing of rifles, and in the crowded lanes between tents, among the grinning Indians and their furious dogs and skittish ponies, Aaron felt as though he were in an Arabian Nights caravan, with the cool smell of trampled snow instead of sand.

Though as a missionary he was suspect, as Black Wolf's guest he was coldly honored, and a few of the hunters shook hands with him, smiles working on their weathered faces. Only a few of the children were so scared by this devil-worshipping ghost that they yelped and fled to their mothers.

Sitting on dry grass in the tipi of Medicine Spider, the Wolf's mother, Aaron had a choice late supper, and plentiful, though as it happened to be of roast muskrat, violently flavored, he was slightly sick.

It was too late for Her Door to put up her tipi, and Aaron and the Black Wolf family slept in the abode of Medicine Spider, who was trying not to scowl at the infidel. She had already invited guests: her husband, her own inconceivably wrinkled mother and, since the Two Tree tent had burned up, Two Tree and his wife, their four children, a grandfather, and a catarrhal uncle. That night, in the skin tent twelve feet in diameter, with a central fire whose smoke did not too accurately escape through the hole left open at

239

the top, there slept sporadically, feet to fire, ten adults, five children, and a number of dogs that was constantly altering but was never less than five.

Before they slept, Black Wolf's grandmother told stories of old warriors, and the children listened and squeaked till one by one they fell asleep. It was New England domesticity in a dwarfed circus tent. The grown-ups passed one to another a small-bowled pipe charged with dried dogwood bark mixed with tobacco, and Aaron joined in the smoking, after a calculation of what this Sodomite sin would do to his soul.

He went to sleep between Medicine Spider's twitchy foot and a sharp axe blade. As he drowsed, his muscles began to walk of themselves, itch and jerk and jab, and he was alarmed till he remembered a logging camp and the lively, minute, unbidden guests there. Yet he was glad to be in this jammed and chilly discomfort, an independent man, instead of among the growing jealousies of the Mission.

They moved camp in the morning, without breakfast except for a crumbling chunk of dry pemmican which Aaron chewed privily.

He had believed the charge that the Indian males were lazy and the women did all the work. And indeed the women now struck camp and shared with the ponies and the sledge-dogs in moving the baggage, stumbling through a swamp where their feet were soaked and chilled. At the new site, the women built fires to warm the children, brushed the snow from a circular space for the tent, leveled the frozen ground with hoe and axe, cut saplings and set them up as tipi poles and draped the skin tent round them, found dry grass to spread as combined carpet and mattress, brought wood for the fire, melted snow and got the water boiling, and sat down to instruct the young ones and cheerfully to wait for the hunters—for the men coming home from business, from insurance offices or war or railroading or poetry or plumbing or presiding over the cabinet—as women had always done.

But the men were not idling. They were up before dawn, walking breakfastless, ten miles, twenty miles, and if they wounded a deer and had to follow it another ten, they might not come in for a day and a night of knee-high snow and unfrozen rivers, with envious wolves always circling round them. So the women rejoiced that they had only a dozen or fifteen hours of nice, safe work at home with the kiddies, instead of having to go out and risk life and reputation.

Aaron was a fair farmboy shot. The Indian men accepted him and liked him and, only laughing at him a reasonable amount, taught him the Dakota words for everything in the forest. He found them like the gangs of Yankee builders he had worked with—mostly cheerful, very talkative.

He kept telling himself that he ought to be giving them a holy message, but every hour he was less certain what that message might be. Cold air, deep breaths, flashes of a flying deer, profoundly still forest with snow-stirring wind on the prairies between, himself tramping steadily all day, the feel of a rifle butt at his shoulder, and home to the fire-warmed tipis shining amid the snow like great Chinese lanterns, scarlet and silver and gold—he was serene and natural here as he had never been at the Mission.

In what religion was fresh air a sacrament?

On a long shot, he got a deer in the complexities of a sumac thicket. The nearest Indian applauded him and patted his shoulder and helped him carry the deer back to camp. Medicine Spider forgave him for being an atheist with no belief in Taku-skan-skan nor even in the Wakan Wohanpi feast by which a decent man returns thanks to the gods for their bounty. She told Black Wolf to explain that if Aaron would remain among the Dakota long enough and humbly learn how to share everything with others, how to listen to the spirits of animals and streams and winds, he might yet become a saved soul and a Man.

But he had to get back to the Mission—at least, so he told himself. On his last night in camp, he felt that he must give to Black

Wolf the magazine article from Luna Speezer. The Wolf might some day become a statesman among his people, and he ought to learn to endure critics.

"I'll read it later, when I feel strong," said Black Wolf, merrily.

Unimpeded by any luggage save his rifle and the borrowed buffalo robe, Aaron tramped to the Mission in fourteen straight hours, without having to camp, worried all the way by the enormous clouds pregnant with snow, feeling small and unimportant, with no evangelical message for anybody, even Mrs. Speezer. He landed at Jake's cabin late at night. As he sat down to cold pork, Huldah fluttered into the room.

"Oh, my dear, I had a feeling you'd be coming tonight, and I was watching from Mercie's room for a light here," she exulted. "Can't I make you some tea?"

"No, no, this is fine. How is Mercie?"

"Near the end. That's made me all the lonelier for you, Aaron. No one to talk to—about how we young people must put new fire into religion—how we must fight God's battles, side by side! I did miss you so!"

He kissed her and her lips were moist and he was losing his senses and his sense when she gently pushed him away with her mechanical, "Oh, don't—not now."

They sat talking of Mercie, with no official recognition of anything like kisses.

37

HULDAH was wiping Mercie's forehead. The Squire, standing at the foot of the bed, was mourning, "Some folks may claim you've been frivolous, Mercie, but I know that in your heart you have lived for God and not for the world, and so your life has not been altogether wasted. And our love has been a sacrament that..."

In a shaky little voice, Mercie insisted, "Balthazar, you and Huldah skip out, and let me talk to Brother Aaron."

She seemed smaller, with her body all one hot coal, but she was still trying to smile at him.

"Ah, that confused soul, Harge; still trying to court me and still uncertain whether I even like him, and still heavy about it. But I'm light now. I can float away. I used to think he and his religion would weigh me down, but I'm escaping."

"Don't, Mercie!"

"Honestly, I haven't complained to anybody but you, Brother Aaron, not even to Huldah, and she's so kind. But she's becoming all breezy and brave and Western. I know you will, too, but to me you're still the New England ways, narrow ways, dear ways—so dear!" She was crying a little, hopelessly. "The prairie is always the same round. It never changes, except from green to gray to green. I long for *moving* things—clouds on the hill, waves in the sun."

"But there's fleets of big clouds here."

"No, I won't have it; I refuse to see them. No clouds."

"And splendid sunsets."

"Not a sunset. No. Never seen one. You can't have a real sunset unless there's a smell of coffee—real *coffee* coffee! Your clouds and your sunsets here are too big. They have no humor. No. I want to see the layer of apple green over the black hills at twilight, and dories in the inlet. Well—I won't." A surprising laugh, with no malice in it but with terror for Aaron. "But maybe there's some kind of personal immortality—all these preachers say there is, and they ought to know. And then maybe I'll look down and see the lilacs in May—or be so seraphic I won't care whether I do or not. That'll be nice—Big Mercie, Number Three Angel!"

"My dear!"

"Would you like to hear all about me? I won't be around to bore you much longer. Would you? I want to relive it!"

"*Yes!*"

"You did that very nicely and warmly! . . . Well, my people have been in Maine ever since there was one—and I think the Lord created it first thing on the eighth day, and used up all the rock and foam he had left. Rock and foam and soaring wings—Maine! My people were sea captains and farmers; my father is a lawyer and a soldier—they call him General, but I don't know as he ever was more than a captain—in the Second War with England, that was. He's sort of gusty; awful dignified in court but jolly at home, like our house—it's awfully stately but lots of secret cupboards and picture books inside.

"I suppose I was kind of frail as a little girl, and he took such care of me after Mother passed on. There was a grape arbor, with a cracked brick floor in it, and we'd sit there and look at the cove, with the piles of lobster pots.

"Well, the General is a good churchman, except maybe he doesn't believe any of it. Then there was this lawyer that had turned missionary, Harge. He came to town to preach a couple nights, and he stayed with us. It was summer. He was thirty-five and I was only twenty, and he'd been married before, to a Pennsylvania Dutch farm girl that up and died quick. He took one look at me and married me. I think everybody was against it, including me, but he was such a bull for passion and determination that none of us got a chance to say anything, and by Christmas I woke up and found myself right *here* and stuck for keeps, and the children kept coming so fast it made my head swim and—here we are. Only you don't have to stay, remember that!

"Oh, I guess for maybe a minute, at first, I was in love with him, whatever that means. He'd already been out here, looking over different Indian villages, and he was planning this station and he made me believe that within ten years (that'd be three years ago!) this would be a real city with an Episcopal bishop and a hairdresser and everything! I thought he was heroic, so strong and physical and yet so pure—he *told* me he was—but then he forgot it when we went to bed.

"Darling Aaron, am I shocking you? Am I being a lady cad?

"Missionaries may want to put down lust, but they're around the house an awful lot, and God does seem to expedite their babies specially and . . . Look! If they really try to imitate Jesus, why do they hate the sinful heathen?"

Aaron protested, "They don't. They just hate the sin."

"Oh, yes. I see you're getting on! . . . Aaron, be careful of Huldah. She's a good woman but she's as hard as a she-bear. She'll defend her cubs, and she'll see that she gets cubs *to* defend. And . . .

"Luna Speezer hates her husband, and everything connected with missionary work. Everything! But she has grit. She'll stick to it longer than better people, like Huldah or Harge. But it is kind of funny! Back home, Luna thought missions would be a picnic, lemonade and cold chicken on a buffalo robe beside a river, with a cabin like a Swiss chalet and all the Indians adoring her and calling her their Fanny Wright.

"Still, the missionaries are better, honester people than any of the other whites that come out here, and just as brave. Maybe they hate the Indians for laughing at them, but they don't try to steal their land—*most* missionaries don't."

She was coughing now, horribly. She begged, "Go quick, my dear.

Isn't it the silliest vanity—I don't want you to see me again. I'm not pretty any more. Oh, get yourself a really nice girl, Aaron, and kind and not too much piety and ambition. I would have been such a good wife—for the right person. Quick, my dear, and all my blessings!"

He found Bessie hidden in the stable, lying on the hay and weeping.

He did not see Mercie again till she lay in the coffin he had made for her; so small a coffin, as smooth as his sandpaper could make it. He had hesitated and then lined it with the inner bark of the silver birch.

She seemed waiting, and he waited for her to speak again. It was not possible that so frail and little a face could be dead.

Squire Harge and Jake and Aaron with pickaxe and shovel dug through the frozen ground to make a grave for her, and they left her in the rough new cemetery on the ridge above the Mission, among the mounds of lone and forgotten children. Over her later was a wooden slab that in ten years would fall to earth and molder away with her. Today no one knows just where Mercie Harge lies, between the prairie and the muddy river.

38

SQUIRE HARGE had been too shaky to preach Mercie's funeral sermon by the grave, in the dreariness of that sluggish snow-fall. Mr. Speezer had spoken. He threw away his scholarly super-ciliouness and cried in pain, "Lord, be very tender of this girl whose smile was often the only sunshine we had."

As they walked back to the Mission, Harge was unseeing and stumbling. Huldah herded his three children and tried to make death in raw winter sound blessed.

Aaron heard him mutter to her, complainingly, "I suppose you'll be moving back to Jake's house now, Huldy?"

"I suppose so."

"You've been wonderfully good to my family."

"I wanted to do everything I could for dear Mercie."

Aaron thought she looked slightly plump and smug about it, but the Squire was moved to cry, "Oh, the Lord will bless you for your manifold charities, Sister Huldy, and richly reward you, where we can only give you our earthy thanks."

"Oh, it's nothing."

"I confess I don't know how I'm going to get along, and the children. The Word says that it is not good for man to live alone. Nor woman neither."

"That's so."

Huldah was a little too cordial about it, felt Aaron.

"It isn't," the Squire lugubriously went on, "that I need anybody to help me personally. If it is the Lord's will, I can cook my own vittles, sweep my own floor, sit alone all evening, studying the messages of Scripture. But being without help would interfere with devoting myself to the savages. I don't know, perhaps all my prayerful efforts are in vain."

"Oh, no, Squire!" trilled Huldah. "None of us could do anything without your wisdom and guidance."

"I'm glad if that is the case, Sister Huldy, though I have but a low opinion of my abilities today—forlorn, deserted, lost."

"Dear Squire, we'll all do our best to comfort you. Just count on us."

"Oh, I shall, I shall, Huldy, bless you!"

Aaron snarled, "God Almighty, they might wait till they get home from the funeral!"

He was alarmed. It had not occurred to him that Huldah might not go on being his own especial encouragement and refuge. He did not (he assured himself) want to be selfish about it, but surely Harge was too old and stubborn for Huldah, who had saved up her youth and could yet spend it gaily. He saw that it was not inconceivable—merely a little nasty—that Harge should win her over by his loneliness and the frightened confusion of his children.

How long would *she* last?

He wanted around him the faint splendors of Huldah's ecstasy and he did not want to lose her support. He decided that on the hunt, with the Indians, he had fallen into the sin of Doubt, and that if a Charles Grandison Finney were about, he would get converted all over. Only, he wouldn't be a worm and enjoy writhing again; no, he wouldn't!

At Jake's, with Huldah back home again, the Squire appeared constantly, and it was a different Squire, a wooing Squire, a high-stepping Squire, a Squire who begged for tenderness. Sometimes he told Huldah (and publicly, for nearly everything had to be public in that cramped cabin) how the Reverend Jacques Pugh, of Evergreen, New Hampshire, had volunteered that the Squire's sermon on enduring providence was the most soul-stirring plea for missionary work that he had ever heard, and there had been over fifty-seven dollars in the missionary collection. Sometimes he merely told Huldah that his three children missed her, and that Bessie had cried for her all night.

Whenever Huldah walked through the Mission grounds, the Squire dismissed his confirmation class (of one Indian widow) and trudged after her, his step firm but a little slower than her excited tripping.

All this her sister Anna observed, with precision and displeasure.

With Huldah, Jake and Aaron at supper (pork and corn pone and coffee made from toasted bread crusts), Anna hooted, "Huldy! While you was over to the Indian village, your beau come around— Brother Harge. They say it's the young fellows that get all het up, but looks to me like it's the old rams. He was pawing the ground and bellowing. And a new cravat—least *I* never see it before!"

Said Huldah, "Now you stop!"

"And I'll bet the Old Man hasn't saved a cent. Any female that married him would have to take in washing, when he retired back to the States—if she lived that long!"

"Stop it, I tell you!"

"Oh, you're one of these delikit mystics I hear about; all visions and flirting around amongst the clouds. You wait till you're seven months pregnant and your hair stringy and your bowels running, and that old goat still prancing around, and you won't be no mystic no more. That's what'll happen if you marry him."

"I *tell* you, I have no intention . . ."

"If you got to get married, you get a good husband that wants to stay to home in Connecticut, where a body belongs. Missionary work is just no good for a Purdick, with nutmeg dust in her hair.

"When we first started teaching 'em spinning and weaving here, the Injuns would come around and learn. I thought we was really doing something useful. But since then . . . I do get so sick of their insulting us and chopping up the girls' nice dresses. Some day, Jake and me are going to pull out of this and have a farm of our own, and if any Injun brave hoves in sight, I'll chase him a mile with a hatchet!

"Oh, if I thought the Lord Jesus really wanted us to stay here, I'd be willing to stick. But I think all this farming is a waste of time for the missionaries. They'd do better to ship us hired hands back home and bring in their bread and potatoes, and tend strictly to preaching and study.

"Before she passed on, Mercie and me agreed about this, but she begged me not to say a word that would discourage the Squire. As if anybody could!"

In this fortunate diversion from her own affairs of the heart, Huldah managed to get away, to go up to bed. Then Anna became really earnest.

"Aaron—Neighbor—you got to do something about Huldy and old Harge. Maybe she'll listen to you; she won't to Jake and me. She's awful fond of you, and looks like you're about halfway stuck on her—looks like she could depend on you. You've certainly given her reason to think so!"

"Well—yes—I suppose . . ."

There is no man in history who would not have been disturbed by the words, "You've given her reason to think so."

Aaron escaped also, to a bedtime of thoughtful dread.

He saw that Harge was ardent about Huldah, if it showed in nothing more than his way of handing her a hymn book. In 1848, a woman who had a hymn book handed to her like that was already compromised. Harge came constantly to ask Anna about the care of his "babes," but it was Huldah at whom he looked while he was asking it. And whenever he saw Huldah and Aaron talking, he would open his mouth as if to blast them, and then be cloudily silent.

Under this unconfessed rivalry, Huldah blossomed and shone and was excusably arch as she listened to Harge on epistemology or

Aaron on rabbit-hunting. And Aaron, between indignation at Harge for his despotism and pity for him as a lonely and futile old man (he had almost reached the senility of fifty), was certain only that it was his duty to help the generous Huldah . . . He was moved when he saw how gaily she helped Bessie make a snow man.

Aaron had excitement now in winter's coming, in the drama of storms. As a Berkshire Hills boy he knew the arts of keeping warm, yet he was ignorant of prairie blizzards, of gales coming unchecked across two thousand miles of Northwestern plains.

Except at blatantly sunny noon, the entire world, Mission and river bluffs and lake and prairie, was flattened out on one gray level. The earth had been decreated, and the Mission buildings were dots on the vast anonymity of snow. Back home, at its bleakest, there had always been cheerful objects close at hand: hillsides and barns and stone fences and cedars coated with cake-frosting, but Aaron's world now was all of distances and planes and contemptuous gray.

He was an outdoor man, not too much bewildered by this frigid unfriendliness, and he began to read the prairie lore. He knew now the untidy reed-piles of the muskrat houses beside the slew ice, which was cloudy where the snow was blown away. After a great snowfall, he learned, the sumac bushes were like the pictures he had seen of cotton blossoms. The smoothness of the fresh snow, with diamonds beckoning all over it, became pocked and scurfy from the unrelenting wind till renewed snow came to cover the untidiness of the Mission yard . . . as, Huldah pointed out, God's mercy covered sin.

Aaron was won to this open, wind-scourged West by the sunshine after a deep snowfall, when the birches were webs against the streakless blue and the lonely pine trees seemed to be holding out drooping, white-mittened hands in appeal for friendship. In the late afternoon, the slopes were rose and gold before sunset but mauve under the trees, and a diffused pink glow spread over the whole world and the snow-robed trees were glorified . . . like, said Huldah, the persevering saints.

But her own enthusiasm was all for lamplight flung out on the snow, and this she shared with Aaron. What Huldah dreaded and what he came to exalt was the winter prairie itself in its vastness and cruelty, with no horizon on sullen days and seemingly no sky, but only an intolerable continuation of the lifeless snow, fogged with aimless flakes.

For these nature notes, Squire Harge had no sympathy. What *he* said, ten minutes after the snow had quit falling, was "Why ain't you got the paths dug yet?"

Though all the stoves were gluttons for wood and he was kept trotting with the sled laden with chunks of maple and ironwood, the several houses were always cold. Bathing had never been luxurious nor frequent at Bois des Morts, but now it was only a dab with a towel, while you stood shivering on a rag rug. Brother Speezer was the only man who could be counted on to shave every day, and going to bed was a calculated leap from a pile of clothes into a pile of blankets like icy slabs. Almost every night the snow sifted in on the top blanket and made a striped pattern on the floor. Noses ran in irritating reality while you were trying to be full of idealism, and bruises from falling on the glare ice were as common as the constant hoot of coughing.

The children were entertained all day not only by sliding but by getting electric sparks out of one another's ears and noses, and there was general joy when Bessie, who was admired but feared, just after an address to all the children on the wickedness of disobeying one's Papa by throwing snowballs at the Speezers' cat, put her tongue to a hatchet and took all the skin off its tip.

Aaron found this winter highly domestic as well as scenic, and there were few higher lights than when Huldah gave him a pair of red woolen wristlets she had knitted for him.

He saw now that cold, hunger, dullness of diet, risk of being lost in storms, were to the missionaries lesser hardships than anxiety about their relatives "back in the States," with letters struggling through once in two months. But the heaviest cross was Fear.

They were all afraid of hunger if the potatoes should go bad and the storms prevent hunting; the women and children were afraid of lurking wolves and the men not too happy about them; and though Harge scoffed at any danger from resentful Indians like Black Wolf, there were constant frontier rumors of gangs of Wahpekute and Yankton Sioux who had broken away from their tribes and become outlaws, shooting, burning, raping.

Never was a group at Bois des Morts so secure on a snug evening, so serene after singing *Beulah Land,* that they did not pause rigid and hearken when an icy tree cracked or the lake boomed or the wind tried the shutters. All night long, in the clamorous silence, Fear crept around the houses like the creeping cold. Fear slid under the doors, Fear whispered and rustled, and by your bed stood Fear.

Along with fear of the menaces outside, there was always the insistent fear of sickness.

Speezer was the semi-official doctor; at least, he had read more books about medicine than the others. It may be that his remedies were not altogether scientific; he lectured that "a good purge relieves influenza and bleeding cures pleurisy." Yet he did have the confident quiet hands and the resolution of the born doctor.

Even Squire Harge "reckoned that Herby was a good sawbones," and that was much, for the Squire hated Speezer, in the strain of compulsory brotherly love through these months of prison.

39

Mr. HERBERT HENRY SPEEZER (M.A.) was writing a revolutionary book. Aaron suspected that the masterpiece still consisted of only a few notes, and the title: *The Torch in the Thatch, or The Efficacy of Evangelism Demonstrated by Examples of Its Persuasiveness over Heathen Superstition among the Sioux or Dakota Indians.*

The Squire snorted to Huldah and Aaron, "Funny thing. When missionaries haven't got many conversions to report, they usually jump into writing books, to have something to show for their supposed labors!"

Suddenly, out of this dubiousness of reputation, Mr. Speezer vaulted into glory. Isaac Weeps-by-Night, who was doing his own private deer-hunting nearby, was attacked by a lynx and brought to the Mission. His right leg showed the bone. Speezer looked pale, rubbed his jaw and said, "We'll have to amputate."

Isaac's Indian companions agreed.

Jake Wherryman proved to have, hidden away for a year, a bottle of whisky, which he brought out regretfully, and Isaac was put into a heroic mood almost immediately. He was laid out on a kitchen table in Harge's living-room, and Harge, Aaron, Jake and an Indian held him down, while Speezer operated.

Here was a new Speezer, cool and precise and commanding. He had a small surgical kit, well kept, but he had to use one of Jake's handsaws, sharpened and boiled. He cauterized the smaller blood vessels with a hot poker—the raw flesh sizzled.

Anna was nurse, checking the flow of blood with linen sponges from an old sheet, but it was altogether a bloody butchering, with the grate of the saw pushed back and forth through living bone, and Aaron was extremely sick.

Isaac came through it and Mr. Speezer was very modest and professional and Aaron had an hour's worship for the hero priest-scholar, the magician carving human flesh and conjuring the human spirit, and in that mood he was more willing to listen to Speezer's disquisitions on theology.

And indeed throughout the Mission, to make the slow and hostile winter tolerable, they were as much given to gossip about theology and rival clergymen as to popcorn and quarreling and hymns. If their pious shoptalk was no more elevated than that of judges or bricklayers, it was at least as lively.

That December Sunday afternoon, Harge preached to the staff and to three Dakota women, none of whom understood English. He had chosen his text by sticking a knife into the Bible and taking the passage on which the point rested. So he found himself fated to preach on a puzzle out of *Revelation:*

"When he had opened the third seal, I heard the third beast say, Come and see. And I beheld, and lo, a black horse; and he that sat on him had a pair of balances in his hand. And I heard a voice in the midst of the four beasts say, A measure of wheat for a penny, and three measures of barley for a penny; and see thou hurt not the oil and the wine."

The Squire lined it out, reading and expounding each sentence in English and then in Dakota—what he hoped to be Dakota, what he believed to be Dakota, but which the three astonished women did not seem to recognize as Dakota.

Aaron did not know what the passage meant, in any language, though it did have a charming sound to him of a child's game played with beans. He looked along the line and guessed that Huldah did not understand it, and that the Speezers' enlightened smirks did not

255

necessarily mean that they understood it either. And from Harge's working brow, he was certain that the chief was completely lost.

The three Indian women seemed gratified. They were used to Shining Wind's incantations and they expected a good measure of mystery and beautiful nonsense from their medicine men.

"But *you*—what are you doing in this sorcerer's den?" his inner malice demanded.

The Mission staff gathered at the Speezers' for supper, that Sunday, and Luna with demure spitefulness suggested, "Squire, I was so much interested in the Scripture that you expounded this afternoon. I'm sure it was most helpful to those squaws."

"Sure enough?" Harge was pleased and considerably surprised.

"Oh, yes. Squire, do you feel that section could have been a prophecy of the coming of the Mormons?"

"Why, I'll tell you, Luna. The whole of *Revelation* is a mystery. It just can't be explained."

Then he explained it.

When he had struggled on till Jake was falling asleep and Aaron was falling awake, Huldah rescued the Squire by chirping, "Oh, it's too wonderful, Squire! You mean these visions are a symbolic interpretation of the supernatural, which can only be expressed mystically. It's perfectly clear, now!"

The Squire beamed fondly on her. Luna glared at her, but she could not afford to quarrel, because Huldah had promised to make a pork-apple pie for the twins' birthday. She did help herself to a heavy sniff though, looking somewhat like the Witch of Endor and somewhat like a countess, in her skinny erectness and her fashionable beaded cap.

"So! You see how it is!" shouted the Squire, so relieved that he was not suspicious when Herbert Henry, in a sinister manner, observed, "Exegesis!"

Luna attacked again:

"I'm afraid I'm not poetical enough to appreciate mysticism—

256

like Huldah! I have a mathematical mind. A Calvinist is so conscious of the doom menacing us every minute. And how fierce that will be!" She lapped her lips. "I have just been re-reading Jonathan Edwards' 'Future Punishment of the Wicked Unavoidable.' How clear! How powerful! Listen!"

She had the book handy for bedtime reading:

" 'Imagine yourself cast into a great furnace . . . Imagine that your body were to lie there full of fire . . . and that after millions of millions of ages, your torment would be no nearer to an end.' "

Luna gurgled, "There! That's the scientific truth that we have to face!"

Anna objected—though she was quaking a little—"I never did think that would be just of God."

"My dear, *dear* Anna! Not just? Listen further to Dr. Edwards:

" 'Thou hast despised the mighty power of God . . . Now why is it not fit that God should show the greatness of his power in thy ruin? What king is there who will not vindicate his royal majesty in executing vengeance on those that rise in rebellion?' "

Jake grumbled, "Folks don't believe that way no more."

"Let me tell you," Luna screamed, "there's just as many purehearted believers in the eternal torture of rebels as there ever were!"

Aaron objected, "You sound so self-satisfied about it!"

"Siddown and don't try to show off, young man!" yelled Harge.

Aaron sat down, without quite noticing whether he was sitting down or not.

——I'll get kicked out by Mr. Harge, come springtime. No, I won't! I'll walk out by myself, and I'll take his Huldah with me. And I won't count myself a failure and run back East. I'll stay in the West and build churches that he'll beg to be allowed to preach in!

The sturdy Anna was confronting Luna: "Are you a good enough Calvinist so if your brother were reprobated and you stood up there in heaven, looking down at him screaming forever, you could be happy about it?"

"Yes, I would! The fact that God could condemn my beloved

brother would prove how gracious and just he was in showing mercy to *me!* . . . Course I never did have a brother."

"And your children, Luna? The twins? Could you stand seeing *them* tortured, and you all cool and jolly?"

Luna protested, "Now hon-est-*lee!*"

A good evening of the New Theology.

The missionaries no more discussed theology all the time than sailors did Noah. They comforted themselves vastly with shoptalk.

Squire Harge was businesslike—and very indignant—whenever he had a letter from the secretary of the ABCFM, their Vatican. He was reading the latest encyclical to the staff:

"With the growing demands upon generous benefactors, we again urge on you the most scrupulous economy. It is certainly according to the will of God that we count the costs before we begin to build."

The Squire howled, "Good God, if we'd counted the costs, think any of us would be here? I made almost two thousand a year, when I was a lawyer, and now I get four hundred and a barrel of second-hand clothes! Economy? Why, we save souls, or we would if we could land any, at the lowest cost per head in the entire mission field! All Boards are alike. They sit by a nickel-plated stove and pull their whiskers and tell us what to do! The trouble is, we been eating too many potatoes. I better cut us down to one a week. Look at Huldy! She's too pretty and well fed to be an earnest missionary!"

Aaron had noted that in all their gatherings, Harge made Huldah his queen-consort, turning to her for admiration whenever he made a point. Aaron was not without jealousy.

The shoptalk became most lively when the Squire had a letter from Mr. Martindean, the American Board missionary to the Chippewa, near Lake Superior. He wrote triumphantly that he was now having an average attendance of almost sixteen Indians at his meetings. Both Harge and Speezer took pencil and figured out their own average—one made it nine and the other eleven, while Jake grunted to Aaron, "Six would be more like it."

Mr. Martindean had written, "We are having difficulty keeping track of our Chips because so many are hiding out in the woods in fear of your contumacious Soos. Can't you manage to keep them home, so our persecuted tribe will no longer be scared but will tend to corn-planting and religion?"

"What do you think of that!" said Harge, who the day before had been shouting that their local Sioux were the most war-hungry scoundrels on earth. "*Our* Indians contum-whatever-it-is? It's *their* Indians, those blasted Chippeways, that always start the trouble. Our boys would behave themselves like the gentlemen they are, if 'tweren't for Martindean's murderous ruffians! One good thing— our Indians can lick his any day! Oh, he may have these big, over-grown meetings like he boasts of, but don't look to me like they're learning much about the Prince of Peace!"

It was all right. It was the talk of their trade. Only, Aaron saw now, it was not his trade and not likely to be. Why had he come all the way from Massachusetts?

He shivered.

Yet he would not go back to his cozy Yankee mountains. This new country was his battle; that old one was his impotent childhood.

He forgot Harge and Speezer and metaphysics and the business of church-keeping as he tramped through a transcendentalism of snow to the untrading Huldah.

40

THE older people at the Mission considered Christmas a rather pagan feast and highly wasteful of food, but the children clamored after it, and Huldah had introduced a tree, cut down by Aaron, into the Squire's living-room and was making ornaments out of pine cones.

Holiday peace was thick and glittering at the station, when Black Wolf came back with fire and threatenings. They heard that he had returned early from the hunt, along with his wife and son, and that he had brought a wealth of furs to Lanark. Aaron was zealous to see him, but when Black Wolf showed up at the Mission, he was gruff; he answered Aaron's greetings with "Huh! I'm here begging for a pencil and some kind of paper book I can write in. You know, Indians are always begging!"

"What are you so angry about, Wolf?"

"That magazine essay you gave me—what ruffians all Indians are."

"I'm sorry I gave it to you."

"No, it's good you did, Gadd. I never saw anything that told so completely what the whites think we are. Now, I'm going to write an answer. It will, I should think, wipe out the whole white race. So will you help me to get it published?"

Aaron's notions about publishers were less exact than his notions about archbishops, but he did presume that they would have no lively desire to bring out a document by a Sioux brave in three unlaundered cotton shirts. He bumbled, "If there's anything—I don't know how you go about . . ."

"You're as bad as the rest of the whites!"

"No, no, honestly . . ."

"I shall write my book in English—oh, I'm a college man, with honors in horseshoe-pitching—but it will be translated into all the Indian tongues, and when they read it, I think they will combine, all over North America. I shall not lead the fighting—I have had only a couple of raids on the Ojibway, though I did do a couple of good killings. I shall be the prophet, and our Napoleon will arise. Kill them all! Though you, you shall be saved and adopted as a Dakota, along with your round-faced Huldah, because you are my friend, and because you are going to give me this pencil and paper."

Aaron affected to be amused in a gentlemanly manner. Oh, let this poor fellow write his book and get it all out of his system!

He obligingly stole from the chapel, which was also schoolroom, a couple of exercise books and two priceless pencils, and gave them to a not singularly grateful Black Wolf. Two days later he went over to the village site and found that Her Door had set up their tipi in which Black Wolf was squatted, writing on his knee. It then first came to him that the Wolf really meant this nonsensical hatred of the white race, and that there was nothing in his Bible which stated that the European-American whites could go on ruling the unwilling majority of the world forever.

He was nervous. The Mission could be wiped out in five minutes. He vaguely wished that he had never got into this business of being a Liberal and betraying his own Totem.

Caesar Lanark said to him, again at dinner—rabbit and wild rice now, with winter beginning to pinch—"Have you considered my very commercial offer, which you had to climb up on the temple pinnacle to refuse?"

"Vaguely."

"I trust that the poison of common sense has been slowly working on you. I don't want to coerce Selene—I am only too good at coercion, and I don't like to start it with this exceptional joy of mine. So if she goes on declining to come here to the wilderness, I may compromise and meet her in St. Paul next summer, and set up my citadel there, with my activities circling far around it.

"I might be able to train you to take over here at the Bois, with Leon Simonet translating for you and advising you. In St. Paul, which is certain to grow vastly, I shall venture on banking, shipping, lumber. My future is big with the future of the state that is to be.

"I have been watching you—first-hand or otherwise—ever since you came. You are still a cub, with no knowledge of what you want to do, and you are much too good-natured with mouthy fools, white and Indian, but you are patient and strong and reasonable, none of which are my virtues. My boys tell me that with a limited Dakota vocabulary, you have a not-bad accent. And Miss Purdick—Huldah, is it?—will be a sturdy and useful wife for you.

"Can you consider this now without getting Scriptural? By the way: don't feel that I have to have your aid. Canada and the East are full of young men who would rejoice in such a chance. *Well?*"

"I . . . Mr. Lanark, if I'd only wanted to make money, I could've stayed home. I was on my way to becoming a successful builder. I'm not lunatic, maybe not lunatic enough, but I do have—I am chased by what some call a Vision—probably a poor one."

"Aaron, I'd like to give you a new vision, that of a new sort of royalty, the Merchant Prince. If you came in with me, but wholeheartedly, you might share that vision, you might even beat me . . . try and do it!

"I was extremely poor, in Canada; my people were mostly dominies and merchants, but rat poor. So I've had my share of servitude, and now, I'm *Master,* and intend to go on being so. Now that this new land is opening, I intend to take it over, from the start.

"Today, the man of business is not only nobility but judge and priest and scholar and soldier. Out of his means he supports all the poets and thought-mongers, and he can command their supposedly independent knowledge and judgment. He is the only man who can rove the world as he wants, or even read as he wants, because he is responsible to no one.

"To prove that, I'm going to start you reading just the sort of metaphysicians who would wipe me out, if they could! They start out as rebels, sniping at me and my tribe from behind rather ill-trimmed hedges, and end up as our court jesters. I like them, because they enlarge the imagination, and today, in this strange and utterly altered New Age that is wiping out the plantation barons, it is the man of commerce and manufacturer who is the man of imagination."

Therewith lending Aaron *Sartor Resartus* and Emerson's Essays.

To Aaron, in his ragged room, Emerson was a proclamation that a man could be religious, could be of God, without the rage of Harge or the twisty oracles of Luna Speezer. Swaying a little to its tune, he read the Divinity School address of 1838:

"I once heard a preacher who sorely tempted me to say I would go to church no more . . . A snowstorm was falling around us. The snowstorm was real; the preacher merely spectral. . . . He had lived in vain. He had no one word intimating that he had laughed or wept, was married or in love, had been commended, or cheated, or chagrined."

Now it happened that on the recent Sunday when Squire Harge had been trying to explain *Revelation* to the Indian women, and had become all red and angry over his Dakota vocabulary, the snow was falling outside and effortlessly speaking all languages. Aaron perceived that Emerson was his man, and he made schemes to go and call on him, in a Concord just over a hundred miles from his own Clunford . . . where he had heard of Emerson only as an infidel.

But when he tried Carlyle, Aaron could not read him; found him too florid and whimsical for a farmer-carpenter, who was concerned not only with metaphorical snow but with the real article, which hourly soaked his booted feet.

He went back to Lanark, as bidden, and wondered, "Don't it

worry you to have those fellows so strong against you and your power?"

Said Lanark, "The merchant is the only ruler today who is so strong, so much in the spirit of the revolutionary age, that he can afford to patronize even the rebels against him. If, or perhaps when, I become rich enough, I shall endow colleges—I who went to school for only three years—and I shall laugh as I watch the professors who hate me kissing my toe. . . . Well, are you coming with me or not?"

Aaron shook his head.

"Are you going on teaching Wahpeton warriors to paint china?"

"No. Maybe my own trade—carpentry. Then, when Minnesota is organized as a territory, I might go into politics, and work for some of the things I want."

Lanark was really sorry for him. "My boy, the Territory, and later the State, will be run by *my* sort of people, no matter what kind of pietists or leathery frontiersmen we permit to be elected. We'll give you an honest government, but firm, and no indulgence to abolitionists or cranks who want to give the suffrage to women and Negroes, or to Indians with their absurd hope to keep farmers east of the Mississippi."

"Is it true that all this land will be taken over, whether the Indians protest or not, as Black Wolf says?"

"Of course—though legally—even if we have to invent some new laws. Your friend Mr. Wolf, by the way, is turning into a nuisance. I have a personal duty to do something about him—he is distantly related to Selene's mother. But to return to the opportunity I have offered you . . ."

"How would Miss Selene like my working for you?"

"My dear young man, she would undoubtedly snub you. I consider myself very fortunate when she doesn't snub me!"

He thought, after he read on in Emerson:

"Yes, let a man stand on his own feet, not as a pink man or a

264

yellow man, not as a Christian or an infidel, not as a Yankee or an Englishman, not as a merchant or abolitionist or gambler or carpenter, but as a Man. I came to the West by accident, but here I stand, here I stay, here I build."

Then, secretly and by evening, Black Wolf brought in his completed "book." While the Wolf waited, Aaron read it, aghast:

41

I, BLACK WOLF, son of Shining Wind, of the Wahpeton Council Fire, being a pure-blood Dakota and a member of the medicine lodge, but having attended a school of the white people, am herewith warning my people what the ghosts are like, so that we may take measures to clean out these Hunnish invaders, or to pen them, like maniacs, behind a boundary line.

Religion and Superstition

Most of the whites believe, or profess to believe, in Christianity, which is an idolatrous religion with many gods. Their Catholic sect has thousands of mysterious divine beings ruled by what they call the "Trinity," which consists of Father, Son and Mother Mary. The Protestants have no trinity, but a four-god council consisting of Father, Son, Holy Spirit and Satan.

As to the superstitious welter of their other gods, it is impossible to tell when the Christians consider them real and when they are indulging in fables. Christians are fanciful rather than imaginatively spiritual, and a great deal of their theology is either amusing make-believe or the obvious manufacture of their power-seeking medicine men.

Among their demigods are Santa Claus, Luck (whom they worship by striking wood), saints, angels, seraphs, witches, fairies, vampires, evil spirits, the spirits of the dead, tombs and statues, the cross and a magic book called the Bible.

Like us, the Christians perceive that all animals, birds and plants have individual spirits; that in every creature, be it the mighty grizzly or the timid mouse, there is some spark of the Supreme God. This is indicated in their talking to cats, dogs and horses as

266

though they expected intelligible answers, by their fondling and even speaking to the more handsome trees and mourning their demise, and by their poems, rather silly effusions about lakes and rivers at night.

The universal superstitiousness of the whites is manifested in their investment of their chieftains with names bearing talismanic values and so gullibly prized that men will cheat, lie, labor to obtain them. Among these names are king, president, senator, governor, general, sergeant, doctor, judge, boss, the honorable, reverend, lord, sir, star, maestro, skipper, champion, foreman. They also have orders of initiates in which such magic terms as "thirty-second degree" have a superstitious significance.

Indians, of course, have no "theology," and indeed no word for this system of credulity in which the white priests arrange for God, who must be entirely bewildered by it, a series of excuses for his failures.

Naturally, as we know that our God pervades every inch of space, we do not set off any particular place as sacred to him, but the Christians, cowering in their fear of the unknown, dare not worship together unless they have built a shelter insulated against evil spirits, and this they call church, chapel, temple, prayer-closet or whatnot. And instead of expecting every soldier to breathe a brief and manly prayer of his own before plunging into the delight of battle, the Christians are so feeble spiritually as to have hired hands, known as "chaplains," to do their praying for them.

They also have one special day, their "Sabbath," which is sacred to their chief God, while to the Indians every day, hour, minute is filled with duty and gratitude to God. His voice is in every breeze, every flowing water. He is to be revered and pondered upon as much on a Wednesday midnight as on a Sunday noon; and whensoever a Dakota youth is ready to enter upon the obligations of manhood in the rite of *hanmdepi,* he stands high and alone without priestly interference till he hears a holy message.

The Christians even consider certain churchly garments and vessels as having magic, and they are terrified without the use of the formulae which their medicine men repeat in order to drive evil spirits away from couches of the newly married and the corpses of their dead. That it is doubtful whether the Christian barbarians can ever be civilized is indicated by their fear of black cats, of walking under ladders and of the number thirteen.

Yet it is not these moral dwarfs whom we should rebuke, but ourselves, that we should endure being cheated by them, that we do not rise and cleanse the world by eliminating them.

Improvidence and Dirtiness

The whites, who insist that the frugal Indian is "shirtless and shiftless," are so wasteful that they have come near to ruining the world. In twenty years, any white farmer will move ten times, because he is so incompetent that he cannot provide continual sustenance.

Where the Indian builds a light tent that can be destroyed for cleanliness, the whites live in structures of cracked wood or brick which in a year become horrors of vermin and incrusted filth and which are littered with the tons of supplies which they require to keep from freezing and starving.

The poorest Indian will invariably make a steam bath, with just a couple of stones and a gourd of water, but my experience of the white frontiersmen, including the missionaries, is that they do not get a complete bath once a year, and so develop the characteristic odor which the more intelligent races find so revolting.

Senseless Love of War

Instead of such gay and knightly contests as the Dakota have with the Ojibway, in which our young men are trained to valor and loyalty and not so many as a dozen are killed in a year, all the whites have constant *mass* warfare, Americans against British.

French against Spanish, with the godlessness of artillery, so that millions, women and children along with the men, are slaughtered. Nor are they brave, like the Indians, but cower in large forts till they are forced out to fight.

Greed and Commercialism

Most Indians hold in common everything except clothes, weapons, tents and food, and even these, by custom and our pure hearts, we constantly share. Especially, we hold in common all land, as lent to us by God. But the whites devote their highest energies to taking possessions from one another, greedily hiding such supplies as they cannot use.

The idea of "commerce," of a lifetime of profiting by the needs of others, is so incomprehensible to nearly all Indians that we do not quite grasp its horror even when we see it close at hand, among the white traders. The whites snarl at what they call our "begging" when we are hungry, yet they extensively do the same thing, under the name of "selling."

This is a form of begging based not upon humility but upon bullying, deceit and a vulgar cultivation of that mental corruption called "the Fashion." Of recent years, I am told, this form of begging is developing into something called "Advertising," which is too corrupt for me to explain.

Gambling and Lying

Many Indians are given to gambling but almost never to the extent to which it prevails among all "civilized" whites, who risk their very children's bread not only with cards and dice but in such gigantic games as stock speculation and real estate. It is probably this recklessness which breeds their almost universal lying. Among us, a liar is often driven from the tribe, but the degenerate whites regard the skillful lying of their political leaders with amusement and even admiration.

Lack of Common Sense

This is nowhere else so well shown as in their voluntary endurance of such rackingly uncomfortable and ridiculously ugly garments as boots, corsets, rigid hats, tight collars. If they so torture themselves, is it any wonder that they torture others?

Lewdness, Incontinence and Position of Women

An astounding unwholesomeness universal among the whites is their practice of keeping up, by disgusting stimuli, the creative instinct which, among the American Indians and all other decent peoples, is entirely seasonal, as a response to nature. Where a Dakota answers the mating call as does a bird or a wolf, among the whites a vile and itching lewdness is aroused all the year round by women's unchaste dress, by perfumes, by indecent dancing and, most horrible of all, by the suggestive rites and hideous jesting of public marriage.

Among us Dakota, marriage is a strictly private business between a man and a woman who, if they find themselves sanely attracted to each other, steal away for a time to the sanctity of the grove, the valley, the wind-harping mountaintop, and there, in the sight only of the stars and clouds and Wakantanka, consummate their holy union. That such a mystery should be attended with the giggling and lip-smacking of a pack of nervous clergymen, tittering children, prurient virgins and vicariously orgiastic old men and women is, to any Dakota, the final devil's dance of white shamefulness.

Whether as cause or effect of this unnatural parade, among the whites a woman is merely a slave, though she may ostensibly be crowned with poetry and insincere honors.

Our women are entirely "feminine." It is they who tell our toddling children the graceful Indian tales of the exploits of animals which so strongly contrast with the grotesque white fables of ogres and giants. Yet socially our women have absolute equality. They vote in council, they own the family tent. They work hard, but it is by their own desire, for they regard the idle white woman, sitting among her provocative adornments, as a prostitute.

Indians are shrewd observers, and find the pompous white men laughable, and one of us should now devote himself to the study of whether the childish or disgusting traits of the European-British-American whites are not due to their lack of any native religion of their own. Their present faith they took from the Jews, which is why, in their feeling of guilt, they treat the Jews so badly.

It is not the smallest source of our hatred for them that they should urge their borrowed and fable-crammed religion (or rather, set of clashing religions) upon us as being superior! It is as though Mohammedans should conquer an Ohio village, seize the land, announce that all the villagers are dirty and superstitious, and then expect them humbly to accept Mohammed as their loving redeemer!

We do admire the figure of the Lord Jesus Christ, whose humble life among peasants must have made him very much like any Indian today. Like us, he was democratic, uncommercial, fond of stories and feasting and laughter. It is my notion that we should add him to our religion, and we certainly could do so with propriety. When Christ died, there were no "Christians."

Those sour and grasping zealots do not deserve a beautiful young god like Jesus. He would enjoy belonging to one of our soldiers' lodges. He was gay, yet he must have been hard and reasoning and warlike as we are, for he faced death on the cross grimly, as a Dakota would. Ours is a religion for *men,* not for soft and whimpering women kneeling before a gilt statue or a text lettered with forget-me-nots.

Perhaps, however, Jesus already *has* lived among us, many times under many names, without our understanding him any better than the whites do. But at least we would not associate him with damp little boys smirking over Sunday-school cards in a chalky classroom or a priest buttoned in black or a wheezing clergyman with liver spots, but with great storms and waterfalls and the shining brightness of the snakes.

We should adopt Jesus boldly, and send missionaries to explain him to the whites, except that no Indian except one very old and sick and never much good in warfare would be pompous enough to tell alien peoples what he thinks they should believe.

Bible Belongs to the Indians

I have been studying the Bible which was given to me at Oberlin, and it has become clear that the ancient Hebrews were among the ancestors of the modern Indians, and that their book, the Old Testament, belongs to us. The Hebrew ideal of the manliness and joy of war, as carried on by a few brave champions going out to challenge the enemy and not by hordes of men armed with cannon, is that of the Indians today and not of the whites.

Pursuing this further, I made a discovery which should startle the world and perhaps revolutionize history, and it is this: The Old Testament condemns the whites for their future treatment of the Indians and definitely prophesies that they will be wiped out.

The coming of the false white invaders is thus prophesied in the book of *Habakkuk* in the Bible:

"I raise up the Chaldeans, that bitter and hasty nation, which shall march through the breadth of the land, to possess the dwelling-places that are not theirs. They are terrible and dreadful . . . their horses also are swifter than the leopards and are more fierce than the evening wolves."

And in *Joel* is an astounding picture of the future railroads, which will be the last stage of the devastation of the Indians—*unless we rebel!*

"Like the noise of chariots on the tops of mountains shall they leap, like the noise of a flame of fire that devoureth the stubble . . . The earth shall quake before them; the heavens shall tremble."

But also in *Joel* the promise is given by God that we shall in time drive out the white invaders:

"Then will the Lord be jealous for his land, and pity his people. Yea, the Lord will answer . . . 'I will remove far off from you the northern army, and will drive him into a land barren and desolate, with his face toward the east sea, and his hinder parts toward the utmost sea.'" (That is manifestly Lake Superior. "' . . . And I will restore to you the years that the locust hath eaten. . . . Then shall Jerusalem be holy, and there shall no strangers pass through her any more.'"

So there, my Indian brothers, is the sacred promise of what is to happen to the white devils, once we arise like men, like the men our grandsires were, and drive them from our land forever! Ponder it, tell it, repeat it, in every coulee, every canoe, every lodge! The Lord is with us and bids us strike for him and for our homes!

Aaron laid down the manuscript book, stared at Black Wolf and wondered, "Do you honestly think that all of this—*any* of this— is true?"

"It's as true as anything you ever read by white people about the Indians!"

"Mm."

"Will you help me get it published?"

"No."

"It might move the white race to get out of our country. They must have *some* decency left! Will you?"

"No."

"Or it might warn them what could happen. It isn't just a playful argument! If all the Indians on the continent unite, there won't be one white man alive from Hudson Bay to Mexico."

"Then we'll have to fight you, even those of us who hate it. I'll do all of the little I can to bring justice to the Indians—I agree they haven't had it—but I'm not going to betray my own people and spy for the enemy, even if they have a good case. I don't love traitors for virtue's sake any more than I do traitors for pay."

"Will you show my book to Harge?"

"No."

"I demand that you do."

"No. I'm your friend, even if I'm not your fellow-traveler on this desperate journey. The Squire would certainly send to Fort Snelling for soldiers to arrest you."

"On what charge?"

"None."

"The bastards!"

"Wolf, you can't first declare that all whites are swine and then be surprised if we're a little swinish. I oughtn't to do even this for you, but I warn you that you better take your book out of here and hide it before I tear it up."

"You think you could?"

"Oh, yes."

Black Wolf studied Aaron's hands, shoulders, eyes. He snatched up his manuscript and clumped out of Aaron's room.

"I wonder," mourned Aaron, "if a good many of the crazy things he wrote aren't true?"

42

THE subtleties of treason bedeviled him for days. It was true that the Dakota had been robbed and ridiculed, and to refuse to help Black Wolf might be treason to that truth. But to help him, conceivably in some small way to share in an Indian uprising which would kill thousands of whites, would be treason to his own roof-tree, and that—not being utopian to the splendid degree of insanity —he could not do.

He tormented himself with "But suppose you were a Southern planter and became convinced that slavery was evil, and there came a war. Which side would you be on?"

Never after that, though he was to be known as an abolitionist of parts, could he hate the Southerners with the rage that was to be stylish among the Radicals and the Lowdowners and the High-handers and the Perfectionists in general.

On an evening when he sat alone with Huldah—the Wherrymans had gone over to the Speezers' for a good racy game of jackstraws and a little breadcrust coffee and Calvinism—he groaned, "Why have I got to be a traitor to *anybody?*"

"Whaaaat?"

"How did I ever get into this reform business anyway, and get made a traitor?"

"Aaron! My dear! What is it that's worrying you? Tell Mother!"

She stretched her arms wide and, unthinking, he laid his head on her shoulder, conscious of the round of her breast, and she affectionately closed her arms around him.

"I just get unhappy about our bullying of the Indians," he said. "And then, prob'ly I'm lonely here. But not when I'm with you. You're very comforting!"

"Am I, Aaron? I want to be. And . . . Listen!" She whispered it, lips warm and moist at his ear. "The Squire has proposed to me. Shall I marry him?"

"Oh, no! That old stuff?"

His open palm lay on her knee, and she let it lie there while she murmured closely, "He needs me, and I don't think you do. Nobody needs me but Balthazar."

"Bal-tha-zar! Oh, no! In his silk hat!"

"Aaron, you don't love me the least bit!" He kissed her shoulder, though the coarse woolen of her dress scratched his lips. She was warm and arousing, and he was sure that in a moment he would be muttering, "Let's slip up to your room. They won't be back for an hour."

But he could not mutter it, could only half-think it. A vast emptiness and inertia held him. He longed for her, but hated his longing; he embraced her again, but snarled at himself, "Stop it! Don't get trapped! For her poor decent sake. And yours. Don't! But I want to sink deep, deep into her. I love her! I do . . ."

And at a noise at the door he sat up with the utmost alacrity and relief.

Black Wolf had come in, and Black Wolf looked hostile. Aaron was pleased by the safety of a probable battle.

"Gadd," said the Wolf, "I got news that there's one of your damned white men sick at a Yankton camp, over beyond Big Stone Lake. They think he's a missionary. I'll guide you, if you want to look after him. Coming?"

"I am!" cried Aaron, smiling lavishly on Huldah while he was sick inside with the thought, "A traitor to her, too!"

At five next morning, in a grayness of falling snow, in slippery darkness, he was riding a pony behind Black Wolf's, stooped over the pony's head with a buffalo robe covering him. When they camped that night, he discovered that the Wolf had his polemic manuscript with him, and while he did not insist, was willing to discuss it further. . . . And Aaron learned that the avoidance of literary criticism is grimmer than hunger and trails lost in the snow.

The Yankton tribe of Sioux were still dependent on buffalo hunting. Their permanent camp was on a sandy river edge, their tipis shrugging shoulders under the snow blasts of the plains, and they considered the Bois des Morts Wahpetons and the other Minnesota Indians as effete Easterners. They had had no wars with the Wahpetons in many years, but there had always been little matters of horse-stealing, and they looked bleak and waited coldly when Black Wolf rode in, guiding Aaron.

The Yankton dialect of Dakota sounded to Aaron thick and inelegant as they talked with Black Wolf, who presently explained, "They say this ghost they have here is a real *wakan* man, very sacred, even though he is white and quite young, and they wanted to know if you could be trusted to take care of him. God forgive me, I lied, and said you were loyal to the Indians and to compassion. You! You are loyal only to Lanark and Harge and your invading army!"

Aaron was impatient—also cold. "All right, all right! I'm a traitor! Let's see this lost white man."

The Wolf shook his head. "Gadd, I used to think you were with us, seeking the truth!"

"So did Brother Harge. Come on—*come on!*"

In a tipi, on a pile of blankets on the softest of dry grass, with an ancient Yankton woman sitting by him, was a boy of twenty-one or -two. He was half-unconscious; the Yanktons said he had been so for days, perhaps in a holy trance. There was no doubt of his being "white," once they had washed his face, weather-buffed and yet pale white, pearl white, with small and precise features and a pointed widow's-peak of black hair above his student's-forehead.

He was fragile, apparently not very tall, and his closed eyelids

277

were unusually heavy. They opened once, and the lost youth seemed to be studying Aaron in bewilderment, and his small, soft mouth pursed in timid supplication. His eyes were large and dark, and his wild look full of anxiety. When his lids slowly closed again, his face was blanked out as if by death.

"Why, this is a girl!" cried Aaron.

The Wolf, who had been standing in wonder, his hand on his mouth, doubtfully translated this to the close-edging Yanktons and the proprietary beldam. They chuckled, and the Wolf explained, "No, she says this is no girl!"

The old woman pushed down the blankets a bit. The boy was wearing what seemed to be the tattered and muddy remnant of a monk's robe, such as Aaron had seen in pictures. To his questions the Yanktons answered, through Black Wolf, that the boy did not seem to be ill. They thought he had been lost and nearly starved; they had found him lying in a coulee. He had no identification except one small book, which Aaron found to be a New Testament with a cover set with ivory but with no name written in it.

On the boy's shoulders Aaron noticed something like furrows from a whiplash. This looked dangerous; he was worried. He ran his hand over the shoulders, encountered a thin strip of wood, and found that bound to the boy's back, set with short, blood-crusted spikes, was a wooden cross.

He looked sharply at the Indians. They nodded as though, yes, this means of penance and torture was quite the correct thing for a *wakan* man. Aaron reflected angrily, "My God, yes, for all of Black Wolf's pious rhetoric, their religion is inhuman! I hate them all! Encouraging this young fanatic to torture himself in their insane idea of . . . Oh. Oh, yes! It's *our* religion that did *this!*"

The Yanktons explained that the cross was evidently a means of *Hanmdepi* mortification. They had been afraid to take it off or even to bathe the boy. They also said placidly that if Aaron interfered, they would have to kill him—right now.

278

Black Wolf suggested, "Try to look like Harge—solemn and half-witted—and I'll tell 'em that you're also a *wakan* man, of the same lodge as this initiate, and that it's your sacred duty to take that torture instrument off him. Oh. Remind me to read you something out of my book about the superstitions of the Christians, will you?"

"Oh, shut up and get on with your mummery, will you!" said Aaron furiously. He was not serene. It had come to him strongly that he was walled in by hostile Indians.

Now Black Wolf was the best orator of the Bois des Morts band, and it was evident from his speech and his gestures that he was presenting Aaron as more holy and insane than the unknown boy, and Aaron guessed from the italics and quotation marks in the Wolf's voice, when he used the word "missionaries," that he was being presented as an enemy to those intruders.

The Yanktons nodded, put a pot of snow on the fire in the tipi, and stood in reverence while Aaron and the old woman stripped the boy to the waist and bathed him. Covering the cross of torture he wore only a buckskin shirt under the monastic robe. His white back, gridironed with scars, was as soft as a baby's.

He opened his eyes, and Aaron fed him rabbit broth from a horn spoon. He went amiably to sleep, and all night Aaron and Black Wolf sat cross-legged near his couch, very stiff, falling asleep, jerking into wakefulness. It was toward morning when the boy said, as quietly as though he had never been asleep, "I feel better. I think I'm going to be all right. I don't know who you are, but our Lord's blessing on you for visiting the sick."

"My name is Gadd. Aaron. I'm at the Plan of Union Mission way east of here."

"Oh, not a bloody cackling Presbyterian dominie!" The fanatic yet collegiate voice was unearthly, in the skin tent with only the tight little fire for light.

Aaron said stiffly, "I am the carpenter at the Mission."

"That's better. Though I've wondered how any man *dared* be a carpenter, like Jesus. For me, it would be too high a calling."

"Mm. Yes. Who are you, Son? All right, I won't call you 'Son' if you don't like it. But . . . Huh?"

The boy's story came out slowly, over a day and a half, while the good Yankton broth and pounded roots (along with what sounded very much like muttered heathen incantations) brought him back from near starvation.

His name was David Queenslace, and he was twenty-two.

He had been born in South Carolina. His father was not wealthy —he insisted on that—but he was well-to-do: a lawyer-planter with a dozen slaves. His father's brother was an Episcopal bishop, throaty but fairly kind. David had once tried to save the bishop's soul, and His Lordship had not liked that.

At ten, David had come on a secret meeting in a locust grove in which an abolitionist from York State risked lynching by instructing the neighborhood slaves over what route to escape northward. Hidden, listening, David had for the first time seen that there were no "Negroes," but only human beings, and that they might not like to be penned like cattle, no matter how charitably. Later, he knew that he had always had some submerged sense of guilt because for three generations his ancestors had kept slaves.

For a few years after that he brooded over his inheritance of sin so frenziedly that he dared not talk about it to his silvery mother, his hard-riding brothers, his father whose favorite phrase was "hard common sense." He did not feel himself one of the family, but a queer foreigner boarding there. He thought that perhaps he was illegitimate.

He went to William and Mary College and was kicked out for preaching abolition. He tried a Quaker college in Pennsylvania and was almost happy there, though he found it too gray and placid, with small sympathy for the visions of God's sensible appearance which were now startling him.

He wanted to be a monk, though the bishop uncle still so menaced him that he had to be an Anglican monk. He heard of Nashotah, a High Church divinity school in Wisconsin, which had been founded equally to prepare missionaries to the Indians and to preserve celibacy and the fine high note of the Anglo-Catholic communion.

In Nashotah, which had wooden walls along with a stone-Gothic feeling, he felt that he was through with trifling. He insisted on wearing a monk's habit, on fervently starving himself, on reading the visions of Suso and St. John of the Cross aloud to his irritated classmates and on fastening to his back the spiked wooden cross.

When his superiors at Nashotah told David to "quit acting like an hysterical virgin," and he said, clear-faced and joyful, "But I *am* an hysterical virgin, as our Lord must have been!" they were irritated into shouting, "Will you quit showing off!"

They also ridiculed (though very nicely) his special monastic garb, pointing out that it combined a little of the Franciscan with the Dominican with the pure South Carolina, and suggested that Heaven might be just as well satisfied if he paid more attention to apologetics and less to scratching his back.

He put away his private robe. They suspected him of wearing the spiked cross at night, but they did nothing till they found that he had gathered in two or three followers, and these young men were spending whole ecstatic nights in prayer, with their arms about one another.

They fired him. Courteously.

He determined to join the Indians. For, he said gently to Aaron, "it was shown to me that they are to be a vessel of God's word and reveal the mystic brotherhood of mankind even to stiff-necked Pharisees like you."

Black Wolf, on the tipi floor, his hands on his ankles like Huldah, squealed, "David! You are the first white man to see the truth!"

David was not quite sure where he had wandered after he had

fled by night from Nashotah. In his robe and sandals, his cross gnawing at his back, a crucifix in one hand and in the other his mother's ivory-bound Testament, he had somehow begged his way across the Mississippi, across Minnesota, across Big Stone or Traverse Lake (Lac Travers it was then), and into this plains country. Apparently he had been "out of his mind," but certainly he had never been out of his soul. The Indians, considering him holy or insane, which to them were the same thing, must have passed him on from tribe to tribe, for perhaps a year now. The last thing he remembered definitely was wrestling with literal devils (they had all been in scarlet, he said, with faces like his father's overseer), and then coming to in this tent, with Aaron looking at him.

David ended, with his somewhat too pretty voice hoarse and weak, "I understand why God preserved me. Now I am to write a new book of the Bible."

"Mm," said Aaron.

"Why not? God's inspiration couldn't 've run out."

"That's so, but . . . "

"The time has come for an Indian or a Negro prophet to lead the bewildered world. We can't conceive any new materialistic ideas, so it is time to turn back to an age of pure faith, under the guidance of an unEnglish race. Black Wolf, perhaps your book . . . You and I will take it and make out of it a new book of the Holy Bible."

"How did you . . . " Aaron had never seen the cool Wolf overwhelmed by astonishment or by affection before.

"I don't know how I knew of your book," David marveled. "It must have come to me from God, in my trance. I don't know how I knew your name, but Wolf, we shall write the book together and it shall change the whole world—and the good Gadd shall be our first disciple, eh?"

"Yes!" rejoiced Black Wolf, while Aaron vigorously said nothing. He guessed that, without meaning to lie about it, David had heard them talking of the book in the night. He wondered whether St. Paul's friends had been as hostile to his inspirations as he was now to David's and the Wolf's.

All the way back to the Mission, to which the fast-recovering David rode on a borrowed pony, Black Wolf and David made a business of new, wonderful and unchecked prophecies, while Aaron felt more out of it than he ever had in the house of Elder Harge.

43

WHEN David Queenslace was brought to the Mission, Squire Harge was surprisingly cordial. He croaked, "I'd far rather see someone who was mad for love of Christ than all you critical know-it-alls!" He looked fondly at David, now wearing an old corduroy suit of Mr. Speezer and meekly holding a skein of yarn while Bessie wound it.

Said Aaron privily to Harge, "Do you know who he makes me think of? Mercie!"

A shock of loneliness and loss and futility came into the Squire's blunt face as he groaned, "Yes, the same unworldliness, like a flower; not like us tough battlers against Satan. I miss Mercie—great jingo how I miss her! Sometimes in the watches of the night I cry to the Lord that I don't know how I can go on without her. That's why I need the sympathy that Miss Huldah has been kind enough to give me.... Young man, I hope you see how God's work here would suffer if I didn't have Huldah upholding my hands."

"Oh, yes." Aaron got a fair degree of fervor into it, while he hastily tried to remember whether his own current policy was to love Huldah or to escape her.

At the other end of the living-room, Bessie—and it must be remembered that she was now almost twelve, which is an age of responsibility, in a frontier mission—was attending to the mystic:

"Why, David, you do so believe in the Pope!"

"No, I'm supposed to be an Episcopalian."

"Supposed to be! What kind of talk is that? You have reservation of the host, don't you?"

"Not in most of our churches. Some."

"There! You see! You're a papist! And the Pope is the anti-Christ! *Everybody* knows that! I'm scandalously busy with all the baking and the mending, but I'll have to take time and make you a Presbyterian, David. It feels so good when you know you're the only denomination that ain't going to burn in a hell just like a lovely stack of marsh hay burning!"

It was, inevitably, Huldah who most nursed and soothed the still shaky David. He confided to her, early, that he had been blessed with a supernatural sense, and she answered busily, while she knitted socks for him:

"I'm so glad! I'm a mystic, too."

"*You?*" But civilly.

"Oh, yes, and there's so few of us. I can settle down any evening, about a quarter to nine, if there isn't some work I have to do, and get into the presence of God in not more 'n ten or fifteen minutes."

"Really? And what procedure of mysticism do you use, my dear?"

"I sit on the floor and get all easy and comfy, with my ankles crossed . . . "

David was yelling with unmystical mirth. "Oh, Huldah, my dear sweet baby, you do tickle me so! Comfy! Sweet, I'm so sorry, but you couldn't be wronger if you tried to. You're making your body the master of your spirit and trying to placate it, instead of getting rid of it entirely so that its bestial grossness can't imprison the pure *you*. The recommended way is to lie flat on the ground or a cold stone floor, fasting, scourging yourself—though perhaps it's better to stop before you actually faint—and so get rid of all desire, so humiliate your disgusting body, that it seems to die and frees your spirit to rise and plunge into the Universal and Eternal."

Huldah breathed, "Oh, yes, I see. I'll have to try that. Do you think it would be better to torture myself quite a lot? I don't know as I'd sleep so well if I did."

"But none of this," said Davy, "is so important as the philosophical concept. Mysticism is the ecstatic intuition of the ineffable one, which rays out from its supra-essence an image of itself which constitutes the idea of the perceptible world."

"Oh, *yes!*" Huldah said admiringly.

To Harge's distress and to the worry of Aaron, remembering Black Wolf's threat, the Wolf came constantly to see David.

That busily moral bisexual monastery, the Mission, dissolved into layer beneath layer of religious fantasy, with the Wolf and David being messianic, Harge skittishly trying to persuade the Young Southern Gentleman to become a Scotch reformer, David leading Harge to the Gregorian chant and Huldah tenderly embracing both sets of fratricidal doctrines.

——Huldah and the old man both going crazy. Couple of temporary virgins that don't like it. The Lord sure calls me to do something.

It was a relief when Harge took him aside with:

"Aaron, I need your help. I been thinking I'd like to marry Huldah, and I believe she'd have me, except she listens to your hooptedoodle so much. Then I'd retire from mission work, in couple years, and get me a nice little white church somewheres, say in Ioway, and advance the Kingdom among decent white folks, for a change. Will you quit foolin' around her and help me—really help her, too, by lettin' her get settled?"

"I'll help you if I can."

"That's mighty fine of you, my boy, mighty fine and Christian! And how about you? It's struck me sometimes that you don't really have the final calling to go on and be ordained. How about law? If you'd study and get admitted to the bar, you'd be on the spot when Minnesota Territory gets going. Be glad to help you— *me and Mrs. Harge!*"

Aaron had a crawly thought of Huldah as *Mrs. Harge,* ironed out as the sharer of Harge's apocalypse and Harge's bed, taking on that pulpy plumpness which is the same as arid skinniness, and all her bounty dissipated as the Pastor's Wife. He found his part in this holy plot excessively distasteful. But he could express it only by a stumbling:

"No, no, thanks, Squire; haven't got any special fancy for the law, and—uh . . . Look! You understand I've got nothing to do with how Huldah makes up her mind!"

"Oh, manifestly, my boy! All I mean is, don't go foolin' and fumblin' around with her when an earnest servant of the Lord has given her his trust and affection!"

Aaron coughed.

He gathered that Black Wolf and David thought they wanted to go far west to the Tetons, most obdurate of the Sioux tribes, and among them found an Indian theocracy. He was astonished by their ingenuity in religion, their courage in adventure, their childishness in government.

They wanted him to come along as a future ambassador from their New Zion to the savage white nations.

"Yes, yes, we'll see," he told them, speaking as a ripe man of fifty.

The Speezers invited him to supper. They were hot with the latest thing in theology: a young Dane named Kierkegaard. Herbert Henry sighed:

"To handle this New Theology—combine science and revelation —that could be my meat just as much as any tow-headed Danish farmer! Him and his existentialism! It makes me want to wander again in the jeweled garden of theology. Why, I almost forget the precious words—monophysitism, Agnoetae, henotheism, homoiousian.

"I don't want a church in the States. I tried it! Cranky old women.

and bankers trying to run you. One noble comfort carries missionaries through everything: we're so obviously superior in every way to all of these barbarians around us.

"I would like to show the world how a man can be a modest missionary and at the same time a big-bug theologian, translated into all languages, with all these famous church-orators copycatting him. Oh, how I could knock out these confounded Arminian Methodists, with their crazy Free Will! I could do them up brown!

"Now, Aaron, if you could just study yourself and get ready to be ordained, then you and Mrs. Speezer and me could make a partnership of it. Get Harge sent back east—the old fellow really deserves a rest. But you could keep Huldah, if you wanted to. Nice woman, I'm sure—quite a steady worker. Well, what do you think, Brother Aaron?"

A month before, Aaron would have told him what he thought, Brother Herbert, but he was becoming appallingly well trained in canonical politics. Well, he said—yes, he said—well, he'd *see*.

At home he contemplated the embarrassing truth that Harge, Huldah, the Speezers, Lanark, Pascal Jones, Father Gear at Fort Snelling, Black Wolf and David had all told him that he was an uncommonly fine fellow and they wanted to use him.

"But I don't notice any of them begging me to be the captain. I must be a born corporal!" he jeered. "Huldah is the only one that thinks I might do something on my own—and I've given her up to Harge, to warm his slippers for him."

He was finding the simple frontier too complicated, and it increased the complication to have Huldah look timidly at him that night, lips defenseless, and to whisper that she had, for the third time, refused Harge's hand in honorable matrimony.

She was clearly waiting for him to say something pertinent. He was frightened. He really did not want to cheat Harge nor to join any conspiracy against him.

He bolted.

With David Queenslace for guest, the women of the Mission had an extra joy in their preparations for Christmas. For the tree they gilded pine cones, made grotesques out of the lead foil from a tea chest sent in a donation box from the Waterbury Missionary Society.

The gifts were to be mittens, moccasins, red hair-ribbons—luxuries which had been hidden away for months. Squire Harge drew Aaron into his study-workshop and in huge palm displayed an old gilt locket edged with seed pearls.

"What do you think, Son? This is about the last treasure that Mercie had left. Got her father's picture in it. I don't approve of Christmas—it's a pagan holiday, and at this critical time when the rage of Satan threatens to overwhelm the bulwarks of true religion, we can't afford to temporize with paganism. But . . . Shall I give this as a Christmas gift to Huldah?"

"Don't!" cried Aaron, while Harge stared in surprise.

Two days before Christmas, Bessie worried to Aaron, "I can't find Davy anywhere, and he only had what clothes we gave him."

Assembled in alarm, in moccasins and blanket coats, the men searched every building and the ravines and scanty woods nearby.

"That youngster could 've gone out of his head again and wandered way off," said the Squire.

Jake discovered wind-sifted double tracks leading off across the lake. "I'll bet Black Wolf come and got Davy and took him off to his tipi," he suggested.

They plodded through a vexation of slanting snow to the tipi and found there only Her Door and her son. She would explain nothing till, in bad Sioux, Aaron recalled to her that he was Black Wolf's friend, and Davy's, and could wish them nothing but good.

She burst out (Speezer translating) with, "Soldiers coming from Fort Snelling. They will be here tomorrow. A Dakota spied them and ran here to tell us. They are going to arrest Black Wolf because he talks against the Government. David and he took food, rifles, blankets, and went off to hide. I don't know where. I don't know! You can torture me, but I don't know!"

"Davy could die, out in the snow," said Aaron.

All of day before Christmas, though it was the Sabbath, the whole Mission talked furiously and quite futilely about where David might have gone and what to do about it. They were at Harge's, late that afternoon. Looking out the window, Mr. Speezer squealed, "They're coming! Soldiers! Black Wolf was right!"

Down the bluff to the Mission, on snowshoes, dragging supply sleds, trudged a file of six dragoons. When they were close at hand, Aaron saw that their leader was no sergeant but no less a warrior than Captain Amos Pipman of the *S. B. Dr. Franklin,* that mighty man of mighty black mustache.

Indoors, the Captain said, "How do! How do! I take it that this is the Bois des Morts Mission. My instructions are to find Doctor Harge."

The Squire was pleased by being doctored as only the non- or recently-doctored can be.

"And if it isn't my dear steamer friend Albert Gadd! *Well!* This is a sight for sore eyes, amid the untenanted wilds, to find a true Protestant mission. I was sent out with this escort, which from a military standpoint is a damn-fool waste of manpower, under instructions to find a young divinity student named David Queenslace. He's wandered off, crazy, and his uncle, who is a bishop—an office savoring of papistry—is raising the Old Ned with the Government. Soldiers sent out making a ruckus just when the Indians are all fidgety! But there you are—orders is orders—or so I hear. Have you got him concealed anywheres about you?"

Upon explanation, the Captain grunted, "If the young gentleman has come to his senses, such as they are, and gone off again deliberately, nothing I can do. I'll go back to Snelling. Oh. Here come the rest of my escort. And a passenger."

They opened the door to look out on a sergeant with three more soldiers and a dog sled jingling with Christmas-sounding bells, and seated on it, bright-eyed under her sable cap, waving her sable gauntlet to them, was Miss Selene Lanark.

44

HULDAH—Harge—the Mission—mystic exercises—Black Wolf—David—they all blew up as he looked at Selene and stood alone with her on a mountain top in a storm of exploding stars.

She sprang from the dog sled and came skipping into the Squire's living-room, throwing open her beaver coat to display a New York traveling-costume of brown wool, up-to-date and daring, with the skirt at least three inches above her feet and with a row of brass buttons from neck to hem. With the cordiality of the New York aristocrat, she held out her hand.

"*Dear* Squire Harge, it's *wonderful* to see you! What *wonderful* new buildings you've built! ... And *Aaron!* I didn't know whether I'd *find* you here! Isn't it *wonderful!*" Her warmth dropped fifty degrees. "How're you, Bessie?"

Reflected Aaron, "I do love her, I guess. But why does she have to be so hoity-toity?"

He watched Huldah watch the fluttering fashion-plate—a Huldah grave, serene, less irritated than pitying.

Squire Harge tried to be disapproving of Selene's airiness, but anything so young and feminine delighted him, and she brought out just the right proper regrets for Mercie. He held her thin hand, his smile expanding and warming.

She had not seen the Speezers or Huldah or Jake and Anna since she had been a lamb of fifteen, but she exclaimed now, so that they almost believed it, that she had dreamed of them, missed them *oh* so much. They shone on her, even though she did distinctly call Anna "Hannah."

But it was on Aaron that she lavished most of her amiability.

"When I see you, it's just as if I were back at Eliot House, in the dear hills. I vow, I do get homesick for it!"

"Then you didn't care so much for New York?" he said hopefully.

"Oh, I did *so!* And I'll have you to know—" She curtsied. "—that I was a monstrous success in that dizzy whirl! My aunt has *the* most elegant house—on Thirteenth Street, very fashionable—and I met the Astors and Brevoorts and everybody, and I went to *so* many dances—oh, I loved 'em—cotillions and contra-dances and the three-step waltz—and I will request you to note, Mr. Aaron Gadd, that a real Italian count, or *conte* as we say in Italian, fell most howlingly in love with me, but he was very poor and I gave him the mitten.

"Oh, New York is *the* most *exquise* city, and I'm going to make Papa take me back there to *live!* That's why I've come. An *agonizing* journey! And now, dear Captain Pipman, will your men be so sweet and darling and take me on to Castle Lanark?"

She was off, shaking her sable muff in farewell.

"Heartless!" said Luna Speezer.

"Play actress!" said Anna Wherryman.

"No. Just young," said Huldah. "Young and motherless. A half-educated, half-heathen-Sioux, with a sneering father, and us gossips gawking at her like owls! No wonder the poor child tried to show off!"

Aaron wished, then, that he had not promised Harge to fall out of love with Huldah. Of Selene he could only think, with an agitation returning and fading every moment, that she was *there.*

The private soldiers were inviting themselves to lodge with Caesar Lanark, but Captain Pipman, that joyful Baptist, begged to stay at the Mission, and he rubbed his hands at the thought of Christmas Eve among the Children of Light, though of the dimmer or Presbyterian light. In the honored Harge guest-room he stripped

293

off the fur coat, fur cap and dungarees he had worn on the trail, and came out in dress-coat with epaulets and sash and sword; a true West Pointer, big, red-faced, mustached like a handful of tar; a veteran of the Mexican and Seminole Wars.

Huldah, glowing to find this Son of Mars also an evangelical of the most virtuous brand, urged him, "Now you've helped civilize the Mexicans, you'll follow the path of peace, won't you, Captain? You won't stay in the Army?"

"That's my call to duty, Sister Purdick."

"But it says in the Word that they that take the sword shall perish with the sword."

"Well, you don't use swords much in modern machine warfare, and anyway, you wouldn't want to perish with chicken pox in bed, would you?"

"The Lord told Peter to put up his sword."

"Of course. Peter was just a volunteer—curse of the army."

As Huldah had no other military texts immediately available, she merely looked annoyed, and said spitefully, "I'll bet your wife doesn't feel that way."

"Haven't any wife, Ma'am. Got struggle enough trying to be a student of the impenetrable ways of both the War Department and the Lord, and trying to make my fellow-officers and the men curry their language. In this modern era, when so many folks are trying to put their reason in the place of God's revelation, most of the army get pretty sluggish spiritually—drinking and blaspheming— better on their toes than on their knees—think they can bully the Sioux into morality, instead of praying with them, as you and Dr. Harge do."

Luna Speezer inquired nervously, "Are we going to take all the land west of the Mississippi away from the Sioux? What do they say at the Fort?"

"Don't you worry your lovely head. Stands to reason that the

Government of these United States, a nation founded on the rock of freedom, ain't going to rob and abuse a lot of unfortunate Indians—not without giving them a handsome present in return. That's what we're known for abroad; our strict justice to every race and condition of man."

Christian philosopher though he was, Captain Pipman was full of manly fun. He set the delighted Bessie on his knee and told her of saving Mexico from the horrors of monarchy and Catholicism; in chummy talks with Harge and Aaron, he admitted his worries about salvation, the breeding of cavalry horses and the surprisingly frequent gas on his stomach.

And without too much prodding from Aaron he said that though Miss Selene had been fluttery at first, she had taken the cold journey from Snelling like a Viking.

The special church service on Christmas morning was joyous. They sang *When I Survey the Wondrous Cross*. Captain Pipman stood lofty, with his long saber at his side, raising his great head to stare reverently up at the thin rafters and lifting his great voice in song to challenge Satan. He insisted on sharing his hymn book with an old Dakota woman who stood next to him. She looked at it gratefully. She could not read.

She peeped round at his sword, then up, way up, in wonder at his mustache. Suddenly he winked at her and joggled her arm, and the old woman dissolved in giggling.

Aaron thought, "That's a splendid fellow and no prig. Ought I to become a soldier?"

Halfway through the service, just as the Squire was starting to preach, he stopped like a man with a heart-attack, he gaped at the door. Aaron turned about to see Selene bountiful with smiles and Caesar Lanark like a grand-opera Russian, with tall astrakhan cap and a broadcloth coat over which cascaded the splendor of his beard, that awesome natural phenomenon. The congregation, white and Indian, gave one soft sigh and watched the imperial pair in full sail to a seat.

So Brother Harge, who had begun to prove in the Dakota language that Christmas was a proof of divine providence, switched to an even more vigorous protestation in English that God is less impressed by any beauteous ballet-girl than by the virtuous daughters of the poor. The sermon kept hovering, fascinated, about the eye of a needle.

Lanark knew the closing hymn; he joined in it, and his assured voice, Aaron regretted, made Pipman's sound a little boisterous and simple.

Selene just hummed, and smiled at Aaron, and he did not quite know what to do with the smile.

The Indians quickly slipped away after service, apparently less in awe of the priests than of the trader. Pipman seemed to know that Lanark was a man of light and leading, an unofficial part of the Government, and when Lanark thanked him for escorting Selene, the Captain shouted, "Oh, it was a privilege! The young lady certainly brightened our dull military company!"

The Aaron who had just been envying him thought, "Pipman is a clodhopper! No, I'll never be a soldier! Toadying to those gilded peddlers! Selene so lovely—so cold—so vain!"

Lanark spaciously addressed them all: "I'd like to have everybody come to my fort tomorrow, Tuesday, about six, for a modest Christmas feast to welcome my child's return."

Captain Pipman said, "I'm truly sorry, sir, but I must get my men started off early tomorrow."

Harge was staring at his flock. The Speezers looked regretful, Jake and Anna and Huldah looked chilly, Aaron felt that he probably looked blank. Harge said gravely, "I don't think we'd better, Mr. Lanark."

Aaron rejoiced, "The Squire has courage! Hurrah! We'll show

these money-changers!" Then he saw that all the Christmas merriness had fled from Selene's face. She pleaded, "But *you*, Aaron?"

Everybody circled on him; everybody stared. Huldah shook her head at him like a cautioning wife, and Harge shook his head like a partner at cards. That helped.

——Oh, these little people that figure they can get more out of the rich by snubbing them than by sucking up to them! To make Selene suffer because her father's a swindler . . .

"I'll be glad to come, Miss Selene," he said stoutly.

The entire Mission spent a happy evening forgiving him for being a traitor. It seemed to be his metier.

Captain Pipman had not used all his time at Bois des Morts in being melodious. He was a competent detective. He had inquired of everybody at the Mission and of all the Indians whether David Queenslace was sane now, and well enough to take care of himself.

Aaron took him over to the Indian village, and they were uneasy. Black Wolf's wife was gone, with their tipi, their child, and nothing could be learned of their hiding-place.

Captain Pipman said placidly, "So? Brother Gadd, when the Indian rebellion comes, it will cut quite a caper, I reckon."

45

ASHE listened to the dinner-talk at the Lanarks', Aaron was convinced that this was the way a salon in Paris would sound. And he did not want it.

The dinner itself was not conspicuously grand: buffalo meat, beans and turnips. But Selene wore what must have been one of the New York dresses from her trunk, very grown-up and rich and enticingly prim: tan silk with a basque and a horsehair-stiffened skirt. It had lace undersleeves and an embroidered linen collar fastened with a brooch and, final devastating charm, on her right shoulder was a cluster of artificial lilies-of-the-valley.

After months of seeing linsey-woolsey, this splendor overwhelmed him, but the talk finished him off. They continually asked what he thought, and he knew that neither father nor daughter supposed that he was thinking anything at all.

They went brightly into the character of Louis Napoleon, the results of the surrender of Abd-el-Kader and whether Victor Hugo was a better dramatist than Shakespeare, and all the while Aaron wondered how he could have surrendered Huldah to old Harge. He felt so contradictory by the end of dinner that when Selene flourishingly played Mendelssohn's *Songs without Words,* he could not hear the music; he could think only of nasty things to say which would crush the Lanarks and bring them to their knees begging his pardon for—he wasn't sure for what, but begging it, anyway.

"*Papa* tells me," said Selene, "that you like my cousin, Black Wolf. Isn't he *too* romantic!"

Her father took over: "There are no romantic Indians. They merely seem so because their occupation of hunting appears less tedious than selling cotton goods over the counter—I say *appears,* because an Indian goes to his hunting just as prosaically as a factor goes to his office or a dull preacher to his pulpit. As for danger, any Indian sensibly takes care to avoid it. Our utopian and darky-loving and redskin-hymning friend Gadd will for once agree with me."

Aaron was certain that Lanark was sneering at him and that Selene was joining in the sneer, as her father pontificated on:

"The typical Dakota is Isaac Weeps-by-Night, who is merely a little ahead of his fellows in giving up hunting for plowing, building a wretched shack and getting drunk on forty-rod whisky. That's what the children of Black Wolf will do . . . if they get born and survive . . . of which I am not too certain, if your dear second-cousin goes on shooting off his mouth!"

Selene looked at Aaron uncomfortably, almost intimately, but he still felt that she would sacrifice him to her father's vanity.

"No, my dear Selene, the romance of the Indians is like the bogus romance of the pioneers. In any state, the first settlers are always the trappers, who are conveniently wiped out by disease and accident and alcohol, then the humble traders like me, then the farmers. Travelers love to picture the farmers as singularly sturdy fellows, but actually, six out of ten breakers of land are no good—otherwise, they wouldn't have fled to the wilderness. They are remembered only on wooden markers in lost prairie cemeteries.

"It's usually the third or fourth possessor of the land who succeeds, after other men have killed the Indians and torn up the buffalo grass for him. It's he who's later known as the founding father. And it's he who will see to it that the squealing of a Black Wolf will get the same attention as that other moan of progress— the bellow of the annihilated buffalo."

"But Mr. Lanark, where do the missionaries come into your picture?" said Aaron.

"They don't!"

"I think you're cynical and horrid!" Selene wailed. But she said it with such fascinated attention that Aaron felt more out of it

299

than ever. With admirable force he vowed that he would get-out-of-this-and-never-come-back-here-again.

It was during his fidgety preparations to get away that Lanark's voyageur, Leon Simonet, came hastily in. In an unsteady hand he held a message penciled on birchbark.

"Letter, sar, from Blackie. He say he hide out. He say we got to leave beans, gunpowder, for him at the spring in the coulee, or will be trouble."

"How did you get this preposterous missive?"

"Stuck to the warehouse door—by an arrow!"

"Where is Black Wolf hiding?"

"Truly, I do not know."

"Find out. Understand?"

Simonet nodded, looked at Aaron with dislike, and slipped away.

Selene was sighing, "The silly Wolf—running away from the soldiers that have already left!"

Lanark's snarl was smooth: "Not utterly silly, my dear. I might have presented him to the military. I still may do. Your Dakota hero is quite insane."

Then Selene looked angry, and Lanark waited for Aaron to go.

When he arrived at the Mission, Aaron found all the adults sitting up, and the Squire trumpeted, "My boy, we would like your blessing! Huldy and I are announcing our engagement!"

"Ur . . ."

"We'll leave for the Fort in a month or so and get hitched there." The Squire jubilantly embraced Huldah, and if she did not look jubilant, she did look content. She said to Aaron with the suavity of whipped cream:

"Yes, I have accepted Bal—the Squire, and we've been waiting up till you saw fit to leave your rich friends, in the hope that you might congratulate us."

Aaron fumbled, "Of course—this touches me deeply—my hope that you will have—and for the Kingdom!"

They seemed to understand him, which was more than he did.

As Huldah and he went up the same ladder to bed—after sister Anna had looked at him with reproach and with an unspoken comment that somehow made him blush—he wondered whether he might kiss Huldah, whether he ought not to. He lay abed longing to perform the pleasant and neighborly deed of going in to call on her. But he forgot Huldah as he reflected that beneath the froth of dinner at the Lanarks' there had been an angry current between father and daughter.

He ought to pacify them. Only, how could he, when he had walked home vowing all the way that he would never see either of them again? Now that he had lost Huldah—and what a fool he had been!—he would go off to St. Paul at once ... Could he catch up with Pipman and his soldiers?

For two days he zealously kept himself from going to the Lanarks' and then, naturally, he went. Early in the evening.

He walked in on a magnificent quarrel between Caesar and Selene.

46

SELENE was not dressed now for the public; she wore a cerise dressing-gown with a gold cord. Aaron was not shocked because he could see so much of her bosom, but because she had been so extravagant. "Young girl like her throwing away dollars and dollars on a vain gaud like that and . . . Aye, but she's pretty in it!" reflected young Mr. Gadd.

Selene threw at him, "You got to help me! I want Papa to come live in New York with me and be civilized! Theaters and museums and broughams and calashes and yellow marble fireplaces and lobster and ladies with ivory parasols and ships going to Europe and everybody talking about the new ideas!"

"Quite!" Mr. Lanark was sardonic. "And don't fail to mention the handsome young men in velvet coats!"

"Papa, you have plenty of money put away so we could live there."

"Yes. I have."

"Oh! You have?"

"Certainly. Aside from my humble depot here, I have dabbled in St. Croix Valley land, in half-breed scrip and in—shall we call it illegal or merely *unofficial* lumbering in the Chippewa country? And you have been my only inordinate expense. I am ready to take a suitable social position, but—*but,* my dear Selene, I do not intend to be lost in the morass of New York or Boston.

"I shall presently adopt the coming metropolis of St. Paul, which is destined to be the largest city west of Cincinnati. In time, I shall be a United States Senator, after I have seen you safely married to some rich but thrifty young millionaire—after I have seen you reigning as the duchess of that charming settlement."

"Pop! I won't do it! I've just seen your St. Paul. It's a heap of logs in a mudpuddle!"

"It will grow so rapidly . . ."

"I don't intend to wait for it. I'm not going to hang around till I'm an old woman of forty before it even has a hotel with velvet sofas! And your idea of a millionaire for me—he'd chew tobacco and wear boots and cal'late as how they's good money in them thar white pine logs!"

Lanark did not sound merry. "Is that your conception of my standard of taste?"

"Yes, for me—not for yourself. You'd just use me to help you get in with the big-money hogs!"

Lanark had shaken his head at her to indicate that she must be discreet in the presence of this young oaf from the Mission. She had ignored the hint and now, in a level fury, he forgot his own caution:

"I need no one to help me! I do use people, and I shall do so far more, but they'll be giants of commerce, not a pert, greensick, half-educated girl, whose only extraordinary trait is her lack of gratitude!"

He stalked to his throne-chair, while she followed him and stood raging: "Not safe to be grateful to you, Pop. I learned that at ten. The only way to handle you is to fight you. You're a little back-woods bully that wants to hang me on the wall and show me off to your fellow tin Caesars in—in St. Paul!"

Aaron intruded and, in a manner not so unlike Squire Harge, re-buked her, "Now, Selene, I've never heard anything so ungrateful!"

"Keep out of this," said Caesar Lanark.

"Go home," said Selene Lanark.

At that moment, Black Wolf and David Queenslace were in the room, not so much entering as materializing. Lanark, on his throne, moved his hand only slightly but in his lap was a long pistol.

David was dressed in something like Sioux costume, but he did not look in the least like an Indian; he looked like a high-school actor playing Indian, eagerly and very badly.

Aaron assailed him, "Where the deuce have you been? We were worried outrageous! Are you all right?"

David's gentle answer was scarcely heard, in the storm Black Wolf was making:

"Lanark! Why didn't you leave the supplies in the coulee, the way I asked?"

"My bellicose young friend, in our humble shop we do not deliver purchases and . . . What the devil do you mean, trying to give orders to *me?*"

"It was careless of me, Colonel Lanark. I merely wanted to save my life from the soldiers—and to prevent any investigation of your business methods. Greetings, Cousin Selene. This is my friend David Queenslace. His father is president of South Carolina. Let me assure you David is fit to meet even the Princess Selene, and he is a priest—the first white prophet to join the Dakotas."

"Now don't you scold me as you do Papa," railed Selene. "I've always loved you very much." To Aaron: "When I was a little girl, Blackie was kinder to me than anybody else. He taught me the little Dakota I know. But he loves making-believe—like Papa. I'm so glad you're grown-up, Aaron. And don't you dare step one step away from here till I've finished my argument with Papa!"

Black Wolf was saying to her, fairly politely, "Did New York seem very great and wise?" when Lanark interrupted him, to question David like a police sergeant:

"Who are you?"

"I'm a divinity student, sir."

"Of course I knew you were at the Mission, but what are you doing on this forbidden ground?"

"I wanted to see if there was anything I could take to the Indians. There isn't! They already have valor, kindness, religious fervor, imagination."

"Quite—quite. Don't you know that this is Indian domain, that you have no right to be here without a license from the agent at Fort Snelling?"

"I didn't think of . . ."

"Then kindly do think! Black Wolf, with his silly trick of hiding

304

you, might have got us all into considerable trouble. Where do you come from?"

So self-confident and magisterial was Lanark that Aaron could understand how, with no guard save his own vigilance and will, he could rule the Indians. David caved in before Lanark as he never had before Aaron or Harge:

"South Carolina, sir."

"Queenslace, I believe the name is? Who's your father?"

"Not a 'president,' as the Wolf generously made him. He's a planter and a lawyer."

"Important at the bar?"

"I don't understand what . . ."

"David, don't get uppity with *me!* I have neither the need nor the desire to pry into your affairs. I want to get the picture of your background, to know how to deal with you. For instance, what sort of money does your father make?"

"I don't know. Twenty or thirty thousand dollars a year, I should think."

"No vast wealth, but he could do something very pretty with Minnesota lands and town-sites, once we get the territory and the larger Indian treaties. . . . Now, my boy, I'm going to send you back home to your father—"

David and Black Wolf gurgled protestingly, together.

"—or else send to the Fort for the soldiers to ship you off—rather less courteously. Meanwhile, you will stay here with me until I can arrange an escort."

David wondered, "Do you know my father?"

"I know everybody! Why?"

"You two talk so much alike. Pomposity without point, and geniality without friendship. You frighten me, as he always did. I think I'd rather go to the brig at the Fort."

But now Selene fluttered down on David, begging him to stay. She knew no one here—well—except for Mr. Gadd. She was lonely.

David and she would have such good talks! He would tell her all about the Dakota and religion and—and everything. Please stay!

She was dizzyingly lovely, and David muttered, "Well—perhaps . . ."

Aaron was eroded with jealousy. These two children of wealth and family libraries were of the same charming age, while he was almost twenty-six now.

Lanark melted. He would talk with David, he promised, about getting the agent's permission to stay, about his learning more of the Indians and, when he should be ready, returning to some Episcopal seminary and being ordained.

David was surprised that Lanark should know he was an Episcopalian.

"Meantime," said Lanark smugly, "we'll get a little more flesh on those bones of yours."

"And get you to smile and not look so holy and woebegone," chanted Selene, most musical, most magical, most sweet.

While Aaron writhed.

"If the Wolf thinks it's all right?" said David.

Black Wolf consented, as though he and Lanark were David's worried uncles. Himself, he was going back to his hiding place, for no matter what they thought, it had been him that the soldiers had been hunting. And he'd just take those supplies along.

Lanark laughed at him.

The Wolf sounded like a wolf. "I warn you people that when you make the big treaties and take all our western lands, we won't find it's worth living, to become second-rate citizens when we would have been first-rate if we'd stuck to the bow and arrow. We're going to fight what you call Civilization and what all the other races call Slavery. Lanark, you've been decent to me—in your nasty way. I warn you to take Cousin Selene and get out of this. The Christians sing about bathing in a fountain filled with blood. They'll get it!"

Black Wolf was gone and, as soon as he saw how Selene hovered over David, so was Aaron.

That night, as he listened to the winter cracklings that do creep through a log cabin, Aaron lay rigid. He knew there might be something more than bluffing to Black Wolf's threats, and he could hear the snap of burning timbers, the screams of dying women. The uneasiness was still over him next morning when he was prosaically chopping wood and Selene appeared, glossy in furs, rosy from the wind, panting from running—and terrified.

"Aaron! I'm a homeless beggar! I mean it! My father has thrown me out!"

"Wh . . ."

"We had such a scene, after you had gone last evening and we'd sent David to bed! I guess it was my fault, I guess I'm spoiled. I said dreadful things. I'm ashamed of everything I've said to criticize him, especially when you were there. But he's so cold, and so *arranging!* I idiotically went on insisting we go to New York—I don't really care one bit about it—I could be happy right here, if he thought I was a girl and his daughter, not just a filly to draw his coach.

"I said I *would* go back east. I'm afraid I stamped my foot. Oh, is it very bad, Aaron, to stamp your foot? I guess it is. But not bad enough to break a girl for, is it? He went all quiet, and he reminded me that by white law I'm a bastard."

"Oh, no!"

"He was only married to my mother by Indian custom—maybe not even by that now, because she up and left him. He told me he'd stayed here in the wilderness and worked so hard for me, and then, like a fool, I said it was only because he enjoyed showing me off. Oh, it's true, but I don't guess we Indian bastards tell white fathers the truth!"

"Dearest Selene!"

"Then he almost hit me. He reminded me he really *is* a Caesar here, and he said by God he'll send me back to my mother's people—I'm to go live in a tipi, where I belong, and haul wood—me that don't speak ten words of Sioux! And then he smiled, so chilly—all his teeth—and he pretended to get awful polite, and he said there was one other thing: Davy has a rich father, and Papa said if I could manage it to marry Davy, I might get forgiven.

"And then he walked out and went to bed, and this morning he's still in his room, and Aaron, I'm scared to death, and I'd rather be a squaw with a drunken man than marry Davy—he's just a sick, desperate child. I'm *scared!*"

Aaron threw wide his arms; she came trustingly to burrow her wet cheek against his shoulder. They clung together like terrified children. She was his pleasant companion of the meadow at Eliot House, and suddenly she was nothing of the kind; she was his girl, his love, of whom he had dreamed passionately all these months of barren chastity. He touched her cheek. Her body was hot and smooth in his arms and they tightened about her; she was flesh, with a fire transmuting flesh.

He was shaky with the desire to have her close to him, within him, after all the distant longing for her. Every inch of his hands upon her shoulders was conscious that he was actually, no more only in dreams, touching the one magic and strange and familiar flesh in the world.

His "Oh!" had more sound of fear in it that of affection—it was not tepid affection at all but a love that would make him kill for her. He tried to laugh at himself for putting on the brute but he knew that there was no question that he would take her from Lanark.

She raised her head to look at him, so close, in confusion. They laughed together, but it was high-strung and uneasy.

He muttered, "I didn't know it could get me like this. My dear!

I'm sort of trembly—insane. And yet we two are the only sane ones in this holy madhouse!"

But he remembered that Huldah, Anna and Jake showed traces of sanity too and, holding Selene's hand, he led her to Jake's cabin and begged of Huldah, "Take care of her till I get back."

But it was Anna who answered, "You bet!"

He quickmarched to Chateau Lanark and into the living-room. Caesar Lanark was being airily conversational with a silent David. Lanark looked at Aaron and yelped, "Oh, for Christ's sake, is it you again?"

Two months before, Aaron would have been touchy and bellicose. Now he said cheerfully, "That's right."

"What the devil do you want?"

"Mr. Lanark, you're a complete bully."

"That sparkling analysis of my hidden ego doesn't answer my question."

"Quite!"

Then Lanark really was furious, for he knew where Aaron had stolen his *Quite,* which is the vitriol-in-the-face of conversation, from the recipe of a gentleman in the county. But Lanark was in bad form. He stammered, "Y-you . . ."

Aaron spoke with a placid evenness which he did not feel at all:

"If Selene has been impertinent, it's your fault—your training in polite viciousness. And if her mother has gone bad—"

"Damned impertinence!"

"—that's your fault, too. Any woman would, living with you. I knew Selene at Eliot House—she was completely gay and excited and innocent. Now you'll find this very funny, Mr. Lanark, but I consider myself her protector, and I intend to keep her safe at the Mission, and don't play with that pistol! If anything happened, we Indians might revive torture at the stake!"

However spurious it was, Aaron had managed to put on something of Lanark's own playful cruelty, and Lanark was not used to that from others. While he hesitated, David sprang up, affectionately put his hand on Aaron's shoulder and urged:

"Oh, Mr. Lanark, Aaron doesn't mean to be saucy. He's such a wonderful friend!"

Lanark's seething stopped. He teased his beard and stared at David like a butcher examining a lamb, and it was to David that he spoke, so lucidly:

"Oh, yes. I see. How naïve I have become in the backwoods! Now I understand, Queenslace, why you could not be more interested in my daughter—or any other female. And I had supposed that it was merely religious mania that made you so skittish!"

What this meant, Aaron had no idea. Apparently David did, for he flushed and ran out of the room.

Lanark looked after him with evil delight, and that gave Aaron time to step quickly, very lightly, to the throne and pick up Lanark's pistol. He stuffed it into his pocket, and neither of them mentioned it as Aaron spoke:

"I see our friend Leon Simonet is hanging around that inside door. Looks like a fight, doesn't it! I haven't had a good one for a year. But that *was* a good one. It was with carpenters' mallets."

Lanark was laughing. "You're a stout lad—for a Calvinist begging-friar. Yes, yes. Not a large chap, but very compact, well coordinated. I think we shall have to give up the delightful vulgarism of a fight."

"All right. And now I want all of Selene's clothes and things. I'll take them to her at the Mission."

Then Caesar Lanark did go maniac:

"You miserable cowshed rustic, you manure-hauling lump—not even good enough to be ordained, like that sod, Harge! You crawl down my chimney and thrust yourself into a discussion between a gentleman and his daughter, whose shoes you ought to be cleaning; you encourage her to make a spectacle of herself and . . . Yes, by

God, I shall give you her things! You've probably had *her* already, the lousy squaw!"

If Aaron did not hit him, it was because he could not—not yet—beat the father of the Selene whom he loved completely and without doubts.

"Take her clothes, and never let me see her or you again!"

Insanely, Lanark was dragging from Selene's room, throwing out of the door, all the dresses she had proudly shopped for in New York. She had packed them so neatly, so excitedly, for her journey to her father, and now they were wrinkled, torn, scattered over the snow.

"Tell that wench if she ever comes sniffing around here again, by God, I *shall* send her off to the medicine feast!" shrieked Lanark, and slammed the door.

Aaron tried to pick up and smooth out the cocky little bonnets, the garments of muslin and linen and silk, which were so frail and charming that he pitied them, and wept for them as if they were living things.

47

SELENE cried quietly as she tried to stroke the wrinkles out of the silk garment lying on her knee. Aaron remembered that it was the tan basque she had worn for her first party dinner at Castle Lanark. She tried to shake the dirt out of the deep embroidery of the lilies-of-the-valley on the shoulder.

"I loved it so, when I got it in New York!" she whimpered.

Huldah trudged into the room and Selene held the dress up pitifully. "It got all ruined!"

Not very sympathetically, Huldah grunted, "Most of us never had any fineries to *get* ruined! We were too poor."

The imperious Selene said sturdily, "Well, if I work at it, I guess now I'll have a chance to be poor as anybody!"

Yet it was Huldah who suggested to her future happy consort, Squire Harge, that they make a place in the Mission for Selene till spring, when she could go east to supposititious relatives.

"And you and me will be going east, too, eh, only for kinda different purposes!" puffed Harge amorously. "So then we'll keep Selly till spring."

Selene was calm. "You may have to keep me a lot longer than that. I better become the best mission-worker that ever was, so you'll want me. I'll have to learn my own Dakota language from you Yankees. *Ega gaga-bazii-ga ha!* I got that from Jake."

It did not sound to Aaron like Jake-Dakota but like Dakota-Dakota. Huldah obligingly inquired, "What does it mean?"

" 'Don't do that to me!' It's a sentence I'll maybe need from now on!"

The Squire was delicate with Selene, as he sometimes was with his own daughter. Regarding reprisals from Lanark, the old county attorney puffed, "I don't intend to take any sauce from him. I feel responsible for having let her come from the decency of Eliot House to the den of that mocker."

When Luna Speezer pantingly hinted, "Is this Lanark girl illegitimate?" Harge said gently, "Was our Lord?"

Between Harge's encouragement and her own kind-heartedness, and possibly a desire to show Aaron what a real woman could be, Huldah adopted Selene complete. She helped Selene mend and iron out her befouled wardrobe; made for her a gingham dress suitable to log cabins; taught her to cook something besides lobster patties.

Selene insisted that she was grateful, and Huldah amiably disbelieved it. But one morning when Aaron got up very early (and at the Mission that meant before half-past-four) to look at a sick calf, he found Selene voluntarily washing Huldah's shift and humming, her stainless hands soaked in rainbow suds. And kissed her!

Huldah shared her room with Selene, and Aaron now had both of these desirable young women rustling at night as they undressed fifteen feet away from him. All that was patriarchal in him rose, and he felt that he would be willing to do chores and hold yarn for both of them forever.

He went to sleep to the faint laughter of the two girls or to their low singing, and realized that the Selene who a week ago had been so airy about "these wonderful new *Dichterliebe* songs of Schumann" was mastering the hymns of the Covenanters.

He said privily to Huldah, "I tell you she has real grit—washing overalls, peeling potatoes, bringing in wood, after the stylish way she's been raised."

"Oh, yes, she's quite brave—only a *bit* spoiled by too much wealth—but we must see how long it lasts. Girls do anything for a while, just for a prank," Huldah explained, a little too sweetly. "She certainly hasn't entirely turned to the path of Satan, like her father, and we must all get together and take care of the child, because she is so ignorant of the simplest truths of the Gospel . . . and she isn't *that* pretty, you know!"

Black Wolf made his inevitable slippery entrance, and before the assembled staff knew he was in the room, he was challenging them, "What have you done with Davy?"

Aaron was anxious. "Isn't he at Lanark's?"

"No. I've scouted the place. Simonet says he ran away from there after something Lanark said. (I'm going to kill that Lanark!) He never came to my cave. Find him!"

Aaron and Jake examined the groves along the lake, the site of the Indian village. They found no trace.

Selene cried, "That boy, out on the prairie, freezing, trying to get to Traverse des Sioux, freezing to death! Unless my father killed him. He might have."

"Silly! Why?" Aaron insisted.

"You're a dear, sweet boy, Aaron. You don't know people that kill just for the fun of it, like a cat. I do. It's in my blood."

She had a note from her father, delivered by a blank-faced Simonet:

"I was rude and intolerant with you, Daughter. If you care to forgive me, it will be a mature act on your part. As I live among slaves and must be ready to crush revolts, I have become somewhat hasty. I regret it.

"I had with parental fondness conceived of you and me in a rapidly expanding St. Paul, enjoying the fruits of my long toil. Your contempt for this fancy made me slightly violent. But it was vulgar drama in me to drive you forth into the storm, complete with shawl, when there was no Unwanted Infant, and I apologize for my tastelessness as well as for my ire.

"Come home!"

She showed the letter to Aaron, shivering, while he kept an arm secure about her. "I tell you I'm *scared* of him! Must I go?"

"You must not! We'll get the Squire's backing."

Harge was beautifully angry. "No! I'm not going to see a fine Christian girl delivered over to that wretch! You'll stay here, my dear child. God help your papa if he thinks that because we can pray we can't fight him and his hireling Injuns. I was a high-class squirrel-shot once, let me tell you. And you're going to be the finest seamstress in the Mission, Selene. I can see a lovely future for you, in a lowly but clean and Christian cot! You stay!"

She stayed.

There began then for Aaron a life of such quiet reasonableness as he had never known. It lasted for three days, which is a good deal in one human existence, and then God laughed.

Aaron was out in the marsh along the Isanti River, searching for a stubborn and cynical stray cow. Entering the marsh was a creek swift enough to keep an open pool in the coldest weather, and he went cautiously; at twenty below zero, it was not safe to go home wet. He stopped short. Floating in the pool was something like a black scarf. Then he saw Davy Queenslace looking up at him steadily, open-eyed. Only, he was dead.

He was bluish of face, on the surface of the chilled water, and for his chosen death he had put on again the ragged monk's-habit of his days of mad and blessed wandering. His clenched right hand, frozen to his thin left shoulder, still held a crucifix.

Aaron was running, screaming "Selene!" But he did not run twenty feet. He turned angrily, stepped into the fire-cold pool, shuddering with the pain of it and, with his mittens soaked and slimy, he pulled out the stiff, fragile body and swung it to his shoulder.

He ran, stumbling, desperate, carrying what was left of David's passion for God horribly against his chest, against his neck. It occurred to him that he must not shock Selene with sight of this mockery, and he bore the body into the log stable.

Jake was pitching hay. He looked, he said, "Good God Almighty —get them duds off you!" He tore at Aaron's clothes—Aaron's own fingers were too stiff to unbutton them—threw round him a horse-blanket prickly with hayseed and smelling of dust, and began to rub his hands, his legs.

While Davy's body lay neglected, the drip from the pool already stiffening into a shroud of ice.

Aaron was trembling with shocks of cold electricity, shaking, helpless, till the blessed warmth of life came back and he was gasping to Jake, "Can you help me make a coffin, quick, before They can see it?"

By They he knew he meant Selene.

It was the sturdy Harge whom they summoned first. Before he knelt to pray over Davy's body he grumbled, "I'm sorry for the boy —mighty blame sorry. But just goes to show what happens to a decent Christian if he gets mixed up with all this foreign mysticism. I've made Huldy promise she won't monkey with it any more, but stick to the straight hard path of the Holy Ghost. . . . Uh—Aaron— did you find the cow?"

Over the coffin, that early twilight, the women wailed, their hair loose, their hands clutching the bare bright pine wood—Selene, Huldah, Anna, Bessie, Luna Speezer—but Aaron saw that Selene was the only one of them who seemed broken and helpless, identifying herself with this menacing death. The others had that delight in death with which all bored and provincial women break the monotony.

They buried Davy in a pit chopped out of stone-hard earth, next to Mercie's little headboard, which was already leaning a little, with the painted letters already a little blurred by the gales. They shivered about the grave in the defenseless prairie, in a slow, ceaseless falling of snow.

Next day Black Wolf came to Harge, snarling, "I just heard!" He was clearly quite insane. "You killed my friend with your magic! I'll be revenged on the whole bunch of you!"

Jake said afterward, "That don't worry me none. I notice when a fellow says he'll be *revenged,* he ain't going to do nothing but enjoy hisself being mysterious. If he says, 'I'll get even,' why then, I'm scared."

"But if he's gone mad?" fretted Speezer.

Squire Harge, who so rarely went near the house of Caesar Lanark—the Idolatrous House of Rimmon—stumped over to report Davy's death and Black Wolf's hatred. He said to Aaron, on return, "Maybe we're wrong about Brother Lanark. He was real nice—said he hoped Selene would learn the plain way of Dorcas from us. But he says, watch for Black Wolf. You're the fightin'est fellow we got, Neighbor. You better keep an eye out."

But calm was over them again, and Aaron was well content to see how Selene was learning the Mission work: sewing, washing, playing the melodeon in chapel, Sioux phrases . . . and trying to get up early without violence . . . and trying to say nothing of New York and her lost glories.

"I've never worked before. I think I like it!" she said.

She would, perhaps, never work as steadily as Huldah, but she had an air and a flourish that none of them possessed. Huldah complained of her taking so long with the unnecessary polishing of glasses, and when Selene made a dress with hemstitched border for one of the Indian children, Huldah protested, "Oh, none of these Injuns appreciate fussy clothes like that. They're satisfied if they get their hides covered."

"You're wrong. I'm an Indian myself!"

This by day. At night, so vulnerable in their desert huts, they noted that they had heard nothing from Black Wolf since his threat. They listened all evening to the wail of passing snow-devils, to fingers prying at the shutters. They pretended to laugh at the Wolf, but now and then, amid a jolly conversation about Hell, one

317

of the men would grunt, "I suppose *he* could get some of the Teton and Yankton to join his Wahpeton. Tough raiders, too." Except for Aaron and Selene, they felt righteous and indignant and Christian that the Indians should feel righteous and indignant and Wakantankian and want to rule the land of their ancestral graves nor gladly pass the bones of their dead children over to a fine Vermonter for fertilizer.

Sometimes Aaron was heartily for Black Wolf; sometimes he complained to Selene, "Oh, what's this sentimental idea I get now and then that the Dakotas are better off hunting with frozen behinds than sitting in a nice farmhouse like we'll help 'em build, if they behave?"

But about one thing he was not confused . . . he thought. To him, Huldah was as dear a sister as Rebecca, but Selene was his deathless love . . . he thought.

His plans for her changed every hour. They would both become missionaries (Congregational). He would somehow take her to New York and—strictly for her, not for any carnal display—become a millionaire. They would go back to Clunford, the only sensible place to live.

More publicly, Harge was making his plans to get Huldah out to the States and marry her. (Huldah herself did not show any hurry.) The whole Mission so forgot Black Wolf as to become quite normally quarrelsome again. Speezer was complaining that Harge's Presbyterians had taken advantage of the Plan of Union to steal two thousand decent Congregational churches, while Harge stated bitterly, "Herb would do more for the cause of Christ if he read less about patristics and got Bessie's shoes mended quicker."

In February the local band of Indians returned from the hunt and set up their tents. Furs were joyfully carried into Lanark's warehouse and the Indians had new shotguns and rifles. Their children came to the Mission school, and Selene, proud to be a schoolmistress and no longer a schoolgirl, helped Huldah and the Speezers drill

318

them in English spelling and arithmetic and sewing and Bible stories.

This winter of 1848–49 had been remarkably cold, but spring blew up early and grateful.

March struggled in with early crows and red-winged blackbirds and hints of green grass. Even a few of the cautious gophers peeped out of their burrows. That crabbed weather-croaker, Jake, insisted that winter would return, but the rest of them frolicked in the gentle warmth, and Aaron walked unabashed, hand-in-hand with Selene.

They all felt released, they all loved one another and the Faith, and then the news came, by a frightened, flying Leon Simonet, that on the evening before a dozen shotgun blasts had been fired from darkness at the palisade of Castle Lanark.

48

I T WAS Aaron who heard Black Wolf's speech. The Wolf was standing out, as the Indian custom was, among the tipis in the darkness, and he made oration that all the Indian nations must unite and get back their old free hunting.

Aaron understood enough of it to be frightened. He went to Harge to report, and heard that Jake had seen, way out on the prairie, Caesar Lanark talking to half a dozen Indians who looked not like Sioux but like their enemies, the Ojibway—the Chippewa.

There was firing from the village, the evening after, and the men stood guard at the Mission. Isaac Weeps-by-Night dotted up on his crutches, crying, "Attack by Ojibway! They sneaked up in dark! They have shot Black Wolf. They have killed him. He is dead— our prophet is dead, and we are finished!"

Aaron and Isaac ventured to the Indian village. On a pile of blankets among the tipis, lighted by pine-knot torches, Black Wolf lay, and his face was gone. He had received a shotgun blast full in the face, and the Ojibway had taken time to scalp him complete, down even to his ears.

Her Door was crouched in a ball beside him, wailing.

Said Isaac, "Two days ago he come out of hiding, with Her Door and the boy. It is a strange thing: the Ojibway attacked no tipi but Black Wolf's; they rushed in and killed him and scalped him and burned the tent and his book he wrote and ran away and did not try to get other scalps."

Aaron remembered Jake's report of Lanark and the stray Ojibway. He said foolishly, like a white man, "What are you all going to do?"

Isaac was astonished. "Do? Look about you! All the warriors are painting themselves for the campaign. We take out after the Ojibway at once."

"Not you."

"Yes, me! But I won't come back. I am a wretched, one-legged man. I'll leave that one leg and my scalp among the Ojibway. It is my duty!"

"Isaac! You can't! You're a Christian!"

"I go to smite the Canaanites, and I'll kill them and kill them and kill them and then they will kill me. Now I put on my warpaint and take my Testament and my rifle and go!"

As he hastened back to the Mission, Aaron hated all Indians and was terrified of them while he yet loved Black Wolf and was dismayed that his revolt had been ended by an outlaw murder. Nothing seemed clear except that he must, at once, get Selene safely away.

He did not know it, but on that day, March 3, 1849, the Congress had passed an act admitting Minnesota as a territory. On the next day, Zachary Taylor, who had once been commandant at Fort Snelling, would become President. Minnesota was now a part of the walled world, while Aaron stumbled through alder thickets and over the ice to Selene.

She sobbed, "Black Wolf was so good to me when I was a little girl! I want to wear mourning for him. I haven't any. Am I going to need it often now?"

It was after ten, very late for the Mission, but Leon Simonet appeared at Jake's cabin with a note for Selene. Jake and Anna and Huldah had gone to bed, disturbed about the death of Black Wolf yet not markedly grieving. Selene read the note with her left hand clenched, and passed it on to Aaron with "Now he's going to try and get *me*!"

This was the note:

"Do you think you have been wise not to answer my billet assez doux? Nor come to see me? I resent boorishness, and I usually do something about it. You need a more rigid training than your delightful dalliance at the Mission.   C.L."

She spoke without hysteria:

"My father is going to do dreadful things with me. He's insane with pride. I think he did have Black Wolf killed. I think I'll be kidnapped."

"Not if I . . ."

"Kidnapped and taken off to some Western Dakota tribe—maybe where my mother is—do you realize he won't ever tell me if she's alive or dead? I'll become an Indian. I love the Indians now, but I wouldn't be much good cooking a dog in a pot. He might marry me off to some brave who's an agent for him and who'd beat me."

"He won't!"

"He might, if we don't run. Fast! I'm terrified of him!"

So was Aaron. He sounded reasonably plucky with "I'll fight him," but she wailed, "You can't! He has too many badmen. You've got to take me away from here—now—first thing tomorrow—you've got to! Darling, please!"

It was not at all hard to persuade Aaron, when she was in his arms, against his shoulder, so yielding; when her frightened voice accepted him as her final refuge. He was convinced that her fear of her father was reasonable, and that there was no protection against the hundred Indians controlled by Lanark. Aaron did so want to be heroic, he did so delightfully picture himself, single-handed, driving away from the Mission a regiment of Indians with torches, and Squire Harge praising him as a Minnesota St. George, but he knew that the Mission would be much safer without the presence of his singularly innocent Helen of Troy, and that Harge would not conceivably consent to their flight.

He kissed her. He muttered, "Get your stuff together. Make sure Huldah is asleep and don't wake her—she'd be full of good advice. I'll steal the grub and wake you at dawn. Don't be scared, Selene, my dear! And I'll have a gun!"

322

She crept up the ladder, looking down at him with trust. He brought a haversack from his room, and from Anna's supplies he took food enough to last to Traverse des Sioux, where he could count on Narcisse Jupon, the trader. He took rice, parched corn, tea, a horn of sugar, strips of jerked buffalo meat, a spoon and a tin kettle and a couple of tin cups and plates. In his room he had his own shotgun and paper shells, and he added to them two blankets and a block of sulphur matches.

He had a brief ethical colic about his thefts, and cured it by deciding that the months when he had worked without salary would make up for the Mission supplies he was lifting. . . . Not that he was particularly fussy about this high problem of virtue, with Selene's life in balance. It was harder to be willing to desert the Mission when the Indians might attack, but if he were here and they did come, he could not hold them off for an extra minute, and Selene would be caught, be spiritually mutilated in captivity.

He was still not happy about it, but he told himself sternly, "I can't parade my heroism and make her pay for it. I'm doing better! This time, I seem to be a traitor to only one side!"

He was surprisingly easy about leaving forever all his friends at the Mission, even Huldah. They were stuffy and futile, he told himself. Yet he knew that he had a vast affection and admiration for all of them: Sister Huldah, the courageous and yearning Harge, the slippery but amiable Speezers, Anna and Jake who were salt that nothing could dampen, the Bessie who was inevitably going to be the ornament of some mission or some dancehall or some home with ten children. They were Good People. They were a benign moonlight which exorcised the black and evil shadows of men like Lanark.

Then he laughed.

He reflected that in the morning, when Selene and he would be found missing, the Good People would run together and decide that they had been "dreadfully deceived in that young man, Gadd, that seemed so pure, and him running off with a rich heiress to betray

323

her!" They would flock over to Lanark's and let him know that the culprits were gone, to the end that Aaron might get an arrow in the dark.

They must move fast. Once at St. Paul or Fort Snelling, Selene would be safe. He'd see to that . . . somehow!

All night he was so compounded of exhilaration over his flight with Selene and of nervousness about the duties of possible wedlock with that mercurial child that it was a nice question whether, had the Indians attacked by dark, he would have picked up Selene and run ten miles, or have bounced in among them, yelling, and have slaughtered the entire mob.

49

H E WAS up before dawn, and Selene must have been equally sleepless, for when he inched down the ladder in his socks, she was waiting for him.

Without even coffee, they swung their packs to their shoulders and crept from the house, headed eastward. They had nothing to say.

From the bluff he looked down through fog and darkness and imagined that he could see the forlorn buildings of the Mission like gray shells. He had been defeated there; perhaps he had been disloyal, perhaps treasonous, to the quest for God and to the Day of Small Things. Well, God must be more patient than Squire Harge.

Already, Harge's name was something old and forgotten.

"So! Let's go on."

Selene fell into the long loping of a prairie gait. She kept even with him, not twittering nor asking sympathy. Three or four miles from the Mission, they cheered as the sun rose and the prairie springtime was mist-scented and fresh-colored. They laughed.

This was real spring, said Aaron, though it was two months early. The greening buffalo grass was set with tiny pools, the creeks were melting, the sky was high blue. Crows were emphatic in their perpetual soapbox speeches and the piles of snow remaining in the shade were edged with glitter.

They had to strip to their bare legs to ford the east branch of the Isanti, but when they had rubbed their chilly flesh with a corner of a blanket, they were flushed again with youth.

"We'll stop for a cup of tea, Selene, and then let's keep pounding on, case your father starts some horsemen after us. Uh—by the way —if you could just look back now and then and sort of help keep an eye out for anything that might be moving?"

They boiled their tea on a tiny fire of buffalo chips and hastened on—not quite so skippingly. They were farther from their signboard, the channel of the Minnesota River, in a wash of spring prairie, like two cormorants in a round of green ocean.

As they went on, Aaron was uplifted by a countryman's pride in the fact that his girl, even if she was not quite so powerful as he, was as determined. Perhaps, he thought, this was the first time when her sleek yet wiry Scotch-Canadian-Sioux body had ever called up all its energy—except when she had danced all night with her putative Count! They would reach Traverse des Sioux and refuge in four days, maybe three, and somewhere beyond that Selene and he would build a Brotherhood of Man in which Caesar Lanark would sit down with Charles Grandison Finney, and keep sitting.

Practically, neither of them knew the art of keeping alive on the prairie.

He was wearing his pilot-cloth overcoat and muskrat cap—both of which seemed too warm—with a long scarf, his broadcloth Preacher's Suit, and boots, since it had seemed too warm and too muddy for moccasins. She was as inappropriately warm in a blue cloth dress with a row of silvered buttons, a heavy velvet cloak trimmed with beaver, a quilted hood, fur gloves and fur-trimmed bootees. It would have been a good sensible costume for New York streets on a cold day, say thirty above.

Her only fool-of-an-heiress trick had been to bring so large a bundle of her finery, but Aaron carried it along with his pack and said convincingly, "Never mind, dear—don't weigh a feather."

She confessed, "I guess I was naughty to take all that, but I just couldn't leave my tan silk—the one with the lilies-of-the-valley. It's all freshened up again. Or the bottle of Lyon perfume that my aunt gave me, and *the* two sweetest things: my bonnet of Italian straw and oh, what a shawl—rose and blue Hernani brocade! I do love them so! But if we have any trouble, you throw them right away.

. . . But I did have such fun buying them, and they're the only dainties I have now, and we must look nice, mustn't we, when we get to St. Paul!"

Her *We* exalted him.

When they had quarter-stripped at the ford, he had felt a quite unbrotherly admiration for the brown shine of her legs. But until she was safe, they were boy and girl racing together on the blue morning, and they were also a God-seeking man who had been slapped and a young woman in danger of horror and the smell of death.

But mostly they were jolly and triumphant. With the sunniest joy he thought, "I'm utterly in love with her! No man in all the poems was so lucky! Byron? A woodchuck! She's lovely and I'm with her and it's a glorious day and I can smell the earth and the rivers and I love her and I'm hungry and we'll stop for some tea and corn!"

They had breakfast-lunch at eleven, in a curving coulee. They boiled the parched corn and ate it with salt, greedily, and soaked slivers of the dry buffalo meat in their tea. They were sleepy, and he wanted to drowse near her, but she commanded, "Come on, Cap'n! On to Vera Cruz!"

As they came out of the hollow, they realized that the sunshine was gone, the sky veiled with a film that minute by minute grew thicker. Half a dozen times each of them said, "It might snow." The bleary sun promised to return, but each time less confidently. The cold was stealing in; the coats which had been a burden of heat were only decently warm now. The temperature, Aaron guessed, must have dropped twenty degrees.

The wind rose steadily. It hummed in the dry grass which no longer, in that drained light, seemed green at all. The first snowflake came from nowhere. It tacked comically in front of them, vanished, and was instantly followed by another, another.

Then Aaron let himself be afraid. He let himself think of the one word that on the prairie was as fearful as Fire—Blizzard.

There could be no blizzard without snow, but in half an hour that was coming fast enough. He wanted to strike at the snow, to kill it.

"What do you think we better—eh?" Selene trembled.

"Get some kind of refuge. But I don't see any groves ahead."

He tried to remember what clumps of woods there were in the cruel stretch to Traverse des Sioux, still a hundred miles away. "Oh, we'll find some place—no trouble," he said cheerily.

He recalled the rule Jake had given him: in a storm on the prairie, camp at once, before you lose the way. Where? There was only the bare grassland before them, without a sizable hollow.

Selene was saying with spurious courage, "Could we manage to rest soon? My feet are a little sore."

"Oh, sure—soon," he lied.

His own feet were cold, and his insteps seemed to be breaking under the stricture of his boots, and he kept on. The fear of the blizzard grew, and he kept on. The snow was thicker, harder driven against their faces by a vicious wind, and they kept on, and now they began to stagger a little and to weave. Aaron heard, clearly, coldly, very coldly, "You two could be frozen to death, here on the prairie."

The hurtling snowflakes, not soft squash but hard pellets, had been just an annoyance and a confusion, but now there was pain in them as they stung his forehead, his cheeks, and ridiculed him by snapping at his nose. He saw that Selene was shaking her head, bewildered by them, and in her eyes were tears—perhaps of cold, perhaps of fear and torment.

He was sure that it was down to zero now. He could not get his breath; he was panting and each minute less sure that, in their stumbling, they were keeping due east. He could not see the Minnesota, their guide; not see anything save the whirl of flakes.

His legs were aching, a fine thin agony spreading up his calves, and he guessed that his feet were blistering. She would be no better. Stop—camp here in the open? His decision might mean her life.

He put his lips close to her ear, to shout: "I'm going to keep right on to shelter, if you can stand it. 'Bout blizzard strength now. Shall I try to carry you?"

She actually laughed. "Dear me, no! Let's keep going, reverend—dear reverend father!"

Then—it might have been for half an hour, it might have been for an hour, with time and place and bodies lost in the growing white whirlpool—they lumped on, and they were not living at all, and their only philosophy was, "I die, therefore I have not died yet."

Then, in exultation, they came to a rash of little willow trees and what looked like the river beyond. It had no more shelter than a brushpile, but it had to do.

She flopped down, hysterical with relief, and he kissed her frigid cheek, cold and smooth and memorable.

He scuffed the snow away with his aching feet. He tore the dead twigs—his hands trembled—out of a hollow at the foot of a dwarf willow. He motioned to her to hold out her cloak as a shelter, and carefully, tearing from a block a sulphur match which lit and stuttered and stank till it turned from evil blue to healthy flame, he set fire to a handful of dry leaves. Then the twigs caught, then the branches.

He dug into his wraps for his ancient turnip watch and found that it was only three. But in the blizzard there was growing night. While Selene nursed the fire, he dragged up all the fuel he could get, hacking at willow boughs and a small cottonwood with his knife. (It had been enterprisingly shipped from Connecticut as a Scalping Knife for native use.)

By the minute blaze, they had tea and dry meat and felt safe. He spread out both blankets, with their two coats under them, and they huddled together, arms about each other, babes in the woods, too warm and sleepy and sore to wreck their trust by any ineptitude of speech.

When he awoke, his cheek against the kerchief about her hair, he did not know whether it was day, evening or morning; only that it was dark and the blizzard shrieking, and their fire was out. He roused her. "Got to get a fire, quick, or we'll freeze! I'll scrabble around and try to find some more wood. See if you can get a fire started with what wood we got."

He dared not go more than a few feet from her, nor dared take off his mittens but, fumbling in the gale-channelled dark, he gathered a few more skinny boughs. A glow rose behind him, and he turned his stiff neck to see that Selene had managed to get a fire going with a small heap of twigs. He smiled. The silken Selene, wrapped in blankets, her face tiny among the clumsy folds, was a grizzly bear with the face of a wilderness-spirit.

She was looking at the fire musingly, her bare hand on one knee, holding the sulphur matches. A dry strip of bark blazed up around her hand, and she convulsively dropped the match-block. It exploded among the burning twigs, scattering them, and when it went out, there was nothing left of the fire but wormlike glows running up and down the twigs.

And—he felt criminal—they had no more matches, and no flint and steel.

She was wailing, "Oh, I didn't mean to—I didn't!"

He spoke with a curiously mature sweetness: "Course you didn't. Don't worry a bit. We're all right."

That was a lie, and she had the sense to know it. There was bitterness in her weeping confession: "I've probably killed you, Aaron! We'll freeze. Or starve. I was a fool at home, an idler in school, a booby in society—me boasting about my Count—but honestly there was one, but he was a stupid dancer. I was a bad seamstress at the Mission, and now I'm an idiot in the wilderness, and I've killed you—and I love you!"

With countless little murmurings of comfort, he made her curl up under the neatly tucked-in blankets. She relaxed in sleep beside him, and he was unafraid now.

50

HE MUST have gone to sleep. He had again no notion how much time had passed when he was awakened by the cold and by the strain on his arm about her. He tried to ease it, and heard her voice, just under his chin, steady and all awake:

"Cold? Darling! Oh, we *are* lost children! Maybe we're going to die here. So ... I do think I love you. I didn't know, when I saw you at Eliot House, so alive and so gentle, and so dear and funny and ignorant! My brother Aaron, my only brother, and that fool, Mr. Thingamajig, that invented the theater! This is a queer time to find out I love you, just when we're going to freeze ... And we can, too!"

She sobbed, but was immediately laughing. "Do you know what I was dreaming about when I woke up?"

"What, sweet?"

"Francesca da Rimini."

"Fran ... ?"

"She wasn't much like a prairie blizzard. She was a lady who lived in Italy, long ago, and she was in love. I always wanted to see Rimini, the Adriatic and the old towers and the olive trees and the secret gateways, and then I go and drop all our stinking matches and we're like to freeze stiff, God damn it!"

"*Selene!*"

"Excuse. But a preacher like you ought to know this is God-damn if anything ever was!"

"I know, but ..."

"But nothing! For sure! ... Oh, darling Brother Aaron, you can pray, can't you? Even without a book, I mean. Pray us out of this—pray us to Rimini in the sun!"

"How would I get along there?"

"You're probably much more like the golden Paolo than I am like Francesca—a skinny brown Sioux half-breed that drops matches—oh, darling, I didn't mean to drop them—I didn't, I didn't!"

Then she was really whimpering, very cold, somewhat frightened, all story-telling romance gone out of her, and she clung to him trustingly, her breast was alive against his, and he knew something of what he wanted in life, something of the God for whom he had been seeking in thin words, now that they were likely to lie dead, body to body, their bones cold on the indifferent cold prairie.

He took her petition for prayer seriously but not for long. He had unhappily noticed at the Mission that when he had most hotly prayed, it had been a way of escaping a decision, of frivolously passing the lot to God. The only prayer he could find now was a mechanical "God help us." He was too conscious of Selene's dependent presence, and of rage that, in his young vigor, he could do nothing for her, yet of joy, too, that he wanted to do great works for her, not for his personal salvation. He was at last united to another human being. In devotion to her he had now first escaped from dread of the Father who was Uriel, Harge, Jehovah.

In half-desperate, half-blissful brooding he must have drifted into sleep again, for he was conscious of awakening just before he saw the fire in the snow-shot darkness where no fire could possibly be.

Fuzzily outlining a hillock west of their grove was a distinct glow. He started to cry Selene awake, with the joy of rescue, but stopped, colder than cold. What fire-maker was this? Black Wolf? But Black Wolf was dead, and a terror seeped from his death and spread round Aaron. Were they Sioux, over the hummock, sent by Lanark to drag them back? Or Chippewa who would butcher them? Or white whisky-smugglers, lowest of brute men, who would knife him but first rape Selene?

He waked her, after the cramp of pulling up his hand to lay it over her mouth for silence, and whispered the discovery.

Of course she said, "Don't go—don't leave me!" She would not have been human otherwise, but only a sprite out of the Malatesta garden in Rimini.

"Got to find out," he said softly.

As he eased himself out of their warm blanket-bed, he was careful to smooth the blankets in about her. He left his heavy coat under her, and the cold came paralyzing through his jacket, more suitable to a village pulpit than to roaring chill on a prairie at night. He stumbled through slippery new snow, up to the top of the hummock. The storm had lulled enough for him to recognize outlines in the fire glow.

He made out thicker woods, more shelter, and the fire. The steady wail of the blizzard slackened, and he thought he heard a human voice, a monologue, then thought that it was the voice of a woman reading from the Bible. He caught some of the words:

"...crowneth the year with thy goodness...pastures of the wilderness and the little hills rejoice...valleys are covered over with corn; they shout for joy."

It was Huldah.

She was crouched compactly in a buffalo robe over a small but competent and lasting fire, and when he galloped down to her, she said, "Well! I didn't expect to catch you so soon. What've you done with that child Seely?"

When she had been following them, the day before, Huldah must have looked like a moving mountain, for she had been toting three pairs of snowshoes, an extra buffalo robe, Indian fire-steel and flint, and a whole round of pork, with extra socks and Wahpeton moccasins for the unfortunate prodigals who had been supposing that they were happy strayed lovers.

She was dressed in a jacket and woolen trousers belonging to Jake.

She sensibly made them change to moccasins before she let them rest and then, with no arguments welcomed, she so divided the buffalo robes that Selene and she were tucked under one and a reprobated Aaron alone under the other. Very cold.

Yes, she had been shadowing them all day. She had made them out in darkness when they were first stealing away from the Mission. She had caught their trail where they had crossed the east branch of the Isanti, and had kept them distantly in sight till the blizzard hid them. She had thought then that she had lost them. She had been certain that they would freeze to death, and she had been praying for them, praying that the Calvinist God (though she was shaky about the theology of it) might have preordained a chance at Heaven even for this fool of a girl and this contumacious, seducing, ungrateful and backsliding rascal.

Neither Aaron nor Selene explained anything, nor did they look at each other. They were too shy in the presence of two hundred years of decent Puritan history condensed in Huldah.

She said that there had been a considerable row at the Mission when she had given the alarm. Luna Speezer had looked like a greyhound on scent, and Squire Harge had wanted to hustle over and get Mr. Lanark and organize a posse to rescue youthful virtue. The only moment during her report when Huldah was something less than blandly omnipotent was when she chuckled, "I don't know if the Squire will want to marry me now. I told him he was an old jackrabbit, always thumping his big feet. . . . Now, Seely, you go right to sleep."

And the exhausted Selene did go to sleep, her head on Huldah's motherly shoulder, not parted from Aaron by anything so brittle as a thin sword but by the whole thick body of common sense, which snorted that Rimini was no longer the haunt of Francesca but only an "Adriatic seapt, int. ruins, fair hotel accom."

While Selene innocently slumbered, Huldah was curt:

"Now, Aaron, we've got to talk sense. I don't know how far you went with Seely, and I ain't going to ask you, because of course you're like all men, ridden with carnal lust and vileness, and you'd lie about it. It's clear that it was God's will that I should be chosen to repair the irreparable damages you have done to the child's reputation and maybe character, this awful godless night."

He tried to protest, but she rode him down. He saw that in her high state of virtue she would not believe anything he said.

"What I plan is this. I agree that it is not good for the child to go back to her father. I'll take her on to St. Paul—if God permits us to live through this storm—and I'll find some honest work for her till her relatives send for her. I'll put her in some Christian household where she can do domestic work and be protected against all these ravening men—including you, my friend!"

——Francesca at the kitchen-range.

"You will go back east, Aaron, after your dreadful failure at the Mission, and I'll pray that some time you'll become a halfway decent man again ... Oh, Aaron, when I gave you all my affection, my most passionate aspirations Godward, how could you do this to me—to her—to God?"

So he was back from the wars and sitting on the same front porch and the folks were rocking and grousing, and nothing was changed and the great voyage had been only a fool dream.

Yes, it did hurt, but after all, what had he to give that wild, fragile child? Huldah and he were an old married pair; never be anything else, and he'd better face it. Had he expected to get a job packing furs and share some hayloft with the fairy child? He'd be lucky if, under Huldah's patient purity, he did ever become "halfway decent."

His inner malice was saying, so wearily, "This is all nonsense and defeat, but I'm worn out by the blizzard, and I guess you'll have to go back to death and the doxology."

Then Huldah slept and Aaron slept. Condemned men sleep on the night before their hanging.

Huldah got breakfast for them—tea and pork—and she gently prayed over them.

The blizzard was past. The sky was not clear, but they felt safe in struggling on. They took four more days on their way to Traverse des Sioux. They did not see any galloping kidnapper, any human being whatever.

The three tramped Indian-file and, without exactly agreeing to it, Aaron went ahead. He could not see Selene without boldly looking back at her past the wall of Huldah's suspicious virtue. At night, Selene always slept under the same robe with Huldah, and before she spoke to him at meals, she looked at Huldah as if for permission. In four days he touched Selene's hand only when he put on her snowshoes—a chancy, romantic service on which Huldah kept shrewd watch.

Yet he was not angered by Huldah but fascinated by her.

In the stress of their journeying, Selene became frowsy, looked cross-eyed with weariness, while Huldah was trim and neat and cheerful. Aaron caught himself thinking, "She's a real woman, rock-ofages, and Selene is a baby."

None of the three was much skilled in the use of snowshoes, and their feet were blistered, the webbing was clogged with wet snow. When they made camp, their hands were too cold for a time to untie the snowshoe strings. There was a day of extreme cold and suffering that went on like torture while they lost their way and staggered insanely, and on the day after that, the sun came out in such dismaying splendor that Aaron was stricken with snow blindness. Huldah made him lie on his back and rubbed snow on his closed eyes till he was relieved, and all the while she told him some reasonably funny stories about Luna Speezer and her plan to convert the Pope to Congregationalism by inviting him to come and inspect God's work at the Bois des Morts.

Aaron sighed, "She has more humor than Selene or me, I guess. Selene might be better off with that Count of hers. Damn!"

At night he lay in his buffalo robe (kindness of Miss Purdick) with his back to the girls, and they were farther from him than California, and the wolves howled all night long.

By day they tramped for many years, a thousand miles to a stage. He would determine to reach that snowy thistle-patch five hundred feet away—then, he warmly promised himself, he would halt. When he got there, he urged himself, "No, just make that next hummock, and then you can *really* stop." And so on till he would suddenly, without warning, find himself squatted on his snowshoes, trying to rest while his knees were about to burst and his calves were striped with agony.

Every ten steps, when he looked back to see that the girls were safe, he was convinced that he had not gone an inch since his last inspection, and he went on shuffle, lift, shuffle, lift, with the band of pain about his cold forehead drawn ever tighter, till he could see nothing before him, around him, but blankness.

He tried to give himself the wry comfort of insisting that the two girls were probably even dizzier, but that low thought was too complicated for him to unravel, in the immense simplification of madness, and sometimes he was not quite sure who Huldah and Selene were or why he should fret over them.

They were all so lost and numb, their heads so bowed, that they must have had the bend of the river and Narcisse Jupon's trading-cabin in sight for two minutes before Aaron came back to sanity enough to realize it, and to bellow, "Look, Huldah! We're safe!"

When they crept, snow-dazed and mumbling, through Jupon's door, that good man was astonished for the first time in a quarter of a century.

51

A T JUPON'S they renewed their supplies. It *would* be Huldah, Aaron sighed, who would have a hundred dollars with her and be eager to share it with them. He himself had $23.70 and Selene had no money at all.

They rested for two days; Aaron in a bunk in the warehouse, safely separated from the log room of Huldah and Selene.

But Huldah had begun to believe his protestations that he had treated Selene as a sacred trust, that he would not think even of kissing her without a license and the public ceremonies of a Plan of Union tabernacle. Indeed Huldah quite suddenly reverted to admiring Aaron as a conceivable junior prophet—Universal Brotherhood his gospel.

"This is a new age of prophets, and what a prophet, what a leader of men and servant of God you might be, Aaron, if you should receive and yield yourself up to a revelation for this terrible era when God may be giving Man his last chance before the Second Coming! I'd love to help—to be the faithful disciple who brought the soul-hungry world to the feet of a new Evangel!"

To be a prophet, with worshippers standing before him by the thousands? To be able, with just a flip of his hand, to get rid of war and hatred? To have even a Harge—even a Caesar Lanark—listen and be changed?

And Huldah could do it! He stared at her, but his inner malice jeered, "Do you know enough to go around preaching to anybody? Do you want to hold sweaty hands, or Selene's cool one?"

Huldah was seized hard by her vision of playing Maintenon to a prophet, and she flooded on, while Aaron saw that Selene was becoming awed, as though he might veritably be a soothsayer and not just her beloved of the storm.

He saw that she had been hurt and broken, like a wounded animal. She was too sick inside, it might be, to be loved as a woman.

So far as he could make out, her repulsion by her father, her realization at the Mission that to Huldah and Anna she was not much more than a useless hanger-on, her exposure and fear in the blizzard, her shock when Huldah had made her happy trust in Aaron seem vile—all this had destroyed the young self-confidence that had been her magic.

He guessed that she doubted her charm, her wit, her elegance, her reason for living. She had once assumed that everybody loved her; now she was wondering whether anybody could endure a person as shoddy as she was—a pretentious half-breed who had been posing as a white lady till even her own father could not stand it and had kicked her out!

She looked at Aaron so apologetically. She did not jeer when Huldah explained to her, "We women think we are the vessels of the faith, but at best we're only weak witnesses to the Kingdom. For a while I was guilty of thinking that Aaron might have corrupted you, when all the while he was pure as snow, standing like a guardian angel with a flaming sword!"

Aaron was suddenly testy at having any sort of sword tied on him. He wanted, without ingratitude, to pat Huldah back into place. He wanted to stir Selene out of her coma. But he was afraid that he might upset her balance still more, and though he rejected Huldah's commission as prophet, he did find himself agreeing with her that they two together must now do something warm and beautiful for the angel-child.

"You'll be glad to know," Huldah confided to him, "that there's nothing the matter with Selene *that way*."

"I don't understand how you mean."

339

"Why, she's so nervous and scared-like, and I was afraid that—it would be back in New York, that bestial Babylon—and maybe some depraved, villainous man had—oh, you know—deceived her, and she was in a *condition!*"

"Hell no!" he said, and Huldah was so scandalized by his calamitous language that he could not go on being scandalized by her calamitous notions.

As they hoisted their packs and started onward from Traverse des Sioux, he vowed that he would do nothing that would bruise this frightened girl, Selene, even if he had to give her up.

It was cold and the snow was wet, but without agonies they trudged on toward St. Paul, and for a pair of days they stopped to rest at Oak Grove, on the Minnesota, the friendly large log cabin that was the house and one-man mission of Gideon Hollister Pond. (Gideon's brick house was not reared for another seven years to come.) Gideon's wife, Sarah, was there, and Samuel William Pond, his older and even statelier brother, come over from Prairieville (which is now Shakopee). Always at least a dozen children were reading or singing or praying or quarreling around the house, and there was a myth that Gideon had once kept a strange child for two weeks under the impression that it was one of his own.

Samuel and Gideon Pond had been the first of the Protestant missionaries among the Sioux, zealous young men from Connecticut, tall and powerful, coming to Minnesota in 1834. They welcomed Aaron, who had seen them at Snelling; they received Huldah as one of their own and, under their broad-shouldered tenderness, Selene became half-assured once more.

In the evening they all sat talking of Palestine, which Gideon so longed to see—and never would. Samuel had the wrinkling face of a great comedian over his prim stock, and he sat with his long legs twisted in a corkscrew. Gideon's face was that of a tragedian, and you could fancy him as a beardless Lear, but he loved to lie on his back on the floor, one elevated foot wagging, while he read aloud—

in French, German, Hebrew, Greek or Dakota. He explained to Aaron that fifteen years ago he too had been a carpenter and still was.

The air of religion in the Pond household was so thick and fragrant that it soaked through Selene and changed her. Late one afternoon, when they were all assembled for family prayer, she cried out, "I have seen the light! The Savior has come to me! I have been lost to God, in vanity and dancing and loose talk, and I merit damnation, but I give testimony to the gracious light of God's mercy!"

The Ponds and Huldah looked stunned, then enchanted. This was the glad outpouring they had been awaiting from the cynical Sioux and rarely getting.

"Hallelujah, bless you!" they cried.

But Aaron found himself hard and angry. "She's hysterical, and grabbing for help. Every word she said she's heard from Harge and Huldah, over and over. It may be the sin against the Holy Ghost, it may bring my own damnation, but I've got to get her away from here!"

Selene was clamoring, "Brother Gideon, I want to be baptized into your church, right now! The burden of sin has been lifted from me, but I want to stay free of it. I want to be baptized so I won't ever go down again into sin and shame!"

Gideon Pond was grave and kind: "We're all moved by God's miraculous mercy, but before you can be baptized, you must be ready; you must understand what you're doing, understand redemption and faith. We'll teach you . . ."

Selene was stubborn and agonized. "The Catholics would just explain things and then baptize me right away, if I needed it!"

There was a Connecticut dryness in Gideon's, "I dare say! By the way, have you ever been baptized!"

"I don't know!"

"By the Catholics, at your father's, perhaps?"

"I don't know!"

"Did you ever have religious instruction?"

"Oh, yes. At Eliot House. Heaps. But I don't know as I ever listened much."

"Well, starting today, I'll try to explain the plan of salvation and the indwelling witness, but now I want you to sit down, Selene, and be very quiet and try to think."

Aaron was grateful for the friendly caution of Gideon Pond, who seemed human, almost free of Huldah's hot ecstasies, Harge's fear, Speezer's sly priestliness. "He and his brother will guide her into solid goodness, I guess, if Huldah will keep her hands off."

Which Huldah would not do.

In the Pond family it was customary for the members to be contemplative about their souls amid a whirlpool of games, songs, theology and the audible collation of Dakota verbs. When Selene sat in a corner, on the floor, meditating, they all let her alone except Huldah.

Invisible in that cabin, hosts of armored angels were fighting one another for the happy soul of Selene. They did not know that they all happened to be on the same side, and that the whole sky-rending battle was over the question of whether Virtue should be spelled with a small v or a capital.

Huldah kept lovingly nursing Selene, petting her and asking what the temperature of her soul was just now. Samuel William Pond may have doubted the value of this tender squeaking. He suddenly held forth to all of them, looking at Aaron as much as toward Selene:

"The true religious experience is, first, an unmistakable perception of God, through the reason and through all the senses—sight, hearing, touch, and a finer sense of whose existence and nature we consciously know nothing more than we do of the instinct that directs the wild fowl on its path unerringly at sixty miles an hour.

"Then, second, it is a wondering realization that God is so much greater than anything else that we know or can know—brighter than light, vaster than the universe yet smaller than the bee, and more tender than all human love together since time first was. And third, it is a surrender to God so complete that you simply can not remember what it was like to have been outside the rapture of its majestic power.

"Yet why do I try to describe the true nature of the Christian experience to you, Selene? Until you yourself have fully experienced it, you can no more comprehend it than the caterpillar can comprehend the nature and joy of being a winged being in the sun. An infidel could no more understand the being and verity of God than a wild hog could understand me!

"You must wait and pray—pray to be able to pray!"

Samuel Pond's manly and sonorous voice had created a spell in which Huldah and Selene and Aaron were motionless. And Aaron was equally awed and afraid.

—— These words of his, even if they're poetic and noble, are still only words! How does he know a caterpillar can't understand a butterfly? The mood she's in could turn her as insane as Davy Queenslace. I'm going to keep Selene from being mesmerized. I'm going to make her keep tight hold on a solid human hand, not on angelic bodies made of cold vapor.

Later he could hear Huldah saying to Selene, with the greatest concern, "The Ponds are wonderfully devout, but in your case, dear, I think they're wrong. You ought to be bathed in conversion while the iron is hot, and make dead sure of your calling. Think! Some day you might help take the gospel to your own Sioux people!"

"Could I? And do you think I ought to burn up all the darling dresses I got in New York?"

To the trained nurse of souls, it was a routine case. "Oh, no. I'd just rip any vain decorations off them and maybe dye them black and make them serve the Lord instead of Satan. My gracious! New clothes so hard to get, out here!"

"The Dakota. My own people . . . I'd like to take a little walk by myself and think. Do you mind, Huldah?"

"No dear, but throw a coat around your shoulders, and don't stay out too long."

Selene obeyed like a timid daughter. Aaron might have followed her out, but Huldah laid an affectionate hand on his arm and held him.

"Aaron dear, I suppose you and I will have to be going on to St. Paul at once, and find some work to sustain us, but I've talked to Gideon and he's willing to keep Selene here for a while and instruct her. Oh, how happy I would be to see that wretched outcast accepted of God and all her cares rolled away! Is it too daring of me?—but I think of her as our child, yours and mine!"

"Yes?"

"We'll find you a lovely job in St. Paul, and you can dream your dreams and start a theological course such as that yapping Speezer couple never thought of, and you'll tell me frankly whether there is anything I can do to help you. I want to do whatever you decide is best for you, my dear. I have a queer inspired feeling that you will be the man who may combine strict Calvinism with a broader humanitarianism—the first great man to unite all races and creeds!"

Aaron felt that he must get out of this, shut off the voice of temptation to leadership and gruesome fame. He choked, "I better skip out and see if she is all right." He fled from the room filled with firelight into a chill nothingness on the river bluff.

He groped, and then Selene was there, confidingly holding his hand and saying in a little thin voice, "Yes, I'll stay, and take the Word to the Dakota. If my father has been evil, I must make up for it."

"We'll both stay, but ..."

"I may get killed by my own people—die very early. I think I want to, and make up for the horrible acts of my father and for my own years of stubborn ignorance and cold pride toward God and the shame, the devastating shame ..."

"Stop it!"

"Aaron!"

"Quit admiring your mud pies—mud!"

"Aaron!"

"I went through it. I felt so remarkably sinful and polluted that I thought the whole business of Heaven must be stopping while the angels stared at me. They didn't! I won't argue with Huldah about this—she keeps cards up her sleeve. But you—you love me."

"The way a sister would—the way Huldah would."

"Don't fool yourself about her sisterliness. That's another piece of her holy play-acting. No. You love me exactly as you did when we were rolled in a blanket and the whole world kicked out!"

"Aaron, I want to pray for you, but how can I when you sneer at a saint like Huldah, when the devil speaks through your mouth?"

"Mouth—mouth—mouth!" he cried, and he kissed her mouth without any metaphysics to it.

He ordered, "We're going to get out of here, by ourselves, *tonight* —go and go fast and keep going. If we give Huldah any chance, she'll make us feel as if we were slapping our mothers. That's what the pure in meanness, that's what the sectarians can do."

"I know . . ."

"You and I are tough carpenters, and we're going to quit apologizing for it. Selene! Be happy!"

"I think I do love you . . ."

"Good!'

"But mere earthly love . . ."

"Selene! Come out of death into life!"

"But . . ."

"Laugh, darling! Laugh or I shall die. I could—so easily. Laugh!"

She did laugh a little, and very ruefully she tried to be funny for him. "But do you know what you're going to say to me, after we're married, whenever you're angry? You're going to say, 'Listen, you little Sioux bastard!' "

"Probably! Listen, you little archangel. If we don't get away from

345

here secretly, they'll argue us down—*I* don't know how they do it! And early tomorrow morning Huldah will be on watch—she knows our pattern. We'll go *now! You* slip in and push your things out of the window and then mine, and I'll catch 'em and pack 'em down to the Fort Snelling road and wait for you. Leave a note for the Ponds and Huldah—very grateful—the lie is that we don't want to give them any more trouble and so we've skedaddled. Now skip!"

"I'll *try* to skip!"

He thought that she was back in the fortress of reality.

As they tramped the trail he said, "I've sat at the preachers' feet and listened to them, faithfully, and tried to make myself become what they said I ought to be. I'm through! I do my own thinking now and my own bossing. And you—you never *were* a flirt or a flibbertigibbet at heart, and you aren't any crawling penitent now. You're a solid woman—you're my wife. Come on!"

"Yes, Aaron."

"And you're neither Sioux nor Yank, bastard nor angel. You're pure essence of girl!"

"Yes, Aaron . . . But I hope you and I aren't *always* going to be creeping off by night—and very cold!"

"This is our last footrace, and we've won it. We've found each other."

They came cheerfully up to the hotel in St. Paul just after dawn. Aaron had marked that even so early in the season, before the steamboats were running, new houses were building. There would be work and welcome here for a young carpenter, and a cook stove and a crown for a young carpenter's wife.

52

JAKE BASS'S St. Paul House was full of fur-traders and lumbermen and insane gold-prospectors who had come up the frozen Mississippi on foot. Bass directed Aaron to a new boarding house, a loft over a wagon-maker's which was so commodious, he said, that they would almost certainly get room to lie on the floor.

"I suppose we ought to get married, first," Aaron suggested to Selene.

She seemed to consider that settled.

They found that Henry Jackson, the trader, held a commission as justice of the peace from the old Wisconsin Territory and that he performed marriages, but he was out of town, buying furs. Then, standing in front of Bass's like a Bourbon monarch surveying a ragged military camp in a blasted forest, they saw that king of the frontier, Joseph Renshaw Brown. Aaron named him, and Selene exulted, "Oh, yes, he's a friend of my father—he hates my father."

The rough-haired, snow-reddened, highbrowed young man and the girl, quick-moving as a brown deer, stood hand in hand before the voluminous presence of Major Brown, who wriggled his heavy eyebrows and stroked his satin lapels and looked benevolent.

"Aren't you a justice of the peace, Mr. Brown? Couldn't you marry us?" mumbled Aaron, as rustic as every lover since the first Phoenician stood with the first Cornishwoman before a priest correctly painted blue.

"My boy, the political structure of this land of promise, which is soon to teem with the wheels of commerce, the palaces of the wealthy and the bellyaching of the poor, is a mess. We belong to Wisconsin Territory, but there is no Wisconsin Territory, since that fair land of cheese and beer and Beethoven has become a state. Like Hell, which many Yankees believe us to resemble in other characteristics, also, we are constitutionless and a no-man's-land. We have sent Harry Sibley to Washington, to petition the Congress to territorialize us ..."

"Oh, you could marry us, couldn't you, Major Brown?" coaxed Selene. "Though my father, Caesar Lanark, says you certainly couldn't. He says you have no authority of any kind."

"How right my friend Squire Lanark is!"

"And he says you're no good of a writer."

"The devil he does! Purvey to your esteemed parent the information that the poems that I haven't even started to write are richer than Mrs. Hemans and wittier than Pope. So you want to get married, child? Perhaps it could be done by bond."

"B ..."

"Come with me. I have made another invention."

At Jake Bass's desk, which was also the hotel sideboard, a steamboat office and a repository for samples of ginseng root, Joe Brown made a space, and in his crooked small script he drew up an agreement. Viz.:

$$In\ re \begin{cases} \text{A. Gadd, Esq.} \\ \text{S. Lanark} \end{cases}$$

WHEREAS the aforesaid are citizens of St. Paul, of legal age, unencumbered by previous matrimonial statuses and of pure minds and hearts, and do in the presence of witnesses announce and maintain their intention of entering into Holy Wedlock for the better furtherance of domestic tranquility and the amplification of the population, one unto another to be wed until death or a duly constituted court or legislative assembly now or in the future to be established should them part,

THEREFORE, in light of their bounden promise, herewith acknowledged, to get married again proper by the first regular preacher that comes along, they being of Protestant faith,

AND in acknowledgment of the sum of fifty cents (.50¢) legal currency, receipt of which is herewith attested, the undersigned, Joseph Renshaw Brown, party of the first part, doth pronounce the said Aaron F. Gadd, bachelor, and Selene Anne Marie Chastelnaveau Lanark, spinster, man and wife, and may God have mercy on anybody that tries to jump this claim.

Heads together, Aaron and Selene read this with considerable awe.

"I'm not a lawyer," said Major Brown, "but I'd like to see any shyster bust that. Where's the fifty cents?"

Aaron had it.

Major Brown held the coin up toward the ceiling as if in salute, took Selene's hand, patted the coin into her palm, kissed her with relish, and crowed, "There's your first wedding present, my dear, and God bless you . . . Jake! Bring your lady wife in here."

So they were married, in the board-lined office, no grander than a settler's cabin, looking into a dining-room that was as much bedroom as dining-room and as much poker-room as either, and three or four dogs yawned and scratched through the whole event. The witnesses were Jake Bass, with a jacket hastily donned but with no cravat to his cotton shirt, and Mrs. Bass, wiping hands dripping with dishwater.

Joe Brown was no longer humorous but of high seriousness as he made up a ceremony of his own and at the end, raising his stout arms of a veteran soldier, he intoned, "With the favor of God and the blessing of all men and women of good will, I pronounce you man and wife!"

Selene looked small and lost and shaky among strangers.

Aaron whispered, "You didn't think your wedding would be like this: no aisles, no bells, no flowers!"

"And I never knew I'd be so much in love with the boy I would marry!"

53

AARON found work so readily that the young romantics were somewhat disappointed. Seth Buckbee, Builder & Contractor, who was almost fifty, which is aged for the frontier, was pleased to engage anyone so young yet skilled as Aaron.

Seth was a Rhode Islander, small and shaggy. He had been here for two years, but he had been too busy building for others (he was the first to adopt balloon-frame construction in Minnesota) to repair his own mansion, an earth-floored log cabin which was his home and office. His wife, who was known universally as Aunt Lou Buckbee and who was as New England as a stone wall, had made it habitable with calico curtains and polished frying pans and a two-volume genealogy of her Folks, the famous Bacons. She was a large woman, firm but fond of jokes, a good Baptist, a good cook, very helpful but not very fanciful. Any community built on Seth and Lou Buckbee would be solid though not volatile.

Seth tried Aaron at making a doorframe, clucked, and offered him an excellent wage, a dollar and a half a day. Aaron would have taken it, but he had the adventurous desperation of a newly married man and he demanded a dollar-seventy-five. Seth choked and looked smitten, but he agreed, and said cheerfully, "St. Paul's going to quaduple in ten years, and we'll build most of it." Aunt Lou had the new Mr. and Mrs. Gadd for noon dinner with, naturally, pork and johnny cake, but also with miraculously early greens from the pasture.

Seth thought that it would be an excellent notion for Aaron to go to work that afternoon, but Aunt Lou said that in her sentimental opinion, a Young Married Pair had ought to have the whole day off, what was left of it, and Aaron and Selene went house-hunting.

The new boarding house recommended by Jake Bass was a completely bare room over a wheelwright's log workshop. On the floor were the mattresses of eight couples, shared by assorted children. One frightened woman lay there all afternoon, in fear lest someone steal that floor-space while her husband was out at work on the levee.

Aaron and Selene were not yet so wealthy as to own a whole mattress, but only blankets (and these they had fondly stolen from the Mission). The wheelwright-landlord made what he called "a nice airy piece of floor" for them by pushing the mattresses a little closer together. Thus was Young Love installed in its blissful bower.

Aaron and Selene, and it was the first undisturbed and licensed long period they had ever had together in fair weather, spent their honeymoon of one afternoon sitting up on the hill where Summit Avenue and all the chateaux would some time appear, looking out over the great valley, the great river and the horizon of lakes and forest. They were sleepy; they did not talk very much; but in his "This is awful nice—I'm glad we got it together" were all the songs since Solomon.

Selene was unexpectedly practical.

"I'm sick of pork. Let's go down along the river and see if we can't catch us one little fish for tonight," she caroled. By the lower landing they found a Sioux woman just coming in with a canoeful of fish. Selene looked at her with cousinly affection, and said "How much?"

The squaw studied them. "You new married?"

"Just today."

"Oh. You take this. No pay!" The Indian handed up a fine dripping catfish.

So that made two wedding presents for Mr. and Mrs. Gadd.

At their apartment house, all the tenants combined or took turns at cooking over the mud-and-stick fireplace downstairs in the wheelwright's shop. The only furnishings the honeymooners had yet purchased were a frying pan and a china plate, plus the cups and spoons and knife from Aaron's pack, but with these they dined magnificently on fish, sitting round their one plate on the puncheon floor downstairs, in the lee of a half-finished wagon. It was good.

When they saw the nine-fold bedroom that evening (quite late, after nine) and the frowsy heads, the rumpled bedclothes, when they caught the reek of sleep and unbathedness, they looked once at each other, caught up their blankets, took them down to the stump-bristling bank of the river and convulsively curled together there, as they had in the stress of the blizzard. They turned to each other complete, without memory and without forethought, abandoned and happy in their chamber of wool where the new-cut pine smelled pungent and the stars were quiet.

Just below them, the river ran darkly from the swamps and the forests of Norway pine down to the bright clattering levees of New Orleans, and of all that simple and magnificent new empire they were a part.

Seth Buckbee, but especially Aunt Lou, let them have for home the low loft over the log stable; there was a stubby ladder up to it, and when Aaron, in one grand spurt of twenty-four-hour labor, had put in a rough dormer window, they had light with occasionally too much air. On Aaron's first two pay checks, plus the $11.62 he had left from the $23.70 with which he had left the Mission, plus a generous view of credit, Selene went shopping at Henry Jackson's and at Louis Robert's, and furnished their choice apartment with a backless double bed, a table, two chairs, a box, a rag rug, a cupboard and a beautiful little sheet-iron stove, two-foot cube. And a Bible and an oleograph of Warwick Castle, because that was how Aaron, in Adams, had thought Chateau Lanark would look.

They were of the city and in it, but they were as truly pioneers as farmer-settlers in dugouts. In St. Paul, casually settled because the commandant at Fort Snelling had driven from the military reservation a group of Swiss-French refugees from the Selkirk Colony in Canada, because a one-eyed bootlegger wanted a situation convenient to the thirsty soldiers and because a Catholic missionary built a log chapel—in this huddle, mittens and jackets were collectors' items, and in spring before the boats from Galena and St. Louis started, potato coffee and johnny cake were as precious as in the wilderness. They all burned cordwood, and for water there was the town pump.

But Seth Buckbee, with Aaron Gadd and another carpenter under him, were already removing as rapidly as they could the first idyllic look of the hamlet. Within months, every log cabin in St. Paul was replaced by a frame shanty or covered over with weather-boarding. The smell of pine and cedar lumber increased, but you still came home from social doings over dewy wild grass, carrying a candle-lantern through a goblin-show of stumps.

The village was a gamble. The Congress might admit Minnesota as a territory and law and real-estate titles be established. Then business men, churches, telegraph wires would follow, and the citizenry presently be able to sit down luxuriously on brick pavements, in the smell of steam laundries, instead of on the grass of a virgin prairie among the unchristianized wild roses.

But the Congress might not pass the enabling act for years. It was held up by the Southern members who wanted more slave-holding states.

"Don't like this slavery, but durn sight rather have Minnesota with a few slaves than not have it," said Seth Buckbee.

And if that bothered Aaron—well, he was busy building.

He was busy building, and Selene busy inventing substitutes for wheat bread. He would have liked to worry out slavery in the light of Scripture, but there was no Protestant minister resident, and he was not intimate with Father Ravoux, successor to the Father Lucian Galtier who had given St. Paul its name.

Ravoux little resembled Lanark's friend, Father Bonifay. He was devout and self-sacrificing; he was also thin-faced and grim-mouthed and given to peering through small spectacles far down on his large nose. Marching through town, sharply striking the beaten-earth paths with his gold-headed cane, sharply looking for the raised Canadian caps which would prove that all was healthy in his spiritual domain, Father Ravoux met Aaron and observed, "I hear you are to build a wooden chapel for the heretics. It is in vain. We shall make St. Paul like Quebec City—a new Rome—all glorious churches and schools and hospitals belonging to the True Faith, to the *majoram gloriam* of God."

"Fine!" said the busy Aaron.

Selene was not so occupied and so frivolous that she sank utterly from her aspiration to be baptized. She worried, "I think I really did learn some humility at the Mission. Aaron, my darling, I don't want to fall back into being the daughter of Caesar Lanark. I want to keep the vision of God and not just a vision of getting ahead."

"We'll both keep it . . . you bet we will!" said Aaron.

But it did seem sounder to build houses which he could build than to teach children a gospel which he did not altogether understand in a Sioux language which he could not quite speak. He reflected, "If I could put over some kind of equality for Mark Shadrock and Black Wolf, that would be enough heavenly progress for me."

"Yes, but . . . oh, Aaron!" was all the passionate Selene could answer.

54

NOT that the daughter of Lanark was unwilling to share in the show of possessions which in 1849 was the American proof of virtue, and it delighted her to have her own house without a penny of aid from her father.

Without even asking permission of Aaron, she marched out and got a job as waitress for Mrs. Bass. She became an expert, quick and balanced and remembering, and in June, when the Rodney Parkers opened Henry Rice's new American House, Selene moved over as assistant head-waitress, at six whole dollars a week.

On the building of this American House, Aaron had worked as both carpenter and paperhanger. There was no more respected young couple in town than these Gadds, nor one more likely to become rich, and the Buckbees loved them.

Though they had come here from Rhode Island only two years ago, though they were near fifty, Seth Buckbee and Aunt Lou were ferocious parochial patriots. "Them folks back east got no neighborliness and no git up an' git. I'm going to sign my check for a million dollars before I cash in, heh, Lou?" His wife, who never listened to him, chirped, "That's right." Seth was of approximately half her size; he spatted with her continually and always asked her advice.

Aunt Lou was built like a Percheron; like Medicine Spider, she was Salt of the Earth, with "more backbone than a pickerel." As a girl she had loved dancing and hayride picnics, with cuddling under the moon, and Aaron suspected that she still would, if only there were any hayrick stout enough to hold her.

Her philosophy, very like Caesar Lanark's but conveyed in more motherly style, was that "the sensible, hard-working folks always runs things, always have. They had ought to be kind to the poor, but the weak sisters ought to be mighty thankful for whatever they get."

She cautiously let it be known that if nothing was ever said about Selene's Indian blood, nobody would notice it, and so it would not exist.

She believed that the Irish and Scandinavians were as shiftless as the Injuns. She would have worked all night delivering a Hungarian baby, but when she said cautiously that "some Canadians are just as nice as Our Own Folks," she felt that she had gone to a perilous extreme.

To Aaron and Selene, Aunt Lou became their new Huldah. But the only original Huldah Purdick was on an adventure of her own.

When she had left the Ponds', Huldah stayed for some weeks at Dr. Williamson's school at Kaposia, then at Fort Snelling, teaching the children of the officers. There she could converse with Captain Amos Pipman about mystical experiences.

When Aaron ran into her, in St. Paul, it was a healthy experience for him to find out how uninterested Huldah was in him now. He went home and told Selene that they must get her over from the Fort for supper, some evening. He said patronizingly, "Don't guess she has much fun now—too bad."

He discovered that Selene was laughing at him.

At the beginning of April there was still so much ice in the Mississippi that no steamer had been able to arrive. Shelves were dusty and bellies turned over at the moldiness of the remnants of pork. Social conversation was entirely of meals they would like to eat, and of whether St. Paul would become the Queen City of the Bountiful West, or a pughole inhabited by a few bootleggers. The whole state-to-be had no decent road, and all food save game and potatoes and a little corn was imported. Eastern newspapers were saying that this would never be anything but a reservation for old blizzards, forever outside the smug brotherhood of the states.

On the evening of the ninth of April, a Monday, so hateful a

356

storm of lightning and wind came up that Aaron and Selene did not even cross the muddy yard to the Buckbees' cabin for a game of piquet voleur. But the gale slackened a moment, and Aaron heard the tiny, strained whistle of a steamboat.

"First boat of the season! Quick!" he yelled.

In mackinaw jacket, with Selene in an aged coat of blanket-cloth, he slopped wildly through the mud to rout out the Buckbees, but they were already running toward the edge of the river bluff, perilously leaving their door open to the tempest.

No place in that embryo village was very far from the bluffs, and in the muck, through the soaking hazel bushes, all the population hurried, peering by lightning flashes at the whipped-up dark-gray river. Then, rounding a bend half a mile away, reeling, as tiny and game as a mudhen in a cataract, the steamboat came.

Yelping, they all trotted and slid and crept down the bluff to the landing, to await the *S. B. Dr. Franklin* 2, successor to Aaron's argosy—their first touch, through all the frozen months since October, with the great world, with their far-off beloved, with their own future.

With the whistle cord held down and the sidewheels hurling up muddy water and all the passengers beaming and screaming at the rail, the *Franklin* 2 wiggled in, the plank was dropped and everybody volleyed aboard, to shout, "Did it pass? Did it pass?"

Captain Harris held up his hand, a rain-shining figure in the lightning. The invaders were silent, and Harris called in a strong voice, "Gentlemen, ladies, the will of God has been the will of Congress. Minnesota has been admitted as a territory! A great state is ready to be born and you are again under the flag!"

The deckhands threw the Eastern newspapers into the raised, reaching hands, but the Minnesotans who had gambled their lives on this outcome had eyes too wet for reading.

"We've been so hungry, we've been so patient, but now the field is ready for the harvest!" said Aunt Lou Buckbee.

The Indians on the river bank, shivering in wet blankets, said nothing.

The Captain announced that the governor of the new territory had already been appointed: Alexander Ramsey of Pennsylvania, a former Whig member of Congress, aged only thirty-four.

On April 18, 1849, and a raw and cloudy day it was, there arrived on the *S. B. Senator* (Orren Smith, master), Mr. James Madison Goodhue, Amherst graduate and lawyer turned editor, and under his arm he carried half his type. Ten days later—part of the delay was because he had to wait while Billy Nobles made a news-chase for him—on a hand-press, among the setting hens in a dirt-floored shed under Lull's carpenter shop, Goodhue printed the first number of the St. Paul *Pioneer,* first newspaper in these hundreds of thousands of northern miles.

On the 23rd arrived two men who in a European culture would have come not two weeks but a thousand years after the first invasion. They were pioneers, but they did not look like fictional frontiersmen and they came in amiably arguing the validity of baptism: the Reverend Edward Duffield Neill, from Amherst and Andover, a zealous but civilized Presbyterian, and the Reverend Euripides Tattam, from Harvard, a civilized but zealous Unitarian.

Both of these venerables were twenty-six, the age of Mr. Aaron Gadd.

Neill looked like a Scotch manufacturer and Tattam like a singularly inquisitive greyhound, tall and cadaverous and active, and he had gold-rimmed pince-nez. The first time Aaron saw him, Tattam's long frock coat was plastered to him by a gust of rain, his straight flaxen hair was dripping, and he was loudly singing *Gaudeamus Igitur* all to himself as he raced through the mud to his mattress at Jake Bass's.

With Goodhue, Neill, Tattam, Joe Brown, the housewives would soon be writing poetry and reading Fichte, in between putting out milk pans to catch the drip through straw roofs and looking interestedly at an Indian arrow still trembling in the hand-hewn doorpost. And with two clergymen on call, Aaron and Selene talked of a marriage more codified than Joe Brown's apparently durable marriage by bond.

"Do you suppose we're really married at all?" considered Selene. "For a respectable girl, I do seem to have more illegitimacy in my family!"

In memory of Huldah, she had become a little timid about Presbyterianism, and they chose Euripides Tattam, the Unitarian, to bind them and he accepted with zest. But Mr. Neill showed up also, boyishly explaining that if there was any bliss around here in such a cold spring, he wanted to be in on it.

This was probably the first formal Protestant wedding ever held in St. Paul, and in the common room of the American House most of the Protestant citizens gathered, without having to be invited.

Selene did not want Huldah. "I'm sure she'd send me back to the nursery, right in the middle of the ceremony."

"She still may, invited or not," quaked Aaron.

As they walked behind the Buckbees to the American House for the service, looking a little shabbier than a month before, with Selene's hands appreciably less smooth, she murmured to Aaron, "Maybe I won't be as insanely in love as I was *then,* and maybe I won't start crying and howling so easy, but I'm so much less scared. Now I feel that the grown-ups really *are* going to let me sit up after nine o'clock and let you stay!"

At the wedding, the Reverend Mr. Euripides Tattam surprised everybody and annoyed several of them by using the Episcopal form, with no airy Unitarian emendations of the original as prepared by King James and God. He sounded like a high-church curate. When Aaron and Selene thanked him afterward (with five dollars in an envelope, which he did not know what to do with), Mr. Tattam confided to them, "I'm so glad you liked the job!

It's the first wedding I ever did. I was for two years with old Philo ffoulkes Abercrombie in Boston, as assistant, but he grabbed all the marriages. Jiminy, I'm glad you liked it!"

They immediately invited Mr. Tattam home for dinner, and though there was not much dinner, just an extra plate of turnips, within half an hour the three young people were calling one another Rip and Aaron and Selene and transcendentally agreeing that people would be all of them wonderful if it were not for people.

So, before the city of St. Paul was quite begun, the young intellectuals had started to reform it.

55

BY THE end of summer, 1849, St. Paul had increased in population from two hundred to twelve hundred. Families just landed
from hastening steamers, grubbing hoe in one hand and parrot
cage in the other, would sleep in tents, in shacks put up in
three hours. Heels were sticking out of the windows in the hotels,
and the American House had eighty extra lodgers in the barn,
but for scenery they could look across the canoe-dancing river to an
Indian village unchanged since Columbus came.

Selene was still a waitress at the American, and if she kept her
fragile eagerness while she tossed trays of pork and fried eggs, she
added assurance and dignity. She received at least one offer of marriage a day from the respectable though unfunded newly arrived
young men, all of whom would become senators, bank presidents
or county treasurers who would end in jail.

Aaron was insanely building houses that were sold before they
were begun. Seth Buckbee sprained his hand, and young Aaron
became working boss. By late July, he was making two-fifty a day,
though he rarely had to work over twelve hours a day—perhaps
fifteen on Saturday. He hired his crews from among the hungry
immigrants who came in toting their tool-chests. He was an
admirable boss, grave but easy, remembering the promises he had
given and as good a workman as any of them. He had already
established himself as a pillar when Governor Alexander Ramsey
arrived in Minnesota.

His Excellency was a young lawyer with dignity and a com-
prehending eye. He looked a good deal like the Reverend Edward
Neill, with the same round face, fluff of sidewhiskers, large nose,

high forehead, solid jaw, and like him was not a holy Yankee but a Pennsylvanian.

His friends in Harrisburg had wanted to know whether he would reach this place, Minnesota, by way of Panama or Cape Horn.

There was no house for him when he came, and his pretty wife and he stayed with Henry Hastings Sibley, at Mendota. He came up for a day to the St. Paul House and in a hotel room with two newly appointed Territorial Supreme Court Justices aged twenty-eight and forty-two, the founding fathers severally sitting on a bed, a trunk and a handbag and using a pine washstand as official desk, he drew up the announcement that the Territory of Minnesota (backed by the armies and navies of the United States) was duly organized, and the election of representatives therewith ordered.

It is not known that the job could have been more tightly done nor the document more classically phrased if the Honorable Mr. Ramsey had worn a red robe with little ermine tails and cut his roll of tobacco with the sword of Charlemagne.

On June 28th a little white cottage was ready-enough (Aaron Gadd had been chief carpenter), and His Excellency & Lady paddled a birch canoe from Mendota to St. Paul and helped carry their trunks from the landing to the Executive Mansion. This was the viceregal procession, American style.

Aaron was hanging the last door in the cottage which was Alec Ramsey's home and Official Residence. The living-room was large, because it had first been planned as a barroom. At one end, Mrs. Ramsey was entertaining the wives of the local bar at tea; at the other end, the Governor was conferring with a series of traders, investors, aggrieved Democrats and, since Ramsey was also Superintendent of Indian Affairs, a knot of protesting Indians.

When they were gone, the Governor said affably, "Mr. Gadd, let me greet you as a fellow-chips. I started as a carpenter, before I became an office-boy and a student at Lafayette. My friend, this is the place and the time for us humble workers!"

Ramsey was so neighborly about it that Aaron, the hero-worshipper, was delighted. Why should he not be Ramsey's lieutenant some day, and his successor? But he thought it over all evening, tapping his teeth with his thumbnail, and he sighed to Selene, "No. Alec doesn't think I'm a fellow-workman. He's too cordial. He'll be a senator, maybe President. He's got the poison of wealth and office in him. I'm going to stay clear of all that."

But this worthy vow was not easy to keep when he was making no less than three dollars a day, and merchant princes like Louis Robert were stopping him on the street (which was no street, but a trail) to implore, "Aary, you just got to get to building my new parlor, and hell with the expense! Like to be in politics, some day?"

Farmers, mechanics, merchants. Loan sharks and gamblers. Doctors who were quacks and a few who were doctors. A native Chippewa minister, who preached once in Neill's Presbyterian chapel, opened in July '49, the first Protestant church in town.

An Englishman aristocratically named Ticks, who wanted a lot of land and wanted it cheap and no saucy American backtalk about it. He said, before he sadly went away, that while he could not consider this chap Charles Dickens a gentleman, the fellow had been quite right in saying that Americans ate nothing but tobacco and raw whisky.

And Hiram Gunstead, who gave up his St. Croix Valley farm to sell furniture in town. He said that two Hungarian families had moved into the Valley, and a lot of Swedes were coming, and it was ruined.

In the same week there appeared in St. Paul a German settler who hated all Scandinavians, a Swedish farmer who looked down on all Danes, a Dane who disliked all Norwegians, and a Norwegian pastor who was hoity-toity about all Danes, Swedes, Germans, Irish Catholics, British, Yankees and Jews.

Of him, Aunt Lou Buckbee said, "I know how that Norske preacher feels. Way I look at it: I ain't got a thing against these outlanders—Dutchmen or even Rooshins or Chinks—but I don't want 'em crowding into my house. I'm sure they'd be a lot more comfy where they *belong!*"

"I simply cannot abide these ugly, awkward foreign names," said Mrs. Tryphosa Bopp Boogus, who came from Gahgosh Falls.

All of them—well, half of them—unpacked their prejudices before they unpacked their hoes and hymn books. So Aaron watched his world missing a chance that was perhaps unique in history.

Among the arrivals there were a few adventurers of the sort known as "romantic."

Selene, the waitress, homeward-bound, was trotting out through the common room of the American House, looking slim and clean as one of her table-knives, when she was halted by a seemly man of forty, with the first waxed mustache she had seen since New York. He was in a gray uniform, with acorns on the shoulders, which she could not identify then or ever.

"I beg your pardon, young lady, but I know so few in this bustling village, and I am wondering whether we might have a stroll."

She was used now to the amiable predatory. She said firmly, "I am a married woman."

"So much the better! I should like to meet the gentleman so fortunate as to have won your heart."

She took him home, to amuse Aaron.

In the dusty light and hayseed-smell of that stable loft, the stranger drank rum and was nobly companionable. With his rolling tales of a soldier of fortune, he won them—up to a point. He was, he explained, Colonel Bohrod Kincardine, of the Maryland Kincardines; a West Pointer, now on special service. He had been in the Mexican War, and he told them all about it, but it must have been a different war from the dust and cactus and greasy women and eating boiled dog which Captain Pipman had reported.

In *his* Mexican War, Colonel Kincardine had rescued three beautiful Englishwomen from the ravening Natives who were, it seemed, cannibals; he had stopped a volcano eruption by dropping in gunpowder; he had advised General Scott to march right on to Panama and regain for the United States the luscious lands that belonged to us by right of wanting them. But most of his time he seemed to have spent in exploring a hundred-mile-long underground temple of the Aztec god Wakawetl, whose priests put in their time chanting dirty songs and sacrificing virgins.

Aaron and Selene were glancing at each other, but Kinky (as he generously begged them to call him) was such a pleasant fellow.

"You ought to try some adventures here in Minnesota, Colonel," said that patriotic citizen, Mr. Aaron Gadd.

"Adventures? Here? Why, my dear boy, nowhere have I found more heart-thrilling escapades, and as a result I am engaged to one of the most radiant and highborn damsels in the outfit west of here —the Princess Selene Lanark!"

"Oh!" said Mr. Gadd.

"Never heard of her," said Mrs. Gadd.

"My beloved little Selene! What damask cheeks, what ruby lips, what eyes like bluest sapphires! She is the daughter of General Cicero Lanark (her title, of course, is derived from her mother, the Spanish Princess—uh—Martinez y Monterey—a Bourbon). I shall never forget my delicate Selene."

"You won't?" said Mrs. Gadd.

"That's why I'm here in St. Paul—waiting for her to join me. Her father, in his great stone castle where he lords it among faithful

Indian slaves, is reluctant to let her go. But Bishop Cretin of Dubuque has begged me to let him inaugurate his regime by marrying us."

"Oh. This Selene woman a Catholic?" inquired Mrs. Gadd.

"Naturally. She'll never forget the day, I'll wager, when I fought for her. We were out picnicking on the vast prairie—rustic joys— just a modest pavilion, but silk. Silk! Suddenly a band of Indians are seen circling round. I put her behind me in the door of the pavilion. I draw my sword—I happened to be wearing a claymore that day—you know, on official affairs—and believe me, I made that mighty weapon sing round my head. The Indians rode on —on!"

"*On!*" whispered Mrs. Gadd, in her excitement.

"I lunged and pierced the foremost steed to the heart. The Indian chief rolled off. I could have slew—slain—him as he lay there, but it is the part of a gentleman and soldier to protect weaklings, even Injuns.

"They attacked again. I decapitated the foremost marauder. They were beginning to fall back when, oh, what luck, the sword broke right off in my hand. But it took me only a moment to pick up the tomahawk of my fallen foe, and when they saw me brandishing it, no doubt they believed that my fearlessness was the gift of the gods, and they fled as one man.

"So, seizing Selene, throwing her across my saddle bow, while in the west sunset piled ruby upon gold, I raced madly toward the castle."

"What became of the pa-pavilion?" fretted Mrs. Gadd.

"Ditched it! . . . Well, there we were, racing for the castle, when, Heavens! what should I see right across our path but the thin, creeping line of flame that threatened a prairie fire—dread menace of that savage land!"

"Worse 'n blizzard?" inquired Mrs. Gadd.

"*Much!* Well, my steed trembled, she balked, but I put my

spurs to her, and cried, '*Sans peur, mon cheval!*' She understood, if not the words (which were in French), at least the resolution in my voice. She shook like a leaf, and then, putting all her gallant heart into it, that little mare flew like a bird over the river of fire, galloped on—on—and the Princess Selene was safe!"

"Golly, she was lucky!" exclaimed the simple Mrs. Gadd.

"Ha, ha, modesty forbids, but *she* seemed to think so! Yes, you two must go out some day and revel in my Sioux country."

"I dunno. No place for a raw girl like my wife, that's never known anything but waiting on table," said Mr. Gadd.

His wife turned on him with a choking, "You ... you ... " Then, diffidently, to the Colonel, "Did you ever happen to hear of a frontiersman out there—lawyer or judge or something—they called Squire Harge?"

"Knew him intimately. Poor Squire, he's passed away."

"From what?"

"From drink."

They never saw Colonel Kincardine again, but in future time they heard that he had—under the name of Benjamin Kinkle—become bookkeeper at a flour mill in Winona. When the Civil War came, though he was over age and had never in his life fired a gun, he enlisted in the First Minnesota and was made a corporal.

He was killed at Bull Run, when he stooped to rub his itching toes.

56

ON SEPTEMBER 3, 1849, Huldah Purdick had a resounding military wedding (Episcopal) when she married Captain Amos Pipman.

And on September 3rd the just-elected Minnesota Legislature began its first session at the Central House, the latest hotel. The members had sprung from the North Atlantic States, Canada, Ohio, Michigan, Virginia and Missouri.

The nine dignitaries of the Council met comfortably in the "Ladies' Parlor," but the eighteen Representatives had to use the dining-room. Daily, after the hotel breakfast, they lugged in their rough desks and became legislative, but at half-past eleven they had to push the desks to one side for the dinner-hour, while they thrust the official papers into their pockets or their hats—not invariably removed during the meal.

They went at it again in the afternoon till the head-waitress yelled, "Scat, boys! Suppertime!"

At night most of them slept in that same elastic room.

On the frontier, men cast longer shadows. This gang of farmers and fur-traders, surveyors and storekeepers, with a blacksmith, a country schoolteacher, a tailor, a doctor-druggist and the missionary Gideon Pond, with Joe Brown for unofficial pilot, were supposed to have enough knowledge of economics, history, geography, law, morality to found a just, orderly and enduring commonwealth.

And by God they did!

The fur-traders did not give themselves any the worst of it, but it was to be several sessions later before the expert lobbyists for flour and lumber would appear.

In a hundred years the commonwealth was to be filled with

electricized bungalows, big red dairy barns and villages with radios and chromium café-grills. Yet the future history of Minnesota, like that of every other state in the Union, would be the inept struggle of mechanics and farmers and shopkeepers to get back a little of what they had never intended to give away in the first place.

But none of this was apparent in the ringing fall of 1849, when the half-cleared forest of oaks and poplars and maples pushed close to the parliamentary Central House and the Reverend and Honorable Gideon Hollister Pond was introducing a bill to punish deckhands who sinfully unloaded bread and Bibles on the Sabbath.

By January 1, 1850, there were in St. Paul four physicians, three tailors, a silversmith, a gunsmith, and sixteen carpenters. It was a reason for pride or for alarm that there were also fourteen lawyers.

Now came the land speculators, and the money-lenders who charged five per cent. per month, ten per month, sometimes thirty, and got it.

Off in the green mysteries of the backwoods there were the more familiar activities of the frontier: breaking-plows, dances at barn-raisings—fiddle squeaking, swing your par'ner, feet astomping, *Money Musk*. But these touched the future less than the men who were tired and old while they were yet young, and who were paying high interest on money that they never saw, in order to buy land which the seller did not own, and which would later be lumbered off by Yankee or German Christian Business Men, who didn't own it either, and be left as burnt-over sand wilderness for a heritage to their grateful great-grandchildren.

Yet through the early 1850's there were still a majority of settlers who worked. Among them was the firm of Buckbee & Gadd: General Builders: Carpentry, Brickwork, Stonework, Glaziers, Interior Finishings: Seth Buckbee, prest; Mrs. Lou Buckbee, secy & treas; Aaron Gadd, vice-prest, genl mgr and supt of construction.

In the summer of 1850, when their baby was coming, Aaron saw that Selene was not so strong and quenchless of energy as he had thought. Her face had always been thin; it was pinched now. He insisted, long before she would have thought of it, that she give up her authoritative bustling in the American House dining-room.

She protested, "I've got to have something to *do!* I can't just sit around our little hole in the wall."

He went in that same hour to Seth Buckbee and insisted that he be allowed to buy the four-room cottage which they had just finished on land which they owned speculatively. Seth and Aunt Lou were appalled at such recklessness, for Seth's boast was "I sell houses; I don't waste my substance livin' in 'em." The Buckbees—though Seth publicly proved his prosperity by wearing a diamond stick-pin in his flannel shirt—were still living in the now weather-boarded log cabin which had been their first home in St. Paul.

Next morning, Aaron led Selene into their wonder house, a story-and-a-half high, a white Cape Cod cottage looking down to the Mississippi. In the living-room was a handsome cast-iron fireplace, and it was all pine-smelling and sweet and fresh and home, and outside the windows stood a box-elder tree.

Selene exclaimed, untruthfully, "This is all a woman's heart could ever want!"

She went shopping for the new home. So richly had the St. Paul stores expanded, these seventeen months, that she now could—and did—indulge in a Ne Plus Ultra Garnet-Plush Tete-a-tete with Gilded Walnut Frame, a rosewood sleigh bed, a parlor stove with isinglass windows, a Brussels carpet, a silver-plated pie-knife, a set of oyster-plates with marine views, a dozen buffalo tongues, a pound of Candy Superieure à la Français, and a Family-size Bottle of Dalley & Connell's Magical Pain Extractor.

They held a housewarming, attended by no fewer than eighteen young married couples. The *Pioneer* referred to the Aaron Gadds as "one of the most substantial of our pre-territorial pioneer couples, who in their modish new home set an example of industry, thrift and exquisite taste."

This for the God-driven orphans who had fled hand-in-hand through the blizzard.

It was ninety above in August, and Selene poked about the house and became anxious and faded, and Aaron was the heir of two hundred thousand years of husbandly ineptitude. But when Dr. Dewey was summoned, late on a September night, Selene rallied to resolution and, in that meager new bedroom with the Mount Vernon wallpaper, with Selene screaming—that cool gay girl of Eliot House mangled and triumphant—their son, Ethan Allen Gadd, was born.

Selene had a fanatical devotion to the baby, and she no longer went out to work. She helped the Indian woman-by-the-day, and in the evening read Tennyson and tried, without much success, to revive her schoolgirl French and music, while Aaron studied books on engineering and Greek Revival architecture, Gibbon and Macaulay.

On Sunday they walked out on a boulevard that was still only a sandy trail through the weeds, and Aaron wore a beaver high hat and pushed Ethan in an Orient Mosque Fancy Model Baby Carriage. By paying their Indian helper twenty-five cents to stay in for the evening, they were able to step into Society, dances and lodge meetings. Society in St. Paul would never again be so lively, for three-quarters of the citizens were under thirty, and given to balls, cards, horse-racing on the ice of the winter Mississippi.

Because he was their friend, and because they would have felt guilty if they had gone to no church at all, every Sunday Aaron and Selene attended the Reverend Euripides Tattam's Unitarian meeting in one or another unsanctified hall.

Selene pondered, "I love to hear Rip preaching—that about Mr.

371

Webster—but I can't skip away from the fact that there is such a thing as a gross burden of sin. I saw Mr. Gideon Pond on the street and I didn't dare tell him we're sitting under Rip and not under a true Presbyterian like Mr. Neill."

Aaron said comfortably, "You don't think your medicine can be any good unless it's bitter!"

"No, I don't! I'm a come-ye-outer! I'm like my father. When I take up a thing, good or bad, I follow it right through to the limit. I don't change coaches like you—you *heretic!*"

She looked at him with anxious love.

Doors were not often locked in St. Paul in those days, and while they were reading on that early-spring evening in 1851, the man was able to walk in without warning. He had the stealth of a Black Wolf devastatingly revived.

They looked up, and just inside the door, staring at them in the clear light of their whale-oil lamp, was a man tall, erect, clean-shaven, ironic of eye, with a cane cocked under his left arm—a figure out of Boston.

Selene sprang up with a hand at her leaping breast and fled to Aaron with "It's Papa!" Standing with his arm about her, Aaron saw that incredibly this was Caesar Lanark, more sinister without his beard than he had ever been with it. There was no shadowing now of his contemptuous twist of cheeks.

But his voice was very civil, a little amused:

"Precisely, my dear girl. It is the prodigal father, with an interest in well-fatted calf. I am glad to note these signs of petit-bourgeois comfort, and I hope to see my grandson, of whose rarity I hear almost hysterical praise on every hand. Oh, yes, I have been poking about town for twelve hours—time enough for a man of resolution, cleansed by philosophy, to do many amusing things. For instance, I have just come from the charming log cabin of Mr. Seth Buckbee, from whom I have purchased enough of his stock to give me a controlling interest in Buckbee & Gadd—or Lanark, Gadd & Buckbee, as I presume it will now be christened."

Selene was shivering. "Aaron! You won't let him! We had such a good, decent business! Not let him ruin it!"

Lanark said placidly—only, Aaron did not think he felt so placid —"Since we are in the teeming metropolis and haven't the leisure that was the one virtue of the illimitable wilderness, shall we not waste time in an ethical debate, but just recognize at once what inevitably will happen—that, after deprecating my tendency to tyranny, you will note my ability, and permit me to fructify your fortunes along with my own!"

Aaron said steadily, stroking the frightened Selene into silence, "That may be true. I'll insist on a contract so that you can't interfere with my specifications as builder. Lanark: Did you have Black Wolf killed?"

"No."

"Honestly?"

"That's a silly sequel."

"I suppose so. Anyway, I'm not going to have you play with my firm as one of your side activities."

Lanark was grave. "Agreed. I shall *have* to take it seriously. I am, as I once boasted to you, a man of some substance, but I have recently been associated with two Eastern gentlemen in certain dealings in Wisconsin lumber land. They had the sagacity, along with the ineptitude, of the tenderfoot. They never risked their lives in portages and desolate camps, as I did—they never needed to. Without any effort they put me in my humble place. And while they didn't reap all my sowing, they obtained a quite creditable harvest. Selene . . . "

Neither of them had seen Caesar Lanark look lonely before.

"I have been well slapped. I am not repentant, not of *anything*, but I would prize your friendship. If I have not been a good father to you, perhaps I can be a good grandfather to ... I don't even know my grandson's name!"

A week later, when the articles for Buckbee, Lanark & Gadd (sic) were drawn up, Aaron was almost as hard in his demands as Aunt Lou Buckbee, and at home, when Lanark played prettily on the floor with Ethan Allen, Aaron was nowhere near so misty-eyed about it as Selene.

During the week after that, Lanark wangled the contract for a four-story building, produced the money for hiring new painters and laborers and insisted on having the office of the firm moved from Seth's cabin to a two-room suite on Third Street, with handsome roll-top desks not only for Mr. Lanark and Mr. Buckbee but for Mr. Gadd, the General Manager, to whom had veen voted the unbelievable salary of three thousand dollars a year.

57

IT MUST have been early in 1852 when Dr. Alfred Munce introduced in the West the full gospel of Synthesism, with its gratifying promise of universal reform, and when the Aaron who had determined to be a Reformer gloomily realized that he could never have much to do with Reform if he had to have much to do with Reformers.

The Firm had received from "Synthetapolis. nr. Hudson, Wis." a letter considerably decorated. At the top of the sheet was a wood-cut of large Grecian buildings, a dozen of them, variously labeled "Phalanstery," "Lecture & Concert Hall," "Palace of Applied Sciences," "Hospital, Hydropathic Bower & Nursery," all ringed with gardens, fountains, orchards. At the bottom was the portrait of a gentleman resembling Pompeius Magnus with side whiskers, identified as "Dr. Alfred Munce, D.D., LL.D., M.D., H.D., N.C.D., graduate of Buffalo, Paris, Jerusalem, etc.," along with the slogan, "Synthesism—one for all and all for one—all starbeams in one radiant orb."

Dr. Munce had written to invite bids upon the construction of the dozen buildings already pictured. "I better go look at the outfit —over and return in a day, horseback," said Aaron.

He invited Selene to come along, and on that April day they rode over prairie and hills to Stillwater, on the many-curved and pine-arched St. Croix, and crossed to Wisconsin. Aaron reflected, "Why should it be plumb impossible that this Dr. Munce might have started a city that will carry out all these ideas of freedom and brotherhood that we've gabbled about? Maybe we'll make our pile and go live there—bring Al up to fight for justice as we never did?"

"Al" had, lamentably, become the nickname of Ethan Allen Gadd.

At Hudson they had somewhat vague directions to Synthetapolis. They found a large sign decorated with primitive paintings of stars, roses and clasped hands, announcing "Synthetapolis 5 mi.," but after that the road became a one-track trail through brush.

They came out on a burnt-over desolation of charred stumps and thin gray soil like ashes.

Reluctantly hoeing and resting more than he hoed was an immensely tall and skinny man with a watery beard and hair down to his shoulders. He wore linen trousers and nothing else.

"This way to Synthetapolis, Cap'n?" shouted Aaron.

The man with the hoe trotted toward them. "Friend, fellow-spirit —and wife—you are *at* Synthetapolis! To the inner vision, marble towers and golden highways and choiring choirs already stand here, though just now we have to hold our devotional classes and symbolic dances and dine and sleep in the Phalanstery over there."

"Over *where?*"

The skeleton pointed, and Aaron and Selene saw a long broken-down log stable, roofed with moldy straw. Mr. Gadd, the builder, was outraged. *"That?"* he hooted.

"That and some quite adequate sheds adjacent," said the hoeman placidly. "Prophet Munce permits me to have one shed all to myself for my church—the Roman Quaker Church. I'm the founder and archbishop—I guess cardinal, too."

"R . . . "

"Great suffering cats! They's a Roman *Catholic* Church, ain't there? Well, mine's the Roman *Quaker*. Can't you understand?"

He sounded less golden and much more Connecticut.

"Ain't but one member—me. Thousands upon thousands have tried to git in, but I says to 'em, 'No, *sir!* Ye don't git in till you fulfill my commandments, and God's, that ye be exemplars of perfect purity, beauty, benevolence, diction, amativeness, uncombativeness, fortitude, abstemiousness, philoprogenitiveness, cosmic communitiveness and grit, as determined by my improved sacro-phrenological chart . . . "

The Quaker cardinal was still talking, faster and faster, as Aaron and Selene rode away.

The Phalanstery was divided into three sections: the men's dormitory on the left and the women's on the right, with the private quarters of Prophet and Doctor Munce in the center. In this puncheon-floored vatican, cross-legged upon a bearskin, wearing a white-wool robe and faded gilt sandals, was the Prophet. He was a short man, remarkably like a bartender Aaron knew in St. Paul; his cheeks were a map of large red veins and his eyes were red but sharp.

"About those buildings?" said Aaron.

"No, no, my young friend, positively not till we have had our noonday collation. I want you to see our worker-comrades—lot more than you would expect."

Some sixty worker-comrades straggled in for a not particularly satisfying lunch of mashed peas, whole-wheat bread and lemonade, and Aaron and Selene saw the millennial movement of the mid-nineteenth century in its ultimate glory.

Sitting at the long and gritty pine table set up in a grove of cottonwoods there were spiritualists and non-resisters and neo-Buddhists. There were hydropathic curists and Fourierists and vegetarians.

There were abolitionists and phrenologists and mesmerists and non-Brigham schismatic Mormons. There were women's righters and Non-Episcopal Wesleyans and remnants of First-Day Pre-Millennian Millerites. There were Grahamite Dietists and Plymouth Brethren and Post-Messianic Hebrews and Prophetic Pyramidists and pacifists and foot-washers.

There were occultists and nudists and semi-nudists and eloquent opponents of taxes, capital punishment, music at worship, eating fish and England.

377

The Prophet bade each of them explain his gospel, or gospels, *briefly* (which was impossible) and Aaron the Seeker fell into considerable agony.

Here were examples, or at least burlesques, of his own beliefs: abolition, equality for women, hatred of racial hatred; and yet as he heard them advocated by idiots and grabbers, he was suspicious of them, and aghast to see how much he could dislike an honest, patient, wistful-eyed, starved, sackclothed, dirty-necked martyr who had been giving up his life to the service of Negro freedom.

Prophet Munce explained, "There are several colonies nowadays where noble souls experiment with a civilization free from dross and superstition, but this is the only place where we try to combine *all* of the new discoveries and liberal faiths."

When they were back in his holy chamber, Prophet Munce put on a smile and a slight giggle and approached business.

"Brother Gadd, you don't have to call me Prophet, if you don't want to. You can just call me Professor. Well, you've seen a few of the Children of Light. What do you think? My idee is, if your firm and me can go in on cahoots—I can't advance any cash, but I'd be willing to give you up to fifty per cent. share on profits, and if we could put up a handsome bunch of buildings like I depict on my stationery, then we'd pull in the True Believers by the wagon-load."

"How have you been financing this set-up?"

"On the sound principle of Socialism: from each whatever he's got, to each whatever he needs—when we got it. The brethren here have been pleased to trust me with their savings. But if you boys could run up the buildings and put in some cash, we could get in the colonists that I haven't been able to touch—the pious widows with lots of wealth and the old coots that want to pour out their money to make up for the way they got it."

Aaron sounded belligerent as he rose, while Selene bobbed up

378

doubtfully beside him: "In other words, you're a scoundrel, and you want me to join in your swindle."

"My dear sir, I certainly do not! Up to a point in history which is known only to me, I have predestined myself to use worldly methods, but the fact is—I am God!"

"Well then, all right then," said Selene as they rode. "What *do* you believe in?"

"Didn't you notice at the Mission that there's something damp and dripping in too much mouthing about salvation and about love for your fellow-man? Believe?—I *don't* believe in fear of divine vengeance, and I do believe in justice and equality—but let's try not to use the *words!*"

"Darling Aaron, it sounds so cold! Where's the beauty and passion that Huldah has, that we thought we had?"

"I reckon, dear, you'll find lots of beauty and passion around the Southern plantations, keeping the slaves happy and keeping 'em slaves. Maybe justice is an unemotional proposition, like building a woodshed that'll last, and will keep the wood dry."

"And God—have you left God out? Can we only have dry woodsheds now? Can't we have temples? Don't you believe in God?"

"Selene, stop drinking *words!* I can answer that when you tell me which God you mean—Squire Harge's or Father Ravoux's or Black Wolf's or Ralph Waldo Emerson's or Prophet Munce's. It bothered me when I was a youngster at the Mission and asked about God, and Harge could only roar and Speezer simper. I don't know. I do know I build good woodsheds. An ugly woodshed that's *there,* right on the ground, is handsomer to me than a ten-story temple that isn't there."

"Maybe it's your eyes that aren't there. Inside my mind I can see temples, all ivory and fine gold, with towers like sunsets, and just as weatherproof as your woodsheds, you sweet, stubborn mule!"

"I guess that's the regulation answer. You and Huldah and Brother Speezer sit in front of a nice fire, with wood from my woodshed, and claim you can see spires and diamond windows, and you want credit for your superior vision. But you never give me any architect's plan."

"You are so smug, and I do love you, but I want to *know!*"

They rode for a long while before Aaron meditated, "One of the brightest Christian virtues is humility, and so I say with humility, 'There are many things I don't ever expect to know, and I'm not going to devote myself to preaching about them but to building woodsheds so true and tight that they don't need ivory and fine gold—straight white pine, cedar shingles, a door that won't bind —glorious!' "

58

ALL through '52 and '53, as the firm took on new workers, Aaron insisted that they try "these foreigners"—Germans, Irishmen, Bohemians and a Frenchman who had been a boy soldier of Napoleon and said that he did not remember any eagles but only lice and hunger.

The Buckbees objected to the outlanders, men without baked beans, but Lanark so heartily backed him that Aaron tried to make out what was wrong. Was it worse to have bad men join you in praising what you thought was good, or to have very good men, delightful and solid men, advocate faiths which you thought were horrible?

Aaron tasted the latter on the evening in April, 1853, when they gave a party to celebrate the two new bedrooms built on their house, and he listened to his friends, promising young pioneers, gloat over the money and the political power they were going to capture.

Ed Cale, who had been a river-steamer clerk and was now organizing a stage-coach line, crowed, "Transportation, that's where the money is! We'll have railroads in another ten years, and I'm going to be in on them. When Seth Buckbee signs that ole check of his for a million dollars—I'll cash it! You boys will cut the lumber and grow the wheat, but they ain't any good without I move 'em, and I can charge you what I like and you'll say, 'Thank you, Colonel Cale, sir.' "

"How are you going to get the colonelcy?" asked Major Amos Pipman—who, curiously enough, got *his* title by being in the army. He was staying at Fort Snelling, with his radiant wife Huldah, preparing for a trip of exploration to the Red River Valley.

Ed Cale boasted in answer, "The Governor will have to gentle me down when he wants me to move you sodger boys."

Aaron's early St. Paul friend, Billy Phillips, the lawyer and vocalist, first prosecutor of Ramsey County, said indulgently, "And when you get all your money, Ed, you'll pay me half of it to show you how to keep the other half. And then I'll be a judge, sitting up there while you get grease on your hands. Dignity, that's the caper, like our Mr. Justice Dave Cooper wearing a dress suit on the bench, with a ruffled shirt and shoes with silver buckles. Dignity and ideals, that's what us pioneers got to have. And money! I'll be a United States Senator, when we get statehood, and some day an ambassador. And Pip, here, will be a general."

Mrs. Pipman—Huldah—a woman ample and confident in embroidered satin, a woman whom you suspected of having been a homebody and a companion to her rich retired father and an enthusiast in the altar guild at St. Jude's on the Hill before she was rescued from home by the military, sputtered, "Oh, Pip and I don't care one mite about rank; just duty and service to our country. People have such a wrong idea of the army. Real professional soldiers aren't one bit interested in fighting but just in exploring and building bridges and guarding our outposts so the Indians and these other outlaws won't *dare* fight.

"People can say what they want to, but slavery will be settled without any Southern secession or any other kind of trouble, and why? because the real army, the West Pointers and their faithful old sergeants, won't *permit* the South to act naughty!

"Oh, we in the army are the real pacifists, the real priesthood, and America is no longer led by the dollar sign, like in the old days, but by the sword and the cross, indivisible!"

After that, Huldah told them about her children, who had been arriving automatically.

It was a considerable astonishment and gratification to their guests that for refreshments Mr. and Mrs. Gadd served fried oysters and champagne.

Major and Mrs. Pipman were teetotalers, but as everybody

pointed out to them, you couldn't give the go-by to champagne. Huldah sneezed over hers, but the Major, who had a slight secret smile throughout the whole affair, seemed to have no trouble.

The Pipmans stayed after the others had gone, and the Major said, "Aaron—I couldn't speak of it while those folks were here—have you got a brother named Elijah?"

"Sure! Haven't seen him for years. Quite a little older 'n I was. Left home because Dad killed my dog. Why?"

"A prisoner in the guardhouse at the Fort claims he's your brother."

"Huh?"

"Must say he doesn't look like you—thin fellow, hollow cheeks, thin black beard."

"Could be him. Guardhouse? Why?"

"We think he's been tampering with the Sioux—inciting them to rebellion. We don't know whether to turn him over to the county sheriff or just ship him out of the territory. Poor galoot—seems kind of helpless."

"That's Lije! We'll get Billy Phillips and get him out. Quick! Selene!"

That substantial householder, Mr. Aaron Gadd, and his genteel spouse were flying like mallards. In their light buggy, following the smart gig driven by the Pipmans, they called in to pick up Counselor Phillips and, even so late at night as eleven, drove up to Fort Snelling. The young commanding officer, Lieutenant Macgruder, had gone to bed but he came out, looking not very martial in his flannel nightgown, and agreed, yes, he would be willing to release the prisoner who called himself Elijah Gadd if so respectable a citizen as Mr. Aaron Gadd would give parole for him.

Frankly, the C.O. was not sure about the propriety of holding the suspect, who had been found talking to a known seditious Sioux and who would not explain himself.

The corporal stationed at the guardroom chuckled, "Fella still settin' up in there, Loot. He can't sleep and he don't drink and he won't pray and I don't know what the hell he does with hisself all night long. Maybe *think!*"

In the barred guardroom, where two drunken privates snored, in the hazy light from a lantern, Elijah Gadd sat unmoving on a stool. He looked like John the Baptist in the dungeon. His hands were folded in his lap. His cheeks were sallow and unshaven, thick with short black hairs, and only his dark eyes were living.

Aaron moved quickly to touch his shoulder and say affectionately, "Elijah? This is Aaron! Welcome home! We'll go to my house."

Elijah's limbs seemed only loosely fastened to his body as he rose, but his voice was deep and quiet and resolute:

"Is this your wife? I am fortunate to see you, Sister, though I don't know your name." He kissed Selene's cheek, very lightly. He smelled of imprisonment.

The commanding officer, who was a very nice young man, given to ideas, said hospitably, "Perhaps you gentlemen would like me to rout out Mr. Gear, the chaplain, for prayer."

Elijah rebuked him, "Prayer to whom?"

"Why, to God, I suppose. Aren't you one of these come-outers?"

"I shall have no covenant with God till he has released all suffering souls in prisons and slave-pens and Indian reservations and houses of shame, everywhere in the world. If he is too snobbish to hear their humble cries, why should he hear mine?"

"Rather! Just as you feel." The C.O. was trying to be polite and merry. "Probably the Padre would just as soon not get waked up anyway. Good night, gentlemen."

Till now, Advocate Phillips had not been called on. He couldn't stand it. He advanced his plump hand toward Elijah, and rejoiced, "I am your lawyer, and I'll see you get a square deal!"

"And, as a lawyer, how would you know one?" said Elijah.

Mr. Phillips choked, and indignantly stood in a corner.

He had, said Elijah, known that Aaron was here, but he wanted to learn what sort of human being his brother was before calling on him.

"I have heard that you are a just and decent man, but utterly ignorant of the world-revolution."

"Anyway, I'm your brother, Lije."

"Who knows who his brother is?"

They talked late that night. Ethan, now two and a half, was allowed to crawl out of bed. His Uncle Elijah had urged, "Let him sit up and listen. I believe children understand more than we know. A lot of our 'education' of them is just putting earmuffs and blinders on their natural senses and wisdom."

Elijah had, through these years from 1838 to 1853 (he was thirty-eight now) been laboring as a farmer, patent-medicine salesman, ditch-digger, printer, clock-maker, tanner. For five years now he had been organizing and speaking for abolitionist societies. He was married, with a daughter, and had a cottage near Lake Oneida, in York State. He had been sent to Minnesota by a committee headed by Gerrit Smith and Horace Greeley, ostensibly to look into the swindling of the Sioux by Government agents, but actually . . .

"My two real tasks are to see whether industries in Minnesota—employers like you—are becoming powerful enough and tyrannical enough so that it's time to start labor unions, and to open up a new Minnesota Underground Railroad for escaped slaves. With the Fugitive Slave Law, the older route through Wisconsin is getting crowded and dangerous. I shall expect your help in this."

"Yes, sure," said Aaron, a little uncomfortably.

"I see from your house that you are not rich yet. But I also see from your confident manner and from the politeness of that lawyer and the soldiers to you, that you will be rich."

"Yes, maybe."

"I don't know that it will kill your natural decency to become rich, *provided* you realize that you haven't earned it, that you will have gotten it from the treasures of exploited nature plus the increase of population."

385

"Yes?"

"There are two poisons for a sensitive man—to be too prosperous and dictatorial, or to be too poor and full of the sneering hatred bred by failure. I think you will escape both of these. Your peril will be abdominal—becoming a Leading Citizen."

"Yes?"

"As such, you'll be expected to make speeches all full of such words as Charity, Ideals, Democracy, Freedom, Faith, Loyalty, Patriotism, Industry, Responsibility, which are like the caresses of prostitutes, warm but vomitable."

"Yes, but don't you use a lot of 'em, too, Lije?" Aaron was recovering from his young-brother awe.

"Undoubtedly. I belong to the people. Only a man who belongs to the people can save them. That's why philanthropists like my boss, Gerry Smith, are useless."

"Yes, might be."

"Aaron, will you run through escaped slaves for us—as Dad did, the old devil?"

"Ye-es, I suppose I will."

"He *will!*" announced Selene—her first offering.

"I know you will. The son of Uriel, son of Hezrai, son of Emmanuel, son of Gath—you'll build, but I don't think you can forget the holiness of destroying.

"But I have a more tedious—eventually more dangerous—job for you. In the East we're beginning to form workingmen's associations to get better wages and work conditions. That's been my chief job. I took part in the iron-molders' strike in Cincinnati in 1847. My doctrine is that here in the New West, the laborers and poor farmers should unite and demand their share right from the start, or else they'll wake up in thirty years and find themselves the serfs of the rich farmers, the manufacturers, the banks, and learn the anxiety and humility that all men feel when they can be kicked out of their jobs any minute.

"I shall return east in a few days, but first I must ask you to commit business suicide by advising your own workmen to form a union. I am your conscience—as Father was. Where am I to sleep tonight, Sister Selene?"

59

SOFTLY, not to disturb his terrifying brother, not to remember his terrifying father, Aaron grumbled to Selene, "I hate to say it, but my brother is nothing but a vagrant, too shiftless to learn any trade thoroughly, and then criticizing us that work seven days a week and stand the heat and cold and risk our savings to get this city going! Easy for him to nag! He's got no stake in our civilization. Labor unions—bunch of cheats!"

Selene begged, with a touch of agony in it, "I need a gospel. We're so comfortable. I miss the hunger we used to have in the Mission, in the blizzard, in that haymow over Uncle Seth's stable. I always feel guilty!"

"Selene! I won't have it!"

"I do. Sometimes I want to run to Mr. Neill or a Catholic priest and confess that I have been—oh, hideously still am—full of selfishness and cheap ambitions, and that I have loved my son's smiling more than the patient face of God!"

"Stop it! That's the way ministers love to have you talk."

"Even if that's true, I have to worship something more than getting three meals a day, even for you. I'm the daughter of the rhetoric-mad Caesar, the cousin of the patriot-mad Black Wolf, the wife of the Aaron that once went out madly to seek for God. I must have some madness, something beyond just letting my blood run in my veins!"

"You better let it go on running, though!"

"I must have a faith. Both of us! These unions of workers—couldn't you respect them, since you're apparently bound and determined not to have any tinsel angels? Can't you see any good in them?"

"Hell, yes, that's the trouble. I do! And I'm scared to death that having responsibility, seeing the money come in, I'll turn Tory. And I still am the boy wet behind the ears, making coffins at the Mission. I want to save my soul—though I will *not* give all I hath to the poor—they'd waste it.

"Oh, damn it, eventually I probably *will* start a union of our men—and get kicked out by Seth and your dad. I love my brother, with his blasted pentecostal beard, though of course he's my father, come back to grab me. I worship him, though I'm not sure I like him. I wish I could be one of these crazy saints that enjoy starving, and starving their wives . . . Would you like starving for right-eousness' sake?"

"I wouldn't mind."

"Sure. You can say that because you know I won't let you. Now quit looking at me like Lije without his whiskers! Quit making me feel guilty! You have no *right* to look hurt and meek and loving—that's an unfair advantage—can't Lije and you fight like *men,* like Caesar and Seth and me? Stop it! I've got to get some sleep, if I'm going to finish Doc Borup's stable this week, and you know I'll finish it whether I save my soul or not!"

He had in, to meet Elijah, his prize intellectuals: the Reverend Rip Tattam and the Reverend Edward Neill.

Mr. Neill held forth, very kind and earnest, pessimistic about God's creatures as only an ardent believer can be:

"This decade ending in 1853 has been the greatest era of liberal-ism the world has ever known—and perhaps the last! What world-shaking changes have resulted from the rapid spread of the railroad, from the agitation for abolition, temperance and the so-called 'women's rights'—and they have all failed—all failed! Many of our soundest thinkers believe that Civilization as we know it cannot possibly endure beyond 1865 or '70.

"All of Europe is in the clutch of confused revolutionaries and

America, hitherto the one hope among nations, is more than likely to be utterly destroyed by a fratricidal war between the North and South. That war will be fought by weapons of whose horror we can only faintly conceive: vast masses of men will be moved by the railroad, with such speed that battles of inconceivable magnitude will be joined; balloons will drop explosives; multiple-fire rifles will slaughter soldiers so rapidly that the entire manpower of the nation will be wiped out! And warships may move beneath the surface of the water and so lay waste the entire seaboard!

"With such an outcome of our quest for so-called 'scientific truth,' no wonder many of our greatest scientists are saying 'Let's quit this impious effort to penetrate God's wisely hidden secrets and flee back to recognition of complete human depravity and faith in God's mercy, whereby alone can guilty mankind be saved.' They perceive that in obedience is the only true freedom, and that the latest note is not the slick 'liberal theology' but the tested and enduring Orthodox Christianity.

"All the honest Thinkers are revaluating truth and order— Orestes Brownson, once the perfect New England liberal, has sought refuge in the Roman Catholic fold. They all see that the secularization of thought and education has not been progress but the greatest crime since Eden!

"Oh, some of the stubborn penny-whistle leaders still protest their shallow belief in the debased trinity of Reason, Humanitarianism and Progress. Despite the testimony of all history to the vanity of any belief in perfectibility, they still boast 'Me, I'll stick!' "

Elijah interrupted harshly, "Me, I'll stick!"

Mr. Neill went home, with somewhat melancholy blessings.

Rip Tattam considered, "If Ed Neill's God is still angry with mankind, he ought to get over it and learn better manners. He's studied our depravity long enough to get used to it. I suspect that man's history goes back two hundred thousand years, and out of this we haven't tried to be liberal for more than ten thousand years—five per cent."

Elijah said gravely, "Mr. Tattam, you seem to be with the people. Why do you waste your time on a plush church?"

"I love any church, even when it's empty, as an actor loves any theater—the smell of mustiness, the hymn books, the pews that suggest friendly people, the pulpit that suggests a chance for me to show off! And most ministers are such nice fellows—dreadfully simple, but friendly and good.

"One thing in which I differ with you labor doctrinaires is that I have faith in Faith, I have reverence for all true Reverence."

Elijah snarled, "Does all that mean anything? Or is it just a rash of words?"

Rip was vigorous: "If you workers hadn't let the preachers and lawyers monopolize the magic of words, you wouldn't be so weak—or so gloomy."

Selene meditated, "I wonder if in the old, old days a hundred years ago, way back in the 1750's, people talked as you boys do, and thought they could settle everything by talking? I always supposed the frontier *then* was all long rifles and caps with coon tails, but maybe people in 1750 talked just as they do now in the Age of the Steam Engine and Freedom of the Sex."

"Lije," said Rip Tattam, "we are witnessing a giant passion—the spectacle of America in search of a soul. The struggle may take another two hundred years."

Said Elijah, "Do you think America will last that long?"

Rip smiled, "Oh, yes, my revolutionary friend! Yes. It will last!"

Aaron said to Selene later—on the night before Elijah sailed away—"I don't know how to choose between Rip's cheerfulness and Lije's bitterness. When I think of you and Mercie and Rip himself, I'm all with Rip. When I think of how Black Wolf died, I'm with Elijah and brimstone."

When they said good-bye to Elijah at the steamboat, when they saw him, small and defeated on deck beside the huge and flashy wheelbox, Aaron said good-bye also to the alien East and to all his youth. Uriel was dead, Deacon Popplewood was dead, Gene Dexter was dead, Elijah was righteous.

The steamer departures at St. Paul have not been hymned by history like the arrivals, when would-be conquerors poured out on the muddy roadways and the plank sidewalks as on the streets of Heaven. On the trips eastward, along with an occasional glossy Ramsay Crooks or Henry Hastings Sibley or Caesar Lanark magnificently going to manhandle New York or Washington, the steamers carried on the back trail all the failures—the farmers who had been burned out or frozen out or who could not take the agony of breaking the matted prairie grass, the politicians who found the trough already full of snouts, the preachers weary of preaching to three half-breeds and a mouse, the storekeepers who had discovered that even on the frontier a stock consisting of one bonnet and a bottle of gin would not bring a fortune, the schoolteachers who could not remember how many t's there were in *kat, a domestic animal.*

They went back to the ague country of Ohio and the uplands of Virginia with tall tales of grizzly bears and of Indians in the parlor, and even the small local history that cherishes an Aaron Gadd has forgotten them.

And with them now was that lean and evangelical Elijah Gadd who had a vision of justice but not much patience. He was gone.

In 1851, in two treaties, at Mendota and Traverse des Sioux, the Minnesota Sioux had been cajoled into giving up all their land west of the Mississippi.

White settlers filled up the prairie about Bois des Morts and, not knowing that it could never be farmed, they farmed it admirably. The Wahpeton were most of them persuaded to confine themselves, with the other Minnesota Sioux tribes, to the narrow reservation along the Minnesota River, where the Government Indian agents, politicians chosen for largeness of mouth rather than of heart or intellect, could exhibit their virtue or stupidity or plain larceny, and guarantee a future Indian rebellion.

The Speezers had followed their Wahpeton to this reservation and started a school; Squire Harge, with Bessie, was building a new mission far to the west, among the Teton Sioux; and Jake and Anna Wherryman had left the American Board and taken a claim of their own in Blue-Earth-County-to-be.

The Bois des Morts Mission was abandoned; a rattlesnake nested under the altar in the chapel; owls perched on the pine bedpost in Bessie's lean-to bedroom; and Mercie's defaced wooden headstone lay flat in the snow, the silent sun.

A few Indians had drifted from the reservation to St. Paul, to live in a ghetto along the river flats. Aaron went there, to inspect a site for a new warehouse. In front of an earth-colored one-room shack, shaky over a washtub, he saw, and could not believe it and looked again and saw Medicine Spider, the mother of Black Wolf, washing hotel sheets in a tub out in the four-foot yard.

He tried to greet her in his jagged remnants of Dakota, to ask her what he could do.

The prophetess looked at him with hatred. She grunted that her husband, the gaudy *wakan* man, was dead; Her Door and Black Wolf's son had drifted westward—might be dead too. No, there was nothing that she would let Aaron do. She snarled like an angry, battle-slashed old cat, and stamped into her shack.

He came another day, with Selene and a basket of food, but he could not find Medicine Spider. He never did find her. He thought of the adjacent swift river, which was less dark than Medicine Spider's vengeful soul.

At home, with Selene, Aaron lashed himself, "Oh, yes, I was going to do so much for the Indians! I've failed *bad!*"

"Oh, quit it! You're no good of a Venerated Reformer. Quit

393

being so egotistical. You aren't good enough to build those heavenly woodsheds and save the Indians and the Negroes, too!"

At this impudent reversal of her usual cry for a gospel, he goggled, and stammered, "But it's you that have been surging around all the time, reminding me that the wages of sin is death."

"I'm more interested in the wages of *work*, just now," she chirped.

60

THE firm had forty regular employees, and at rush-times they used over a hundred. When Aaron told his partners that he intended to invite the hands to form a union and alleged that this would insure the peace of the firm as well as prosperity of the men, there was the riot that he expected.

But that gentleman-anarchist, Caesar Lanark, who ate metaphorical babies for breakfast and reformers for lunch, was less obstructive than the plain and kindly Buckbees. Lanark was not too interested, since he now had half a dozen local investments, and he merely scoffed, "I see you're still the Thresher, swimming very rapidly and just keeping even with the bank." But Seth Buckbee screamed, "I'm not going to have any underlings or outsiders telling me how to run *my* business!"

Aunt Lou was meatier. She remarked, "I ain't makin' any sugar tits for no chisel-stealers." Aaron explained that if she agreed, she would be showing a True Christian Spirit. That did not work—she said she had one already. So he faced his three partners and shouted that if they did not yield, he would quit and start a firm of his own. That did it—beautifully or comically or both. He called the workers together, in the warehouse, to encourage them to organize the first considerable labor body ever seen between Milwaukee and the Rockies.

The forty men sat on sawbucks, benches, boxes, in the long dusty shed; carpenters, painters, plasterers and paperers, brick and stone masons, odd-job laborers, timekeepers. A York State cement worker, the first in Minnesota, rose:

"I'm not much of a hand for piety, but I think we had ought to open this labor meeting with prayer, like we were back home. How about Reverend Stone?"

A few grumbled but no one snickered, and Willington Stone, brick mason and Methodist lay-preacher, known as "Reverend" except when the men were in liquor or quarreling over the borrowing of tools, stood up.

Looking at the tanned, dust-pitted faces of the workers, all of them bent down in prayer, even those of the Fourierists and atheists, Aaron was drawn fine as he remembered the twilight concerts in the Clunford church, the Lord's Supper by candlelight in the pinched chapel at Bois des Morts and Huldah Purdick fondly kneeling beside him.

Bill Stone was a flinty-faced, anxious little man, an excellent bricklayer who enjoyed his constant fiery battles with the Demon Rum and usually won. He prayed:

"Lord God of Hosts, thou who dost bless us in the illimitable darkness of the night, bless us now and give thy sanction to our association as men, as workers and as thy children, and lead us to help, in our small way, all our fellow-servants. Bless us, and especially bless the boss, Brother Gadd, for his kind thought in organizing us. Amen."

Aaron spoke with sharp brevity. Veteran workers like them need not be told of the advantages in forming a union—a custom which he believed would become common in the future. As a fellow on the other side of the fence, maybe he ought to buck them, but personally he'd rather deal with a lot of satisfied fellows than try to cut their throats and get his own cut. He would get out now, and leave them to organize; he would be satisfied with almost anything they agreed on—if they'd just leave him, as boss, the price of a bucket of beer now and then! (Applause and laughter.)

A painter moved the election of Reverend Stone as chairman. Seconded. Passed.

Bill Stone sprang up to complain, "Dunno's it's proper for your chairman to put up a holler, but I can't see where all the different crafts had ought to make an association together. What's a common wood-sawyer got to do with a skilled mason?"

The Big Swede, not long over from the Old Country but now chief carpenter, said sardonically, "Yoost for a beginning, I t'ink us smart aristocrats of labor need a little help from da common fallas!"

They were yelling at one another, hysterically discussing industrial unionism two generations before it had a name, when Aaron slipped out. He felt deflated. He was unreasonably displeased that half of the workers liked him better than they did one another.

Later, he asked the Big Swede how it had all come out.

"Oh—all right."

"Did you get organized?"

"Yaas."

"Why aren't you more enthusiastic, Lars?"

"You vant to know?"

"Prob'ly not, but let's have it."

"A union that the boss starts, dat must be for him, not for us."

"Well, it's a start, ain't it?"

"Yaas, sure, it's a start—I t'ink. G' night."

The result, after a couple of months more, was a union constitution stating that in cases of intolerable underpayment, they would, standing together as men and comrades, go to the boss and complain, "Now do you call that nice?"

Within ten years, more than half of these forty pioneer unionists would themselves become employers, and a half of that triumphant half would be stating that unions were for loafers, while for them the ideal was the truly American ideal of Free Enterprise.

The Reverend Mr. Rip Tattam was not too interested in Aaron's unionizing. He said:

"All associations make me feel crowded. That's why I'm a Unitarian. Too many of our customers are too conservative and too rich —they use in investments the same dismaying common sense they use in theology—but at least our pastors meet only in occasional little flocks and chirp about nothing more doctrinal than the propriety of renting pews. I fear organization and authority. I can

397

love your unions while they're persecuted, but I shall fear them when they take possession of all virtue."

Aaron thought, "There's another of the men who said 'I'll stick' unsticking."

Well, he could carry on so long as he had the faith and love of Selene, the somewhat legendary figure of Elijah, the honorific distrust of Caesar Lanark and some amused, patronizing approval from the union itself.

He'd stick!

61

B Y 1855 the city of St. Paul had a population of forty-seven
hundred, twenty times as great as when Aaron had seen it seven
years before. And he was aware of the whole territory, which was
to become a state in 1858. He had put up buildings in St. Anthony
and Minneapolis, some day to unite beside the power-giving falls,
and in St. Cloud and Winona. He saw the tall Red River carts, full
of furs, squeaking over the prairie from Pembina, along with Joe
Rolette, who came in buckskin and sash as a member of the Legislature.

He thought of the North, lakes and pines and Lake Superior,
horizonless as the ocean, and of Duluth reigning over it from the
hills; of the last of the fur-buyers, still struggling by birch canoe
from Grand Portage to Rainy Lake, and of the first of the voracious
lumbermen, the red-shirters and their dry State-of-Maine bosses.
Of settlers moving over the prairie in wagons as close together as
the buffalo they displaced, living first in sod huts, breaking the soil
behind oxen, threatened by fire and by the Rocky Mountain locusts,
a plague out of a frosty Egypt.

St. Paul was still, for all its growth, only a planless windfall of
wooden boxes, and the growing lumberyards caught fire constantly
and, at night, entertainingly. The red-shirters came in from the
lumber camps to get drunk in ten languages, and the sidewalk on
Third Street was littered with cards from gambling houses.

It was in 1855 that the Gadds' second child, Cordelia, was born.
The event was a success. Selene was stronger now, and given to
running about afternoons for coffee and conferences on nursing,
but she did not make speeches at the Societies for Female Culture
which were springing up.

When the Mississippi was frozen, they all skated on it: Selene in sealskin basque and muff, with Ethan Allen, a solemn, secretive, inquiring boy of five, concealed in a ten-foot red muffler, and Aaron in fur-trimmed frogged jacket and high hat and curly skates, pushing Cordelia, like a woods rabbit, in a sled with a gondola prow.

And it was in 1855 that they moved into their second house and Seth and Aunt Lou thriftily took their old one.

The new mansion was no show place, but the *Press* was of opinion that it "added a new note of long-settled solidity and dignity to our booming city." It was square, with four pillars, like a small-sized Greek temple. In the parlor there were Guaranteed Imported French Tapestries and a marbleized iron fireplace which, if it did not look much like marble, did not look much like iron.

It is not impossible that with this new house, Aaron might have become a somewhat shaded social light. He enjoyed dancing the mazurka and the schottische, and when Henry Rice entertained with *Jarley's Wax-Work*, Aaron enacted a Turkish Emperor, to general admiration. It was Selene who wanted to stay home nights, and to that delight she devoted herself as she never had to being the well-dressed young matron.

After treating it lightly, the Big Swede decided that their union was really meant to be taken seriously.

It was a shock to the firm, including Aaron, when in 1855 the union demanded that if workers should be injured on the job, they should receive care and compensation. Up to that time it had been assumed by both the bosses and the workers that if a man lost an arm on a band saw, he was careless and probably recalcitrant to God, and lucky if after his recovery and after his house had been sold to pay the doctor's bill, he was benevolently given a job as night watchman, at ten a week.

Lanark and Seth said that was the right way, too, and *they* certainly were not to blame if lunatics insisted on throwing themselves into saws and off wet third-story roofs. The men threatened an unAmerican measure known as a Strike, and a parading with ban-

400

ners denouncing the kind firm that had brought them up at its corporate breast. Seth and Lanark screamed that such tricks would compel all responsible Northern employers to join the South and campaign for the admission of slaves to every state of the Union. Slaves did not carry banners.

Aaron was perversely tickled. He had for so long now been so respectable; the most adventurous thing he had done in months had been to skate with the baby's sled. It delighted his eccentricity if not his reason to inform Seth and Lanark, "If they go on strike, I'll go out with them. And I can see how some day there might be a state law *making* us pay injured workers."

The strike was won before it was called, and Seth was sick from unrequited love of twenty per cent. profits and Lanark chuckled at the whole business, and Aaron thought about going into politics. Ed Cale whispered, "Yeh, stupid like a fox, Gadd; made his partners think he was all for these ordinary galoots. Don't you believe no such a scandal. Aary Gadd is a fine fellow. Loves a dollar just as much as the rest of us."

Once the union had by all this general treachery and shenenigans triumphed, it went imperialist-mad with victory. The men talked about getting the daily work-hours reduced from eleven to ten. And in this, at last, Aaron could no longer go with them.

What would uneducated fellows like them do with an extra hour? Gamble and drink more beer? He realized that he had almost reached his limit in liberal sympathy.

Then he was caught up again, thrown high on the tide of abolition and the hatred of Negro slavery.

The first settlers of Minnesota had been too intent on freeing themselves from the bondage of untamed earth to be much agitated by bondage in the South. Back in 1837, when Dred Scott was the body-servant and slave of Dr. Emerson, the surgeon at Fort Snelling, it had not been important to Henry Sibley or the Pond brothers that this slave should be freed in a free land.

401

The peculiar institution came closer in the 1850's, when Minnesota was advertised as a cool resort for summering, and the river steamers brought to St. Anthony and St. Paul a flutter of rich Southerners and their personal slaves. Aaron did not like it when he encountered a Mississippi Baptist clergyman with a rich wife and a Negro slave-valet. When he hinted a certain dislike of seeing a man of God owning a son of God, the cleric said politely, "Sir, you are a scoundrel, an atheist and—" in screaming climax "—a Yankee!"

In that day there were great heroes and maniacs. In 1856, after the burning of Lawrence, Kansas, by pro-slavery commandos, John Brown went mad or went abnormally sane and wound up his bloody dialectic with a saber. It was just two months later—so illusory are time and past and present, slavery and concentration camp, frontier rifle and atomic bomb—that, on July 26, 1856, in Dublin, a cannier and more universal rebel named George Bernard Shaw was born.

The Reverend Euripides Tattam, with his freshman enthusiasms, his professional scholarship, his willowy tallness and gold-rimmed eyeglasses, lover of peace and reason, then most unpeacefully and unreasonably lectured in I.O.O.F. Hall on the glory of John Brown. A litter of red-shirt toughs, with some more decorous citizens who could take slavery *and* let it alone, started to smash benches, but Aaron Gadd, not an especially large man, grabbed the noisiest rioter by the neck and ran him out, silently.

Within six years, thousands of Minnesotans would be fighting in the Northern armies.

After Rip's riot, Caesar Lanark said to Selene, "The reverend gentleman's sentiments are admirable. I am always for the spectacle of virtuous bloodshed. But the pace of his oratorical passion is always a bit dogtrot, don't you think?"

Selene and Aaron were companionably angry together, that evening. Rip's example urged Aaron on to direct action. Ever since the visitation of Elijah, he had been contributing to the small and resolute local abolition society and occasionally acting as a substitute conductor on the Underground Railroad. Now he volunteered for regular subversive service.

Whenever he received the message, he went down to the warehouse of a most conservative and contemptuous merchant who was the station agent at Red Rock and by night he loaded the Cargo.

Most of it he then forwarded to an agent in the North, a West Indian who was a retired factor of the American Fur Company and who was named Xavier Pic.

62

NIGHT by the starry Mississippi ice, night and the winter stillness. Bringing the fugitive home to the pillared house and safety from the driving terror.

Through the thick snow Aaron steered his two-seated cutter, with the nickel gorgons' heads decorating the dashboard, back into town. A solid figure, with his long cigar, his reddish thick mustache, he guided the horses skillfully, just flicking the silver-mounted whip. His son Al—Ethan Allen—sat by him, and in the back were Selene and a bundle covered with a buffalo robe.

Al babbled, "Daddy, why do you give the darkies a ride?"

"Don't call 'em 'darkies'. How'd you like to be called a 'whitie'? Call 'em Negroes."

"How would you like to be called a 'Wegro'?"

Aaron had no answer for this one, and he chuckled.

"Daddy, have Negroes got souls?"

"Sure have, if *we* have."

"Oh, *we* have! Uncle Rip says so. . . . Are you friends with the Negroes?"

"Sure am, when they'll let me. Ain't I friends with you, Al?"

"Well, I don't know, Daddy. We never settled it about that toy cannon."

"What does your mother say on the proposition?"

"Aw, you know her, Daddy. It's no fun getting things out of her. She's too easy."

They were home—they drove up to the solemn brown-and-white portico of their house. Selene and Al skipped out of the cutter, the picture of carelessly prosperous mother and little boy, but there was nothing careless in the quick looks they took to left and right and among the cedars in front.

"A' right!" Selene snapped.

Aaron had been lazily snapping a chain to a heavy iron weight anchoring the horses. He sprang now to the back of the cutter, lifted the buffalo robe, growled, "A' right. Quick, Friend."

Selene was holding the front door of the house open. A figure slipped from the back of the cutter and flitted in ghostly stealth up the steps, inside. Aaron coughed ostentatiously, lingered to light another cigar while he looked sharply all around, and followed up the steps.

Their guest this time was a tall, rather pale Negro with the molded strong hands of a craftsman. On his flight from slavery he had picked up too large a coat in one place and too short a pair of trousers in another, and his linen shirt-collar was worn through to its second layer. But there was nothing comic about him, nor servile. He was competence in exile.

Aaron said gravely, "Welcome, Friend. You are safe. But I think it would be advisable if you stayed a day or so in your room—up this way. I'll bring you a tray of supper."

They conducted the fugitive to their principal guest-room, a fabulous warm apartment with thick red carpet and paper all huge red roses and gold stripes, a dressing-table with gold-filigree toilet bottles and a preposterous rosewood bed with starched and lace-edged pillow-shams.

Selene cheerfully fussed over taking off the pillow-shams and turning down the bed. Al, with lively companionship, demanded of the far-wanderer, "Do you know any stories about spooks and hants and mules that do funny things?"

The fugitive stood rigid. His blank face slowly became human and smiling. He sounded as though he were laughing and then as though he were laughing tenderly, and he said, "Cap'n, I got one of the finest collections of hant stories out of Alabama. I'll be honored to present them to you!"

The boy yelled "Goody!" in admiration for the poet.

Aaron came in with a tray of cold chicken, cold roast beef, bread and butter, milk and a pint of scuppernong wine.

"Like a swig of wine, Cap'n?" he suggested.

The Negro said with astonishment, "I don't know, sir. I've read about it, but I've never in my life tasted any."

"Might as well start . . . Were you a houseman?"

"I worked in the fields as a boy, sir, but I'm a trained bricklayer. My name is Henry Oldham."

"That's the caper, Mr. Oldham! I have a building firm—and you have a job, laying bricks at two and a quarter—"

The man was sobbing.

"—starting as soon as you're rested up."

Oldham had listened as if to the voice of the Lord God, and as shyly as though he feared to offend the Lord he muttered, "Will it be safe, sir?"

"We won't let you out of here till it is. We'll snoop around and find out if there's any slave-catchers on your trail. If there ain't, then by act of John Brown and God, without waiting for the scoundrels in Congress, you are a free man!"

Oldham looked as though he were going to break into hysterical gratitude. Aaron held up his hand, said gruffly, "No, no, it's nothing. None of your fellow-workers at the shop will squeal on you. Maybe they ain't so much for abolition, but they sure God don't like slave-catchers. Good night. Water in that dinky little bottle there, water closet first door on your right and Bible in the highboy."

He said to Al, "Every time we run through a slave, I think of how I used to go with my father when *he* smuggled 'em, twenty-five years ago—a quarter of a century!"

Al was fascinated. "Am I like you were then?"

"Maybe you're a little cleaner."

"Wasn't it any different?"

"Yes. I was scared of my father. Are you scared of me?"

Al giggled.

Aaron pondered, "He didn't want as many things as I do, but maybe he wanted 'em harder."

"What did Grampa want?"

"To be let alone! But I like people. That's an important difference."

To Al, who had been brought up to like all people in all shades and classes, this seemed meaningless, and what astonished him as he went up to bed was the new concept that his father, the all-father, could also be a son, who had once been subject to a father of his own. The mix-up in generations was too much for him.

Perhaps it was for Aaron.

He had sunk into a dissipated habit, this past year; he had a small rocking chair in their bedroom, and sometimes he lounged in it and talked or read instead of galloping into bed as an honest carpenter should. From that voluptuous chair (it had a cane seat, and two elk and a noble Indian were painted inside the top rail), he grumbled to Selene, "I'll always be kind of bogus as a lover of the colored brethren. Did you notice how careful I was to call our friend *Mister* Oldham? If he'd been a white man escaped from Massachusetts, I'd probably have called him *Henry*—and shoved him up in the attic! ... O Lord, let us bestow our blessings with a lighter hand!"

Selene curled on his lap, her head against his chin.

"Hey! Don't rock so hard!" she grumbled contentedly.

He stroked her hair as he went on:

"I wish I had the conceit to go into politics and really do something about the Indians and the Negroes. Ex-Governor Ramsey would like me to get into the new Republican outfit. Not me, I said. Leaders! Showing off, orating, getting their faces known, wanting offices! On my tombstone, darling, you put 'He built solid houses and paid pretty good, and if he didn't like it when the galoots went on strike, he didn't get all sore and sacred about it. Go thou and do likewise.' Then I'll rest easy. . . . if you're near me!

"I'd rather be building the MacSchneider-Fellows Offices—the tallest shack in Minnesota, with more light per square foot—than be Secretary of War. I'm satisfied and . . . And that's a lie! Do you suppose that once you start feeling you have to have some special brand of righteousness, you can ever be satisfied? Except in a wife! I love that kind of a superior leer you have, and the shadow on your shoulder, just like I did at Eliot House. Good night!"

Henry Oldham was a smooth bricklayer. When he had put Oldham to work, Aaron had not thought of consulting the Big Swede, president of their union. As yet, the closed shop was unconceived. After a man had been around a while, he applied for membership in the union if he wanted to, and they took him in if they liked him, and the chief visible advantage of the union, besides the beer picnics, was that members were less likely to be laid off in dull times.

The Reverend Rip Tattam invited Oldham to lodge in his not-uncomfortable harness-room, which had been a hiding-place ever since the Fugitive Slave Law of 1850 had provided that flesh-dealers could go into non-slave states, seize any decent dark-skinned man, take him to court and drag him back south as a slave, if the court was pleased. Often the court was highly pleased. That was why a poetry-quoting Unitarian preacher had a dark double-walled chamber in his stable, with a buffalo-rifle always standing loaded in one corner.

Two nights after Oldham had gone to work, when Aaron and Selene were at supper—chipped beef and cider and floating-island pudding; pink pressed-glass tumblers fretted with knobs, imitation tapestry behind the carved-oak buffet, and the shabby oleograph of Warwick Castle they had loved in the loft over Seth's stable—Caesar

Lanark rolled in humorously with "I'm off to Washington on bank affairs, but I must stop and tell you that when I get back I shall probably find no trace left of our contracting business."

"How come?"

"Friend of Labor, you have trouble ahead."

"As how? ... Sit down and have some cider, Caesar."

"The sportive members of your little union are meeting just now in our warehouse, to discuss walking out on strike tomorrow."

"What about? I may walk out with them."

"I doubt it. They are refusing to work with that colored chap, Oldham, whom you smuggled in. My spy in the union asserts that they 'ain't gonna fellowship with *no* nigger!'"

"Oh?"

"The Scandinavians and Yankees are quite as illiberal about it as the bushwhacker Missourians. Their theory, very sound, is that the Senegambians should 'go back south where they came from and not go taking the bread out of our mouths!'"

"Even Reverend Stone? From New Hampshire?"

"My information is that Brother Stone is the most violent of the lot. It seems that in his version of Holy Scripture, the Ethiopians are not permitted to live alongside white men."

"But I saw Bill and Oldham working together, this morning, and they were getting on just fine."

"Too fine! It appears that Oldham is an expert at herringbone brick, and that is Stone's own pulpit. He does not welcome rivals in the sanctuary, and he's out with a Bible in one hand and a brickbat in the other."

"And the Big Swede?"

"He patriotically maintains that he has no prejudice against the darkies but that the peasants in Scandinavia—the few that may still remain there—have a lien on all jobs in St. Paul before we give any of them to *foreigners,* like the Negroes! How are you going to swindle this one, my missionary friend? Forward our unwanted charcoal friend to Canada?"

"I'll figure it out. Go talk to them. You have to have faith in the people, especially when they're wrong—they need it, then."

"Aaron, I have never concealed from you my opinion that you are a humanitarian idiot, and yet almost thou persuadest me to be a Christian! Some day, if you become too obstructive to the rights of Capital, I shall have to call your loans and ruin you, but till then, *even* then, I shall feel a somewhat comic loyalty to you and to my daughter and to my grandchildren—who will be my heirs in the bank and see that I have a magnificent granite memorial with a mendacious inscription, which will amuse me at my club in Heaven. *Au revoir,* my children!"

Selene said urgently, "I'm going to the union meeting with you. Henry looked at us so gratefully! I know what it is to be kicked out and nobody wants you ... except Aaron!"

From the entrance to the warehouse they listened to the workers joyfully and viciously ridiculing one another's geographical origins: Yank, Buckeye, Canuck, Dutch, Paddy, Svensk. Aaron stormed in and Selene tiptoed after him. More than eighty men were sitting on the new folding chairs, and they were silent at the entrance of the General Manager.

The Big Swede, throned in a kitchen chair on a workbench and looking, Aaron thought, remarkably like Caesar Lanark in his castle at Bois des Morts, said forbiddingly, "Excuse me. Dis is a union meeting. Outsiders are not allowed."

The workers stared contemptuously.

The Aaron Gadd who stood fronting them was not much like the sunny-haired boy of eight years ago. He was clearly a man, still eager but broader, more ready, more formidable; a red-faced fighter with a ruddy mustache. His surprised and candid brown eyes were not changed at all.

He made the first long and serious speech of his life. He was, he snorted, speaking to them as one of a community of men; not boss and hands, not Americans and Europeans, but men.

"You all know that as far as I could, I've worked for you about as much as I have for myself. Well, I learned from the Bible that the way of righteousness ain't easy, but I never read that righteous folks have to make it harder for each other than the devil does. You're good neighbors and workers, and yet you want to squeeze out one of the best neighbors and workers that ever came here, just because you've been simple enough to believe the word of some mudheel that all the darkies are just animals—yes, by God, after you've seen Harry Oldham handle a trowel!

"You, Reverend Stone—Bill—you've been bellyaching that Oldham is no good, and at the same time that he's too good for you. What kind of Mormon gospel do you call that?"

Most of them laughed, glad that it was not they whom the Big Boss was picking out for the lash. Bill Stone looked indignant and then, as he was not backed up by his friends, rather silly, and then pleased, as Aaron went on:

"Why, Bill Stone! And you one of the most unselfish Christians and fine gentlemen and smart craftsmen in the territory! You didn't use your imagination, and think of Harry alone, among men who have wives and kids—lonely and scared and driven—looking to us, the confident and happy, to help him!

"Boys, this evening could be the real beginning of Minnesota history—not the padres or fur-traders or explorers, but decent men getting together to insure universal work and bread and homes. This could be the first day and the heavenly light. Let's make history—let's honor ourselves by honoring Harry Oldham!"

There was large applause; too large, Aaron thought, too derisive or too mechanical, like the applause of cynical voters. He looked about, embarrassed. There were no empty chairs, and no one moved. He sat on a box beside Selene, who gripped his hand.

The Big Swede drawled, "Brudders of the St. Paul Building-Workers' Fraternity and Union, you have been addressed by a Mr. Gadd. Vot is your pleasure?"

Brother Haufschnell, expert paper-hanger and plasterer, who had been born on a pile of sugar-beets in Bavaria, rose to offer (and we leave out his mangling of W and Th), "I move you, Brothers, that visitors be asked to remove themselves, and we proceed to vote on do we strike against making our honored crafts ridiculous by being forced to work with men like monkeys!"

"Against men in the very image of Satan!" added the more or less reverend Mr. Stone.

Then they all gasped—none so much as Aaron—as Selene sprang up and spoke, boldly yet pleadingly, her thin hands imploringly at her breast.

They were all plain people, she said. She had been a hotel waitress and a good one. She herself was half-Sioux, and she spoke for the Indians, the Africans, the Orientals. She wound up, "Harry Oldham is my *friend!* Please!"

Mr. Haufschnell stood up again. He was a nervous little man and sarcastic and given to scratching his nose. He begged everybody's pardon if he had misunderstood, he submitted, but he had been told that here in America, as back in his beloved and highly-educated Bavaria, females were not supposed to make speeches. They were, like the highly respected wife of their boss, Mrs. Gadd, mothers of children, the grace and beauty of the home, the adornment of holy church, but not no rivals of the men-folks in brainwork, never!

He wanted a vote on the motion to strike and, while the Gadds sat helpless, the union voted by raising hands, sixty-three to nineteen, to strike against ever working with any Negro. To show that they were free Westerners and not influenced by Aaron, the nineteen revolutionists carefully did not look at him.

Brother Terence O'Toole made an implementing motion that they should charitably allow their employers twenty-four hours to get rid of Oldham before they would strike.

Brother Stone was denouncing this motion when someone banged the door and came in.

He was a square-faced, dark-faced man with a long black coat and a wide black hat, and with him was a weedy town loafer and drunkard named Lopper. The union meeting stared while the stranger stated, "My name is Ebenezer Ludgate, from Tennessee. I have information that a runaway slave of mine, calls himself Henry Oldham, is hiding here in town, and some of you gentlemen know where he is. I want him, and I call upon you all in the sacred name of the Law to assist me."

There was a curious flutter through the meeting, a feeling of danger and anger which could not be placed. Mr. Ludgate laid hand on a pistol tucked into the band of his trousers as he went on:

"The sheriff has deputized Mr. Lopper here, your fellow-townsman, to help me."

Someone unspotted called, "We *notice* Mr. Lopper, our fellow-townsman!" and they laughed, not agreeably.

Haufschnell was near the door, back of the invading Ludgate. You would not have believed that the jerky paper-hanger could have slid out of the room so shadowily.

Mr. Ludgate tried to bully the crowd. Where was Oldham? Huh? They ought to be ashamed to hide a bloodthirsty and rebellious ape! He would have them all arrested—aidin' and abettin' a thievish scoundrel who would rape all their women . . .

Nobody answered a word. Their faces were still.

Aaron kept starting to rise, but Selene had her hand strong on his arm and she muttered, "Keep still, darling. You'll say too much. Dry up!"

Haufschnell tiptoed back into the room, looking sly, and took the center. He said, clearly and cheerily, "Our sick brother that was threatened so bad by the pox is now all safe!"

They cheered.

Slave-chaser Ludgate roared, "You ain't heard the last of this!" and swaggered out, followed by Mr. Lopper, who seemed unhappy over the heavy stare of his fellow-townsmen.

The Big Swede ordered an apprentice, "Sonny, see if that fellow is out there, hanging around." The boy came back guffawing, "Him and Mister Lopper are marching down Third Street, headed for Tennessee."

The Big Swede ruled, "Brother Haufschnell will now report."

Said Haufschnell, "I hustled to Reverend Tattam's. By now, him and Harry Oldham are halfway to the North Pole, on the Reverend's mare. I'd like to see that horse in a race!"

This time, the crowd's cheer sounded like a cloudburst on a tin roof.

Haufschnell suggested, "I move we yoost forget that strike-vote, without any parliamentary monkey-business!"

The Big Swede said, loudly but sedately, "I appoint Brother Reverend Bill Stone to the chair while I make a motion. I move you, Brothers, that Brother Harry Oldham shall be and herewith is admitted to all rights and privileges as a full and active member of the Building-Workers' Fraternity and Union."

"Second the motion!" yelled forty voices.

When they voted, the only hand raised as contrary-minded was that of a tough apprentice, at whom they universally bawled, "Hey, you ain't *got* a vote, you pint o' nothing!"

The Reverend Mr. Stone was heard:

"Brothers, let us pray the merciful God to speed on his way to freedom our comrade and friend, Mr. Henry Oldham, and bring back in safety his rescuer, the Reverend Mr. Tattam—that is, if you can call an infidel Unitarian a Reverend!"

The Big Swede said earnestly, from the chair, "Boys, I wish somebody should now make a motion to elect Mr. and Mrs. Gadd as honorary members of our union—where they belong! Not with no woting powers, you understand!"

A veteran member was heard: "How about changing that motion and give them the names we like to think of them by—Aaron and Selene!"

"Propose motion, with that amendment!" yelled a bricklayer.

"Amen!" said Bill Stone.

The Big Swede announced, "Motion proposed seconded all favor signify usual manner motion carried—*unanimous!*"

Selene was crying.

AN APPENDIX

AN APPENDIX

THESE are the characters of this novel who were actual historical persons:

Charles Grandison Finney, president of Oberlin College. Riverboat captains Russell Blakeley, M. W. Lodwick, Daniel Smith Harris. St. Paul hotelkeepers Jacob Bass and Rodney Parker and their energetic wives.

Early St. Paul settlers Joseph Renshaw Brown, Vetal Guerin, James Madison Goodhue, Edward Duffield Neill (not Rip Tattam, though; the Unitarians did not actually establish a church in Minnesota until twenty years later). And Dr. John J. Dewey, first physician in St. Paul and first druggist in Minnesota, Henry Jackson, Louis Robert, and the vocal county-attorney William Phillips, who never did become a United States Senator, but disappeared into a Washington bureau clerkship.

Father Augustin Ravoux, Chaplain Ezekiel Gear, Major R. G. Murphy, Lieutenant Macgruder and Alexander Ramsey, who was to be governor of the state of Minnesota as of the territory, then United States Senator and Secretary of War.

The missionaries Thomas Smith Williamson, M.D., and Stephen Return Riggs and their wives, Robert and Agnes Hopkins, the brothers Samuel William and Gideon Hollister Pond and their wives Cordelia and Sarah. Outside the Indian Agency we hear the voices of mission children, and two of them, John Poage Williamson and Alfred Riggs, were to become more powerful missionaries to the Indians than even their fathers.

. . . .

Our "Narcisse Jupon" owes something to the hospitality of the real Louis Provencalle, called Le Blanc; and our Deacon Popplewood takes his heavenly discourse from the historic yet now unknown Deacon David Punderson of Washington, Connecticut.

Mentioned in the story but not appearing on stage are the real Minnesota people Harriet Bishop, the early teacher (she simply could not stand the intrusion of Scandinavians on her private Minnesota), Henry M. Rice, who became senator, Supreme Court Justice David Cooper, Dr. Charles Borup, Danish physician who became fur-trader and banker, William Nobles, the blacksmith who became a national road-builder and discovered Nobles Pass in the Rockies.

And Martin McLeod, the literate but rather sour Canadian fur-trader-legislator; Little Crow, who wanted to live in a brick house and drink his whisky in peace but who was jockeyed into leading the Sioux outbreak of 1862; Bishop Cretin, Bishop Loras, Parsons K. Johnson, Joe Rolette, Ramsay Crooks, Norman Kittson, Hazen Mooers, Colonel Gustavus Loomis, Captain Edmund Ogden, Father Lucian Galtier, who first named St. Paul.

And Lawrence Taliaferro, the Don Quixote of Indian agents and, most shining, Henry Hastings Sibley, trader, scholar, huntsman, historian, general, state governor, first delegate to Congress—so handsome and confident a figure that he is less sympathetic than a courageous but easygoing trader like Philander Prescott, who loved the Sioux, married into them and was murdered by them.

. . . .

The missionary Robert Hopkins was drowned in 1851, during the very doubtful treaty-making at Traverse des Sioux; Sarah Pond, Gideon's wife, died in early 1853, worn out with many children, much toil; and later in that same '53, Gideon married Robert's young widow, Agnes Carson Hopkins. The outcome was cheerful. Gideon lived on till 1878 and Agnes for many years after that.

I have a notion how charming Agnes must have been, both from her pictures and because in 1947 I met and fell in love with the daughter of Agnes and Gideon: Scintilla Sexta Pond Ritchie. Gideon had given her the wild name in humorous protest at the way children did keep coming. She was nicknamed "Till," and when I met her, in her eighties—one hundred and thirty-seven years after her father's birth!—I found Till gay, shrewd, clear-eyed, lovely.

She must, as a girl, have seen Selene and Aaron in Gideon's brick house, built in 1855, which still stands in Bloomington, Minneapolis.

. . . .

The Reverend Edward Duffield Neill, after the period during which we see him, did get around. He was chancellor of the University of Minnesota before it had a president or anything else, and state superintendent of instruction. He was chaplain of the First Minnesota Regiment in the Civil War and then, 1869-70, United States Consul in Dublin. I should like to know what he said to Charles Stewart Parnell.

Neill wrote the first formal histories of Minnesota, and he was president of Macalester College in 1873, but in the end he went beautifully astray and joined something called the Reformed Episcopal Church.

. . . .

Major Joseph Renshaw Brown was even more of a man than is suggested in the novel. If he had lived ten years longer—he died suddenly in a hotel in New York in 1870—he might have been more famous than Henry Ford and have hustled up history by forty years. He devised a steam wagon which was to open up all the West without rails. It actually did run, but the first models were too heavy for gumbo roads. He had just secured a lighter engine when he died. Perhaps as much as anyone he was the inventor of the automobile.

Farther-and-Gay Castle, Brown's huge stone house on the Minnesota River in the wilderness below Sacred Heart, burned by the Sioux just a year after he finished it, remains, in 1949, Minnesota's only (practically) medieval ruin except Fort Snelling.

He has been criticized, been called "Juggler Joe," for his over-hospitality to the swollen claims of the traders against the Sioux in the Traverse des Sioux treaty, yet later he was certainly the most intelligent and useful agent the Sioux ever had. (Oh, yes, he was an Indian agent, along with controlling state political conventions and editing the St. Paul *Pioneer* and founding the towns of Stillwater, Hastings, Henderson and Brown's Valley.) He had more of Lorenzo de' Medici in him than would be supposed by that seventy per cent. of the present virtuous citizenry of Minnesota who know nothing about him, or by the ninety-eight point five per cent. of the general American population who have never heard his name. When the definitive book about him is written, it will be translated into Czech, Urdu and Hollywood.

· · · · · · ·

If I had carried Aaron Gadd's life a little further, we might have met, in Minnesota, James J. Hill, Charles Eugene Flandrau, jurist-frontiersman, Old Doc Mayo and his boys, Jane Grey Swisshelm, who loved Negroes and hated Indians and politicians, Ignatius Donnelly, who loved the people but had to make a living, Edward Eggleston, Hoosier author who as a young man was a Bible-peddler and Methodist itinerant in Minnesota, and Bishop Henry Benjamin Whipple, great gentleman, great actor, heroic defender of the defrauded Sioux, and Anglomaniac snob who never could decide whether he was more happy to have heard the voice of God calling him Disciple or the voice of an English curate calling him Milord.

· · · · · · ·

It is an illusion that the haze on the far-off hills is bluer and more romantic.

In every state of the union, as in Minnesota, we have historical treasures small and precious and mislaid. It is admirable that we should excavate Ur of the Chaldees and study the guilds of Brabant, but for our own dignity, knowledge and plain tourist interest, we might also excavate Urbana of the Illinois and investigate the first labor-organization of the Bronx.

S.L.

DATE DUE